THE PERFECT PLAN

A

NOVEL

BY

D'lo

All rights reserved.
copyright © 2018 Larry Boggan
ISBN-13: 978-0-9862025-4-4
ISBN-10: 0986202541

The characters, incidents, and dialogues in this novel are fictional. Any resemblance to actual events or persons living or dead, you might have known or possibly knew, is coincidental.

Published by Donald D'lo Enterprise Inc.
All rights reserved. This book or any portion thereof may not be reproduced or used in any manner whatsoever without the express written permission of the publisher except for the use of brief quotations in a book review.

Printed in the United States of America
First Printing, 2015
Donald D'lo Enterprise Inc.
PO Box 252 McIntosh, NM 87032
donald_dlo@earthlink.net

ALSO BY DONALD D'LO

Speculative Fiction Novels

Limbo
Blood Worthy
Angels of Anarchy

Poetry

Eidolon Bogey Remember Me

PROLOGUE

The Perfect Plan tells a relevant and riveting story as to the events that shaped our society.

What you are about to read is the Association of Avian Literary Artists (AoALA) publication of an ancient novelistic endeavor called *The Perfect Plan*. Five unnamed human scripters, an unnamed executive, and a high-ranking devil, named Beelzebub, composed the innovative version(s) of history. The AoALA editorial staff has included in the manuscript extemporized notes and transcripts from antiquated videos. The AoALA interjected this material to assist the reader in the elucidation of the original document and as an aid to understanding the primitive human culture and their often-delusional belief in mythical creatures and peculiar religious dogmas.

It may be difficult for some readers to find a consistent storyline in the novel. However, the plot becomes, (despite its semi-linear progression,) a multifaceted advancement of evil that leads to a disastrous event historians call Armageddon. It is that event that begat our society. The bizarre multiple endings contained in *The Perfect*

Plan we believe represent farcical alternatives of history that have little or no import other than to facilitate humans pretentious beliefs of biological superiority.

We owe the discovery of *The Perfect Plan* to Demolition Robots who found fragments of the manuscript in a vault beneath the Chicago Black Ops Building. The robots discovered an assortment of scripter notes, personal videos, secret CIA, and FBI files, newspaper clippings, personal photographs, and satellite images in the vault as well. Segments of the original manuscript, unfortunately, were lost to biological and environmental decay, but with Restore LLC as the primary advisors, our writers redrafted *The Perfect Plan*. Restore advisors in some cases altered the manuscript to clarify and correlate segments of the text especially where pages were missing. All changes made by the advisors, translators and editorial staff mimicked the original text in style and scope.

A tremendous thank you is due to the translator Gobbler Jakobe Jenson E.D.E, who translated the original manuscript from humanities many diverse languages.

Favorable Reviews

Lawton University. "**The Perfect Plan** is a social statement regarding the corrosive power of greed that led to the destruction of an entire race of people."

Humboldt Religious Review. "Amazing how stupid the human race became prior to the Turkey Revolt of 3054. Let us pray we learn from their mistakes."

Tom Tolmie, feather-dresser, philanthropist, and the winner of the Golden Gobble Award. "**The Perfect Plan** has remained on my mind since its first publication."

The Historical Society and Memorial Preservation of Archeological Discoveries of Human Remains. "**The Perfect Plan** is a laughable insight into the surreal and flawed human condition."

"Delightful... Yet horrific... A history lesson to be remembered, well done." –The Chronicle.

"Unsettling... This narrative in a humorous way portrays the possibilities of our own demise." – Politic Nation.

"How else could one look upon horror without the numbing effect of absurdity?" – Charles Barker, Chancellor of the Turkey Topper Bookstore.

"The first telepathic reading of, **The Perfect Plan** was held on December 4th, 3605, An audience in the Old Chicago Theater provided a rousing stomp and gobble for the narrative as presented by the renowned Actor Tom Turnkey. A few cockroaches were also in attendance" –The Animal Farm Review.

Neutral Reviews

"It's okay?" –The Cannabis Book Club.

Unfavorable Reviews

"**The Perfect Plan** is a distasteful and incorrigible hyperbole of invented musings written by incompetent scribes to portray a vapid fool, Jimmie Linguine, as he administrates Armageddon. AoALA should be ashamed!" – Book Critic, Sig from Illinois.

"Lewd, pecker and mammary obsessed writers... A Vulgar composition, not worth the turning of a single page." –The Farther Right Review.

"**The Perfect Plan** is a disaster in literature... What is the purpose of incompetence and confusion?" –The Almanac.

"What is consistent throughout this anti-erudite experiment is its lack of rational development. **The Perfect Plan** is a perfect failure." –The Journal of Art and Literature.

Northern New Foundling Book Review. "**The Perfect Plan** is a festering sore in modern literature and should be amputated. Now!"

"**The Perfect Plan** is a cornucopia of caca planted by robots to undermine our turkey civilization. It is fake and should be banned." The Sovereign Fowl Party.

"**The Perfect Plan** written by an extinct race of decadent hominids is obscene and should be banned—no burned." –Alt Light Pious Revie

Section I

The Beginning

CHAPTER 1

Rocky Cliffs, Raging Sea, and Dead Baby

This was Jimmie Linguine's first birth. His mother, Izabelle Linguine is a distant cousin to the renowned pasta maker and Italian mouth-harpist and porn star, Slimy Linguine. She had taken Chacho, an unemployed drug addict, and snake charmer and his oval-headed opium snake to the bathhouse for a little foreplay. She conceived Jimmie Linguine named after Slimy's father, in the confines of her bathtub as she sat naked atop a submerged three-legged despair stool in Slimy's shoulder-deep horse trough full of goat milk, or what she believed was goat milk.

Interjection: AoALA researchers believe that the origins of bathtub pregnancies, (two (2) are in the Perfect Plan M.S.,) are the result of claims made by Sir Thomas Browne. Reference: Sir Thomas Browne's Vulgar Errors VII.xvi: Circa

The Perfect Plan

1658 B.S. (Before Sainthood.)

— Izabelle carried the baby unwillingly and gave birth unhappily to a small bald bit of a waggling child. Shortly after parturition, Izabelle moaned. Her breasts, swollen with milk pained her greatly but she in her madness refused to feed the hungry neonate.

Instead, she emptied her milk upon the ground and in the half-light of dawn Izabelle carried Jimmie to the sea and placed him, mewing like a starving kitten, upon the sandy beach just inches from the rising tide and without regret or any semblance of emotion, naughty, nice, or otherwise, Izabelle left her infant son there to die.

Breathe.

Odor the Farceur of the Elusion people combed the beach every night looking for certain spherical shells that he frequently used in his magic show. He found the newborn child, Jimmie bobbing in the tangled arms of driftwood. Odor crooned a brief song-like prayer to the Wet Nurse of the Universe, Mother Urdu before diving into the tumultuous sea to save the baby. The Farceur swam plunging below the swelling waves and rising in the watery troughs until he reached the infant.

Once the boy was in his grasp, Odor backstroked through the whitecaps, and landed exhausted upon the beach. He crawled across the wet sand with the child under his arm and laid himself and the motionless child down under the umbrella of an ancient palm. Odor placed his cauliflower ear next to the child's mouth and listened for the hiss of life. He heard nothing but the sound of crashing waves.

He then placed his calloused hand on the child's chest and pumped lightly. The Farceur continued to pump until small spurts of water seeped from the boy's mouth. The child took several breaths looked at the clown face of Odor and began to laugh. Just as the Farceur raised his voice in joy, Jimmie Linguine rolled his small round eyes to heaven, took one last breath, and for the second time died. Odor once again tried to resuscitate the boy but failed.

The Farceur perhaps incorrectly surmised that the boy's double death was a penance administered by God to atone for Izabelle's, sins of debauchery and crapulence. The shameless hussy was, in fact, living an unrepentant and shamefully arrogant life with, as mentioned before, no 'good' thoughts what so ever about her son.

Odor saddened by the boy's death put on the mask of a clownish monkey and took the lifeless child to Mother Urdu. She at the time was with her pack of preborn souls. The little ambiances scampered gleefully around her heels or clung like little apes to the coarse hair on her four lengthy legs. One soul, clearly younger than the rest clung to her opulent breast as she gathered firewood on the beach. Odor spoke to Urdu in a dialect known only to the primitive Achelusion (pre-elusion) people, saying, "Take the child Mother Urdu, and place him back into the world."

Urdu gazed sadly at the infant, "The child must have a purpose to be returned to the world. Odor you know that." The Great Mother gathered the preborn souls and one by one placed the reincarnates on teats that lined her chest and belly.

Odor danced about excitedly and said, "Please give him purpose Mother Urdu."

A bell riding the waves far out at sea clanged a solemn knell announcing Mother Urdu's sadness. Lamenting seagulls swirled in intimate circles above the Goddess. Urdu looked up at the birds then lowered her gaze to the place where the sky and sea met in a thin black line. "How goes your tribe?" The Great Mother asked.

"We are in turmoil," Odor said, "the Eurasians have arrived with their gold. Our tribal leaders have made them kings, and they take our people to work their fields for little or no compensation." Odor's voice trailed off in a long Achelusion whistle.

The children on Urdu's breasts made sucking sounds like tiny trumpets. The gulls circling above cried out harshly, and a distant navigational buoy clanged, ding...ding...ding, in an ever-disheartening tempo as darkness began its slow descent upon the world.

"Mother?" Odor said.

She glanced at the Farceur briefly, raised her claw to her lips, and held her long-nail pressed against her muzzle until the sun disappeared. Odor, quietly, built a fire to warm Mother Urdu and the preborn children. Mother Urdu turned her back to the sea and gazed intently at the land now shrouded in darkness. Odor sat silently alongside Urdu holding the lifeless Jimmie Linguine in his lap. Mother Urdu placed her paw on the dead child and whined periodically throughout the night. She finally spoke as sunbeams covered the boy's baldhead. "He has a purpose," Mother Urdu exclaimed.

"What is his purpose?"

"His purpose in life is to destroy the world," Urdu replied.

"What! When, where...how will this happen?"

"Many years from now," Urdu said in a soft whisper. She paused, scratched behind her ear, and continued in a nonchalant manner, "He, like yourself, will be a clown, a special clown—a clown reporter, and a clown saint, and an incompetent clown president!"

Urdu brushed back her long hound-like ears and raised the boy to her lips. Teary-eyed she gazed intently at the lifeless body. She took a deep breath, gently placed his head from crown to chin into her mouth, and blew life into him. She then expelled the boys head with a loud lip-pop. Linguine's misty soul seeped from Urdu's mouth. She

The Perfect Plan

gently held Jimmie's soul in the depression of her joined paws. Urdu smiled and said, "This is his soul's first rebirth," she gently nuzzled the boy's soul and placed him on the teat below her right front leg. It was her largest teat. A teat reserved for the neediest child, and he suckled there cradled in the bend of her elbow for three days one hour.

CHAPTER 2

At the end of three days and one hour

Mother Urdu looked down at Linguine's misty soul nursing on her breast, then looked up at the birds circling, and then lowered her morose gaze to the place where the sky and sea convened in a thin black line. She needed to speak to Odor. The Farceur received Urdu's platonic invitation to visit via the wind and arrived toot sweet. His look Urdu noticed lacked the pertinacity he exhibited three days earlier. "How goes your life?" The Great Mother asked.

A tear came to the clown's right eye. He blinked it away, "Our Chieftain, Albian, abducted my wife Bordet while I was away hunting and gave her to the Eurasians as a gift." Odor's voice trailed off in a long sad whistle. I am now without a wife and without a legacy. Mother Urdu held Odor's hand and led him into her cave where newly arrived souls were mewing softly in the folds of

The Perfect Plan

Aura's comforter. "This is my handmaiden Aura." Urdu pointed at the young woman.

"She is beautiful," Odor said as he gazed at Aura's lightly oiled body.

"She is without a husband," Urdu said. Aura looked down at Odor, She was a tall woman and gangly with just enough weight to be pleasing to her lovers. Urdu spied a sorrow spot shaped like a starfish on the nether of Odor's head.

She patted him on the dull coloration and said sympathetically, "Aura is available for seventy mud-crystals and I will throw in Jimmie, to continue your lineage, for another ten gems."

Odor readily agreed and extracted a tote bag from within the fold of his armpit. He retrieved eighty mud-crystals and placed the currency at Mother Urdu's feet. "You may use the side chamber," Urdu said. Odor bowed respectfully and took Aura's hand. He led Aura into the bedchamber where they remained for six days. Mother Urdu becoming impatient with the couple's lengthy coupling went to the cistern and extracted a bucket of water. She entered the bedchamber mumbling obscenities and dosed the couple to break the fastening of their limbs and libidos. "Times up," Urdu shouted. She quickly stepped between the couple to prevent reunification. Urdu removed the suckling Jimmie Linguine from her teat and slipped the little apparition into Aura's womb. "Now get out," she ordered in a brash tone.

CHAPTER 3

An unspecified number of years later

Odor the Farceur always said, "The best clown was a serious clown," and Jimmie, his apprentice now twenty-three years of age agreed wholeheartedly with his mentor. Jimmie watched carefully and learned as Odor sung to the Elusion people with his clown mask on and his rattle stick shaking. He sang to his tribesman about the heartless Eurasian invaders. He whistled, birded, bellowed, and roared lyrics describing how the Eurasian's stole land and currency and enslaved Achelusion people with the help of tribal leaders. More importantly, he preached on how the invaders and their accomplices must be overthrown. This, of course, did not fare well with the corrupt tribal leaders, nor the Eurasian intruders.

In an attempt to abort a probable insurrection, Prosperous the Eurasian Commander sent for Loki, the Lothario from the Northlands. Loki arrived on the Island as a hairy wolf-like man.

The Perfect Plan

He was a shapeshifter and a trickster, an accomplished dancer, and according to the majority of people on the island, a man of low moral character. This facet of his personality caught Mother Urdu's attention. She had a proclivity towards worthless men.

Loki took the shape of a sleek broad shouldered muscular Polish dude with a huge pecker. And, as a way of an introduction danced the Jerk, a Polish precursor of the twerk. Loki as a broad-shouldered muscular Polish dude danced naked except for his red-quilled, double-peaked, velvet, hat. Urdu became so enamored by the stranger that she promptly divorced her husband Fyodor the Epistler and took Loki to bed.

Loki, as was the custom in those days, paid Urdu for sexual favors. The amorous handsome man with substantial coinage, quite naturally, distracted Mother Urdu, and she briefly neglected her duties as the mother of returning souls. It was during this time of inattention that the Achelusion King Albian, without her knowledge or approval, made a deal with the Eurasian Commander, Prosperous. Both parties signed the deal branded on the back of Eely Pedi, Fyodor's the Epistler's manservant. Thusly placed on the servant's extreme lower back and buttocks, the agreement stated, in a triangular format, the following:

"I Albian for the sum of fifty-thousand mud-crystals, with the support, and covenant of the Achelusion people of the Elusion Archipelago, do hereby transfer all property, real and personal, and all personages, as slaves, to Prosperous to do with as he pleases for eternity at which time property and freedom will be returned to the people in ass is condition."

The "I, and Albian," was tattooed in red the distance of a pinky finger directly above the servant's butt crack.

The remainder of the agreement, tattooed in blue ink spread across the servant's buttocks. "Ass," which most probably should read, "as is," was placed on the left butt cheek and, "condition," was placed on the right butt cheek. The two cheeks ornamented with blue ink jiggled as the servant walked. He was quite rotund even the 'I' on his back disappeared at times in the waves of fat that undulated beneath the surface of his skin.

Odor, with Mother Urdu's permission, and Loki's abstention, having discovered the pact with the invading Prosperous and his mercenaries raised an army of loyal tribesmen and waged war.

Jimmie became a renowned warrior, feared by all Eurasians. The war raged for seven years with both sides losing a considerable number of soldiers. On a very blue day Prosperous, based on Loki's recommendations, sent Odor a message that he would like to reach an agreement and end the war. The agreement simply stated that Prosperous would return all lands, and free all people,

The Perfect Plan

including Odor's wife Bordet, if Mother Urdu would give Prosperous continuous and unlimited rebirths to affluent parents. In addition, Prosperous wanted Jimmie dead. He considered his adversary too dangerous to live peacefully with the Eurasians. Odor vehemently rejected the proposal and threatened to return to war.

Urdu, in desperation, called upon Loki the trickster to assist her in disrupting Odor's intent to continue the conflict. Loki had just read a manifesto embracing neutrality written by the great philosopher Jihad J. Ready in which he claims that inaction is the prerequisite for accomplishment.

Loki surmised based on his own actions, or lack thereof, that the theory was right-on. His proposal to Urdu was simple. Loki recommended that Urdu accept the agreement and limit Jimmie Linguine's life to thirty years and one day. In each rebirth, he proposed, Urdu should give Jimmie's soul to a mother who *doesn't give a shit*. This short life cycle and the lack maternal guidance Loki believed would cultivate the boy in the way of clowns (similar to Odor) and the boy, due to his lack of parental guidance, would have no ambition what so ever.

Urdu implemented Loki's plan by first providing Prosperous the details of the offer which he accepted without dispute. She then notified Odor in person, at home, while he was performing a coming with his pregnant wife Aura. The sex act, doggy style, Urdu thought was violent, and probably a good indication of Odor's mood. The Farceur angry about Urdu's interruption withdrew from intercourse and left the hut outraged at the proposal. He declared that Jimmie should live a normal life free from such ridiculous restrictions. "If limited to thirty years of life, Jimmie would never be able to see his children grow up, or have a decent career, or have time to become famous, or experience baldness…"

The list of 'or' went on for two moons, and a noon. Urdu finally interrupted, "Okay, Odor I will allow Jimmie to experience baldness plus you will get your first wife back, and—"

Odor raised his hand and reentered the hut. He reappeared after a brief time eating an orange. "Continue," he said.

"I will personally make sure that Jimmie is placed" Once again, Odor raised his hand and entered the hut. This time, he reappeared sipping a beer.

"As I was saying," Urdu said.

Odor raised his hand, "Aura and I have yet to finish our intercourse. It may take some time, but I'll be back." —Once again, Odor returned to the hut. Urdu waited patiently; for three days and an hour; then became angry about Odor's disrespect. She entered the hut. Aura was lying on the dirt floor sipping a whiskey. Odor was lying next to her, tonguing her ear. They were both naked—both appeared satisfied. Odor spoke, "My wife and I—"

The Perfect Plan

Aura interrupted, "We are with child, and I do not want that hussy, Odor's first wife, Bordet in my house. What I do want is," she thought for a moment, "what I do want is Jimmie's soul rebirthed to us. He will be thirty tomorrow, you know."

Urdu thought for a moment, "I cannot. Jimmie must go to an apathetic family—a family that lacks ambition."

"Do I look ambitious?" Odor said.

Urdu smiled, "You led the villagers into battle. You are the tribe's shaman." Urdu paused deep in thought, squatted, and scratched behind her ear with her hind leg, "Tell you what," she said with a glimmer in her eye. "I will give him to your first wife, Bordet. Since she has experienced continuous disrespect by King Prosperous and the Eurasians, over many years she has lost all ambition. You take Bordet back Odor and raise Jimmie as your son."

Odor agreed even as Aura argued vehemently against Urdu's proposal. Prosperous, consummated the deal. He paid Carol Owasso, a professional assassin, fifteen mud-crystals (equivalent to twelve pieces of silver), to have Jimmie murdered. The homicide took place during a rally to impeach the traitor, Albian. Jimmie died while eating a licorice stick laced with poison. As the last hiss of breath escaped Jimmies lips, a baby's cry erupted from Auras bed. She had her baby a girl and named the child Bessy Odor. A week later

Bordet gave birth to Jimmie Linguine.

Out of hatred, jealousy, disrespect, and malice, Aura demanded that Jimmie stay with his mother in a separate tent far from the Odor abode, and she threatened Odor with three words, *Total Sexual Abstinence* if he denied her petition. Odor Complied. Urdu knowing Linguine's curse of repeated limited lifetimes abstained from acting against Aura. It was after all part of his destiny.

Interjection: Pages from The Perfect Plan manuscript were lost or destroyed before sainthood between 2348 BCE and 1750 AD. Tragically, 4,098 years or 136.5 of Jimmie Linguine's early life cycles are missing. Other more recent life cycles mysteriously went missing as well.

CHAPTER 4

The Death of Tecumseh

I was standing in an open field, leaning on my rifle when a reporter took a photograph of me surrounded by dead Indians. What was not in the photograph was Tecumseh's body. The Shawnee Chief's turkey feather headdress fluttered solemnly in the breeze as Governor William Henry Hays rode away from the chief and toward the photographer, Kyle Rivers, and myself. As soon as the Governor left Tecumseh's body, a local militiaman kneeled beside the fallen warrior. He appeared to be clipping the great chief's toenails and placing them in a leather bag-presumably for souvenirs.

The Governor dismounted, walked casually to Mr. Rivers, and said, "Take my photograph?" Rivers promptly obliged positioning Governor Hays near a small tree. After the photo-shoot, Hays approached me, "I see you made it Linguine."

"I did Sir," I replied.

"Have you eaten?"

"No, sir."

"Come join me?"

"I can't sir. I have to be in town by noon." I set my toe against a goat turd and with a kick sent it sailing. "Governor I have a message for you."

"Yes, what is it?"

"The whiskey stock is buried in Jim Beam's grave at the Lord and Savior Cemetery in Lexington Kentucky."

"Who sends this message?"

Mounting my spotted horse, Domino I smiled, and said, "I do," and without looking back rode east toward Lexington.

CHAPTER 5

Jimmie and Dasia

Jimmie Linguine worked the circus tour, on and off, as a clown, He worked for the Pools Circus, from 1775 to 1785. He had known Dasia for five years, intimately for the last three years. She was a seamstress by trade. Her father Lester Delimit was the town's, Blacksmith.

Jimmie Linguine arrived in Lexington around noon on the 4th of July. Upon arrival, Linguine went directly to Slander's Saloon, where he bought several shots of the popular Jim Beam Whisky. He stayed at the saloon a couple hours and left the brothel through the back door headed for Dasia's home.

Daytime visits with Dasia were rare, but Jimmie had been absent from his lover for a long time, and he desperately needed her company. Jimmie, experienced in clandestine meetings, approached the seamstress shop with care. He tapped on Dasia's window. The window slid open and Linguine, tom-cat-like slipped inside. The figure of Dasia was visible in the limited light. She was a stout girl of low color attired in a gray skirt and full corset. She was soft of flesh and lacked both the physical and mental hardness of most country girls. Jimmie peered at Dasia in a wanton fashion and she returned his gaze with the same obsessive lust. Heated by desire, the couple quickly disrobed.

Jimmie and Dasia wrestled together espousing themselves to each other via a fully framed mirror as well as a direct line of sight.

Sadly, while engaged in intercourse a person or persons unknown stabbed Linguine repeatedly in the back. Dasia knocked unconscious during the attack was unable to identify the assailants. The High Marshal believed there was more than one attacker and investigated Dasia's father, Lester Delimit along with Ben Ryan, William Harvest, and his eleven apostates. No arrests were made for this heinous crime, and Linguine's murder to this date remains unsolved. Jimmie was thirty years and one day old when he died.

Jimmie experienced an after death experience when a person or persons dragged his mutilated body piece-by-piece outside the sewing shop and left him in an alley.

CHAPTER 6

Rural Kentucky

Sometime before noon, disregarding the fleas and other biting insects Governor William Henry Hays left his fortress in the Indiana Territory and headed East toward Lexington Kentucky. His three-legged dog, Paradox, accompanied him on the trail. Paradox was a retired circus dog trained to ride, primarily, camels, but he was such an adept equestrian he could, for all sober purposes mount almost anything with two to four legs. Hays provided his dog with one of the smelliest creatures on earth, a goat, named Eventide. The dog and goat, obtained by barter, came from Pool's Circus and Equestrian Show. Hays traded a beautiful Indian Princes for the two retired circus animals and was elated that he could, 'Pull one over,' on the au fait ringmaster.

It was a rosy day, and the air smelled of Jasmine, figs and goat shit. Paradox mounted on Eventide took the lead. There were rumors swirling amongst the natives about hostile takeovers. The indigenous red face people it seems were irritated about the whites' taking their land and animals.

For future reference, even the red and blue-faced turkeys hated the white eyes.

Paradox and Eventide spearhead the invading company of pilgrims to act as political scapegoats in case of a cultural attack by the Red Faces. Paradox, having a close connection with his higher power, prayed that God would disallow such an affront to the white invaders, and punish the heathens if, in fact, there was an assault, and corporate lives were lost.

Evening arrived with a soft breeze and Eventide disappeared into the murky shadows without a trace. Paradox was out in the woods relieving himself and Hays was in his tent contemplating on how he was going to retrieve his Jim Beam Stocks. As he pondered on the issue of grave robbing, his female slave Pardonable provided him with an inappropriate yet nutritious meal of mealworms and chicken breast. Hays, who only ate white meat was unaware of the mealworms included in his supper.

Pardonable at the time of the expedition to Lexington was pregnant but miscarried. She suffered greatly from the loss of her child—Hays apathy over the demise of their baby possibly was the reason why Pardonable fed Hays the mealworms—nevertheless, it was to have been William Hays's first child.

Pardonable had a previous child. William's brother George Hays sired the baby. Pardonable named George's child Renee. George Hays traded Renee to a shoemaker, Ben Ryan, for a mule in Lexington Kentucky. George figured he got the better deal. Renee was an eight year old at the time of the trade. The mule was only four. Pardonable requested permission to visit Renee once she arrived in the Lexington. William capitulated on the condition that she in return would satiate his carnal needs.

___O___

July 4th, 1785 was an extraordinarily hot day. Paradox, while sniffing around the shaded buildings of Lexington for assholes and bitches in heat, found Linguine's mutilated body in an alley behind the shoemaker's shop on Bird Street. Paradox mounted Eventide and spurred the goat into a sprint to search for their master. They found William squatting behind his wagon. Paradox yapped the news to his master, and Hays—even though suffering from mealworm induced diarrhea—catapulted himself over the canvased Conestoga and followed Paradox and Eventide to the alley where his butchered friend lay. William fell to his knees. He embraced the pieces of mutilated flesh that were once his friend, Linguine. That night as fireworks exploded overhead. Hays with the notorious Jacobite and British sympathizer, William Harvest, and his band of eleven apostates extracted stocks from the gravesite of Jim Beam and replaced the shares with Linguine's body parts.

When the burial was complete, William Harvest overheard Hays say in a somber voice, "A fitting companion for Mr. Beam." When Harvest asked Hays what he was going to do with the shares, Hays replied, "These stocks will either save the world."

Pardonable visited her daughter Renee while Hays was out watching fireworks and robbing Jim Beam's grave. When her husband William returned from the festivities and thievery, Pardonable notified him surprisingly, (soon after her recent miscarriage) that she was pregnant.

CHAPTER 7

Pardonable Negotiates for the Life of Bob

William Harris Hays was a conservative and a miserly man associated with the Whig Party. His nickname, *A-Hole Hays* came from the parsimonious treatment of his slaves. He even treated his pets badly.

Paradox complained to Hays, about the cruel treatment of Pardonable by raising his leg to Hays boot and pissing. Eventide being a slave himself agreed with Paradox. Something had to be done about Hays cruelty to slaves and animals. The climax of this confrontation came both physically and vocally. Physically, Pardonable, (early in her pregnancy), took Hays to bed banged him for seven days and seven nights. When completely being vaginally creamed, as they say, she, Paradox and Eventide provided their argument to Hays. Pardonable was the spokesperson for the trio.

"Honey," Pardonable said, "I had a nightmare,

a vision that truth is self-evident."

"What truths are you speaking of?" Hays queried.

"Have you not noticed the disdain that I, Eventide, and Paradox have shown you lately?"

"Why yes, I have," Hays uttered, "Why have I been treated thusly?"

"Because we are not property. We are self-determining creatures and demand our freedom."

"Here, here," bleated Eventide.

"We demand respect. We demand freedom." Pardonable continued.

Paradox showed his fangs and growled.

"Did you enjoy our sex?" Pardonable said.

Hays looked surprised, "Yes, I did very much." He managed a listless smile.

Pardonable clenched her teeth and snarled, "Well that shit is going to stop!"

Hays, taken aback by her tone became angry. He sneered, and glowered, and farted under the stress of her interrogation. He also smirked.

"You had better remove that smirk from your face before I rip it off," Pardonable said. Hays' eyes softened dramatically. No one had ever spoken to him like that before, not even his wife who was at home this very moment having sex with Martin, (pronounced Mar-teen.) Martin is Mrs. Hay's part Spanish, part African-American butler.

"What do you want from me?" Hays asked.

"Freedom," Pardonable replied, "Freedom for me and my child—our child, and freedom for

The Perfect Plan

Eventide and Paradox." She glowered at Hays, "and," she continued, "This baby will carry your name. He will inherit your wealth. One day his line—your line and mine will save the world." Pardonable paused for a brief moment, "Mrs. Hays has not provided you with a son has she?"

"No she, uh, she refuses to have sex with me," Hays confessed.

Pardonable wagged her head from side to side —delivered a scathing stare, and said, with a serpentine hiss, "Wonder why?"

Paradox barked and rolled over in merriment while Eventide bleated gleefully.

"Okay," Hays said, "You can have your freedom, all of you, but, if the child is a boy he must be whitened."

Pardonable weighed her decision carefully, "Okay," she said.

Twenty-seven years later.

Pardonable, her owner William Henry Hays and their son Bob were having turkey for dinner. Bob had shot the 'daddy' bird from a blind made of persimmon limbs. The turkey community did not take it well. This was not the killing season for turkeys. This was deer season, and they filed a complaint with the warden. The warden, on behalf of the Hays family, wrote an apologetic note to Mrs. Turkey and her seven, now orphaned children. The government provided Mrs. Turkey a bushel of corn to keep her quiet. The Presidential

Election was in two days, and the Hays family was nervous. It seems that Bob, during his hunting expedition had forgotten to apply the weekly whitener to his coal colored body. His sudden blackness had caused rumors to flourish.

The electorate suspected Candidate Hays' slave, Pardonable was secretly Bob's mother. Hays vehemently denied the accusation and even offered, as evidence, a statement from Dr. Wind, (a local veterinarian,) verifying Pardonable's virginity. Wind stated and Hays repeated as he addressed the American Indian Veterans Wives Club during their weekly brunch. "Ain't nothing corporeal or abstract ever been up in there." Pardonable did not confirm or deny the claims that Bob was her offspring. The next day, Bob whitewashed himself and miraculously turned whitish, again.

William Harris Hays became President of the United States of America, and the Hays family moved to Washington D.C. ... Sweet!

CHAPTER 8

World War One 1917

Jimmie served in the US Army.

I was born September 22, 1885, to Francine Bogy and Samuel Bogy. I had an older sister and her name was Sadie. I was eighteen when Sadie, purchased a Christ Child. She kept the carbon dated mummified Christ Child in her closet. My sister purchased the child from a traveling salesman for twenty-five dollars. It was the last one, and a steal at that price the salesperson claimed. The child was different from most mummified children; his right hand placed above his wrinkled brow, was frozen in a permanent salute, and in his left hand, he clutched a miniature American Flag. Sadie prayed to the Christ Child every morning and every night. It was during her morning prayer that I got a letter from the Selective Service to report for my physical exam. A week later, I was at Camp Gordon Georgia. Six months later, I was carrying a 1914 Enfield rifle in the dense German forests. Two years and twenty-seven dead bodies later, I returned to the U.S., became an alcoholic, and died at the age of thirty on the streets of Biloxi Mississippi. My sister, Sadie placed the mummified Christ Child with me in the coffin and with a fifty-dollar burial contribution from the Veterans Bureau, planted us both in Arlington. Loki attended the funeral. "All for naught," he said. I agreed nonverbally of course. The Christ Child resisted at first; then said a whispered "Amen."

___o___

I died in 1917 sitting on a bench in Lincoln Park wearing a Woodrow Wilson mask. I died with my hands tied behind my back. I died with a copy of a Jim Beam stock certificate pinned to my shirt. Someone stabbed me. It really hurt. Anyway, that is how I died.

Interjection: Research into the origin of this particular Christ Child.

The six-month-old baby was a victim of mustard gas during WW1. His mother was Wanda Feldberg, and his Father was Lee Domicile. Both parents died with the child. Sgt. Bob Numb found the baby in a ditch. He shipped the child to a taxidermist in Bleeding California where the dehydrated corpse was packaged and sold as a curio.

The years 1918 through 1963 are missing from the manuscript. There are vague references

The Perfect Plan

to those missing years on a bathroom stall, (in a service station,) somewhere around Cicero Illinois.

CHAPTER 9

Mid Twenty-First Century

Politics of the Past involving Jimmie Linguine

She first appeared at the office in January as an office clerk. I was a naive college graduate inexperienced in romance and life in general. The new girl's name was Virginia Fawn. She was beautiful. I was, I must say, shamelessly in love with her. She had been working for the political consultants, Jameson, and Sons two weeks before she agreed to go on a date with me. Our first date was unforgettable, we made out in the back of her car. The short sexual encounter ended when she sighed, and said, "Arise Linguine or I will provide twin nipple pinches to your chest." I was, of course, reluctant to dismount and she did indeed, as promised twist my nipples causing me great-yet exhilarating agony. Once I recovered both mentally and physically,

The Perfect Plan

we left the alley and arrived within minutes at the Corny Karris Concert. Virginia loved his music, I on the posterior of her conviction, found his music too colloquial, and sorry to say dozed off.

Virginia tugged on my ear. I blinked my eyes several times to dislodge the lingering sleep and smiled, "Sorry," I mouthed the words. Virginia rotated the ring on her finger, diamond side down and turned her attention to Corny Karris and his music. A light breeze rustled the yellowing cottonwood leaves above my head. The sound of the wind, I thought, added a delicate nuance to the twang of his enigmatic lyrics. Applause shocked me into a heightened state of awareness. We sat through six more songs. I tried to hold Virginia's hand, but she refused. With my hands nestled comfortably in my lap, we listened as Mr. Karris finished the show with a long bluesy run on his guitar. Virginia stood as did others in the audience and provided a rousing, and obviously, heartfelt ovation.

The Artist provided two more songs as an encore before taking his final bow. He thanked the audience and invited everyone to attend a fundraiser for the homeless at the Back Door Bar and Grill. Virginia brushed my leg as she bent down to retrieve her purse. "Pardon," she said. I smiled. We strolled to her car. She opened the blue rusted door of the ancient automobile and slipped inside leveling herself on the imitation Leopard skin that covered the seat. "See you at the office," she said. I gave a mock salute and attempted to kiss her. She turned the key in the ignition. The engine coughed several times then shuddered to life. My pursed lips returned to their normal linear position. I dolefully waved at her disappearing car and then turned my gaze skyward to thank the stars for our brief intimate experience.

When Virginia arrived at work the next day, she looked like a decadent teenager. Her hair was a mess. She was wearing the same clothes she wore last night, and she reeked of alcohol. Barbara was the first to greet her, "Oh, girl you look a mess."

Virginia leaned into Barbara's ear, "Where is Mr. Tibbs?"

"He's in his office," Barbara paused, "Were you out with Jimmie last night?"

Virginia glanced in my direction, "No," I heard her whisper.

The door to Mr. Tibbs office burst open. Tibbs stuck his curly-uncombed head out, "Virginia Fawn, Jimmie Linguine, in my office, please." I was at my desk reviewing the Farmington file. I glanced at Virginia. She brushed back a strand of black hair, straightened her thin denim vest, and approached the office with a stiff back and eager pace. My approach was more cautious. I frankly, was concerned about this meeting. There had been blowback from Senator Hays concerning our candidate Mr. Lawrence Lighthouse's use of campaign contributions. The FBI was now involved. It took a few seconds for me to settle my nerves.

The Perfect Plan

Virginia had already seated herself by the time I entered the office. "Sit," Tibbs said, pointing to the chair on his right. "We have two days before the convention, and Mr. Lighthouse is under investigation for money laundering and fraud. Do either of you know what's going on with the investigation?"

Virginia cleared her throat, and spoke calmly, "I have spoken with the FBI Director Mr. Flange last night after the concert. He has agreed to postpone the investigation until the primaries have concluded. And, he indicated to me that he is open to recommendations," Virginia gestured quotation marks with her fingers, "if Mr. Lighthouse is nominated to run for president."

Tibbs turned to me, "Mr. Linguine?"

I replied with a nervous stutter, "I got a call from the Unified Teacher's Union. They are withdrawing support for Mr. Lighthouse until this matter is resolved. The Simmons Corporation, however, is totally committed to their support of Candidate Lighthouse."

"Where are we at in the polls?"

"Forty-three percent," Virginia said, "Five points ahead of our closest competitor, Senator William Hays."

"Linguine, check in with our Super Pacs contact the local unions in Concord and see if you can get Governor Madison on board. I understand he is leaning toward Hays." Tibbs turned to Virginia, "Mrs. Fawn, did you get the photographs?"

"Yes, Sir."

Tibbs smiled, "We appreciate your sacrifices"

"Thank you, sir."

"Okay get going guys." Tibbs waved us out of his office, "close the door behind you, Jimmie."

I reached behind me, closed the door, and raced over to Virginia who was sucking on a bottle of water, "Where did you go last night after the concert?"

"That's personal Jimmie. Thank you for joining me at the concert. I appreciate it," she said with a simplistic whine.

I ignored her acerbity, "No problem, maybe we can go out again?"

"You mean on a date? I doubt it, Jimmie." Virginia resumed drinking her water and turned briskly away.

I left work early that day, went home, phoned an airline company and purchased a ticket to Concord. My flight departed at 2:27 p.m. I boarded the plane at 2:00 p.m., signed in at the Concord Hilton, at 4:08 p.m. I was unpacking when the phone beside my bed rang. I let the call go to voicemail and left immediately for the hotel's bar on the ground floor. It was happy hour.

Joe, who I learned was a professional boxer, was bartending. "What do you think of the war?" he asked.

"I don't know what to think." I said, paused briefly; then continued, "Actually, I loathe the war. Our attempt at nation-building has always been a failure." I fingered the cuff of my jacket sleeve. "And, the arms manufacturers and dealers support the war for profit. It has been a cash cow for them."

"What kind of work are you in?"

"I work for Jameson and Sons, a political advisory company."

"What candidate are you backing?"

"Lawrence Lighthouse," I said.

"He's an asshole, a corporate guy," Joe said, wiping the bar top with a small towel.

I looked up from my drink and shrugged. "It's a job," I said, "a man's got to eat."

Joe smiled. The bar slowly filled. A band began to play and people started to dance. The music was foreign to me. It sounded Middle Eastern. I asked an attractive blonde woman sitting next to me the name of the band. She, apparently insulted by my question moved to the other end of the bar. I sniffed my under arms in an attempt to find if body odor was the cause of her repulsion. No odor, strange I thought, then checked again with another sniff.

"What about buying me a drink?" a young woman said. The woman apparently noticed the blonde woman's departure and took the vacant seat. She touched my arm. She seemed familiar.

"I like your perfume," I said. She leaned forward, brushed her hair back exposing her neck. I leaned into a spot behind her earlobe. My nostrils flared as I inhaled the aroma of something akin to lemons, "What is it called?"

"Marmalade," she said in a husky voice. "I'm Luta Coffin," she said.

"Nice to meet you, Ms. Coffin."

"What about that drink?"

"Sure, Jacob, give Luta what she wants."

"Brandy, house brand is fine," she said. Jacob poured her drink. "What's your name?"

"Jimmie Linguine," I said. She raised her glass. We touched glasses, "Salute."

"Salute," I replied.

She downed her brandy without moving the glass rim from her lips and belched. "I just lost my job." She said. Her face began to pucker. A flood of unexpected tears came forth and lines of mascara streamed down her cheek giving her the look of a weeping clown.

I retrieved a napkin out of the dispenser and gave it to her, "Sorry to hear that," I said, and paused allowing her to recover, "Where did you work?"

"At the Simmons Corporation," she whimpered, "They are removing the senior employees and replacing them with minimum wage workers."

A twinge of sadness stiffened my spine, "You are still young. It's just a temporary setback."

"In this economy, are you kidding," she said.

I touched her arm, tried to comfort her. She looked at me. Her chin quivered, and with a soft moan, she once again began to cry.

The Perfect Plan

I removed my hand, "I'll call a cab."

She reached for me, "No, please don't... I'll be alright." She dabbed her cheeks with the napkin and laid the stained paper on the bar top. "One more drink?" She asked. A forced smile spread across her face.

"One more Joe," I said laying a Lincoln on the bar. I picked up her discarded tissue and wiped more of her mascara off. She was actually attractive. "I have to leave, busy day tomorrow," I said. She downed her drink and nodded.

Luta spoke as I turned to leave, "Can I come with you?"

"Better not Luta. I need to sleep. Let me call a driver."

"Okay," she said. I helped Luta to her feet. She was unsteady—almost fell. I put her arm around my shoulder and half-carried her out of the bar and into the lobby. About halfway to the door, her legs went limp. I managed to catch her before she hit the floor. I lifted her wilted body and held her tightly against my chest. She giggled and kissed me hard enough to bruise my lip. An elderly couple stopped to witness the amorous attack.

"Luta c'mon girl stand up, I've got to get you to the driver." She did not respond. I dragged her to the door and waved to a waiting taxi driver for assistance.

He lumbered over and helped me get her to the car. "Where to?" he said with a thick, European accent.

"I don't know."

He looked at me quizzically, "I have to have a destination. I just can't drive her around."

"Look in her purse for an address," I said.

The driver scanned her body and the pavement, "She doesn't have a purse."

"Shit," I said, "What's your name?"

"Charlie Dorff,"

"Charlie, can you help me get her up to my room?"

"Sure," he slipped his arm around her waist as I swung her left arm across my shoulder. We carried her to the elevator. I pushed the up arrow ↑ —

We waited. The elevator landed. Charlie and I with Luta between us pressed through the opening doors. We ascended to the thirteenth floor. The elevator door opened, and we stepped into the hall. A Gallic football team dressed in emerald green shirts and matching shorts jostled past us. They entered the elevator for the down ride ↓ —

We weaved down the hall carrying Luta, still unconscious, between us and arrived exhausted at my room. I shifted my weight, retrieved the keycard from my pocket, and opened the suite's door. Charlie and I carried Luta inside, we placed her gently on the couch, and I covered her with a blanket. I slipped Charlie a twenty, thanked him, and sent the burly man on his way.

Interjection: Scripter 3 opines her pregnancy.

One of the first items found in the Black Ops

The Perfect Plan

Vault was a self-video of scripter 3. The Demolition Robots found the video along with a Z-ray image of a human fetus in a pale yellow file cabinet marked 'Personal #3.' The video begins with a close-up of her tear-stained face as she explains her creative devoir for writing this scene. Her voice trembles as she speaks. "The hotel represents the body. The elevator opening symbolizes the vagina. The elevator rising denotes the ascension of sperm," she sobs, "and the occupants encapsulated within the elevator represents two XY's and one XX chromosome. When the elevator door opens," she uses hand gestures as if opening a door, "the semen floods into the hall. The hall symbolizes the fallopian tube. The sperm," she blushes and waves her arm snakelike, "travels down the hall past previous 'unsuccessful' ejaculates,'" She makes quotation marks with her fingers, "to the hotel room, which embodies the uterus. That is where eggs are kept and one of the sperm breaks down the door and fertilizes the egg... and the woman becomes pregnant with a little girl."

Scripter 3 sighs. She moves the stereopticon (B) downward from her face to her large belly and she moans softly.

Interjection: A stereopticon (B) was originally a sliding picture projector. The machine was later advanced to portray moving pictures against a wall or curtain. At the time of 3's video the stereopticon had evolved into a self-contained viewing device.

—I slept comfortably.

I awoke at seven, showered, dressed, and woke Luta who was snoring like a hibernating bear,

"I have to go," I said. Her eyes sprang open. She looked dazed and confused, "Who are you?" she asked.

"Jimmie, from the bar," I said.

"Oh," she replied, sat up and looked around, "Where am I?"

"My hotel room," I replied, and then blurted out, "nothing happened, you were drunk, passed out. I tried to—"

"It's okay," she said.

"You lost your purse, do you need cab fare?"

"No, I live a few blocks away. I'll walk."

"Your purse?"

"Didn't bring one." She reached into her jeans and retrieved her apartment keys.

"Thank you," she said, "For helping—for not trying-"

"It's okay, are you alright? You were pretty upset last night…about losing your job."

"I'm fine," she said with a faint smile. I opened the door and watched her shuffle down the hall and step into the elevator. My concern, clouded by the departing Luta became robust when I saw

The Perfect Plan

a piece of folded paper on the carpet. I reached down, picked up the paper, and opened the *Termination Notice* from the Simmons Corporation. I placed the notice on the coffee table and spotted the message light blinking on the phone. I dialed the recording service It was Mr. Tibbs. In last night's melee, I had forgotten about his phone call. In his message, he said that he had set up an appointment for me with Governor Dean Madison. The appointment was today at 10:00 o: clock. I had thirty minutes to reach the Governor's Office.

I arrived at 9:55. His receptionist asked me to take a seat. Twenty minutes later a small bald man entered the visiting room. "Mr. Linguine," the governor said as he extended his hand. His handshake was soft, warm, and pliable.

"Good to meet you, sir," I replied.

"Come this way," he said. I followed him to his office. He sat down, "please," he said pointing to a chair in front of him.

"Thank you, sir."

"What can I do for you Mr. Linguine?"

"I would like to speak to you about supporting Presidential Candidate Lawrence Lighthouse."

"He's an ass."

"True," I smiled, "but if elected, he would be a beneficial ass to you and to the State of New Hampshire."

"Can he beat Hays?" Governor Madison asked.

"I believe so, why don't you approach Mr. Lighthouse with a donation?"

Madison raised his right eyebrow.

"Look, Governor, our Super Pac's are raising considerable amounts of money. And. I am sure Mr. Lighthouse is open to any suggestions that you might have that will benefit the party. Let me set up a meeting."

"Have Larry call me himself," Madison said, "I don't need a mediator."

"Okay." I reached for my phone.

"Not now, I've got an appointment in five minutes. Have him call me tomorrow afternoon around five."

"Alright."

"Thanks for coming, Mr. Linguine. Mrs. Bottle will show you out."

I followed the receptionist out of his office and into the hall.

My next stops were at the United Electrical Union, Pipe Fitters Organization, Healthcare National, Inc., and lastly, the Fair Deal Super Pac headquartered on South Central Ave. It was 7:30 p.m. when I got back to my hotel room.

I was in my pajamas, relaxing in bed and listening to music when I heard a loud knock on the door. "Who is it?"

"Jimmie, it's Al Wilson, I need to speak to you." I rolled out of bed, quietly approached the door, and peered through the peephole. A small man wearing thick glasses and an expensive suit was at the entrance. "Hold on, I'm coming," I shouted.

The air conditioner squeaked on. Cold air flushed over me as a raced to the closet and retrieved my snub nose 38. I placed it in the pocket of my robe; "Be right there," I walked casually to the door and opened it a distance allowed by the security chain, "How can I help you?"

"May I come in, it's urgent." He said

"Who are you?"

"I'll explain later." I paused for a moment, released the security chain, and opened the door. He stepped inside, "It's about Virginia Fawn." He paused, thought for a moment, "She's in the lobby."

"Well tell her to come up," I said.

"She can't, she's," He hesitated, "she's with someone. You need to go get her."

"Who is she with?"

"She's with Lighthouse."

"That's where she is supposed to be Al besides what is it to you where she is and what she's doing?"

"Trust me you need to go get her."

Intrigued by his concern, I said, "Alright I'll go take a look, come with me."

Al's face reddened, "No, I can't be seen."

"Go wait at the bar then," I said gruffly.

"Okay, I'll see you in the bar," he replied, "please hurry."

He took the elevator as I dressed. Five minutes later, I took the elevator down. Virginia was in the café having coffee with Mr. Lighthouse.

Her eyes lit up when she saw me, "Jimmie, what a surprise."

"Hello Virginia, what are you doing in Concord?"

"Business, Mr. Lighthouse is going to meet with Governor Madison tomorrow morning. I am here to make sure things go smoothly," she said.

"I spoke with the governor earlier today. It was my understanding that Mr. Lighthouse…"

"I don't care about your understanding- I am here to see the governor on my terms, and at my convenience, not his," Lighthouse said.

"Sorry Sir, my apologies. Well, I will leave you two to discuss politics. Nice seeing you again Mr. Lighthouse, Virginia." I turned to leave when Virginia said, "Wait, Jimmie, I need to speak to you. Excuse me Mr. Lighthouse this won't take but a moment."

She looped her arm through my elbow and we walked to the reception area, "I need your help," she whispered.

"What do you want from me?"

"The real reason Lighthouse is here is to meet with the President of the Simmons Corporation and broker a deal for his election."

"What does that have to do with you?"

"I support William Hays. Jimmie, I want him to win the election."

"Like I said, what do you want from me?"

"Help me," she said, "I'll make it worth your while," she touched my chin, "C'mon baby join us.

The Perfect Plan

Hayes can make you rich. I can make you famous."

"I'll have to think about it," I said.

"Okay, okay, think about it but we need an answer by noon tomorrow."

Virginia released my arm and turned briskly away. "Virginia," I whispered. She turned to face me, "What does Al Wilson have to do with all this?"

She frowned, "Nothing," she said, turned took a step, and turned back around with a gorgeous grin, "almost nothing."

I went to the bar and tried to find Wilson. He was gone. While there, I decided to have a drink, just to sort through the evening's events. Joe was bartending. I was at the bar perhaps thirty minutes when a small man wearing a cowboy hat entered the tavern and walked directly to Joe. They conversed, speaking low. I could tell there was tension in the conversation by their gestures. Suddenly Joe pointed at me. The Man turned his gaze in my direction, shook Joe's hand, and approached my table waddling like a penguin. "Are you Jimmie Linguine?"

"I am what can I do for you?"

"My name is Roy Rice. I am Deputy Sherriff here in Merrimack County. Did you know Luta Coffin?"

"Yes, I met here at the bar, last night," I said, "why?"

"She's dead." His tone was cold, uncaring, and that made me nervous.

"How?"

"Let me just say she died under suspicious circumstances," He administered a stern look at my face and continued his gaze for an uncomfortably long time before he spoke again, "A gunshot wound to the head. How well did you know her?"

"Not very well at all, I just met her."

"Where were you between six this morning and one this afternoon?"

"I went to Governor Madison's Office, arrived about ten—stayed with the governor for about half an hour and then went to the United Electrical Union, and Pipe Fitters Organization, and…"

Roy interrupted, "What about last night?"

"I was in my hotel room."

I knew the next question from Rice's critical stare, "Alone?"

I paused, "No, Luta was with me. She passed out last night. I took her to my room. She left this morning between eight and eight-thirty."

"Did you take her home?"

"No she walked home alone," I said.

"Do you own a gun Mr. Linguine?"

"Do I need a lawyer? Am I under suspicion…?"

"If you think you need one, get one, I am just investigating a probable crime," Rice said.

I thought about closing my statements, and getting an attorney, but decided against it, "Yes," I said, "I own a gun."

"Do you have it with you?"

The Perfect Plan

"In my room," I said.

"Show me." Rice followed me to my room. I opened the door, walked into the closet, reached for my robe. The robe felt light—too light. The gun was missing.

Interjection: A video of the executive in charge's critique of Scripter 3's writing:

Apparently unhappy with the writing of the previous scene, the executive in charge filmed an example of creative visualization to improve, "Scripter 3's anemic writing techniques."

The Executive's Example:

"Jimmie linguine suffers a contraction of his intestines from the loss of his pistol. Due to severe distress, he ejects predigested mushrooms and pulled pork. A clock recites the passing minutes with thunderous drums. In addition, the room that he occupies contracts to a point of near suffocation; then expands to a point of perpetuity and contracts again with loud monstrous noises. All light withdrew into the void of unconsciousness and Jimmie loses control of his bladder." Do you understand? Rewrite the scene.

Rewrite:

— "In my room," I said, trembling as if the walls were closing in on me. I could barely breathe.

"Show me," Rice said and followed me to my room. I opened the door, walked into the closet, reached for my robe. The robe felt light too light. The gun was missing. I puked, the ticking clock became insanely loud. I could hardly breathe.

Breathe.

I pissed in my pants and fainted. I must have been unconscious for a considerable length of time because...

CHAPTER 10

Escape

I awoke sucking on Virginia Fawn's teat. We were in her hotel room. Both of us were naked. She looked great. Virginia placed her finger under my chin and raised my head slightly, but I did not release my nipple-grip, "Jimmie," she said. I rolled my eyes up, "Did you kill Luta."

Still suckling, I shook my head, no. She placed her hand on my forehead and pushed. Reluctant to release my pale pacifier, I sucked harder. Her breast once firm and round stretched; became elongated. She whimpered in pain, paused, stopped pushing, and reached with timorous fingers for her purse. She swung the bag wildly, and repeatedly. After the fourth or fifth blow, she managed to knock me off her nipple. "Damn it Linguine you are Sooo immature," she said, "Get up and get your clothes on." I stepped into my grey jubilee trousers and buttoned my shirt midway so that the single chest hair that I had pampered since my early teens stood proudly as a signpost of masculinity.

"They are looking for the gun you know, you need to get your shit together."

"But."

"No buts, we have to go. Pack and be quick about it." Virginia said.

"But what happened to Deputy Roy Rice?"

"I told Deputy Rice that you suffered from fainting spells caused by Erotophobia, commonly known as sexual incompetence. And that you," Virginia stuck her finger in my chest, crushing the sprig of unaccompanied hair...

"That's a lie. I don't have sexual issues, quite the contrary; the Kinsey Institute for Sexual Awareness awarded me a phallus-shaped trophy for my performance in the short film, *The Art of Love*."

Virginia looked at me, rubbed the index finger of her right hand beneath her dripping proboscis, while administering, with her left hand, a painful slap across my cheek. She glowered, and said as I writhed on the floor in pain, "The deputy will come back and continue his investigation is that what you want?"

"No," I whined, as my spine liquesced.

"Then go get your things."

I went to my room and collected my clothing, made a quick and unsuccessful search for my gun, and then made my way to the bathroom where I

The Perfect Plan

gathered my personal items.

Virginia met me in the hall. "Where are we going?" I asked.

"Nevada," she said, "we are going to Carson City Nevada."

We burst out of the hotel like two convicts in an unplanned escape. Virginia with her dress pulled above her knees arrived at the car well before I did. My pace, slowed by the weight of my luggage hampered my stride. I arrived at the vehicle utterly exhausted. She opened the car's rusted door, shoved me in, took my bags, and effortlessly threw the luggage in the back seat. I had barely fastened my safety belt when she slid into the driver's seat, stepped on the gas, and jolted us from a sedentary position to rocket speed within a few seconds.

We were well outside Concord before I had breath enough to speak, "Why Nevada?"

"The primaries," she said. "We need to meet Senator Hays, and work on his campaign."

"What about Lighthouse?"

"Lighthouse is an ass. We are switching sides."

"What do you mean by we? I work for Tibbs. He assigned me to Lighthouse. I am not part of this —whatever this is."

"Jimmie, Lighthouse set you up. He planted your gun at the scene of Luta's murder."

"What! Why?"

"Something you did to him."

"What did I do?"

"I don't know what it was, he didn't say, but it must have been bad."

I remained silent for the next hour and a half. The contents of my bowels were bubbling, probably a reaction to stress. I farted. It was silent and malodorous. Virginia rolled down the window. I yelled through the cold air rushing through the car, "I have to go to the bathroom."

"I know," she screamed.

Fifteen torturous minutes later, we came upon an ancient service station. A sign, disturbed by a light breeze, voiced a noisy complaint. A light flickered in the small office where an attendant sat reading a magazine. He was an ugly ape-like creature. Virginia went into the station and paid the ape. He followed her out and began pumping the gas. I gave her a backward glance and dashed to the men's room. The doughnut-shaped lid, stained with age and use was suitable in my tenuous condition. Sitting on the sticky seat made me queasy, the odor was ghastly. My mind, however, was clear. I am a wanted man. A criminal. I should have stayed and defended my name, my reputation. A dull brown moth interrupted my thoughts as it danced along the graffiti-marred wall. As I watched the insect rumba around the stall, I noticed a message penciled in bold black letters. The message, dated October 31, 1925, read, "Jimmie Linguine was here." I scanned the remaining wall, and to my surprise found the same message dated 1955, and 1985. It is a tradition, I thought as I

The Perfect Plan

penned the same message with today's date.

"Jimmie, are you alright?" It was Virginia.

"Yeah," I said, "be right out."

She was waiting for me in the car. I climbed in, "Where are we?"

"Somewhere outside of Cicero I think," she said.

The attendant, framed by the storefront window gazed at us intently. His admonishing stare may have been caused by the odor I had left behind. Virginia put the car in gear and drove away. I spent the next five hours trying to recall my previous visits to that particular stall in that particular gas station in or around Cicero Illinois. I knew it was hopeless.

We shared the task of driving and traveled straight through the night, only stopping for food and gas. Exhausted, we found a small, cheap hotel in Oakley Kansas, and spent the first part of the night employing Kinsey's five-steps to sexual fulfillment. I reluctantly stopped at Virginia's insistence to capture a few hours of sleep but resumed humping even though it was a dry hump, (meaning puncturing my pillow,) until dawn.

We arrived in Carson City in the sunny calm of a new day. The rubber tires of the old tin can we were in hummed softly on the black asphalt, "We need to find Senator Hays," Virginia said.

"Do you have his number?"

"Yes."

"Well call him," I said.

She pulled over to a phone booth and dialed his number. Hays answered the phone with a curt, excessively loud, hello. Virginia explained her wish to support him and he provided directions to his hotel. We met him in the lobby of the Plaza Hotel. Senator William Henry Hays was a thin man with a thin face. He rarely smiled, but when he did, his yellow teeth forced you to place your attention elsewhere. The candidate dressed somberly as if he was an undertaker and he had a two-day growth of un-presidential stubble that peppered his jowls and chin with varying shades of grey. His voice carried the peculiar nasal whine of a southerner. "Lighthouse is gaining on me," he whined, "the race at this point is dead even."

"Have you talked to John Myers?" Virginia asked.

"Come let's go to my room where we can talk in private," Hays said.

We followed the thin man to his room. We entered. He closed the door behind us. "No," Hays said, "he is the problem. Lighthouse's people have gotten a list John's girlfriends and are threatening to go public if he continues to support me."

"You mean hookers," Virginia said.

"What can we do?" I asked.

"I don't know?" Hays said.

"Do you think it's time to send in the clown?" Virginia said.

Hays's eyes lit up, "I wanted to save him for later, but yes," he exclaimed, "It is time for the

The Perfect Plan

clown?"

Virginia placed her arm around my shoulder. She, at six-feet-two-inches, was a foot taller than I was and I could smell the cologne she wore. She smelled divine. "Jimmie," she said, "it's time."

"Time for what?"

"The Clown." Hays interjected, "Don't you remember?"

"No, I don't know what you are talking about."

"I was afraid of that," Virginia said.

"Bring the slide projector let's see if we can jog Mr. Linguine's memory."

Hays retrieved a slide projector from his luggage, placed it on the table, and pointed it at the wall. He pressed the play button, placed himself between Virginia and me, and the three of us watched the wall intently.

A date first appeared. The date, March 7, 1775, was written in amateurish white lettering on a blackboard. On the next slide, a title appeared superimposed over a Native American face. The caption read, 'Tecumseh'. The following scene caught me off guard. I was standing (it looked like me) in an open field, leaning on an ancient rifle—a muzzle-loader to be exact. There were bodies lying on the blood-covered grass. This scene segued into a continuous display of photographs. One photograph would appear; then disappear, as another photo would come into view. I recognized Virginia, and Roy Rice, and Luta

Coffin's face. The vast majority of faces and scenes that appeared, I could not identify. "What's going on?" I asked.

"Wait until you have seen them all," Hays said. The photos continued. All were unrecognizable, but one—the last one—that picture was of me. I was dressed in a clown suit, much like the pajamas, I wore as a kid. The suit was lemon yellow. Orange rings laddered the right arm and a light blue ruffled collar circled my neck. I wore a monocle over my left eye, and a purplish wig sat atop my bald head. I looked ridiculous. The strangest thing, however, was that my left ear was missing. The slideshow ended with me scratching my head and saying, "Was that me?"

"Yes," Virginia and Hays answered in unison.

"Okay, what is this all about?" I asked.

"Let me see if I can explain," Virginia said. "You know you are a Weeper soul, a soul that begins and ends at specific life cycles?"

"Yes."

"Well, something happened to you during one of your life cycles?"

"A bomb blast," Virginia said.

"A bomb blast?" I asked in disbelief.

"That is correct," Hays said, "and the accident has altered the stability of your many lives. You can now move forward and back in your life cycles. That is relive say 1955 through 1985, and in the next life cycle you may be in your first or thousandth life."

The Perfect Plan

"You can never complete your purpose skipping around like that," Virginia said. "You tend to modify your life based on the scrambled memories that reside in your head. In other words, part of your past can appear in your future and vice versa."

"Which means?"

"Which means you may change an event so that it makes sense in your current life"

"Like losing my ear?"

"Yes," Virginia said.

"Can you guys help fix it?"

"No, but you can help us fix our past, present, and future," Hays said.

"Why would I do that?"

"Jimmie, I need to be elected to change the world for the better. My legacy will last for a thousand years, maybe more."

"I need to change some things to Jimmie, horrible things that I have done in my life," Virginia said.

"I don't know," I said, "changing things may not be the best solution to your problems, and how do I know what life you guys are in at this moment. This could be my past or future." I thought for a moment, "Or Virginia you could be in my past and William Henry Hays, you could be in my future, yet both of you are here in my present life." Virginia and, Mr. Hays looked confused. "Anyway, I don't think it will work."

"Jimmie, you only have twenty-eight more

days. Please consider our proposal. Let us fulfill our destiny, please." Hays said.

Virginia took my hand, "Okay, no pressure, it is solely up to you Jimmie. Let's go get a room. I am tired and hungry. William here is paying all expenses." She smiled at Hays, "Isn't that right William?"

"Yes, that is right, you guys enjoy yourself- relax, have a good time." Hays winked at me. Virginia pulled me through the door and escorted me to the lobby where she signed for a room. The primary was in three days. Mr. Lighthouse, we were told was headquartered at the Wyndham Garden Hotel. I was certain he had spies at our hotel, The Plaza and expressed my concerns to Virginia. She told me not to worry, "Hays," she said, "had everything covered."

Virginia opened the door to our room. We unpacked I stretched out on the bed. Virginia sat beside me. "Have you called Tibbs and told him we have bailed on Senator Lighthouse?"

"No," she said.

"Lighthouse is going to be pissed." I mumbled, "Tibbs too. We will be blacklisted, you know."

Virginia snorted, "What's worse working for that snake Lighthouse of working for Senator Hays who is trying to do what is right in this world? Or, you could go back to Concord and give yourself up to the authorities."

I administered a brazen glare at Virginia, "I

didn't murder that woman."

"Shush, not so loud."

I sat up, "Well what are we going to do about Tibbs?"

A smile spread across her face. "I'll call him and let him know that we quit the firm if that will make you feel better."

"Yes," I said, "that would make me feel a lot better." Ten a clock that night Virginia called Mr. Tibbs' office and left a message stating simply, "Jimmie and I quit. Deposit what you owe us into our bank accounts. Thank you."

Virginia and I spent two days canvassing for Senator Hays. We spent our nights making love. I must admit Virginia was a talented sexual deviant. She was especially good this morning, it was difficult for me to get out of bed but today was Election Day, and it was imperative that we arrive at the meeting on time. We met Hays at the rally. It was about nine in the morning and his supporters were confident that Hays would win the election. Early polls indicated that Senator Hays had a slight lead over Lighthouse, but by eleven thirty that morning we heard the bad news John Myers the president of the Anthem Corporation pulled his support for Hays. It was all over the news and went viral over the airwaves. The statement given by the corporate spokesperson was that Senator Hays was harboring a criminal. I skulked into an isolated corner as a hush fell over his followers. By the end of the day, it was evident that Lighthouse

Donald D'lo

had won the primary. I remained in the corner nervously eating a licorice stick that I had pilfered from a toddler, and remained in my corner, self-secluded until my arrest and extradition out of Nevada. I did not get a chance to hear Hays's concession speech. I died in Merrimack County jail from an embolic stroke twenty-five days later.

CHAPTER 11

Mother Urdu Decides not to Intervene

I pulled away from her nipple long enough to take a breath and asked, "How many deaths is this for me now Mother Urdu?" I returned my lips to her nipple and awaited her response.

"Let me think Jimmie," She did the math in her head. "You have lived three-hundred-thirty-one very short lifetimes. You are the first and only weeper soul in existence, and I feel so sad for you. If it was not for the agreement Loki made with Prosperous," she wiped a tear from her eye. "You would have lived full lives," Mother Urdu wiped a tear from her other eye. "You cannot live a full life if it is limited to thirty years." She whimpered.

"And one day," I said.

"Yes," she agreed, "thirty years and one day."

"How do you pick mothers for the reincarnates?" I asked; then began nursing again

"Well, in most cases, I pick mothers based on

the soul's need to fulfill its purpose in life. But, in your case Jimmie, you must go to an apathetic mother that lacks ambition. And, I have to do the opposite when I pick Prosperous' mother. His soul's purpose is based on greed. You and Prosperous are the only two exceptions. You two are contraries, *yin, and yang.*"

I spat her nipple out, "What is yin and yang?"

"They are opposites," Mother Urdu said, "Opposites placed together brings harmony." She pulled my little hand to her lips and kissed my fingers. "You are yang, Prosperous is yin," she said. I felt her warm breath on the back of my knuckles and giggled.

"What are you going to do about Loki?" I asked.

"That," she said, "is my destiny—my problem —and my purpose…. well one of my many purposes in life." She hesitated, "I really would like for him to do the right thing."

I fell asleep in Mother Urdu's arms and awoke between the knees of my mother, Liz.

CHAPTER 12

Jimmie Linguine died in Merrimack County jail

You may recall that I died in Merrimack County jail from an embolic stroke. I became aware of my next birth when Liz, my mother farted during parturition. I was about halfway out when the fart rumbled between her thighs and touched upon a singular reality—an Einstein flash of lucidity. That gaseous discharge crystallized into meaning within my infantile mind, and for that, I am eternally grateful to my mother. The veracity of my insight was mind-blowing. The magnitude of thought, overwhelming. This concept, I surmised, is the basic building block of understanding why we are reborn. Until now it was a mystery, until now, it did not matter... but now it does. Wow!

I must admit, I was so involved with my theory, I forgot to breathe, but after a hard ass slap from the doctor, I was pumping air like a blacksmith's bellow. After the shock of life settled in,

I began to decipher my ascension theory. The answer, I understood, as the doctor cut the umbilical cord, is that we are all born with a purpose. My purpose was soon apparent... but never fulfilled.

Because.

As soon as the doctor handed me to my mother, Liz, she dropped me. I hit the floor with a hollow thud. The accident caused blunt force trauma to my head. My cerebrum to be exact, and I never recovered.

The second time Liz dropped me was on the side of the road, and like Anus, the Tibetan boy adopted by jackals, I found a home with a pack of wolves. I was happy for the next thirty years, and because I was living like an animal, I never again developed or presented a serious hypothesis on the rationale for re-birthing or anything else for that matter except food and sex.

I died 30 years and one day after I was born. My demise took place on the road, (near the spot where my mother dropped me off as a baby,) an inattentive motorist struck me as I crossed the newly constructed I-911 Interstate Highway. I was in pursuit of a rabbit.

CHAPTER 13

Hypnotherapy

Destiny Johnson, aka Virginia Fawn, contacted me on a rainy night in October. The purpose of her interaction I found out later was to blame me for the Vietnam War. This is how it happened:

I was twenty-five and working as a part-time street clown and fish scaler, (t'was a Temp Job,) for the Salmon Canning Company out of Seattle Washington. My pay was so meager I had to live in a cardboard box. I felt overwhelmed, emotionally, and decided with prodigious forethought to offer my devastated state of mind to the public. Seeking stability on the metal knob of a fire hydrant, I began my tirade.

"There is no torture as constricted, and hurtful as to be bound, and beset, (It is myself; I am speaking of) in a cardboard box, ill, and without sustenance, or friendship. My medical symptoms caused by intestinal worms and cooties produced a constant itching and bowl discharge. I have also experienced in my life a prolonged financial collapse which in turn led to a mental breakdown. My miseries were so extreme I sold my clown shoes to buy food. That act of disparagement made me withdraw from society, hence my lack of friends..."

Silence.

"I need money!"

Having espoused my situation to a solitary wino I returned to my box. Apparently, that wino had connections because the next night a woman came to the cardboard home in which I lived; she was attractive, well dressed, and personable. Bear with me please; I have inserted the following phrase 'happily' into the narrative to bolster my failing ego. Anyway, I *happily* invited her into my home. She elegantly dropped down on all fours, being careful not to bruise her knees and wormed her way inside the dark confines of my packaging box. I smiled as she held a kerchief to her nose to buffer the smell.

There are two sources of odor in my box. One source is that I scavenge for the primary foundation of my sustenance—fish—from trash cans. Seattle has an abundance of partially eaten fish, which has; I must admit a lingering odor, and 'number two' is that and my dysentery, (my number two,) added to the stench.

The Perfect Plan

I smiled again; she returned my smile with a schmaltzy grin. I noticed her eyes lower to the sardine skeletons and soupy poop on the floor. She gagged once, recuperated nicely without heaving, and extended her hand. I accepted her appendage and administered a courteous kiss on her hairless knuckles.

Oh joy, she was without a ring.

She immediately wiped the kiss from her backhand with her hankie. "My name is Destiny Johnson. My divination reveals that I have known you for a long time, Jimmie."

"Really, I don't remember you," I said.

A clap of thunder startled both of us. It began to rain heavily and water began to seep through the corrugated paper roof.

"Is there somewhere else we can go," she said as she placed her hand as a means of support on the ceiling of the disintegrating roof.

"Your place," I said jokingly.

She replied with an admonishing, "No!" She paused, administered a stern look, and then continued in a casual cadence, "There is a restaurant close by we can talk there." We exited the soggy back-flap of my collapsed home and I followed her two blocks to Dixie's Deli. At first, Dixie would not let me in, but she capitulated with a twenty in hand, courtesy of Destiny. The owner appeared nervous as she led us to a corner booth. We sat opposite each other. "I'll get straight to the point," Destiny said.

"Eat first," I implored and waved Dixie over to our table. I ordered a coconut cream pie and coffee. Destiny abstained, claiming intolerance of C_{12}-H_{22}-O_{11}. I ate while she talked. "I want to know what happened. I want to know why you didn't kill Omar."

"What," I exclaimed spewing post-ingested pie over her beautiful personage.

"I want you to see a hypnotherapist," Destiny said while cleaning pie from her heavily browed face. I loved those dark cryptic brows arched above her dreary yet mysterious eyes. She interrupted my thoughts, "Did you hear me?"

I glanced down at her unbanned hand. "How much are you willing to pay?"

After a lengthy Medusa-like stare, she spoke decisively, "Fifty dollars."

"Okay," I said. Destiny put a five spot on the table, dawned a pair of gloves she held in her purse, grabbed me by the cuff of my clown collar, pulled me outside (it was still raining) and hailed a cab. We arrived at a gothic house somewhere in the suburbs. I admit I was not paying attention to our travels. I was instead coveting my lovely companion's slim body. We arrived at our destination, exited the cab, and paced casually, with Destiny in the lead to a red door. My companion rang the doorbell with her rigid index finger.

An old woman appeared. She had more wrinkles than a Shar-Pei. The hag glared at me through overlapping waves of facial skin and provided a droopy smile, "Come in," the old woman said. Destiny pulled me inside the house. "My name is Beth Wallace," the old harpy screamed over the royalty-free *soothing* music that played on her computer. I had heard the same music a million times at the homeless shelter. "What I would like to do," Beth said interrupting my fond memories of an overcrowded home, "Is to hypnotize you. We would like to discover certain portions of your past."

I noticed snot leaking from Beth's pronounced aquiline nose—t'was a hypotenuse centered between mounds of fleshy-rotund hills. My interest peaked for I too have the same malady. I studied her intently—watched the stream flow to the crest of her lip. I smiled as she cleverly flicked her tongue up and swept her upper lip with the apex of her median sulcus. It was an Ah-Ha moment. I have learned a discreet method of mucus removal. It was well worth the trip to the Gotham House of Hypnotherapy. I wondered if she knew anything about the removal of cooties and or intestinal worms.

"Ahem," Destiny said, effectively breaking my deliberation on the furtive removal of snot and parasitic insects.

"What?" I said.

"Your past?" Destiny said in a low angry voice.

"Give me the money and go for it," I said.

Destiny reached into her purse and retrieved

fifty dollars. I took the money and placed it in my back pocket—a precaution in case someone wanted to lift the cash during the hypnotherapy session. I sat in a well-padded beautifully embroider green and gold Elizabethan armchair. Beth turned the volume up on the pastoral music and told me I was getting tired, blah, blah, blah. She counted down from ten to zero. Beth said in a whisper, "Go back to July 4th in Lexington Kentucky. You met Dasia. Tell us what you see and what happened."

"Close your eyes."
I closed my eyes.
"What do you see?"
"Nothing it is dark."
"Try harder, concentrate. What do you see?"

Silence.

"I see two oil lamps on the small tables on each side of her bed. We are in love, uh, making love. The light from the lamp dances on the cabin walls. The cabin smells like apples. I set my stride for a marathon of plowing. It does not go well. I last maybe thirty seconds. Dasia, in tune with my comings and goings, feels the urgency, predicts my climax and yells *pull it out now!* I am unwilling to comply and cling tightly to her body. She dislodges me with a hefty push. I roll over. My love juice showers the ceiling—it is a low ceiling."

Silence.

The Perfect Plan

"Yes, yes, then what?" The old hag murmured. I hear her accelerated breathing.

Dasia says, "Kill a baby who will become Omar the Librarian and I will give you an above the knees' knob and let you stick it back in."

I say, "Why should I kill a potential Librarian?"

She replies with frustration in her voice, "Because Omar the Librarian is the forbearer of Charles the Magnate who is the forbearer of Johnson the illustrious, and the list goes on until Lyndon Baines Johnson (LBJ) appears. Johnson, as Vice President will have President John F. Kennedy shot, and LBJ will escalate the Vietnam War."

"Did you kill the kid?" The hag asked.

"No, there wasn't a kid there."

"What happened next?" she asked.

"I gaze at Dasia's breasts—her divine nipples, and I say, I will kill the kid if I can find him. She smiles and we get back to it."

"Yes, yes," Beth said, "what happened next?"

"Someone stabs me in the back."

Silence.

"I could have gone another ten, maybe twenty more minutes, but I died before the climax."

"Damn," Beth said.

I heard Destiny give another 'Ahem'.

Beth continued, "Did you kill Omar in your

next life?"

"Nope."

"Are you sure?"

"Yep, I would remember killing a kid. I would remember something like that!"

"Okay, that's it." Beth Wallace snapped her fingers three times, and said, "Wake up." I opened my eyes and smiled at the gorgeous Ms. Destiny Johnson. She seemed unhappy. She clasped her hands tightly together in front of her as if in prayer.

I reached for her shoulder, patted her gently, and said, "It's not your fault." She in response to my kindness reached into the purse cradled in her lap. I was elated—confident that she was going to give me more money. She lifted her eyes and gazed casually at my face. I smiled and extended my hand to receive the cash. She withdrew a gun from the mouth of her purse, and shot me in the eye; luckily, for me, it was a BB gun.

Jimmie's Reflection

I completed my own one-eyed investigation about Omar using **whoisyoursister.com** and **DNA-Yesterday, Today, and Forever Research Center**, with the following results. Dasia's father, Lester Delimit impregnated her, his own daughter—rotten bastard, and Dasia had a little boy.

Soon after the child was born, Lester gave the baby, Omar to settlers headed for Texas. The information Dasia provided about LBJ is true Omar

The Perfect Plan

was LBJ's great, great, grandfather. I guess she was right the death of one child could have stopped that horrible war.

Silence.

I felt somehow responsible. There was another President from Texas, however, that I could have—should have killed, but did not—not my purpose in life. My purpose in life is to stop, if possible, the Turkey Revolt of 3054 and by doing so, destroy the world. Nothing else matters.

Silence.

Perhaps something else did matter—while reminiscing, I discovered another thing—A missed opportunity if you will... Before Destiny shot me, I should have asked Beth Wallace if she knew a remedy for cooties and intestinal worms. A cure would have made my short life much more pleasant.

CHAPTER 14

Fighting Gravity

I was born fighting gravity and arrived upside-down. I mean my mother, Mary Johnston, was upside-down when I was born. The small airplane was gliding bottom-up. Ten years later, my mother explained. "It was, as you can imagine, a messy birth. Lawrence Johnston, my boyfriend, and your father loved to fly. He was a professional stunt flier, a barnstormer his fans used to say. Lawrence and I were flying in a comedic contest. I was (even though nine months pregnant) tethered on the plane and he would flip the plane over, and fly upside-down with me hanging vertically to the ground. This sort of stunt was popular back in the day. It was called 'girl-on-a-wing'." She smiled, "Anyway, there I was hanging when I got nauseous and had a belly cramp, then another, and I thought it was, you know, kind-of-like, um, uh, impacted bowls from inverted flying. I mean you were my first child, I didn't know anything about birthing a baby. Well, it wasn't long after that—that I got another horrible pain.

The Perfect Plan

I thought I lost control of my bladder. Then your little turnip head popped out, all purple and white, and bald. Soon the rest of you came out. You were waving your precious little hand at me. I reached for and managed to grab that little flagging mitt of yours. We hit a bit of turbulence, I dropped you but managed to snatch your umbilical cord, and pulled you screaming like a banshee to my chest." Mother patted me on the head. "We landed a few minutes later, and the crowd roared with excitement." She looked at me lovingly and said, "Got put in the Guinness World Book of Records."

A little bird popped out of the small Bavarian Cabin hanging on the wall and sung, "Coo Coo, Coo Coo, Coo Coo." The Clock was a gift from Lawrence.

Mother smiled and pulled an old black-and-white photograph from the escritoire. The picture was of a young woman (my mother) standing beside a Piper Cub airplane with Lawrence. He was dressed in a leather helmet with dark goggles and combat boots. A banner labeled Linco Flying Aces streamed next to the odd-looking couple. Mother plucked another photograph out of the drawer and pointed to a miniature pilot dressed exactly like Lawrence. "That's you," mother said proudly tapping my Kodachrome captured face.

"What happened to my father?" I asked. It was a ritual question. She provided her answer with a cheerful locution. "Oh, Lawrence changed his name to Larry Incarnate and ran off with a fella named Roy Rice. Seems like your Pa preferred men over women." Mother thought for a moment, "He wasn't your real pa, though. You son are a product of *immaculate conception*, that's clean creation in laymen's terms, or as I like to call it having a baby without a man's participation." She smiled, lovingly and spat into her cupped hands. Mother rubbed her hands together, and then mussed and fashioned a bonnet of spiked hair, atop my head.

I brushed her hands away, and said, "But mama how did I get my name if I don't have a pa?"

Mother stretched her lips over the length of her overbite and grinned. "There was an important businessman. I can't recollect his name now. I remember he was handsome though. He paid me seventy dollars one night for a date; got me drunk, which, by the way, I thoroughly enjoyed," she winked at me. Her grin spread even wider. "He left a note on the couch sometime during the night that said name the boy Jimmie Linguine." Mother took a deep breath, and continued, "That son is how you got your name."

Interjection: Information provided by the Texas State Department of Child Welfare.

The Texas State Department of Child Welfare in an effort to collect child support completed an investigation concerning the mysterious man who named Jimmie Linguine. The only items

The Perfect Plan

found were a small pile of ashes and a housefly trapped on a strip of flypaper. The current small town consensus is that the Devil's entomologist, Beelzebub did the deed and wrote the note; then destroyed the evidence. Poof, just like that.

Interjection: A handwritten note provided by Roy Rice's sister-in-law, Doris Detent concerning Roy's attempted murder.

"Roy Rice and Larry Incarnate were at a strip and tease joint called the Blues Club when a parochial bastard disguised as an Arab, came into the establishment, and shot Roy Rice. The wound was high and on the fleshy extremity of Roy's hip. Since it was a gay bar, the incident remained under wraps, i.e. no cops were involved. There was speculation however as to who was the shooter. A jealous ex-boyfriend ranked high on the list, as did Roy's bookie for an unsettled debt. Roy's barber was mentioned as the possible shooter due to an unpaid shave, and Roy's cousin Leroy was a suspect because he wrecked Roy's prized Cadillac. The CIA, it was rumored, wanted Roy shot, (I don't know what that was about), and Lawrence's son, Jimmie Linguine was also a suspect."

CHAPTER 15

Ref: Counter Cultural Era

Some Radical Hippie Pals

I found out that I had been adopted when the State of Texas institutionalized my mother. She confessed during a temperate interrogation that she stole me as I lay sleeping on the doorstep of the Saint Croix Church in El Paso Texas. I was fifteen when they locked her up in a psychiatric hospital and placed me in a foster home. My foster parents were Ernest and Mneme Pile. Mr. Pile was a history professor with an ambition for politics. He ran unsuccessfully for Marfa City Councilor but failed to garner enough votes. I stayed with the Pile's for three years before moving to Austin, then to Chicago, where I went to work as a junior reporter for the Blue News, an underground newspaper. The news chief asked me to cover the antiwar movement. His contact suggested that several groups including the Maladies planned to protest the Democratic Convention in Chicago's International Amphitheatre.

The Perfect Plan

I met Adonis Baxter at a coffee house on 3rd street. He was wearing beads and a checkered tabletop poncho fresh off a booth in Derry's Dinner. His hair was a rat's nest of curls and tangles with twigs and other unidentifiable 'shiny' material, perhaps tinfoil, embedded in his unkempt mop. I was clothed in jeans and a t-shirt. I wore sandals and recently dyed a strip of my head-hair purple. It was a real attention getter. Adonis brushed his hands on his pants scattering white powder in a widening circle around him. He extended his arm, provided a vigorous shake, and said, right off the bat, "My name is Adonis Baxter, and I am the Clown Prince of Radicals." He had a reassuring smile.

"My name is-"

"I know your name," Baxter interrupted. "You are here for the Convention, yes?"

"That's right," I replied.

"Great, by the way, I like your hair. C'mon lets walk and talk." I hesitated, briefly and glanced warily at the surrounding buildings. "Don't freak out Jimmie, I'm cool," he said as he put his arm around my shoulder and we swaggered down the sidewalk like a couple of beautiful Benjamin's. As we strolled along Adonis said, "I do revolution-via-the absurd."

"So I've heard."

Adonis smiled.

"The attempted left-wing alignment of the

Pentagon was... different," I said as I tried to stay in-step with Adonis.

"Yeah," Adonis chuckled, "but, I couldn't get the military to surrender."

"And the New York Stock Exchange! What was that all about?"

"Some radicals—Hippie pals and I went to the stock exchange to protest the War, capitalism and of course, corrupt corporate controlled big government. It was crazy. We walked in there like a bunch of badasses and tried to exchange monopoly money, for real cash. We had a blast. It got weird though when the cops arrived. They took us seriously." Adonis kicked a discarded beer can down the sidewalk. We marched on.

"What happened?"

"Spent the night in the hoosegow." Adonis looked at me and smiled, "Hey do you want to meet my chick?" He gave the can a final kick and sent it sailing into the gutter.

I returned his smile, "Sure."

We walked another five or six blocks and entered a rundown flophouse. His apartment was on the third floor, number thirty-five. The door was open. A waterbed stained by brews and assorted human seepages sprawled like a busted rubber raft on the floor. I heard the toilet flush as we entered and out came this great looking girl in tight red short-shorts.

"Here she is, Candy Courtney, the love of my life," Adonis said.

Candy strutted to her lover, placed her arms over his shoulders, and said, "Oh, my Clown Prince of Radicals." Then they commenced kissing. While they were lip-locked, I leisurely scoped out the room. The whole place was filthy. I returned my attention to the couple they were still at it—the French kiss had become repulsive.

"Um-hum," I said. They unlocked for a moment and looked at me as if annoyed. She turned, walked to a nightstand, and retrieved a half-smoked joint. Candy scratched a match across the scarred tabletop and held the flame to the joint's tip. The tip glowed red as she sucked in the acrid smoke and propelled it in two wispy ribbons from her nostrils. Candy was wearing a loose blouse that perfectly displayed the shape of her apple-sized breasts. As she raised her hand to pull the doobie from her painted lips, I noticed her hairy armpits; then glanced lower to her unshaven legs.

"Candy, this is Jimmie Linguine," Adonis said.

"Nice to meet you," Candy exclaimed as she approached me with hand extended. We shook hands, and I must say my eyes lingered on her slightly parted blouse. She wasn't wearing a bra. She noticed my gaze and stuck her tongue out of her lips like a snake seeking prey. I was breathless. A telephone rang. Adonis stepped between us, sat on the deflated mattress, lifted the phone from its cradle, and said, "This is Adonis... okay," was the jest of Adonis' part of the conversation. He hung up the phone and grinned, "We're going to Shitsville for the convention." Adonis said, "You coming Jimmie?"

"What, where is Shitsville? What's going on?"

"You will have to come with us if you want to find out," Adonis said.

Candy grabbed my arm, "This is going to be a blast." She brushed against my thigh, "You coming?"

"Sure."

We jumped into Candy's VW bug and headed east. She drove to an abandoned garage on Chicago's south side where we met the renowned James Robin, Phil Dean, and other radicals that I did not recognize. They were in an old dented station wagon carrying, to my surprise, a turkey imprisoned in a wooden crate. The turkey gobbled an ardent complaint about his confines as we jousted each other for a seat.

"I'll go with Jerry." Adonis said above the turkey's gobble, "You guys meet us at the Civic Center, in front the president's sculpture." James stepped on the gas. Adonis laughed, the turkey gobbled frantically, and the remaining protestors provided a parade wave as we peeled out and roared off in a plume of noxious gas.

By the time Candy and I arrived, the demonstrators had already unloaded the turkey. A large crowd of activists surrounded the caged bird. The activists carried signs and placards that read *Dethrone the President-elect,* and *This Turkey is the most Qualified Candidate.* James was in the process

The Perfect Plan

of reading the Deceleration of Independence when the cops arrived. The police arrested Adonis and five other protesters. They went before Judge Wilmore. The magistrate charged Adonis and his pals with disorderly conduct, disturbing the peace, and violation of city ordinances. The violation was for having unpermitted livestock at Chicago's Civic Center. Wilmore released Adonis and his fellow Maladies on a twenty-five dollar bond. Candy and I met Adonis at the courthouse steps. He entered the car laughing.

"What's so funny?" Candy asked.

"One of the cops said the turkey offered his life for the Maladies freedom. Can you believe it a cop with a sense of humor?" Candy planted her lips on Adonis's lips. He continued his laughter. It sounded like a turkey gobble, (corny but true,) as Candy's tongue worked its way down Adonis's vocal cords.

We hung out at Candy's pad a couple of days getting stoned—primarily on weed, but had a little acid too. Numerous people came and went. Including members from the National Conference against War, and Students for a Free Society. The groups were organizing the protest during the Democratic Convention. I left for my pad two days before the convention and reported to my Editor Mr. John Checkoff over the phone. I notified him of the current affairs, i.e. my relationship with Adonis Baxter, and promised to have the story on radicalized youth ready for his review in a week. I was not aware that the FBI followed me, nor that they had bugged my phone. Sometime around midnight, I got a phone call. It was Candy saying that the FBI had picked up James, Phil, and Adonis. I asked her if she needed company. She said yes. I left immediately and arrived a few minutes later to find her door open. She was on the bed crying. A man was standing over her with a rubber house lifted above his head. "What is going on here," I yelled.

He dropped the hose and pulled his gun, "Identify yourself."

I stepped back with my hands raised, "Jimmie Linguine," I replied.

"Do you know this woman?"

"Yes."

"Did you know that her friends are wanted for murder?"

"Whose murder," I said.

"Mr. Turkey," the man offered a sly grin, "Gotcha," he said. He and Candy broke out in uproarious laughter.

Candy seemed to levitate off the bed, "Jimmy you came for me."

"I did. I thought you were alone... I mean I thought you needed help."

"I do Jimmie, I do." I glanced at the man. She followed my gaze, "Oh, this is Charles Davenport, a close friend." Davenport holstered his weapon. "Charles is with the Chicago Police. We met at a bar on Seventh Street."

The Perfect Plan

"Lovely," I said.

Candy opened a bag and rolled a joint. She retrieved a lighter from the table, flipped it open, and lit the doobie. I noticed Davenport scrutinizing her body as she sucked the smoke to the bottom of her lungs and held it there—when she exhaled these smoky words flowed onto the flat of the table, "I'm sort-of a reporter too. I work for Mayor Daily as an undercover agent." She coughed and took another drag.

"Seriously?" I said.

She exhaled creating another cloud and said as the swirl of smoke levitated, "Seriously, I want you to join us, Jimmie."

"Why would I do that?"

"We need to win this damn war, my friend. We need to show the Commies that we can kick their ass." She thought for a moment, "We can't allow a bunch of draft dodgers and hippie freaks to fuck this country up."

"I don't know Candy. I cherish the right of free speech, and I'm not the kind of person that... well, that misrepresents the truth." Davenport laughed. Candy gave him an unsupportive, almost hostile look. "Jimmie," she continued with smoke flowing from her nose, "this war is backed by some influential people and powerful companies. It is politics, and power Jimmie—always has been." Candy placed her shoulder against Davenport, "This anti-war movement is just a phase. It will end soon. I assure you."

"I have to go," I said and quickly turned toward the door.

"We will see you at the demonstration then Jimmie," Davenport said as I walked through the door, down the hall, and out of the building. I stood on the sidewalk, hailed a cab, and went to my hotel room confused, and disturbed about Candy's motives and Davenport's intent to disrupt the anti-war demonstration.

___0___

The August air was electric with emotions. The demonstrators had split into two camps the (SFS), Students for a Free Society and the (NCAW) National Conference against War. I attended the SFS rally. The poet Arms Long was the speaker. The speech was not inflammatory; on the contrary, it was passive and centered on love and peace. As a precaution, however, the SFS provided LBJ masks to the protesters as a disguise in case parents, employers, or the government was viewing the protest on TV. The NCAW took a more militant approach. The leader Jim Jury spoke into a bullhorn chanting, "Pigs are pussies." I walked a short distance to the NCAW camp and to my surprise saw Adonis raising his fist angrily as he chanted along with Mr. Jury and the other protesters. I approached Adonis from behind and tapped him on the shoulder. He turned. I pulled my mask down and showed my full face to my friend. He smiled his patented smile and embraced me. "I thought you were arrested," I said as I replaced my mask.

"I was my attorney got me out."

"Where's Candy?" I asked testing his knowledge of current events.

"Don't know she wasn't home when I got there."

I decided to leave his ignorance undisturbed. Adonis tapped on the LBJ disguise, "Where did you get the mask?" I pointed to the Students for Peace camp. He laughed, and said, "Pacifists."

A turkey gobbled. I glanced down at the caged bird at Adonis's feet, "He's alive?"

"I bribed a cop," Adonis said. He smiled, "We couldn't let our candidate Mr. Turkey remain behind bars."

I laughed. The humor was short lived.

A swarm of cops arrived suddenly in patrol cars and motorcycles but most of the cops were on foot. All were in riot gear. They formed a line, "Disperse," a cop, yelled from inside his patrol car, "You do not have a permit to gather, disperse immediately."

Adonis had collected an assortment of stones at his feet. He was the first to cast a stone. The rest of the NCAW rushed the cops. The clash was immense. Tear gas came first, and then gunshots and screams. The cops marched forward with batons and shields whacking and slashing at the retreating protesters. The police pushed the NCAW protesters into the SFS group who were watching the carnage from a small parking lot, both groups were pinned against a chain-link fence. The cops went to work. They were relentless, merciless, and arrogant yelling, "We have had enough of your hippy shit, and its jail or hell for you bastards." Eight people, six men, and two women were bludgeoned to death before the police van arrived.

I turned and hauled ass. Two cops singled me out as I tried to flee they gave chase, caught me within a few seconds and began to hit me with their batons. One strike to the back of my head knocked me unconscious. I awoke in a pool of blood and saw from a prone perspective, masks, and bodies lying everywhere. The cries and moans of the injured and dying were horrifying. I tried to rise but a foot planted on my back halted my attempt to escape. "Where do you think you're going?" It was a familiar voice—Candy's voice. She reached for my hands, pulled my arms backward to what I thought was a breaking point. I felt the cold metal of the cuffs, experienced the tightening circle on my wrists, and groaned as she grabbed a purple lock of my hair and jerked me, with the assistance of a fellow officer, to my feet.

CHAPTER 16

Adonis Pulled a Pistol

Agent Candy and her associate grabbed my collar and jerked me to my feet. The turkey gobbled to my left. Sirens blasted on my right, and helicopters dawdled above with an egg-beating rumble. "Where are you taking me?" I yelled, still dazed from the traumatic blow administered to the back of my head.

Candy placed her lips to my ear, "Someplace safe," she whispered. Agent Courtney escorted me to an unmarked car, opened the door, and held my bloody head down as I slid into the back seat.

"What about the turkey?" I asked.

"Davenport will catch him," she paused, "We'll baste the bastard in sarcastic drool and have him for supper tonight." She laughed.

I did not think it was funny and snorted "Bullshit."

The interior of the car smelled like cigarettes and boiled eggs. We, via back alleys and less traveled streets, arrived at a quaint little bungalow on 6th Street (I think), numbered 609. Candy pulled me out of the vehicle and pushed me to the front door of the cottage. She elbowed me aside and rang the bell. A black-clad maid with a ruffled headband opened the door fully and allowed us to enter the house. Candy, with a gentle push, guided me to a large interior door, and said, rather quietly. "Mr. Hatton I have him. He is here with me now."

"Enter."

Candy opened the door. An old man was sitting at his desk in his bathrobe. A spotted dog was at his feet, and a mid-fiftyish woman stood behind him with her hands resting on his shoulders. "Please sit," the old man said. The rasp and wheeze of old age modified his voice. I sat down. Candy stood behind me. "My Name is G.D. Hatton," the old man said.

"What do you want with me, Mr. Hatton?" I asked.

"Your involvement with politics, radical politics will be your undoing," he said.

"I am trying to do what is right—what I believe I was called to do?"

"By whom?" the old man wheezed, clearly agitated at my chutzpah. The woman behind him patted his shoulder to calm him. He patted her hand in return. "Look, Jimmie, it's all about money—always has been. War is an economic tool. It helps raise our standard of living as well as keeps us safe from our enemies."

"We are our own enemies. Greed is our enemy." I said.

"Damn it, Jimmie, you are a smart boy, join us we can make America strong again."

"Why should I, and what is it that I have that you obviously want?"

The old man laughed, "Your abilities Jimmie that's what we want."

"What? ... What kind-a-shit are you slinging old man?" I was near hysteria. Blood rushed to my head. I felt dizzy. "What do you mean abilities? ... What abilities?"

"Your connections with people and disconnection with time. You can create change- you can change reality, change the future as well as the past... so to speak."

"That's not true?"

"You already have."

"How so?" I said loudly.

His eyebrows rose in a thin arch with the question, "The whiskey stocks... Hays?" The old man replied.

A spotted horse and dead Indian flashed through my mind.

"Hat, you in there?" someone said from outside the office door.

"Yes, Ben, come in," The old man replied. The door opened and a young black man entered the room. He was well dressed, probably in his early twenties-kind-of-a preppy college kid with a huge afro. "Jimmie, this is my stepson Ben Dearing. Ben, this is Jimmie Linguine." Ben shook my hand.

"Sorry to interrupt, but I have a meeting with the Young Republicans on campus, can you spare twenty for gas?" Ben said.

Hatton stuck out his long index finger. It shook involuntarily, "Suzan will take care of it. She is in the kitchen."

Ben turned to me, "It was a pleasure meeting you Mr. Linguine."

I gained enough composure to speak sensibly, "Same here."

Ben left the room. Candy closed the door and asked coldly. "What do you want to do with him?"

Hatton coughed violently then tried to regain his breath. His aide retrieved a tissue and handed it to him. He took the flimsy paper and hacked up a wad of phlegm, spat it in the tissue, and said, "Sorry," he tossed the tissue in the trash, and then continued, "How old are you, boy?"

"Twenty-nine," I replied.

"When will you be thirty?"

"My birthday is in a week."

"Well, we can hold him for five or six days until he dies or turn him loose and kill him early in his next thirty-year cycle." Hatton tapped his feeble finger on his desktop, "Turn him loose. Ben can handle it the next time." G.W. said, "Besides I have plans." The dog provided a mixture of barks and subtle growls as I turned to leave.

Candy escorted me out of the house and

placed me in her cruiser. She got in, sat contemplatively for a moment, and lit a cigar. "Do you remember anything Jimmie, I mean about your past and future lives?"

"That is none of your business," I said.

"You don't remember me. We worked together?"

"No, not really."

She took a long drag on a cigar, "Hum, too bad."

"Where are you taking me?"

"To my place," she said.

I traveled perhaps twenty minutes before we arrived at her apartment. Candy parked in the shade of an elm tree behind the apartment complex. We entered through the back door. My hands cuffed behind my back made climbing the staircase difficult and my breathing became labored. I focused on the vacilation of Candy's ass as we ascended two flights of stairs. I was breathless by the time we arrived at her apartment. She unlocked the door, nudged me inside, and closed the door behind her. "Are you going to remove these cuffs?" I asked amid gulps of stale air.

"In time," she replied. She approached me cautiously. I backed up. She stepped with me. I continued to retreat. She accelerated her advance, and before I could react, she shoved me violently. I fell backward on the mattress. She straddled me and began to loosen my shirt.

"Am I interrupting?" Adonis said from the

doorway. Candy failed to lock the door behind her. She turned her head, and a wicked little giggle erupted from her mouth, "As a matter of fact you are, do you mind?" she said.

"Take the cuffs off Jimmie," Adonis said.

"Or what?"

Adonis pulled a pistol from behind his back, "Or, I will shoot you."

"You don't have the balls." Candy said.

Adonis fired. The bullet hit Candy opening a golf-ball sized hole in her chest. The bullet's impact twisted her torso. She faced me with a look of surprise. Candy collapsed on me and convulsed as if the sex act denied an instant earlier came to her in death. I heard a hiss of breath escape from her mouth. Candy died with a strange almost, how should I say this? Pleasurable orgasmic moan.

Adonis searched her body for the keys to the handcuffs. He found them in her pants pocket and unlocked the metal bracelets. With a swift wave of his hand, he motioned for me to follow. Saddened by Candy's death I hesitantly trailed behind him. My mind rumbled through the reasons, of why he killed her. She was no threat to me or Adonis. It could have been good, the sex I mean. It could have been very good, but now I will never know. She did not deserve to die by any expanse of reality. "Hurry," Adonis said as he clamored down the staircase.

My inward thoughts dissolved in a moment of panic, "Where are we going?" I managed to say.

The Perfect Plan

"We have a safe house," he said. Adonis jumped the last few steps and landed on the floor with a thud. I followed suit in an Adrenalin rush fueled by anxiety. He burst out the back door. I leaped and landed in stride. He was already inside the car. "Get in," he said. I opened the passenger side door. The car was moving as I stepped inside. We were roaring down the street at an incredible speed by the time I fastened my seat belt. I noticed blue and red lights flash in the rear-view mirror the cops had the apartment surrounded.

The safe house was a travel trailer on the south side of nowhere. Barrel fires spotted the abandoned construction site. The homeless surrounded each barrel with hands extended zombie-like over the flames. "We will crash here for a day or two before we once again engage the enemy," Adonis said. The travel trailer was adequately maintained, not clean, but functional. Adonis went to the fridge and peeled a couple slices of baloney out of the plastic wrapper, "Hungry?" he asked. I shook my head no.

"Why did you kill Candy?" I asked as the baloney started to sizzle in the frying pan.

He turned his head, gave me a brief stoic stare, and turned back to his frying meat. "She is or was a cop, and an enemy to our cause," he paused, "and a traitor, a whore… a liar, uh, and deep down she hated me."

"What does Hatton have to do with all this?"

Adonis inclined his ear in a genial manner towards me, "You know Hatton?"

"We just met. Candy took me to his home. He said something about whiskey stock and William Henry Hays. Even Candy asked me if I knew her at some point in her life."

Adonis looked surprised, "Then you don't remember me?"

"No."

"Sure you don't want some fried baloney?"

"No."

"Get some sleep, Jimmie. We will talk more in the morning." He pointed to the top bunk with his fork and winked. I climbed the makeshift ladder to the top bed and promptly fell asleep. There was an explosion. A man, a medic, Bemire was bending over me. "Jimmie," It was Adonis, "you had a dream," he said, "are you okay?"

I rolled over and faced the travel trailers wall paneling, "I'm okay," I said.

Dawn the next morning, the barrel fires had died out, the homeless had not yet risen. I was taking a leak behind a partially demolished corrugated tin building when a black car approached. A man got out. It was Office Charles Davenport from the Chicago Police Department, and to my surprise, the African American kid, Ben Dearing. Officer Davenport pulled his pistol as Ben politely knocked on the trailer door. Adonis opened the door and the two entered. They remained for perhaps fifteen minutes and left. I hesitated before walking to the trailer and cautiously opened the

The Perfect Plan

door. Adonis was sitting at the small table in the small kitchen sipping on a cup of coffee. The cops had handcuffed one of his hands to the table leg, leaving the other free. He glanced up as I entered. "What was that all about?" I asked gazing somberly at the cuffs.

"The enemy has come to our door to arrange an agreement. They want us to cease and desist our confrontation against the 'War and elected officials,' Adonis made quotation signs with the fingers of his free hand. They said there have been too many deaths, too much property damage," Adonis lingered briefly to develop his next statement, "If we stop, they will not charge you."

"What if we don't agree?"

"We are no longer safe Jimmie. They know the location of every safe house. They know our plans. They have a list of our supporters, our financiers. They know everything."

"Candy?"

"I will be charged for her murder and stand trial." Adonis took a sip of coffee. He wiped tears from his eyes with his shirt sleeve. "You are a reporter Jimmie, not a protester. Use your talents, report about this illegal war. Report about the crooked politicians, and corrupt government. Be our voice Jimmie that is the only way we can stop these criminals."

"When are they coming for you?"

"They have the camp surrounded. I asked them to wait until I talked to you. If you do not agree to forsake the cause, they will arrest you too and charge you as an accomplice to Candy's murder." There was a sudden and startling knock on the thin-skinned trailer. "It's open," Adonis said. Officer Davenport and Ben Dearing stepped inside.

Dearing scanned the place intently as Davenport spoke in a subtle whisper, "What are you going to do Linguine?"

"First, I want to say I had nothing to do with Candy's death."

"I don't give a shit?" Davenport said with a smirk, "Are you going to stop marching and protesting. Are you through with the Maladies, the Students for a Free Society and the National Conference against War?"

"I wasn't marching I was reporting," I said.

"I need you to sign these papers denouncing the Maladies, the SFS, and the NCAW, and also sign an agreement to testify against Adonis Baxter."

I looked at Adonis. His face was stoic, unreadable. I hesitated. "Now," Davenport yelled.

"Okay, okay I'll sign the papers."

CHAPTER 17

Rescuing the Maladies

Ben Dearing chuckled as I signed the papers agreeing to testify against Adonis. He reviewed my testimony and my denouncement of the Maladies, SFS, and NCAW. Davenport handcuffed Adonis and shoved him through the trailer door. Adonis hit the ground with a thud and moaned. "Get up," Davenport yelled as he grabbed his prisoner's collar and pulled him to his feet. A few minutes later Adonis was in the back seat of the unmarked car. Davenport drove away leaving me with Ben Dearing. "Let's go," Dearing said in a gruff voice.

"Where are we going?"

"You'll see," he replied.

We drove through town, past the sprawling Chicago suburbs, past Racine Illinois, and stopped somewhere on the trash infested shore of Lake Michigan. Ben got out of the car and started gathering wood. I sat in the car and listened to the soothing sound of waves. Ben started a fire and extended his hands over the flame to warm them. "You can join me if you like." I hesitated but figured that if Ben meant to do me harm, he would have done it by now. Besides, I was cold, and the fire looked inviting. I sat opposite Ben. He looked up from the fire and grinned. His teeth shone like pearls in the firelight.

"What are we doing here Ben?" I asked.

"Waiting."

"For what?"

"Whom, we are waiting for whom."

"Who then?"

He picked firebrand from the Campfire, the tip glowed a reddish orange, "Them," he said pointing his stick in the direction of the road. I looked in the direction he was pointing and saw headlights coming.

"Who are they?"

"Friends," he said.

"You know them. They are the remaining Maladies, James Robin, and Phil Dean," Ben said. The automobile stopped a few yards from the fire. Ben and I stood and waited anxiously for the two men to exit the automobile. The passenger door opened and James stepped out, and then Phil. Both were somber, bearded, and smelled horrible. We shook hands. Before we had a chance to sit, James asked Ben if he had any food. Ben went to his car and retrieved a box of girl scout cookies. The two ate the brownies like ravenous apes, each unwilling to share the smallest crumb. I was concerned a fight would break out. Ben, however, cooled the situation, "Don't worry boy's I have another box." Both Phil and James looked at Ben and then at one another, and without speaking resumed the gastronomic art of gluttony.

"More," Phil mumbled while ingesting the last brownie.

James licked his fingers to remove the gooey chocolate residue, and in support of Phil's request, said, "Please."

After the second box of brownies, the four of us gazed silently at the flames before Phil spoke. "We are on the assassination list." I looked at Phil without speaking. He continued to gaze at the fire.

"Hatton put us on the list," says James.

"Who exactly is Hatton?" Phil asked Ben, "and why did he put us on the death list?"

Ben focused on a distant light far out at sea, a fishing boat perhaps. "Ben, who is Hatton and how are you associated with him?" Phil repeated.

Ben spoke calmly, "He is the President and CEO of the Black Op Corporation, a subsidiary of the National Shield Corporation. I am his stepson."

"What does he want with us?" James asked.

"He feels that you guys and what you stand for are a threat," Ben said.

"To whom?" Phil inquired.

"To the corporations to our or should I say his way of life," Ben said.

A thought came to me suddenly, and I abruptly changed the course of inquiry from Hatton, to Ben, "Why were you with that cop Davenport?"

"Yeah, and how did you find us?" James added.

Ben Dearing turned his gaze back out to the distant flickering light. "I am a student dissident reporting on corrupt cops." Dearing paused and looked at me.

"You are a dissident?" I asked wide-eyed in disbelief.

"Yes, a member of the Students for a Free Society," Ben said. "As for you two." Ben looked at James and Phil. "Adonis told me how to find you. I placed a call, provided a car, and directions, and here you are."

"You could have put some food in the car," Phil said.

Silence followed Phil's kvetch.

"I need to go back to Chicago," I said.

Ben looked confused, "Why?"

"Something is going to happen. I do not know what exactly, but I need to be there. Can you help?"

"I can try," Ben said, "but it won't be easy."

James stoked the fire with a crooked stick. "What about us?" he said stabbing into the fire, sending sparks adrift in the darkness.

"Leave," Ben said, "I promised Adonis I would find you and send you guys to a safe place. I have written the address down." He handed Phil a

The Perfect Plan

folded paper. "It is close by, and they are expecting you." Ben stood. We stood along with him, doused the fire, shook hands, said our goodbyes, and went our separate ways.

Ben enlightened me further as we traveled back to Chicago. He told me of his abusive stepfather, and how awful Hatton was to his now deceased mother. He would lock her up for days in their bedroom, but it got worse as soon as Spot arrived. It got a lot worse. Ben suddenly turned the vehicle in which we were riding off the road and into a convenience store parking lot. He rolled up his sleeve showing me the pink burn marks on his dark arm. "Son of a bitch," I said.

Ben replied oddly by saying, "Son-of-a-bitch should be sung, not said. Singing the phrase gives it greater emphasis." Ben provided his melodic rendition of Son-of-a-bitch. I agreed entirely. Profanity does sound more resolute when sung.

Ben went to the store and purchased a couple of sodas, a pack of bologna, mayonnaise, and bread. We retraced our route back to Chicago—drove to the safe house, (same small trailer,) as dawn was breaking in a pinkish glow over the treetops.

"Remain here," Ben, said, "I'll be back later this afternoon."

"Is this safe? I mean this is where you guys found us to begin with." I said.

"This camper is all we have for now. I'll be back." Ben reaffirmed with a slight nod of his head and drove off.

The trailer was as we had left it. I could still smell the fetid fried baloney. I guess no one came to clean the little camper after our arrest. I was exhausted, crawled onto the foam mattress, looked at the familiar wood paneling on the trailer's wall, and fell asleep.

A blasting car horn jolted me from a pleasant, and I confess erotic dream of Candy. The sun flooded unabridged through the thin plastic windowpane. I squinted into the bright light and saw Ben leaning casually against the side of his car. He was smoking weed. "C'mon, we haven't all day," Ben, yelled.

I stepped out of the trailer, and said, "Where are we going?"

"A friend has agreed to take you in for a while."

"Cool," I said. We drove downtown, stopped at the Liberty Café for a bite to eat, and then proceeded to Montclair a suburban neighborhood northeast of Chicago. A man in his mid-fifties or early sixties and a younger woman greeted us as we pulled into the driveway of a modest ranch style home. Ben introduced us, "Jimmie, this is Wilson Ortega and his daughter Molly."

"Hello," I said.

"Nice to meet you," Molly said, "Come in, please."

Mr. Ortega opened the door for us to enter, "Food, drink?" he asked.

The Perfect Plan

"No thank you," Ben replied, "We just ate."

"So you need a place to crash for a couple of days?" Mr. Ortega said.

"Yes Sir," I thought for a moment, "What day of the month is today. I have lost track?" I said.

"This is the twenty-sixth day of August," Molly replied.

"Could I stay until the twenty-eighth?"

"Sure," Mr. Ortega said.

"How do you guys know Ben?" I asked. Molly and her father looked surprised.

"We came here in…" Molly began.

"Some time ago," Her father interrupted. "I went to work as a custodian, a janitor, if you will, for the Black Ops Corporation. That's where I met Ben's father, Mr. Hatton."

"We came in search of a 'woman'," Molly put a strong emphasis on the subject of her remark. The comment, I noticed, drew an angry look from her father.

"Oh," I said.

Ben stood abruptly, "I need to go," he said. "It is getting late. Father will be expecting me."

We all followed Ben out and watched as he got into his car, "I'll be back tomorrow."

"Great," Mr. Ortega replied. We waved as Ben backed his car out of the driveway and drove away.

As soon as we entered the house, Molly said, "Let me show you to your room." She led me down a hall, opened the door on her left, and said, "This is it, I hope it is comfortable enough."

"I'm sure it will be," I said.

She closed the door, "Super will be at seven. Try to get some rest." Her voice percolated through the door's thin veneer.

"Okay, thanks," I replied a little louder than normal.

I sat on the bed and listened to an unintelligible conversation from another room, by the tone and cadence of the conversation the two seemed to be in some sort of disagreement.

CHAPTER 18

Interjection: Searching for Hatton: A reminder, Mother Urdu asked Jimmie to find out how Hatton in 1968 received an unauthorized soul.

The heated tête-à-tête between Molly and her father appeared to have been resolved. They were at last smiling and speaking jovially.

Ben arrived at the Ortega home around noon with news, "Father is dying," he said without emotion.

Wilson Ortega looked at his daughter. She returned his steady gaze. Ortega spoke in a sympatric tone, "Hatton has been a good friend, and I want to see him before he passes."

"No, Wilson, you can't, Hatton made it quite clear that he wants to be alone, and remain unvisited," Ben, replied.

"Where is Hatton at?" I asked.

"Mercy Hospice on Lancaster Street," Ben said.

"I am so sorry," Molly said tearfully.

"Thank you, Molly. I just wanted to let you all know. Now I'm afraid I must be going. Hatton left me in charge of the funeral arrangements," he checked his watch, "and I have an appointment with Mr. Gooding, the funeral director in thirty minutes."

"Keep us posted," Molly said.

"I will," Ben responded as he walked to his car. We stayed outside and watched him leave. "How sad," Molly said. Ortega and I remained focused on Ben as he rounded the corner and disappeared behind the Episcopal Church.

Ortega led us back into the house. I went into my designated bedroom, packed, and called a cab. "I've got to go," I said as the cab arrived. "I'll call as soon as I'm settled." I ran out the door and climbed into the cab. As the cab was pulling away, I heard a turkey gobble and though no one was outside the house, I thought I heard someone say, "Toodle-oo."

"Where too," the Cabbie said.

"Mercy Hospice on Lancaster Street," I said. We arrived. I paid the cabby and walked to the receptionist desk where, according to the nameplate on the counter, Mary Myrtle was working. The woman behind the counter was heavyset. "Excuse me," I said, "are you, Mary?"

"Yes, what can I do for you?"

"My name is James Jones. I noticed that you guys have an opening for an orderly, and I would like to fill out an application."

The Perfect Plan

"We do?"

"Yes Ma'am, according to the bulletin board you do," I said.

"Here," she said pulling an application from a shelf behind her. "Take this to the waiting room, fill it out, and bring it back to me with the pen." She emphasized pen as if it were a gold nugget.

"Yes Ma'am," I said.

I began to fill out the application. I studied the nuance of each question, wondered why my middle initial was so important. I also questioned the need for three references. I didn't have one, much less three. While scratching my head and pondering whom I could use for references, a young man came to me, "Do you smoke?" he said. "I need a cigarette."

"No, sorry, but uh, do you know where the restrooms are?"

He pointed and said, "Down the hall and to your left."

"Thanks." I traversed the hall on tiptoes and turned left into the Men's Room where I remained until the five o:clock shift arrived. The employees barged into the building like a herd of spooked cattle and flowed through the halls of the building. I joined them and we mauled our way down the corridor. There was to my right a cafeteria. It was empty, and I was hungry. I broke from the crowd and entered the kitchen. Luckily, someone had left a pan labeled potato and broccoli soup on the counter and I helped myself to several servings. My investigative skills and intuition led me to the Nutritionists Office. The door was open, and I entered, slick as a cat, into the semi-dark interior. A large dry-erase board hung on the wall in front of me. I found Hatton's name and room number 666 and traveled a short distance to his assigned room. I hesitated, thought about Mother Urdu's request, and with added determination, knocked. There was no answer. I peered into the private room. It was dark except for a small table lamp on the nightstand. Hatton was in bed, apparently heavily sedated. His face was pale, his breathing erratic. A broom closet was the only place to hide. I slipped inside, made myself as comfortable as possible. I left the closet door slightly ajar sat on a mop bucket and waited.

It was six-o-two p.m. according to my watch when the alarm went off. A nurse rushed into the room, took Hatton's vitals, and reset the monitor. Another person came into the room. I overheard their conversation, the nurse said, "He doesn't have long, please notify the family."

"Yes ma'am," the second person, perhaps a nurse's aide, said. She immediately left the room. The nurse, I could see her kindly face now, gently rubbed Hatton's baldhead, checked the I-V tube and bag, and then unexpectedly pulled on the old man's exposed toe. Hatton did not respond. What happened next shocked me. The nurse, let's call her Betty, bent over, lowered her head, opened her mouth, licked her lips, and... Someone knocked

The Perfect Plan

on the door. The nurse stood upright and said, "Yes," She was calm.

"You are wanted at the front desk," the nurse's aide said. He had a southern drawl.

She covered Hatton's foot with the blanket, patted his foot gently, and said, "Be right back."

At 6:45, a beautiful young woman entered the room. She was carrying a spotted dog. One look at Hatton and she began to cry. Ben arrived a few minutes later. He kissed the woman on the cheek, and said, "Suzan, are you alright?" She nodded, blew her nose, and gingerly placed the dog at Hatton's feet. Ben sat down on one side of the dying man. Suzan sat on the other side. I could see her face clearly through the crack in the door.

I felt gastrointestinal pressure begin to build. Damn broccoli at work, I thought. Another alarm went off, and the nurse Betty' came into the room. I could not help but notice how, once again, she gazed at Hatton's feet before attending to the alarm. "I am sorry," she said, "he is gone."

"Can you give us a moment?" Suzan said.

"Certainly."

"You too Ben, I would like to be alone with Hatton. Just for a moment, please."

"Okay," Ben said and left the room. Loki entered the room through an open window. "Yes, yes," Suzan said as she saw the hairy man swing his furry leg through the window.

He was nude except for his coat of fur and a fanny pack buckled to his waist. Loki pulled something resembling a pistol out of his fanny pack and aimed it at the dog. Spot sat up and seemed to smile or grimace—whatever facial expression dogs have under stress. The wolfman squeezed the trigger and a stream of fluid hit Spot squarely in the face. Spot began to convulse and unbelievably began to change. His transformation was rather rapid. In less than one minute, Spot morphed into a naked, slimy slug. Loki picked up the slug and placed the creature into Hatton's mouth. The old man's complexion immediately began to change. His appearance began to improve. He began to breathe. He opened his eyes. I farted.

CHAPTER 19

A prelude to Hatton's soul transfer

Chacho, Jimmies first father, the bastard, OD'd in the back of a black 57 Ford automobile. Mother Urdu disliked the man's use of opium, in part, due to his abandonment of Jimmie Linguine and his mistress, Jimmie's despicable 'original' mother, Izabelle. Urdu had repeatedly given Chacho opportunities to do the right thing—yet he continued to misuse and abuse himself, children, and dogs. Mother Urdu had no choice in Chacho's soul transfer she was legally bound to find a home for every soul under her care. She decided to transfer Chacho's soul to a hermaphroditic slug and did, in fact, place Chacho's soul in a selfless, meaningless, useless, worthless gastropod. The slug, Chacho, lived in Louisiana. Loki by chance was visiting an old girlfriend, Charisa, who lived and worked in the Mount Bayou cucumber farm. The slug lived in a nearby forest called the Adjacent Woods. He/

She/It dined primarily on hallucinogenic mushrooms. Loki was taking a stroll in the Adjacent Woods to clear his mind of abstract thoughts when he came upon Chacho nibbling upon the spongy dome of a mushroom. Loki stopped, mid-stride, knelt cautiously down on the moist brown loam, and addressed the slug with a finger wave and a verbal greeting, "Hello," Loki said.

"Hi," the slug replied.

"What is that you are eating?" Loki said as he placed the ends of his fingers one against the others, which seemed to the slug a modified finger placement for prayer.

"Magic mushrooms," the slug said.

"Will you share? I have a fondness for mushrooms and magic," Loki said.

"No!" the slug exclaimed.

Loki detached his fingers, "I have no coin, but I can provide favors."

Chacho stopped chewing, "What can you do for me?"

"What do you want?" Loki replied.

"I am tired of being a lowly-slimy-slug, a 'less of a thing.' I yearn for the pleasure of sex with another thing preferably human..." The slug paused to consider other options, and then added, "or dog."

"Are you sure? Being a mammal has its drawbacks." Loki remarked as he gazed intently at the slimeball.

"Yes, but..."

The Perfect Plan

"I can change you from a slug to a roach." Loki interrupted. He provided the slug with a wolfish smile, "It would be a manageable step-up."

"I don't want to be a roach," Chacho said.

"A fly?"

Chacho considered the possibility of flight, "Perhaps, but I prefer to be returned to a human form. I was once human and enjoyed that life-form very much." The slug said.

"All right, for a load of magic mushrooms, I will give your soul, via a fortuitous route to a man!"

"What fortuitous route?"

"Dog first, then man."

"Done!" Chacho said and extended his slimy self to touch the hand of his, (in a non-biblical sense,) savior. Loki waited three days for the slug to die from a self-inflicted dose of insecticide. Loki extracted Chacho's soul, harvested the slug's magic mushrooms, and set out to find a suitable recipient for the slug's soul.

CHAPTER 20

Jimmie's death and Hatton's Soul Transfer

I was hoping for an exciting death, something heroic, but it did not happen that way. I died from an intestinal blockage caused by an allergic reaction to the potato and broccoli soup I had consumed at Mercy Hospice.

Suzan remained with Hatton long after the soul transfer. Spot aka the hairy man gave his respects to Hatton and left.

I know I am incoherent, the pain and awful smell. The gas has made me delirious...

A spark of light flickered. I died passing gas in the broom closet—

During the passage from life to death, I emancipated an absorbing thought.

Death is like copping a feel on a beautiful redhead while roller-skating uphill...

—I suppose I should stay grounded. In reality,

The Perfect Plan

soul separation during death is like falling asleep and reawakening with lips around Mother Urdu's supple nipple. I suppose one would prefer a beautiful redhead's nipple, the source of my fantasy, but it just doesn't work like that.

While processing the redhead's image, it became clear to me that after so many deaths, the world had not improved, and it became even more transparent to me that my travels have become more and more distorted. I was having difficulty remembering the details and sequential events of my life. Everything had become malformed, uncoordinated, and disharmonious within the natural order of things. I mumbled my complaint to Mother Urdu while fastened to her teat. She patted my bald head, understandably concerned about my dilemma, "Now, now," she said, "everything will be alright."

Feeling secure, I suckled on Mother Urdu's Mammary gland—the big one beside her right front leg. After a belly full of Mother Urdu's soul lactation, she posed the question I had been dreading. "How did Spot transfer his soul to Hatton?"

"Well, you see..." I glanced up from Mother Urdu's breast. Her jowls wobbled with excess curiosity and excitement. I described the ape-man and his pistol to Mother Urdu.

"What was in the pistol?" she asked.

"Looked like water to me," I said; then thought about the smell, "I was farting a lot, but there was the undeniable smell of rotten broccoli and... and sulfur," I exclaimed.

"Hmm, sulfur, the antecedent compound of cocky serum, used by tricksters and shape-shifters." She looked down and smiled. Strings of drool escaped her lips and fell on my forehead, "Whoops," she exclaimed and wiped the saliva from my unwrinkled brow, "What did you see next?" she asked.

"I saw Spot change into a slug," I said.

"A slug?"

"Yes, a slimy slug."

Mother Urdu tapped her long curved black claw on her chin, "Did this man—the man with a pistol have a hairy ass, long penis, stood about six-foot-six and look like a werewolf?"

"I just remember he was very hairy, I didn't notice the other stuff."

"What about his toes, where they clawed or nailed?"

"Don't know Mother Urdu," I said.

"Hmm," she said, "Fully naked?"

"Yes."

"Would you recognize him if you saw him again?"

"I think so."

Mother Urdu pushed all the nursing souls away and went to a compartment in the rock wall. She reached deep into the crevice and withdrew what looked to be a photo Album. She returned to her throne and opened the book. The first picture

The Perfect Plan

was a huge hairy penis. "Does this look familiar?"

"Not really," I said.

She turned the page to a picture of a narrow hairy ass. "What about this?"

"No," I said amazed at the amount of hair on the creature's tush.

"Okay, Look at this one," she said and turned the page. It was a man's figure. It looked familiar.

"Maybe," I said.

"Look closely," she replied.

I examined the photograph meticulously. Then I recognized the blunt nose and pointed ears. "That's him," I exclaimed. "That's him, the hairy man, it is him."

Mother Urdu smiled and drooled once again. She didn't bother cleaning up this time. "It is Loki," she said, "Loki," she repeated softly. She looked up. I thought I saw a tear form, "Son of a Bitch," she whispered in short choppy words.

"Son-of-a-bitch should be sung, not said." I provided an example. Mother Urdu clapped her paws together excitedly.

CHAPTER 21

Suzan Sandal gives birth to Jimmie Linguine, in New Mexico

It was already dark when Jack Rare, a local rancher, phoned concerning the stray dog that had become a threat to his livestock. Jack gave Ortega the location of the mother who had pups and advised him, "To get them tonight," because he was going out at first light to dispose of the animals.

Determined to save the animals Wilson Ortega turned off Highway fifty-five at Rare's goat farm and drove exceedingly slow down a dirt trail called Rare Ranch Road. He drove for miles through pools of moonlight and clusters of cactus whose needles scratched eerily upon the metal fabric of his truck. Finally, he spied a red ribbon that fluttered from the low branch of a juniper tree. "I'll be damned, here it is," Ortega said somewhat surprised he found the spot so easily. He turned his truck off the road and parked between

The Perfect Plan

the tree and a low-lying growth of sage. Ortega retrieved a flashlight from the trucks glove box, walked to the north end of a drainage culvert, and peered inside. The flashlight cast an eerie light that swayed along the corrugated metal tube. He could see that the mother of the pups was dead. Her tongue hung from her mouth, her open eyes had glazed over, and blood had pooled in an odd harpsichord shape around her head. All but one of the pups lay motionless around her. The only survivor whimpered and ever so slightly moved its hind leg. The puppy Wilson observed from the dimming glow of his light had a spotted coat, a pudgy flat dappled face, and small speckled ears that bent forward and dropped down like the wing of an origami bird. Ugly in a cute sort of way Ortega thought and involuntarily smiled.

Ortega was a large man too large to enter the culvert. He looked around for an object long enough to reach the pup and found a cedar limb lying on the ground. He inserted the leafless branch into the culvert, stretched his arm, and strained with a progressively reddening face to reach the pup. It was difficult, but he managed to pull the mewling puppy to him. Ortega grabbed the pup, cupped the small speckled body in his hand, and smiled. The hungry critter nuzzled Ortega's palm for a teat, found the man's pinky finger, and attempted to suckle. "You, my friend, are perfect for my little girl," Ortega said, as he placed the puppy inside his jacket for warmth, and left for home.

Wilson Ortega saw the fire as he returned down the isolated road. He had passed the abandoned house an hour earlier. It was Rare's aunt, Gretchen Lamar's, old adobe. The home now abandoned was leaking smoke and flames from its windows. Ortega stopped the truck, a safe distance away from the fire, placed the pup on the car seat, and went to investigate. As he approached the blaze, he heard a scream. Ortega ran lifting his legs in higher, longer arches until he reached the burning house. He stopped. The heat was intense. He shielded his face with the flat of his hand and happened to see with some difficulty a young woman through the billowing smoke. She had collapsed outside the building.

Ortega removed his jacket and placed it in front of him as a heat shield. He slowly advanced toward the young woman. The girl whimpered as he covered her with his coat. He then carefully lifted her and carried the teenager away from the burning house. Ortega stumbled and went to his knees but arose quickly to advance the girl to a safe location. He reached the road gently placed the girl beside his truck and fashioned a pillow with his jacket to cradle her head.

Trained as a medic in the Korean War, he was familiar with the resuscitation process and quickly began CPR. There were no burns, no apparent injuries. He noticed the swell of her belly. The girl was pregnant, late-term he figured. He had to

The Perfect Plan

work fast to save the teenager and her baby. Ortega began with chest compressions. He counted aloud. One, two, three, and repeated the compression of her chest ten times. Ortega lifted the girl's chin forward to open her airway, pinched her nostrils, and began mouth to mouth. Two breaths he remembered then resume chest compressions. He quickly checked her pulse and once again resumed the procedure. The girl coughed and suddenly began to breathe. She coughed violently again and then curled into a fetal position. She began to whine. Then she screamed. She clasped Ortega's arm as fluid gushed from between her legs. Her water had broken.

"Oh, Jesus!" Ortega exclaimed.

The pain and trauma that the teen was experiencing brought forth unsolicited memories. She saw red flags popping in the wind. She heard monkey chatter and the cry of a peacock. She saw a man—felt the man rape her. She screamed again.

"Shit!" Ortega exclaimed. He tried to lift her to her feet, but she was too weak to stand. "Shit," he repeated. Ortega hoisted the girl to the seat of his truck. He moved the puppy close to her—got behind the truck's steering wheel and began to drive. Albuquerque and the hospital were an hour away. The girl during a brief respite from the pain reached over, gently lifted the puppy, and brought him to her breast. The teen's contractions became stronger, more severe, she screamed, the puppy whined. Ortega drove onto the shoulder of the road and stopped. He grabbed his flashlight, ran to the passenger side, and opened the door to assist with the delivery. She was lying on her back. He positioned her legs, lifted her skirt, and removed her panties. What is your name? Ortega asked.

"Suzan," the girl replied.

"Well, Suzan you have to push."

"It hurts," Suzan screamed,

"Push," Ortega spoke with a courteous insistence and patted the girl's arm.

Suzan gently held the puppy to her chest and complied with Ortega's request. She continued to scream. The babies crown appeared. Ortega clasped the small flashlight between his teeth, slipped his hands beneath Suzan's skirt to catch the baby when it came. Suzan continued to push. The child slipped out into Ortega's open hands. The placenta followed, and Ortega cut the umbilical cord. He took the puppy that Suzan had been holding throughout the delivery and handed the child, a boy, to his mother. She reluctantly took the baby. "I need to get you to a hospital," Ortega said.

"No," Suzan replied, "I do not want to go."

"You have to," Ortega said.

"No, I want to die," Suzan, whined.

"You are going whether you want to or not." Ortega took the baby, wrapped the boy in his shirt, and offered the child to its mother. She refused to take him. Ortega shrugged, mumbled an instantaneous string of profanity, and placed the infant on the truck seat beside the spotted puppy.

Disappointed about Suzan's refusal to take the baby Ortega got into the truck, slammed the door shut, and without speaking drove to the University Hospital in Albuquerque with the calm urgency of a disciplined soldier. They reached the emergency entrance within forty-five minutes. Ortega left Suzan and her baby in the truck and hurried inside to notify the first nurse he saw about the crises. The nurse retrieved a gurney and called upon two orderlies for assistance. Ortega followed the hospital staff to the truck and stood by as they helped the dazed young mother onto the gurney.

The nurse lifted the baby from the truck seat and Ortega followed the entourage inside the hospital. A middle-aged nurse placed a gentle hand on his bare chest and stopped him from entering the emergency room. She asked in a soft almost inaudible tone, "May I get you to fill out this form?"

Ortega unconsciously took the clipboard. He watched as Suzan and her child disappeared behind the closing emergency room doors and then reviewed the form. "I don't know any of this information!" He said.

Nurse, Belinda Gomez, interrupted, raising her finger upward, "Wait a moment, I'll get your shirt," and before Ortega could reply, the nurse turned quickly pressed several buttons on the wall and disappeared through the opening doors. She returned with his bloodstained shirt. "She will be fine, now go home. Come back tomorrow if you like."

"What about the form?" he replied.

"Give me your number. We will call if we need anything, now go!"

Wilson Ortega filled in his name and phone number and handed the clipboard to the nurse. He reluctantly left the hospital and drove his normal five miles per hour below the speed limit until he arrived home. Molly greeted him at the door, "What took you so long?" she asked, but before he could answer she said, "Did you find them?"

"Only one baby." He pulled the tiny spotted creature from his jacket.

She took the pup ran her fingers over his soft fur coat, "He's blind Papa."

"He is young. He will open his eyes soon," her father replied. "Come on let's prepare a bottle and feed the puppy."

Father and daughter mixed corn syrup and canned milk in a cup and heated it on the stove. Wilson stuck his finger into the mix and smiled. "Just right not too hot nor too cold. Get an eyedropper, Molly. Let's feed the baby." Molly went to the bathroom found an eyedropper in the medicine cabinet, rinsed it off, and handed it to her father. Wilson stuck the glass tube into the milk, drew in a portion of the liquid, and placed it into the pups open mouth. The pup squealed with pleasure. Once the puppy had eaten, Ortega explained to his daughter what had expired that day.

The Perfect Plan

Molly began to cry. "Shush," her father said, "It is late, let's go to bed. I will check on Suzan and her baby first thing in the morning." He kissed Molly goodnight, reminded her to feed the pup every three hours, and then went to bed. He dreamed he was in Korea. Bombs were exploding all his comrades were dead.

Ortega arrived at the University Hospital midmorning to find Suzan and the baby was gone. He inquired about her at the front desk. The nurse explained that Suzan and her newborn baby had simply disappeared.

CHAPTER 22

Luck is a beneficial circumstance. Fate regardless of the outcome is destined to happen

Ortega needed time to think. He headed home on the meandering Old Salt Station Road. It was a longer but more scenic route. He hadn't gone a mile when he saw Suzan. She was barefoot and still in her hospital gown. The gown, he noticed, was open in the rear. Ortega pulled off the road behind her and honked. She turned, recognized him immediately, and began to cry in a troubled way. The baby in her arms was crying too. Ortega exited the truck, gently embraced Suzan opened the door of the vehicle, and said, "Get in, I'll take you home." Suzan, still sobbing slid into the truck. As soon as Ortega moved under the wheel, and buckled his seatbelt, she reached over and kissed him on the cheek. It was a lingering, appreciative, kiss.

"Where's home?" Suzan said in a recognizable southwestern patois.

The Perfect Plan

"Estancia," Wilson said over the baby's crying. He gazed affectionately at the child, "I think the baby is hungry." Suzan ignored his comment. "You need to feed the child," Ortega said in a more forceful tone. She did not reply. She turned her head and gazed out the window. Ortega parked in front of Mr. Redding's Country Store. "Stay in the truck," he said as he entered the old clapboard building. He returned shortly with a baby bottle and several cans of formulated milk. Ortega opened the hood of his old truck and placed a can of milk on the hot engine. He waited until the milk was warm cut a hole in the top of the can with his knife, poured the milk into the bottle, and gave the bottle to Suzan. She refused to accept the bottle. Ortega became angry, "What is your problem," he shouted and took the baby from its mother. He directed the nipple to the baby's pale lips, and the tip soon disappeared within the newborn's mouth. As soon as the baby finished eating, Ortega started the truck and headed home. Suzan sat on the seat beside him. She was quiet, uncomfortably quiet.

Molly met her father at the door. She was surprised to see him with a baby in his arms and equally surprised to see the inadequately clothed young woman standing beside him. "Molly, this is Suzan-Suzan, my daughter Molly."

"Hello," Molly said.

"Hello," Suzan replied with a timid glance in Molly's direction.

"Molly, show Suzan to the guest room. She is about your size. Can she borrow something to wear?"

"Sure," Molly said, "Follow me." Molly led Suzan to the guest bedroom. "The bathroom is here." She pointed to the bathroom door, "Go ahead and clean up, I'll get you some clothes and leave them on the bed."

"Thank you," Suzan whispered as she turned toward the bathroom.

"What's your baby's name?" Molly asked.

"He doesn't have a name," Suzan replied slightly above a whisper Molly gathered a pair of jeans, blouse, and blue laced panties for Suzan. She laid them on the bed and returned to her father. Molly starred affectionately at the child, in her father's arms. A precious gift she thought. She touched the baby's tiny hand and was shocked to feel him clutch her finger. He was strong. The baby opened his large eyes, gazed silently at her unfamiliar face and smiled. "Coochie Coo," Molly said and tickled the boy's chin with her finger. The baby giggled.

Later that night after a meal of pork chops and potato salad. William asked Molly to get the pup. It was feeding time. It was a ploy. William hoped that the pups nursing would trigger Suzan's maternal instinct and she would feed her child as well. What happened shocked Ortega and Molly, instead of nursing her baby, Suzan gave the infant to Molly along with a warm bottle of milk. She

The Perfect Plan

then took the puppy from Molly's lap opened her blouse and allowed the puppy to suckle on her milk-swollen teat.

Ortega advanced his thoughts in a careful manner, "Tomorrow," he said, "I will take you and the child back to the hospital." Suzan did not respond. She turned her head slowly and gazed out the window at the growing storm.

That night massive cumulus clouds covered the moon and stars. Suzan took the opportunity during the darkest night ever recorded in Torrance County, (according to the Estancia Ranchers Radio Show,) to abscond with the spotted puppy and her unnamed child.

She departed Mr. Ortega's home, confident she was doing the right thing. She did not want to leave the baby with Ortega. He had saved her life, and, she surmised, he did not deserve the hardship of raising a bastard child, the son of a rapist.

Suzan with Spot in her arms and her newborn baby in a basket caught a ride to El Paso with an elderly cowboy driving an El Camino. The cowboy said, "My name is Bob," and with a courtesy offering of his snuffbox, continued, "Would you like a dip darling?" Suzan declined. Bob, except for his whistling, remained silent for the remainder of the trip. He did, however, cast long frequent glances at the baby boy sleeping on the seat beside his mother. Suzan held Spot close to her breast until they reached El Paso Texas. The cowboy turned off the highway and for no apparent reason drove to the bus station on First Street. As he applied the break, he said, "Get out darling. This is as far as you go!" Suzan thanked the old man as she opened the door. She turned to leave and began to walk away. "Wait," Bob said, "You forgot the baby." Suzan turned grabbed the child, gave Bob a caustic smile, and slammed the door of the vehicle. Once again fate intervened and led Suzan to the doorsteps of the Saint Croix Church of God. She was breastfeeding Spot when she left her baby boy at the church and headed via the 'thumb' to 113 Margin Road. That was the last known address of the rapist and father of her child.

    The baby left behind, strong of lung, and hungry, alerted the Reverend Brighton of his whereabouts. The Reverend took him into the church but within hours, (for reasons unknown,) he delivered the baby, via taxi, to the Texas Family Penury, an Evangelical Orphanage.

CHAPTER 23

How Wilson Ortega and his daughter Molly came to Chicago

Wilson Ortega and Molly were distraught when they woke up the next morning to find Suzan Sandal, her baby, and the puppy gone. It was clear to Ortega that the baby was in peril. He decided to go back to the University Hospital to see if Suzan had left any evidence as to her destination. He met Nurse Gomez at the reception window and proceeded to inquire about Suzan and her escape. Nurse Gomez explained, in great detail the hospital's policy about the patients right to refuse treatment. Ortega held his hand up to halt the conversation and requested, with an even temperament, if she had any idea where Suzan might have gone. Nurse Gomez gave a negative response with a measured shaking of her head. He then inquired if Suzan had left anything. The nurse thought for a moment, suddenly disappeared, and returned with the clothes that Suzan wore. She began to rummage through Suzan's pockets. Her face lit up as she retrieved a newspaper clipping. She read slowly, mouthing the words silently. The article described the circumstances surrounding the rape of a fifteen-year-old girl in El Paso Texas. The incident happened a little over eight months ago. John James Gilmore, the accused rapist's trial was set for Friday of next week on January 13th. She handed the clipping to Ortega. He read the article, noticed reddish-grey smudges on the paper, and out of curiosity, flipped the paper over to find an address, 113 Margin Road, El Paso Texas, written in pencil. After a brief discussion about the relevance of the article, Mr. Ortega jotted down the address and left the hospital promising Nurse Gomez that he would keep her informed of his findings.

Molly greeted her father at the door. Judging by her mannerisms, she was apprehensive about any news her father might have. Ortega explained to his daughter his belief that Suzan would go to Texas to testify against John Gilmore, her alleged rapist. After lunch, Ortega called the El Paso District Court and inquired on the status of John Gilmore's trial. The court's secretary told Ortega that the accused was out of jail on a twenty-five-thousand-dollar bond, and his trial was still set for Friday the 13th.

After a visit, first, to the church for prayer

The Perfect Plan

and confession he then went to visit the witch Senorita Juanita Rosa Montoya Izquierdo who was well *known and seldom wrong* as indicated on her business card. Senorita Izquierdo read one's future by twisting balloons into curious shapes. Ortega paid the witch two-hundred dollars to locate Suzan. Senorita Izquierdo's hands moved quickly, and she confidently constructed the 'object', shaped somewhat like a dog. The dog's head tilted to the right revealed a Southeasterly direction. The dog's legs, which seemed to indicate a fast trot, or run, implied, that the seeker should go in great haste. Also, something of great importance was divulged to Ortega. Juanita disclosed that the dog changed somehow. The canine for some unexplained reason died and became something else-something like a slimy hairless creature without legs or ears or pecker. The results of the reading? Based on the Bruja's interpolation of her craft, Ortega and Molly must go to El Paso to search for Suzan, her child, and just as importantly, the dog. The analysis provided by Senorita Juanita Rosa Montoya Izquierdo was as all omens are, *open to interpretation*, Juanita cautioned.

Ortega and Molly were ready to travel, and travel they did, quickly and with considerable forethought. They understood they needed more information and visited Ortega's old friend Ellison Bogdan at his ranch close to Bootstrap New Mexico. Ellison, a rogue nuclear physicist, sported a fine-full-black beard, and long black hair. He wore a biker-type red and white bandana around his forehead and reeked, Molly, noticed, of marijuana.

Ellison raised goats some of which participated (involuntarily) in experimental Latin classes for the undeserving. Ellison Bogdan defined 'undeserving' as without the ability to speak. The class taught telepathically, also included a few dogs and one turkey named Evan. The turkey, Ellison exclaimed, performed very well given his limited aptitude. The ability to communicate without speaking became so effective that the government purchased the mental formulas and used them in its current war against communism. The platform later used in the Vietnam War provided poor results. Ellison Bogdan claimed that the tropical climate interfered with the electron and neutron absorption by brain cells, which reduced the brain's ability to send and receive data.

Evan, now in his late teens, was mentally exhausted and was of little use to the (TEP) Telepathic Educational Program. Ortega, despite Ellison's claims of the turkey's exhaustion, offered to purchase the turkey if he, the turkey could pass a pre-purchase test. The test he proposed consisted of asking a silent question, or questions, to Evan and wait for an answer. Ortega, to legitimize the experiment, placed the turkey in a cardboard box, and asked Evan the mental question, "Was Suzan's child still alive." He waited for the answer beneath

The Perfect Plan

a juniper tree with a case of beer at his feet. Seven hours and eighteen beers later the answer came to him, "Yes."

Ortega paid seven dollars for Evan. The turkey came with a Certificate of Telekinetic Fluency. Both Ortega and his daughter were elated. Ortega and Molly bid their friend Ellison goodbye and resumed their journey to El Paso. Molly drove, while her father slept off the effects of the telekinetic conversation. Eight hours later, they arrived in El Paso. It took twenty minutes to find 113 Margin Road and less than a minute to call the cops. John Gilmore was dead. Shot thirty-seven times which, in Ortega's mind anyway ruled out suicide. The Ortega family had reached a dead-end, literally.

Now comes the miracle. Having given up all hope of finding Suzan, her child, and Spot. Ortega, Molly, and Evan, after a brief voiceless conversation, decided to stay the night at the Blue End, a small motel on the outskirts of El Paso. They checked in, ordered out, and ate pizza before retiring. Evan, unable to sleep, due to his reactivated telepathic energy picked up his favorite newspaper The Chicago Times and began to read. The newspaper inadvertently provided a clue in the form of an article and photograph. The article referenced an incident last night in Chicago. It seems that the cops interrupted Bobby Breen's concert when the singer, allegedly stoned, disrobed on stage. He and his entourage, including a teenage girl and a spotted dog, fearing an imminent arrest, fled town after the concert. There was no word about Suzan's baby. The photograph was of Suzan and Spot standing at a Bobby Breen Concert in Grant Park Chicago Illinois. Evan relayed the vision to Ortega, and the trio left posthaste for Chicago.

By the time they reached Dallas, however, doubt began to creep into Ortega's mind. He once again communicated silently with Evan who by the way no longer rode in a box. The turkey had gained full liberty in the vehicle. Ortega's silent question was a repetition of the first question, "Is Suzan's baby still alive?" Evan bobbed his head and answered once again with a silent, "Yes." After a prolonged silence another message from an unknown source, perhaps it was Senorita Juanita Rosa Montoya Izquierdo, said to Evan with a heavy Latino accent, "Ola Turquia, have Ortega go to Mr. Hatton's Office at the Black Ops Corporation in Chicago, and apply for a job!"

Interjection: A security camera and stereopticon (B) video found with the manuscript provided the following account concerning the intrusion of telepathy into the story.

"Pardon," said Scripter 1.

There was an upheaval of shifting eyes from the writing table. "Here we have a cerebral dialogue between Ortega, a turkey, and now a witch." 1 lit a cigarette. She clasped the rolled tobacco firmly between her index and middle finger took a drag and exhaled a smoke cloud. She rubbed her eye with the crook of her thumb, and said after she yawned, "Have we exceeded the limits of reality?"

3 spoke in a perfunctory manner, "Who among us can quantify reality. If I go to bed with a character whom I shall not name, does it mean that I have not fucked him?"

"The man is real, the character is not." 2 said.

4, "But they are the same!"

"No," 3 said, "the man is permanent, the character is not."

"The man is the character when he is in character," 2 exclaims.

"Well, if that is the case reality is based on time and space," 1 said.

"We all know that you fantasize about screwing Linguine," 5 declared, "That's the reality of it."

"Enough," The executive exclaimed, "Who can answer the question posed by number 1?"

"All those who agree that we have exceeded the limits of reality raise your hand." 5 said. 1 raised her hand.

In the meantime.

Beelzebub who had heard that there was going to be a death in the next scene stopped by to eavesdrop on the scripters. It was business, Beelzebub wanted to know what chance he had of taking a soul back with him to Hell.

The security camera recorded Nob as he listened.

Beelzebub laid his bat ear on the thin-skinned trailer and listened to the scripters opine on reality. Beelzebub knocked on the door after the vote. The executive in charge opened the door, and the Nob came and examined the room without offense, but with plenty of diligence. His perfumed neck caught the attention of scripter 3. She smiled from an immediate desire, (the craving she later disclosed to scripter 1 was that she, Linguine and Beelzebub, were engaged in a threesome.)

Beelzebub's head sunk into the cup of his collarbones and his eyes shone forth like startled sentinels from their red windows. "Hello," he said. A lump of dried mucus blocked his nasal passage making his words seem spoken by a bluegrass bard. "I have been listening to your conversation concerning reality."

"So," replied 5 in a condescending tone.

"Do any of you think I am real?" Beelzebub whined.

Scripter 3, knowing her involvement in premarital fornication, and illicit fantasies, replied, "Yes, I mean I hope so."

"Me too," answered 2, expressing guilt for his immersion in the drug trade.

4 gave a lengthy confession to murder. 5 admitted to stealing his wife's prophylactics. Only 1 was a nonbeliever.

The Perfect Plan

Beelzebub placed a long crooked finger against his nostril and blew out the wad of desiccated snot. The bugger landed in the executive's coffee cup. He was distracted at the time by 1's animated butt scratch. "Well," Beelzebub said, "I guess I will see you all in Hell. Even you, number 1, for lying."

The executive in charge raised the coffee cup to his lips. No one warned him of the submerged bugger.

CHAPTER 24

The FBI arrested Suzan Sandal for the murder of Agent John Gilmore

Ortega got a job at the Black Ops Corporation in Chicago. Molly enrolled in public school, and Evan took a well-deserved vacation to visit his former owner Ellison Bogdan.

Ellison Bogdan, while building a bomb shelter, received a call from the Bureau to assist in the investigation of Suzan Sandal. She had refused to talk even under extreme torture and they needed Evan's help in reading the defendant's mind. Bogdan accepted the offer on Evan's behalf for money and country.

Evans now famous statement, "Suzan, Suzan, Suzan, what now girl? John Gilmore did not rape you. As a matter of datum, you seduced him. Pulled a Lolita on his ass."

"Start from the beginning," Ellison Bogdan

said.

Evan delved into the defendant's mind, "Suzan met Gilmore at the El Paso Zoo. She was in the La Cueva Marching band. El Paso Mayor, Ralph Rochester asked the La Cueva New Mexico Band to participate in their annual Thanksgiving day parade. Gilmore, his wife, and six children moved to El Paso from Galveston Texas three years ago. His attorney James Corny stated his move was a business venture sex toys for the Russian toy market. In actuality, he was an undercover agent for the FBI investigating aficionados of illicit companionships. Suzan was fifteen at the time, quirky and irresponsible." Evan fluffed his feathers, shook his beard, and cocked his small red naked head to the right. His eyes appeared to be tiny brown buttons stitched to a blueish smear on his otherwise red-head. Evan focused his burnished buttons on the FBI Agent and admonished him for thinking dirty thoughts about Suzan. Mr. Chung's face grew taut as he realized Evan could read his mind. He apologized profusely.

Evan continued, "Suzan like I said, met Gilmore at the zoo, and immediately began to seduce the handsome, well-dressed man. He was at the zoo studying monkeys as part of a creationism theory he planned to present to his church. Suzan walked up to John, unexpectedly, and showed him a picture of her backside. She asked him if her butt looked like a monkey's ass. He said 'no,' and then she showed him a picture of her front side and asked does this look like a monkey's vagina. He studied the photo diligently and replied no-"

Agent Chung interrupted. "Cut the crap." He had a bulge in his pants, "get to the specifics."

Evan gobbled in disdain at the agent's bad manners. Ellison translated the gobble and decided to omit Evan's remarks about the Agent's abnormally small testicles and his discolored crooked teeth. Evan continued, "All right Mr. Magic Man, Dickhead, FBI Pervert," Ellison removed Dickhead and Pervert, but allowed the rest of his statement to remain. "Cocksucker," Evan added. Ellison removed that as well.

"Evan," Ellison said telepathically, "Keep it clean. No more profanity aimed at the FBI Agent. Now continue... and... please abbreviate the story like agent Chung requested."

Evan ruffled his feathers, stamped his feet clearly agitated by Ellison's support of the Agent.

"Okay, you and the pervert want it short, I'll make it short. Suzan first seduced the zookeeper, stole the keys to the animal cages, and while playing the tuba, (inside the monkey cage,) she managed to disrobe, and while still blowing her instrument, had sex with Gilmore. That animalistic action caused the monkeys to behave like humans, and well, there was an orgy."

Evan eyed Agent Chung in disgust. The man, clearly aroused by his brief description of events, sought relief in the Men's room. He returned a few minutes later more or less relaxed—perhaps relieved is a better word.

"Continue," Ellison said telepathically.

"On January 8^{th,} Suzan dropped her unnamed baby off at the Saint Croix Church of God in El Paso Texas. Then proceeded to 113 Margin Road where she shot John James Gilmore thirty-seven times while he sat helplessly on the toilet. He was reading the December issue of Reader's Indigestion. She picked up the magazine, noticed an advertisement for non-specific work-related opportunities with the Black Ops Corporation in Chicago. She robbed the First National Bank of El Paso, the one on 22nd Street and flew to Chicago where she met Mr. Hatton. Suzan, after providing Hatton with an introductory fellatio, immediately became the Office Manager of the Black Ops Corporation. She learned karate; wing chun, jujitsu, yaw-yan, and her personal favorite Nguni stick fighting. She also became proficient in small arms fire. Within the first three weeks of employment, Suzan had killed seven people, James Robin, Phil Dean, Lucy Mae, Ralph Dunmore, Charles Hope and two brothers Bob and Sam Roberts. All were members of the Maladies, a group of protester's against the war. There you have it Mr. FBI, Secret Agent Man... Asshole." Evan said.

Ellison omitted, "Ass hole."

Bogdan took a deep breath, "It's all here

Mr. Chung. Based on our contractual agreement for my services as moderator, translator, and transcriber, that will be seven-thousand dollars. Evan's service as a snitch is forty-seven thousand dollars. If you need us as expert witnesses, our fee is eighty dollars an hour—that is a piece. Any questions?"

"Not at the moment," Chung said, "I will give you a call if something comes up."

"Our money?"

"A government check will be in the mail by the end of the month." Chung smugly replied.

"Ass hole," Evan said. Ellison relayed Evans message to Chung who quickly dropped his smile and replaced it with a glower.

Suzan sat stoically on a bench in her jail cell listening to Evan's damaging testimony. Hatton with his new soul and Suzan's attorney Bernie Shell sat beside her. Both took copious notes on the testimony. Bernie broke the silence, "Nobody is going to believe that turkey." Hatton nodded in agreement.

CHAPTER 25

Three Tidbits

1. The Trial of Suzan Sandal.

Suzan and her attorney Bernie Shell sat before Judge Sam Caliber. The Governments Attorney Mr. C.H. Wad and Agent Chung were also present. Hatton sat in the audience. Judge Caliber called the courtroom to order. He immediately asked the opposing attorneys to come before the bench; spoke briefly to the attorney's, then, Judge Caliber sent them away. "Case dismissed." He yelled, slammed down the gravel, promptly stood, and left the courtroom. A turkey's testimony according to section ninety-nine of the Northeastern American Penal Code cannot be allowed in a court of law.

Evan made a statement to the press. "This is another example of humanity's unjust and discriminatory treatment of turkeys."

2. The Future of the Black Ops Corporation.

Hatton and the Black Ops Corporation were elated about Suzan's freedom. Hatton especially was overjoyed. He missed Suzan's fellatio, and perhaps more importantly, the company had become less profitable without her leadership. He was sure once she was back in the saddle the company would revive. His assumption proved correct. The Pentagon handed out a multi-million dollar contract to the Black Ops Corporation as a supplier of military equipment and arms.

3. The Turkey Uprisings

Evan, angry about the disrespect and unlawful treatment of Turkeys began a campaign to stop the murder of millions of Turkeys all over the world. The so-called Gobbler Campaign of 2035 was the first organized campaign by turkeys, now called the Turks, to demonstrate against the cruelty of humans. Seven thousand turkeys marched on Washington D.C. At exactly one p.m. Mountain Standard Time. A coordinated riot broke out all over the world. Glo-

The Perfect Plan

bal News reported seventeen turkey deaths in Washington D. C., fifteen deaths in Paris, Five in Russia, eight in Beijing, and seven in London. One turkey died in McIntosh New Mexico as he carried a protest sign in front of the Post Office. The turkey later plucked and eaten by the Post-madam was the pet of the famous child actor Edna Estancia. There were no reports of human causalities during the confrontations.

Skirmishes between humans and turkeys continued until President Cardner signed the Disco Treaty, which gave the turkeys seven hundred acres of free rangeland in North West Alaska. None of the five-thousand-seven–hundred gobblers, hens, and chicks survived the first winter.

Then came the Turkey Wars of 2055. The US government called out the National Guard in Ohio. That state claimed to have slaughtered 45.5 million turkeys within the previous year. The turkeys' heard about the slaughter of their innocent companions and held a nonviolent demonstration. The protest was simply a peaceful march. The birds carried signs and gobbled "Freedom." The National Guard attacked the protesting turkeys on the day before Thanksgiving. The military murdered 200,000 turkeys and sent their bodies, overnight delivery, to Walmart.

The Black Ops Corporation, by the way, provided the National Guard with their weaponry. Evan was irate and proclaimed a holy war against the hostile humans. He had a plan.

Interjection: Turkey resistance has changed over the years. The Turkeys' developed methods like car bombs, and improvised explosive devices, IED's, designed to kill soft targets. This form of terrorism gained popularity in the early 2000's by Muslim extremists.

CHAPTER 26

Linguine's first mother and murderer, Izabelle did not like or appreciate her rebirth. She rebelled in a surprisingly sadistic manner

Understand, ladies and gentlemen, before elucidation that sex is a random selection, based on chance and certainly not preordained. Having said that, Mother Urdu broke the rules and placed Izabelle in the womb of Molly, the wife of Brother Fordham Dally with the belief that a good Christian doctrine would temper Izabelle—that is calm her soul's malice. That contradiction caused this— ↓

Reverend Dally evangelized his entire life in the hills and hollows of rural Bunion County Georgia. Molly named her child William—William the Demeaning she later told a deacon during the boys baptismal.

Reverend Dally came home after a two-week stint in the backwoods preaching the gospel to two hedonistic, bands of Scottish immigrants, the McNider's, and the Smiley Larder clan. The patriarch of the Larder clan, it just so happened, invented the first battery-operated dildo. Papa Larder called it a massager in those days. The Reverend Dally purchased one of the wands to massage his arthritic feet. The cucumber-shaped machine, however, became popular among women as a sexual stimulator, especially in their husband's absence. Molly, in a most jovial fashion, found the device and began to use the vibrator for self-gratification.

During his late infancy, William began to take an interest in girl things, dolls, barrettes bright colored clothing. Queerly, the thing he loved the most was the buzz of his mother's dildo. One day the reverend walked into the house and saw his son, little William with his pants down. The child was attempting to insert the dildo between his butt cheeks. The good preacher took a switch to his son's backside and confined the boy to his closet for three days.

William, by the nature of his character, rebelled against the person he was becoming, and with a severe case of self-loathing, he plotted in his mind at least, the unatonable murder of his family. On Friday the 13th during the spring rains of April, William the Demeaning murdered his father and mother. The crime was committed thusly. William, after an altercation with a classmate, returned home crying. Molly, being a caring mother, tried to console her son. She fed him bananas and oatmeal, his favorite food, and sung *Blessed Assurance* his favorite gospel song. In reality, he hated that song. He ate patiently and listened calmly, all the while scheming against his mother for raising him in such a restrictive environment.

"Mother," William whispered.

"Yes, child?"

"Where is papa's pistol?"

Molly looked briefly at the roll top desk in the living room; then turned her gaze quickly back to her child, "Why do you want to know the location of your father's gun?"

"I want Papa to teach me how to shoot."

Molly was ecstatic that her boy wanted to learn how to shoot a pistol. "I will tell your father as soon as he comes home. I am sure he will show you how to shoot." That afternoon Fordham came in from the field. He had been planting strawberries; His wife met him at the door with the glorious news. "William," she exclaimed, "want's to learn how to shoot."

"Wonderful," the Reverend Fordham Dally said, "where is the child?"

"In his room," Molly replied, "playing the *Hunter Games* with his pet rabbit."

"William, come here," his father yelled. Fordham's voice penetrated the thin plank walls of the house with a booming and clamorous shaking.

"Sir," William said in a meek mousy voice.

"Come," his father, said. William walked into the living room, gave his mother a gracious curtsy, and embraced his father's waist. "Mother says you want to learn how to shoot a gun." His father said with pride.

"Yes, father I do."

Fordham walked over to the roll top desk, opened the drawer, and retrieved a revolver. He opened a box of shells, put a handful of cartridges in his pocket, and walked outside followed by William. Father and son marched to the nether side of the pasture where Fordham placed a coffee can on a fence post. His father stepped off ten paces, leveled the barrel of the gun at the can, and fired. He hit the can dead center. "Okay, your turn," his father exclaimed. William took the pistol from his father and pointed it at the can. The kick of the weapon startled William, but his aim was true. A dime size hole appeared between the F and O letters on the can. William, elated by his success pleaded with his father to allow him to continue shooting. Father and son, for the first time, felt comfortable in each other's company. They practiced marksmanship together until Molly called them in for supper.

Later that night, with the dildo buzzing in his buttocks, William shot and killed his mother and father while they slept.

Interjection: Beelzebub

The Perfect Plan

Beelzebub at this point stuck a tobacco-stained finger into the structure of this story and in this manner caused a gap in the narrative. "Sigillography, sir," Beelzebub stated, "I have studied the seal of Izabelle's documented birth." He sat at a plank table among unfriendly ants who chose to leave rather than speak to the devil. Beelzebub was unconcerned. He understood abandonment, besides ants he believed lack empathy, so he spoke to God, "She is my daughter." Beelzebub lit a pipe, crossed his legs in a leisurely fashion being careful to amend the position of his bifurcated tail. His tail had a tendency to lash out uncontrollably during periods of self-analysis. "Look," he said with eyes uplifted. "It is not my fault she turned out this way. I am not responsible for his or her, (meaning Izabelle's,) misdeeds." He uttered maledictions in a grave undertone and in an upsurge of self-pity, he appeared to reflect soberly on his clubfoot. He then sighed. "That is all I have to say. She is my daughter and I love her."

___O___

Beelzebub had surgery on his clubfoot, and he is doing well in recovery. He wanted to thank everyone for the get-well cards and especially thank those who offered their prayers.

CHAPTER 27

During the Peak of the US Whaling Industry

Mother Urdu decided that Izabelle's next placement would be somewhere remote, sparsely populated —better still somewhere where no one wanted to go. Urdu made her decision based simply on what was best for the development of Izabelle's soul. It was not a salubrious location.

Izabelle's father, known as Tubo de Estova was a doctor. He was a local oddity in many eyes, for the tall hat he wore. His real name and title according to the ship's ledgers were Doctor David Nottingham of Fowey England. David and his pregnant wife Cabana were sailing to Cuba to open a hospital. The ship was lost in a horrific storm, and Cabana became a castaway on the Isle of El Gran Vacio. She was the only survivor of that tragic event. Cabana's baby was born thirty-one days later.

Izabelle Nottingham Cortez was born on

The Perfect Plan

a night illuminated by a corpulent equatorial moon. The birth was without difficulties and the child appeared healthy. The infant grew under the thoughtful care of her mother. Strange events, however, occurred when the child—at two years of age—began to talk. She spoke in a strange language, a language steeped in darkness, and laden with consonances. Words like eull, zull bondon and muvel, heavy words neither Spanish nor English nor a combination of the two. In addition, Izabelle delivered her speech with a defensive animal sound, something akin to a growl. She retained this language until she was in her pubescent teens. After her first menstruation, she began to speak fluent Spanish as well as English. Cabana, of course, was elated about her daughter's conversion to recognizable languages, and she and her daughter spent every night after the evening meal recounting the dull happenings of the day. On a particularly boring night, Izabelle began to make up strange stories. She spoke about eating the island's sand until her home was gone. She also spoke of wooden water monsters and flying insects with metallic skins and copper wings. Cabana attributed her daughter's strange stories to their isolation, specifically her daughter's lack of interaction with children her own age.

Later that night as the moon's reflection lay upon the ocean's surface. A whale's body floated through the perfect sphere of moonlight and came to rest in the island's shallow waters. Cabana saw the waves animated by ravenous fish. She considered the dead whale to be like Izabelle a holy mystery, a creature cursed and consumed by circumstance. The next night a huge title wave roused by an unseen and most mysterious host washed over the island. Cabana and Izabelle frantically climbed the solitary palm tree, to escape the pounding surf. The rising waves pushed the whale's carcass with firm and assiduous force, against the inhabited tree. It remained stuck against the tree, a foul mass of flesh—in conservative jargon, a stinking tree hugger.

As soon as the sun appeared, Izabelle and her mother clamored down the tree, crossed the only solid section of the animal, its skullcap, and made camp on the starboard side of the island. The odor combined with the sun was so overwhelming that by mid-day, Izabelle collapsed. To protect her daughter from the intense sun, Cabana fashioned a small shabby umbrella of palm leaves and tied the foliage to a driftwood frame. She stood above her daughter and provided shade by rotating the umbrella with the sun's passage across the sky. The constant standing, the heat, insufficient water, and awful smell took its toll on Cabana. After two days of suffering, Cabana collapsed and died. Soon after her death, it began to rain. Revived by the rain, Izabelle cradled her mother in her arms and lamented in a mournful-hollow-whisper. After three days of soulful weeping, she buried her mother in the sand. Izabelle sat on the beach waiting and wishing for her on death. She felt insecure, betrayed, abandoned, and lonely. Her mind vacillated in and out of a dark place where demons of sex and death tittered in a cynical fashion about life and one's purpose therein. Death (portrayed as a skeleton) heard her cries. She spied him lying comfortably on the sandy beach. He, with his leg bone balanced across his kneecap, swung his shin bone back and forth in a most casual rhythm. In his skeletal hand, he clasped an open book titled, *The Gymnasts Guide to Life and Ecstasy*. Izabelle listened intently as the skeleton read lewd and lecherous passages from the book. After the turn of four or perhaps five pages, he abruptly slammed the book shut and snapped his bony fingers together creating a loud noise equal to the breaking of a dry branch. He stared at Isabelle with his vacant hollow eyes and said, totally out of context, 'Useful are the dead,' he then issued forth a musical chuckle, so loud was the chortle Izabelle had to cover her ears.

Izabelle, remembering the sex demon's words found a sharp-edged stone and began to disembowel the decaying whale. She cast the viscera into the ocean and used the whale's ribcage to make a small shelter. Izabelle covered the shelter with whale skin and fashioned a water catchment system from the animal's hide. From a small whale rib, she fashioned a bow and made arrows from driftwood. She killed seabirds feeding upon what remained of the whale carcass and using bone hooks and whale flesh she captured fish from the ocean surf. Her situation was improving. She no longer felt insecure, betrayed, or abandoned,

But,

She still felt lonely, and her loneliness, caused Izabelle to return to speaking the dark language of her youth. She also practiced intense acts of violence against herself. Today, this day, after slashing her skin with a cutting stone, she removed her clothing and began to rock back and forth in a rhythm similar to the swinging of deaths leg. She was in this horrible state of abstraction when the Capitan and crew of a whaling vessel rescued her.

However, when the ship docked in the Boston Harbor, all the sailors on board were found dead- bludgeoned to death with a whalebone. Also, it may seem trifling or strange to some, but all the deceased seamen were naked when found by the Harbor Patrol.

The first five days in the new world was uneventful. Izabelle's survival skills honed by island living prepared her for the task of leisurely living in a wasteful and excess city. It was raining the day she met a slightly overweight hawker named, John Oliver at the B and B Carnival. He was selling popcorn. She was selling sailors clothing, among other nautical items. What is notable about their meeting was that within a day Izabelle was speaking lucidly again. Even more remarkable, two hours after regaining her speech, she guided

Mr. Oliver through the seventy-seven sexual positions listed in Death's book, *The Gymnasts Guide to Life and Ecstasy*. It should be noted that Izabelle and John spent many hours perfecting the moviegoer position.

Interjection: The Gymnasts Guide to Life and Ecstasy is a graphic novel written in Hell (date unknown) by a British porn star, Linda La' More.

Interjection: Annotation by the AoALA editor and his associates: Four pages of the transcript were missing. There was a bloody fingerprint found on the bottom of the next page.

— The two fell in love, got married, and she and her new husband, after honeymooning two days at the Wayfarer's Inn left Boston. Izabelle based her decision to leave the city on a cosmic appearance of whale clouds drifting across the sky. The pod of light fluffy whales sailed west along the Mystic River. She and John followed the whales to Mystic Lake, and there, in a reflection on the lake's placid surface, she saw the image of an Alpaca standing beneath a *Welcome to Madison Ohio* road sign. It was an omen—a very good omen she believed. The couple hand-in-hand hawked sailors stuff out of a duffel bag for six-hundred miles. They reached Madison on April first and bought a house on April second with the money they made selling sailors gear. Happily, John got a job as a parts manager at the Tecumseh Lawn

Mower Plant. Izabelle became adept at reading tarot cards and set up a psychic studio in her basement. She earned enough money as a fortune teller to pay for her substantial mental health costs.

They were more-or-less happy, but Izabelle's dark side would appear (thus the psychiatrist,) usually during periods of moderate to extreme happiness. John found ingenious ways of giving her space during her episodes of dark speech, and flashbacks. For instance, at night, during her bouts of whalebone bashing, he would go to Joe's bar and fondle the waitress. Or, if Izabelle's episodes happened during the day, he would go to the golf club and fondle the caddie. Either way, his strategy seemed to work for both of them.

The couple over time became socially active. Mr. Oliver especially enjoyed politics and became a member and eventual leader of a rebellious group called The Pious Right. After seven years of marriage, Izabelle and John had a 'miracle' child and moved into the affluent Cheshire neighborhood of East Madison Ohio. A year after the child was born, Izabelle died in a train wreck. No one knew why she was on the train or her destination.

CHAPTER 28

North African Village of Wassup

Izabelle's soul birthed as William Sanders III, trained to be a medic in the Second Social Security Conflict. This theatrical Confrontation, unlike others in the 22nd Century, was bloody due, in part, to the hiring of professional wrestlers as combatants. The wrestlers' instinct for the fanatical and farcical damn near ended the conflict. It would have too if it were not for Sander's and his chemical brew. Sanders while experimenting with hallucinogenic compounds developed a chemical known as fletch. This petroleum-based compound solidified the gladiators' naturally spongy cerebellum making the wrestler's actions more manageable. The treatments allowed the fight to continue in a supervised way and put money, lots of money into corporate coffers. In addition, Sanders also created the pesticide Asspergasp that annihilated every creature, except man, in the Southern

Hemisphere.

But, that's another story.

This story is about how Izabelle's soul placed into Dar's body got to France utilizing pugilistic skills and tight boxer shorts to gain money for travel expenses. Mother Urdu gave Izabelle's soul to Dar by way of his mother, Shanika who was a slim, shy woman with a beautiful afro. Shanika was born and raised in the small North African Village of Wassup with her extended family of fourteen God-loving souls, including her father Sam, her mother Sliver, and twelve aunts and uncles from both sides of the family. Shanika was unmarried and untouched by man. A virgin, reportedly verified by a male nurse named Bartholomew.

Her pregnancy as the Gospel of Paralipsis states was an ill-fated happenstance. It seems Shanika, tired and dirty from her travels, found and sat in a community bath for at least an hour. The previous bather, Dirty Bill Baring, as reported by the villagers' was a sexual pervert. The depraved man soaked in extremely hot water with a magazine in his left hand. The publication (found poolside as evidence) depicted nude women in all sorts of provocative positions and postures. Nurse Bartholomew reviewed the publication, labeled it as circumstantial evidence, and called for a local man named, Bob to testify. Bob danced around Bartholomew, holding his privates as if he had to pee while chanting between gut-

The Perfect Plan

tural snorts, The pervert Bill Baring was sitting in the bath, breathing heavily. His face twisted into a grimace. He held a magazine in his left hand, his right hand hidden below the waves, caused gesticulating water to splash above his belly. He was humping too.

Nurse Bartholomew after hearing, Bob's testimony sent out a posse of vigilant virgins—Nuns of the Shall Not Convent—to convince Baring to return to the village and stand trial for his misdeeds. The sisters returned—how should I say this, unclean perhaps, or sinful, well hell, I will just be frank; they came back knocked up just like Shanika. It was rumored that Bill Baring was responsible for their pregnancies but the sisters, (all 5 of them,) never bathed during their trip. Bartholomew assumed that their 'being with child' was due to Immaculate Conception just like Jimmie's mother, Mary Johnston's single-person pregnancy.

The five sisters returned to their convent in Wassup, while Shanika motivated by circumstance i.e. her condition, left Wassup to be with her sister in Paris. However, Shanika never made it to Paris. The farthest she got from Wassup was five miles bipedally. She crawled the next five miles and slithered snake-like in God-awful pain the last two miles.

Dar was born on the road (more like a game trail) twelve miles west of Wassup. The boy weighed fourteen pounds eight ounces at birth. His weight and rotund figure caused complications during the parturition. Shanika, unfortunately, died while giving birth to her slick-bowling-ball-size-baby. Fortunately, the child survived with the help of six buxom wet nurses (one woman and five goats.) The woman and her entourage found him on the side of the road wrapped in sticky placenta. The woman named Boobs buried Shanika in a shallow grave and carried Dar to her village where she and the goats fed the boy in seizures of more-or-less equal length. He grew rapidly.

Dar stayed with Boobs and her goat family until man-hair appeared on his face, legs, underarms, and crotch. The news of his maturation traveled like body odor on a strong breeze and the Baring Clan having caught his scent in nearby Loadtown sent a dispatch. The messenger, Dar's grandfather Sam, arrived one day on a stolen camel and without dismounting the beast the old man said, "Complete your mother's dream. Go to your Aunt Florence in Paris." Sam turned his camel around, and with great haste struck the beast on his right flank. The camel jolted into a rocking run, achieved ten to twenty yards, and then for no apparent reason, stopped abruptly. Grandfather Sam, thrown from the camel as if a discarded beer can, broke his slender goose-like neck in the fall.

Dar in grief took the stolen camel and returned to Loadtown. His family greeted him with

The Perfect Plan

suspicion. His grandfather, a renowned camel jockey, and romantic had never been thrown, not by a woman during intercourse, and certainly, not by a beast. The villagers completely inexperienced in the reasoning process called for a Priest. The Priest, a portly man with faded wrinkled skin, and a torn loincloth (he was an exhibitionist) took Dar into his tent. The minister questioned the boy thoroughly about the alleged accident and decided after five minutes of meditation that the boy was guilty of murdering his grandfather. He also decided to release the fourteen-year-old under certain conditions. The conditions were:

1. Dar would represent the village in an upcoming sporting event, and
2. Win or lose Dar would be banished from the tribe forever.

Dar reluctantly agreed.

The event, a boxing tournament for junior Olympians, was set for Dajaj the day of the Turkey (next Thursday) tribes near and far brought their sons and daughters to the sponsoring village of Loadtown. Dar trained for two days. His coach, Mohamad Alibaba was extremely disappointed with the boy's pugilistic talent. He commanded Dar to sit in a corner of the boxing ring for five hours minimum and speak to his inner-self. Dar reluctantly complied with the trainer's request, but after one failed attempt at deep contemplation, Dar quit. He felt helpless. He thought, *how in hell does this inner-self crap work*? Dar's reincarnated soul, Izabelle, answered from within, "Easy, I have in one of my prior lives, been a cut man for Max Baer. I know my way around the ring boy, but you will have to trust me." Dar nodded to himself. It was clear in his mind anyway that he was going to get screwed during the fight. "Think positive," his soul Izabelle said.

Izabelle, in Dar's subconscious mind, demonstrated several basic boxing moves and told him to practice. Dar threw two short jabs and a sweeping right uppercut. Exhausted, he threw down his gloves, went to his corner, and sat down on a milk stool borrowed from Boobs.

Fight day arrived. The crowd was large. The people were angry especially his close relatives and eager to see blood, his blood. Dar's opponent, Omar, was a head taller than Dar, and he had seven older sisters. That meant he had experience. Dar lacked ambition and self-confidence. His family noticed his timidity, and they booed, hissed obscenities, and threw things at him as he entered the ring. The referee removed the tires, beer bottles, and spittle from the boxing mat and motioned the boys forward. The two youngsters walked to the referee and listened as he gave instructions, "No biting, gouging, pulling hair, everything else is legal." The Ref sent the boys back to their corner. The bell rang. Omar lunged at Dar and began to pummel his face. Dar reddening under his dark skin and bleeding from his nose ran to the corner and covered-up. Omar followed. "Run," Izabelle echoed from a niche within his head. Dar ran to the opposite corner. Omar approached quickly, threw a quick punch, "Duck," Izabelle said, "Then, swing." Dar ducked and swung as instructed. He hit Omar flush on the jaw and knocked him flat out.

Oh shit! Dar thought, or perhaps it was Izabelle speaking.

No one cheered, quite the opposite. The crowd was awe-struck and silent. It seems that everyone, including the referee, bet Dar would lose. The only person that bet on Dar to win was his aunt Florence in Paris. Mohamad Alibaba collected the money and gave Florence's winnings to Dar, escorted him to the edge of the village, put a boot to his ass and sent him on his way.

Now, about the tight boxer shorts. Dar used his aunt's money for travel expenses as he traveled toward the Mediterranean Sea. He spent unwisely during his travels, purchasing glass beads, fine toiletries, a camel hair suitcase, five pounds of butterscotch pudding, which he ate in a week, a Santa Clause hat, and a pair of satin boxer briefs, equipped with FRY technology to accentuate the groin. Dar reached the beach penniless. With no way of purchasing passage across the sea. He began selling off his collection of excesses in the resort town of Gazette. The boy sold everything but his too-tight boxer briefs. He even sold the fine Gucci suit he was wearing.

Interjection: A Portrait of the Referee, aka Ref.

Art historians have unanimously agreed that the sketch, found at the bottom of a metal spittoon in the Black Ops vault is an original. The description of the drawing is based on a crayon portrait signed by Da Vinci. The artist utilized a style popular in the human decadent period, which lasted for well over one hundred, (human,) years.

The referee is standing in the middle of the boxing ring. He has a short square chin at the base of his rotund bluish—trending nigh purplish—face. Pendulous jowls and bat-like ears reside on either side of his head. His prominent nose extends and bends slightly left between his narrow bloodshot eyes. Red serpentine veins crisscross the orb of his enormous proboscis. The Ref. has an abnormally slim torso. He balances upon splayed bare feet. He clasps his small, delicate, and distinctively Trumpian hands together above his head in either celebration or shock of Dar's victory. The AoALA's consensus is that it is the latter.

CHAPTER 29

The Boxer, Dar's opponent

I will make this particularly sad life story brief. Mother Urdu planted my little Linguine soul in Pam Benloudly. My father, Ray Lee Benloudly was a famous North African boxer who owned a gym in the village of Loadtown. My daddy named me Omar and taught me how to box. My sisters and I were his only pupils. I do not believe my parents loved me. They, however, did tolerate my existence, because I was so talented at boxing. My dad promoted fights and used my considerable pugilist skills to enhance the number of goats our family owned. A kid named Dar beat me in the junior Olympics. My father and the entire village of Loadtown wagered that I would win the fight. The townspeople, with encouragement and support from my parents, recouped some of their losses by selling me into bondage as a bodyguard. A radical poet Mr. C.C. Basely purchased me. Over time, we became close friends and he became my mentor in the art and lack of rhyme in free verse. I died in a plane crash while on a journey to New York to meet a publisher for my book *Eidolon Bogy Remember Me*. I was thirty-one years old, plus a day when I died.

Interjection: Research into the Omar Benloudly Estate:

The estate of Omar Benloudly filed suit in 2018 against Donald D'lo, (an unmentioned reincarnate of Jimmie Linguine,) for copyright infringement. D'lo published Eidolon Bogy Remember Me in 2016. One hundred years after Omar died in a plane crash over the Argentine Alps.

CHAPTER 30

Dar in Barcelona Spain

Dressed only in his FRY enhanced boxer briefs, Dar boarded a semi-functional ferry and landed in Barcelona. He survived in the city by raiding restaurant dumpsters. Naturally, Dar's too-tight shorts during his dumpster excursions became soiled and torn.

The fact that his too-tight boxer briefs were soiled and torn at first may seem irrelevant, but actually, it is essential to the narrative.

Why? Because a famous swimwear fashion designer, Deli de Delores, discovered Dar quite by accident while she dined at the famous Restaurante Desnuda. Dar was dumpster diving while Deli de Delores involved sexually with her hairdresser stepped out of the restaurant into the back alley to practice hip-humping, aka dry humping, aka booty-thrust, pelvis pushing and of course, everyone should be familiar with the term pussy grinding. Anyway, Deli de Delores spied Dar's ass up in a dumpster. She immediately stopped her gyrations, and yelled, "You in the dumpster, come here." Dar backed out of the dumpster unsure of the situation. Expecting the worst, he assumed a boxer's stance, which displayed perfectly his torn too-tight boxer briefs. Delores sighed, giggled while clapping her diminutive hands, and asked, "Cuanto?"

Dar shrugged his shoulders. It was a physical manifestation of his thought, *what the Hell did she just say*. He stared at her.

"Your swim-ware, I love it—I would like to buy the shorts." She said in a thick Spanish dialect.

"Okay."

"Seven Thousand Euros-is okay?"

"Okay," Dar said. Actually, he had no idea what a euro was or how much it was worth in comparison with the U.S. Dollar.

"Yes, yes, okay," Delores interrupted. She opened her purse, and pulled the money out, hesitated, "Remove your shorts." Dar wriggled out of his too-tights and handed them to Delores. She scanned his muscular fourteen-year-old body, "How much for your-um, your body?" She pointed at his pecker.

"Seven thousand euros—fourteen thousand for everything."

"Okay," Delores said, "Come with me." Delores handed Dar the money. He counted the num-

The Perfect Plan

bers carefully. She took Dar by the hand and hailed a cab, leaving her hairdresser Sancho crying in the alley.

Dar Baring purchased clothing via the internet, he especially liked the tie-died knitted poncho and acid washed bellbottom jeans. He also adored his double-breasted red and green striped tuxedo. Dar stayed with Delores a week; then took a train to Paris. He called his aunt Florence, (a clandestine bomb maker he later learned). She picked him up at the train station and took him to her modest home. Dar stayed with his Aunt Florence, became radicalized by the NIC team of insurgents, learned the intricacies of bomb-making, and with detailed instructions from his aunt, Dar carrying Izabelle's soul left for the USA.

Reminder

It wasn't an accident that Dar got Izabelle soul.

Prosperous and Izabelle's soul, it just so happened was with Mother Urdu at the same time waiting for a new birth baby. Prosperous struck a deal with Izabelle while Mother Urdu was napping. The deal was so egregious that Beelzebub himself entered it into the world's most heinous crimes and received a Pull-it-Sir-Prize (sponsored by the popular magazine Readers Really), for the evilest deed recorded, to date, in the history of humanity. Here is the deal. Prosperous, still angry about the thirty years profits lost in the Elusion war and Loki's bargaining on Jimmie Linguine's behalf, asked Izabelle (Linguine's first birth mother) to use   the body given her by Mother Urdu, which was Dar, to kill Jimmie Linguine before his time—it didn't matter how. Izabelle aka Dar decided on the bomb.

CHAPTER 31

The School Bus Attack in Madison Ohio

Dar who stayed with his Aunt Florence, in Paris, became radicalized by his aunt in association with Emad Ben Avid a Taliban Mullah, where he learned the intricacies of bomb-making, and with detailed instructions from his Aunt Florence, Dar with Izabelle's soul, left for Madison Ohio USA.

Dar Baring flashed his Paris Passport and ticket to the boarding agent and boarded American Airlines Flight 119 for Columbus Ohio. He landed at Port Columbus International Airport at 7:47 Sunday evening, hailed a cab to the Columbus Bus Station and caught a Grey-dog shuttle to Madison.

The smoky fog over Madison Ohio, Dar thought, looked spectacular through the unwashed bus window. The window's blue tint added an even more gloomy hue to the surrounding gray air, (Dar loves Gloom.) The terrorist got off the Bus on Capital Street in Madison Ohio and walked to the Café Erie. He strode happily into the restaurant, turning diners' heads as if he were a bowling ball destined for a rack of pins. Dar was wearing a double-breasted red and green striped tuxedo. The suit was a rarity in this blue-collar town. Rumors of an outsider eating at the Café Erie started to spread, and soon a crowd gathered outside the café. Dar ate quickly, pushed his way through the crowd, and spent the night a few blocks away at the Sleep Inn Hotel. The next morning, Dar rented a car, searched for and found Dawson's Mobile Home Park, as recommended by Florence, and rented a trailer.

Soon after his arrival and settlement, Dar met Camden Hart, a local high school dropout, and single mom. After a week, she moved in with the terrorist, and they settled into a seemingly normal life. Camden helped Dar get a job in the Walmart meat market just before Thanksgiving Day. Evan on the same day began to protest in the huge Walmart parking lot. There were seventy or eighty turkeys on a picket line. Shots fired by unknown assailants killed Evan and seven other turkeys. The FBI arrived the next day and completed a background check on every Walmart employee, except for Dar, he hauled ass in his rented car and went to a safe house in Texas. The current theory among Madison's intellectuals is that Dar did not plant the bomb. The belief is that Wild Turkeys blew up the school bus containing Jimmie

Linguine and twenty other children. No one has claimed responsibility for the terrorist attack. However, on the day of the bombing, a school bus mechanic witnessed suspicious looking Indians dressed like turkeys around the bus. As soon as the mechanic called the cops, the Indians mysteriously disappeared.

Evan's funeral was at the Everlasting Church of God's Pauper Cemetery in Bootstrap New Mexico, Ellison Bogdan, his flock of goats, and over a hundred turkeys attended the services. Bogdan placed a marker above Evan's grave. The message scratched on an old weathered plank, carved with beak and claw by Evan himself thirty years before his death said simply, "I will return."

Jimmie died and was buried by an unknown character in what is now known as the Madison Blast Radius.

Interjection: The following is a video message, which includes a verbal exchange between the executive in charge, a chorus of choir boys, and Beelzebub. The location(s) of the speakers are unknown.

The executive in charge says, "Let us pause a moment in silent prayer for Jimmie Linguine and all the children who died or were wounded on school bus TR08." A voice muffled by distance and the lamentations of the crowd cried, "Fuck the Turkeys."

Beelzebub's Counterpoint.

Beelzebub opined a brief summary of his involvement with the Terrorist movement. "I shall stir the dirty water of this stagnant pool called Madison Ohio, and will, so help me Satan, discover by my own voracity the man responsible for this good and noble deed."

Chorus of Lost Souls, "Grand deed,"

"I need a man or woman like that under my commission. If I get resistance from anyone, I will paralyze that person or persons from the knee up using Mephistopheles ball peen hammer and will strike with certainty the vulnerable left hemisphere of his or her kneecap. We are not gender bias in hell are we boys."

Chorus, "Hell no!"

CHAPTER 32

Linguine Returns to Urdu

Within a minute after my death, I was at the entrance of Mother Urdu tomb. The opening, no larger than the birth canal of a cow was damp and slippery. I slithered down the dark fissure until I came to a grand room where charcoal Images of ancient beasts adorned the rock walls. Stickmen gave chase to antlered animals. Crocodiles with mouth agape guarded a winding river where grass huts lined steep muddy banks. A flickering fire cast red moving patterns over Mother Urdu's massive body. The smell of roasted garlic permeated the air. She was lounging on a stone throne. Red and black stripes ringed her face, arms, and legs. Her dreadlocks covered with gold and red butterflies fell to her broad shoulders. Twelve in-process children (reincarnates) navigated her painted body stopping briefly to suckle as they passed her plump breasts. When the reincarnates came too close to Urdu's muzzle and hound-like ears, the butterflies would rise in a mass of sparkling color, hover briefly, and then resettle, like flies to a turd, on her matted mop.

I formed as a pre-clown at her feet and pulled her claw. She smiled, "Jimmie, I've missed you."

I hugged her ankle, "Mother."

She widened her grin, and held it, long enough to show her russet teeth before she spoke, "Why are you here?"

"I have died."

"You cannot die for another..." she looked at her paw and began a silent count on her nails, "seventeen years."

"I died in a bomb blast."

"Impossible."

"Mother, I cannot clearly remember my past, the present, or my purpose. Everything is mixed-up, a blur," I explained.

"It has never happened before," she said, gazing at the fire. "You cannot die Jimmie. It is impossible not until you have reached thirty years and one day. You must go back and serve your purpose."

"What is my purpose Mother Urdu?"

She raised her hind paw, scratched behind her ear, and in doing so, exposed her sex-sprout to me, "It will come to you, have patience," she said matter-of-factly.

Mother Urdu looked at me with her saucer-sized eyes and said, "Coochie Coo." She lifted me from the floor, sat me on her lap, stuck a big nipple in my mouth, and rocked me gently as butterflies whispered, "All he needs is love," above her head.

Donald D'lo

The Middle

Section II

The Rise of the National Island Corporation

CHAPTER 33

The Birth of Alexander

As a reminder, Prosperous, in each consecutive birth, found love in families selected by Urdu. Her search criterion was simple, find families steeped in avarice and ambition, and send the brat to them via high-speed importation. Everyone else went by coach—

There was a heavy frost that morning. Billowing blankets of mist floated between the stone-headed Racine Mountains. Charles Danube, Faience's chauffeur was driving the Fat-Black floater through the fog. Faience Comings III, (nicknamed Trey,) was traveling to see his panicked wife at the Mercy Hospital in Spud Idaho.

Carol waited patiently for her husband in the hospital. She was inherently a nervous person with eyes that swam back and forth like goldfish in a small bowl. She was ghost-like. Her pale grey

The Perfect Plan

complexion allowed her to blend into shadows with little effort. Carol was sitting in the shadows when Dr. Royce entered the waiting room. He searched the cubical until he found her vacillating eyes. "Ready?" he asked.

She nodded a weak affirmation.

"Okay let us begin," Dr. Royce said.

A nurse placed Carol's thin body on the delivery table, lifted her legs, and placed them in the stirrups. "Can we wait for my husband?" Carol whined.

"I'm afraid we haven't the time," Dr. Royce replied, "Debbie and Brenda are about to deliver." Carol was prepared, and the procedure began on time. Carol Screamed. Interns tittered in the background. She screamed again. Even though someone else was having her baby, the fake parturition was extremely painful to the barren woman

Alexander Popped out!

The baby containing Prosperous' soul came to the Comings family by way of Debbie on October 18th. The baby weighed ten pounds eleven ounces. The delivery took thirty minutes. Dr. Royce delivered Faience Comings IV (nicknamed Alexander after Alexander the Great) by a non-evasive system of birthing called Suction 104. The procedure, provided primarily for affluent women, used a surrogate, in this case, Debbie, to carry the child to term.

Carol still sore from the simulated labor had her attendant tend to the baby during the trip back to the Coming's mansion. It was a joyous trip for Trey. Bubbly champagne flowed over Trey's favorite drug-laced peppermint flavored chew-chews. Carol sulking in the back seat noticed, by accident a large cluster of carbuncles on the back of Trey's neck. The pustules seemed to scatter in an unorganized manner and return only to scatter again, no doubt a visual perception brought on by her swimming eyes, never the less she became nauseated and demanded that Charles pull over onto the side of the road. He did. She puked, fainted, and woke up in bed with baby Alexander in her arms.

Interjection: Painful contractions were a preventive measure used by the National Islands Corporation to discourage eligible mothers from having natural births.

— Nine months earlier.

Trey in a drug-induced stupor reflected on his purchase of Debbie Robbins and Brenda Lee Leigh. He bought Debbie to bear his son Alexander, and Brenda to bear Alexander's playmate Alice. He found both Debbie and Brenda in the West Target Holding Compound. He visited the compound once a month to search for possible sex partners. Both Debbie and Brenda were in a group of young women scheduled for purging. Trey purchased

The Perfect Plan

Brenda for her broad hips, Debbie for her enormous teats. He paid a quarter coupon, each and sent both women to the eraser room to have their memories removed and replaced with a loyal domestic worker's consciousness.

Trey was not present when Brenda and Debbie received chemical injections to ensure simultaneous ovulation. He was away playing badminton with the only person he could beat at the game, his chauffeur, Charles Danube. Trey giggled with every stroke at the birdie. He was still giggling when Charles Danube dropped him off at home. His wife Carol, and surrogates, Brenda, and Debbie were sitting and or standing nude in a mirrored room.

The three women were in the Mansion's Ballroom sipping on sexual stimulants. Trey removed his shoes and shorts but retained his racket. So, with his racket in hand, he yelled as loud as he could, "Let the rodeo begin." He mounted Brenda first. She was the most proximate. Trey viewed himself in the reflection of mirrored walls, which of course enhanced his sexual powers. Brenda had a dark brown complexion. Trey had a light complexion. He looked like a Band-Aid on the back end of a buffalo. Trey suddenly left Brenda and attacked his wife Carol, a passionate person who moved in short nervous twitches and spasms. He could not bring himself to kiss his wife; he did not enjoy face-to-face intercourse with her for the simple reason he got dizzy looking at her swimming eyes. He screwed his wife, Carol, like Brenda, doggie style, and to each, he utilized the racket to their backside to initiate a faster pace. As for Debbie, he poked her missionary style. She reacted to his moves with a bouncing madness, and he buoyed in the rough waves of her big round rubbery tits. Trey screamed with pleasure while on the wet wild ride—that is until his wife Carol slapped him across his face. He looked at her critically and asked breathlessly, "What are you thinking?"

Carol frowned, her eyes swam toward each other, a clear sign she was angry. She replied, "You are having too much fun. Dr. Royce could just as easily collected my eggs and your sperm and used AI to impregnate Brenda and Debbie." Trey ignored his wife and resumed surfing on top of Debbie's undulating body. "I know why you selected Debbie and I am sure you have plans to revisit her for sex and nourishment long after the baby arrives. I should never have agreed to this raunchy rodeo."

Trey looked at Debbie's face then turned toward Brenda for a reaction to Carol's comments thankfully there were none. Debbie and Brenda were as obedient as ever. He lowered his eyes to Debbie's breasts; then turned and stared into Carol's swimming eyes, "You wanted this baby," Trey said. "The rodeo was part of our pre-pregnancy agreement."

"You are just like your damn father," Carol

said and sighed as Trey dipped his head beneath the waves and bubbled between Debbie's breasts.

Interjection: There was a legal limit of one child per couple, but the affluent often cheated and had numerous children. A tally by the National Island Corporation's Census Bureau, using DNA samples, found that Trey had seventy-three illegal children. The majority of Trey's illegitimate children lived on the streets most of the youngest had already been purged. According to corporate records, Alexander was Trey's only legal child.

CHAPTER 34

Perversity

Trey's father, Faience Comings II was nicknamed Flush for a good reason. Flush had a phobia about his body's plumbing system. Trey assisted his father during daily anal interrogations. He inserted the hose and operated the intake and outflow electro-pump.

On Saturday 14th, the day Trey became twenty-seven, (legal age in the National Islands,) Trey downloaded an excessive mixture of Smoothie and Drano. His father died from complications of the overdose. There was a cover-up, and Trey after spending a small fortune to maintain secrecy, inherited his father's holdings. The holdings were vast and diversified. The largest asset was Fairies Gadgets and Goo. This Corporation made an assortment of sex toys, and a type of Android called Replicas. Beatrice was one of his prototypes. She was referenced as the Beeline Android and Trey's bestselling model.

Trey, like his father, was an attractive man, and well proportioned, for his small thin size. He exercised daily to maintain his muscular body and active sex life. Not only was he handsome, he was rich, which was one of the reasons he had an active, and perverse sex life outside of marriage of course. The MacAfee Post listed him as one of the three wealthiest men in the world and Alexander grew up in a lavish environment whereas his childhood playmate, Alice grew up in a chattel pod with her mother.

There were seven pods all were glass containers with no interior partitions. The toilet, lavatory, and shower were located opposite the kitchen. Everything else was a combination living and sleeping area. The capsules were under surveillance at all times. Trey was a voyeur among other lucid and lurid things. He made videos of the female inhabitants during their most intimate moments. The capsules were living quarters for women who served in different occupations around the isolated chateau. Debbie, the cook, and Alice, Alexander's playmate, lived in Capsule Five. Trey, for reasons of secrecy only visited his captives in darkness. It would not bode well if Carol found out about his sexual exploitations. He manipulated the Pod's *on-off* switch. When he loosened his belt, the lights would go *off* and fastened his belt the lights would come *on*. He had an insatiable appetite for exotic women and replaced his captives every six or seven months. Debbie and Alice were the only exceptions.

Trey sent Alexander, at the age of thirteen, to Corporate Combat School to learn self-defense primarily, but he also learned military tactics in modern warfare. When Alexander turned twenty-seven, Trey took his son, now General Alexander, to the Chattel Capsules for his birthday. The man-child, upon his father's insistence, attempted to sleep with his childhood friend, Alice. The lights were off details of the event were not visible, but when the lights came back on, Alexander was lying on the floor in a pool of blood. Alice was standing over him with part of his ear in her mouth. Trey's reaction, as expected was dramatic. He sent both mother and daughter to the West Target Holding Compound for immediate purging.

CHAPTER 35

General Alexander

There had been several cost-saving corporate blackouts during the day and most of the *American Island News* reporters had gone home. Elvira, my eighty-year-old, coworker and I, with our omega-powered computablet, were the only journalists left in the newsroom. I had shut down my tablet, but Elvira immersed in her story about the current effects of global warming continued enunciating slowly into the monitor's micro-recorder. A hand-rolled cigar protruded from her unpainted lips, and every time she spoke, a small stream of yellow smoke flowed between the gaps of her missing teeth. I peered through the lemon scented cloud of smoke that engulfed her and noticed her sleeveless beige blouse had parted slightly revealing the black star-spangled X of a Confederate flag tattooed on her withered left breast. I suddenly had an inexplicable erection. She squinted at me through fake eyelashes, "Are you through Jimmie," she said. She smiled and opened her brown eyes to their full-round shape.

"Yep, I'm done," I continued to stare through the haze of smoke into the cradle of her open blouse. She noticed my gaze but didn't bother fastening the two loose buttons of her camouflaged sleeveless shirt. Instead, she, with a flexible tongue, rolled the cigar to the right side of her mouth, placed a crooked finger to her thinly mustached upper lip, and motioned for me to come forward. I stepped to her side, leaned over her shoulder and once again peered down at her gravity-stretched breasts. I wanted to reach down-touch them. She pointed to an embroidered insignia lying on her desk.

"Why the secrecy?" I whispered.

"Use your coder," she replied. I pressed the enter button on my coder and an electromagnetic screen surrounded us. "There may be spies, listening devices you know, one can't be too careful."

"What is this about?" I said, playing along with her unfounded paranoia.

"It is General Alexander's insignia," she replied.

"Really?"

"It was taken from his body."

"He's dead?"

"Killed in Wyoming."

"Are you sure?" I rubbed my bald head. It had become an annoying habit. I made a mental note

The Perfect Plan

to see the company psych about it—that and mention my unnatural cravings for Elvira.

She opened her drawer and retrieved a photo-film. It was the unmistakable body of General Alexander lying in a puddle of blood.

"How?"

"He was killed during the Symbolist Campaign. A traitor gave the generals position away, and the corporation sent out executioners... thousands of them. The general and hundreds of his followers were annihilated." She said.

"He was the last?"

"Yes," she said with an explosion of yellow smoke.

"How did you find out?" I replied.

"I have connections with the NIC."

"The what?"

"The National Islands Corporation," she said. Her mellifluous voice was beautiful. Her malodorous breath was awful.

"What will the NIC do now?" I lowered my gaze to the lip of her skirt; then lower to her slender blue-veined, hirsute legs. The electromagnetic field made the hair on her body stand erect. I, oddly enough, found her buoyant hair sensual... even the patch of hair fluttering from the cavity of her armpits seemed erotic to me.

"I don't know," she said breaking my concentration. "Perhaps the boss will let me investigate."

"I doubt it," I said. She smiled and replaced the photo-film within the dark confines of her drawer.

With the loss of General Alexander, the whole world could be teetering on a dangerous precipice. The last time the NIC had this kind of setback was during the Gas Wars.

"I've got to go," I said despite my desire to stay—to be near her.

"Go, I'll lock up. See you in the morning," she said through a cloud of pale smoke.

"Okay," I shut down the coder and walked slowly to the door. I paused for a moment contemplating the possibilities of a sexual encounter with my enormously desirable coworker. Her hair had suddenly fallen back into place. She seemed different, younger, even I would venture to say, beautiful.

"Go," she said. I left reluctantly closing the door behind me.

It was late and dark. The National Island Corporation had cut off the nonessential streetlights, but I needed a drink, and Skelly's was the only joint in New Chicago open at this hour. I walked to the boozy enclave, located in Bray's Alley, and stepped into a buoyant spectrum of rainbow colored light. It was, as usual, breathtaking.

Jacob was bartending, "Hey Jimmie, what you-be-wagging?" he said and grabbed his crotch. I gave him the thumbs down in response. He smiled.

"Moon Rose Elixir, straight," I said, taking my seat at the bar next to Lola.

The Perfect Plan

Jacob pulled the bottle off the shelf and poured my drink. "Waggener came in yesterday—said he's joining the Global Freedom Party," Jacob said nonchalantly, "You still a neutral?"

"Yeah, I don't care much for politics," I said.

"Are you going to buy me a drink?" Lola interrupted, but before I could say go to hell, Jacob sat a drink in front of her. It was a double; I could smell the one-hundred proof alcohol mixed with ninety percent juju in the large dirty glass.

"She'll reach the termination date tomorrow," Jacob whispered. I nodded my understanding. "She has been unemployed a year now."

"I tried to find work, you know," Lola said defensively.

"My condolences. Who's doing it?" I asked.

"Saint Peter," Lola slurred.

"He's good," I said objectively, "clean and neat." She nodded and forced a smile. I touched her hand. "The next one is on me, Jacob," I said. Jacob swung the bar rag across his shoulder and brought back a bottle of Medici, the cheap stuff. "How are you going to have it done?" I asked while uncorking the bottle.

"In the dark. I don't want to see anything," Lola said, "Saint Peter is going to surprise me."

"That's nice," I said.

"Yeah, nice. He says he likes me, you know—might bring flowers for my cremation," she replied staring sadly at her still youthful looking hands. I reached out the short distance between us and gave Lola a hug. I felt her retch as the contents of her stomach mutinied against the booze, but I was unable to react in time. With a heave, Lola sprayed a foul-smelling concoction of whiskey, juju, pizza, and cauliflower, over my pants and the bar's countertop.

I jumped back, "Shit," I yelled. In my attempt to avoid the puke, I knocked over the barstool. Lola just looked at me dumbfounded and without apology stumbled off towards the women's room. Jacob threw me the bar rag, I wiped the putrid mixture off my clothes and threw the rag back to Jacob. He rinsed it off and began wiping down the bar. "I'm out of here," I said sloshing through the waves of microbial light towards the door.

"Okay," Jacob said, "See you tomorrow."

It took me ten minutes to walk to the Night Shade Apartments; a Corporate owned building housing five hundred sixty renters plus another four hundred illegal relatives and a hundred or so unrelated illegal immigrants. All the illegals paid corporate penalties for unauthorized habitation.

The corporate owned cubicle phone was ringing when I entered my apartment. I let it go to voice messaging. It was Elvira, "Jimmie, call me it's urgent." Not in the mood for conversation, I removed my clothes and stepped into the low-pressure shower. The water trickled over my baldhead and down my body. It felt warm like the corporation was pissing on me. I smiled at the thought and made a mental note to pass the metaphor on

The Perfect Plan

to Jacob. Having lathered with cinnamon soap, I turned the water off and scrubbed, making sure I laundered all the odorous parts of my body. I used the remainder of my one and a half minute water allocation for rinsing.

The cubicle phone rang. I reached for a towel, and while drying walked towards the small illuminated screen. Elvira's wrinkled face appeared, "Hello Elvira."

"Where have you been?" she barked as if she were an infuriated drill sergeant at boot camp.

"Skelly's," I said defiantly.

"Something important has come up. I need to talk to you."

"We are talking now."

"Are you daft? I need to speak to you about the insignia."

"C'mon Elvira, not now, I need to sleep," I said in the middle of an extensive yawn.

"Tomorrow will be too late. If you don't come, I'll go by myself." There was a sense of urgency in her voice and look of melancholy on her face.

"Go where?"

"Meet me at the office!" she whimpered and then click, the call ended.

I slipped into my Broadmoor shorts and Dan David sandals and met Elvira at the office. She was standing in a dark corner smoking her cigar, "Why are you wearing that?" she asked.

"Why not?" I replied.

"This is serious. You cannot travel in those clothes. We are going to the Second Elected Confederacy Headquarters of Poland," she sucked on the cigar making the dibble coin-size end glow like a demon eye, "Jimmie," she said exhaling, "The NIC Commander..." she took a breath, "General Alexander is still alive."

"What?"

"The general is still alive. He faked his death. He plans to attack the GFP's Office in New Chicago. We need to go to the NIC Headquarters in the Warsaw Sub-Office." She inhaled again. "Mr. Delphi is funding the Freedom Party."

"Mr. Delphi? You have to be kidding; he's not a Global Freedom Party sympathizer."

"He is now. The NIC has taken Mr. Delphi's wealth, what they could find anyway, and thrown him off the corporate board. He still has resources and wants to help the Global Freedom Party."

"You mean he wants to get back into the corporation with the GFP's help. It's called a hostile takeover."

"Whatever." The cigar's end glowed again. "Still, it's our chance to record the invasion."

For an extended moment, my eyes followed Elvira as she paced back and forth below the overhead light. She was—well, she appeared attractive, and I was aroused. "Our speeder arrives in fifteen minutes," she said abruptly, "you need to change clothes. Do you know the code to Dave-Davy's locker?" she asked. Smoke streamed from

The Perfect Plan

her nostrils.

"No," I said, "why?"

"Break the locker door and take his clothes, hurry," Elvira said.

I removed the pins from the cabinet hinges and confiscated a black-and-white checkered skullcap, a bright red calmover, and a pair of compressor boots. The boots and skullcap fit, but the calmover was too small. "I can't wear this," I mumbled.

"Yes you can, and you will," Elvira replied, pushing me into the restroom to change clothes. "Hurry," she said, tapping her foot as if playing the pedal drum in a Foo-Foo band. "We're out of time the speeder is here." She grabbed my arm as soon as I stepped out of the men's room. I looked like a hairless ape in leotards. I could not hide my erection. She looked at me, smiled, and pulled me to the window-harbor where the teleport opened. "Let's go," she said, as we crawled through the harbor onto a vacillating light beam. The speeder tilted with our additional weight.

We stumbled to our seats and buckled-up, "Put that out, there'll be no orgies on this ship," a cracked baritone snarled from the brass speakers. I gave Elvira a questioning look. She shrugged, took one last drag, and flipped the cigar out the portal. I watched the glowing ember fall until the speeder jolted vertically, and with a roar shot straight up. "This is your Captain, Larry Incarnate III speaking, sit back, and enjoy the trip." Elvira

Donald D'lo

and I were pinned to our seats by the force of gravity. Both our faces morphed into lumpy pancakes. The speeder stopped abruptly at fifty-thousand feet, turned horizontally and with another blast ripped off toward the eastern horizon.

CHAPTER 36

NIC's Second Elected Confederacy Headquarters

We arrived at the NIC's Second Elected Confederacy Headquarters in thirty-seven minutes. A guard met us at the palace entrance. The sentry stood approximately four and a half feet tall. He had spindly legs and gargantuan buttocks that protruded like kettledrums from his pliable trousers. The sentinel's headwear a giant stovepipe hat, red in coloration, rested precariously on his small square shoulders. The hat contributed the final foot or so of the man's definitive height. The tubular hat that concealed the Lilliputian's head and his facial features to this day remains a mystery. "Greetings," his shrill voice echoed from within the hat.

Elvira saluted smartly and handed the hat a piece of paper, "Our orders, sir."

The sentinel stuck the paper beneath the

brim of his hat and said, "Reporters, huh? Come this way." We followed the short, blocky man down marble floors to a door marked Commander and Chief. The hat paused, stomped his square feet twice, shot his arm out like a Hitler enthusiast, and tapped on the door's metal veneer.

"Enter," a high voice yodeled from behind the door. The hat elevated his hand, finger-felt the brass knob and slowly turned the knurl. He gently pushed the door open and stepped aside as we entered. I followed Elvira's oscillating hips as she moved toward a huge mahogany desk. She snapped her heels together, causing her rear to jiggle in her tight stretch pants. She saluted as I sat down in a nearby chair.

"Stand up and remove your hat," the hat said as he leapt up and slapped the back of my skullcap, knocking it to the polished oak floor. I silently cursed, retrieved my skullcap, and stood. "Reporters Elvira Evers and Jimmie Linguine," the hat said, "Reporters this is General Alexander leader of the NIC forces."

General Alexander returned Elvira's salute with a three-finger lethargic gesticulation that could have been mistaken for an obscene signal. "Please sit," he said. We sat as the hat gave him our papers; then, as graceful as a coryphée, the hat pirouetted into a complete about-face and goose-stepped out of the room. "We have been expecting you. How was your trip?" Before we could answer, the general abruptly said, "Follow me." I pur-

The Perfect Plan

sued Elvira and General Alexander as they walked briskly down a long hall. We stopped abruptly at a green metallic door. Alexander entered a code, and the door swung open exposing thirteen military clad men and women in riotous conversation about the upcoming war. "These are the commanders of the NIC." All thirteen commanders saluted. Alexander returned their salute with his languid wave, "Be seated." Everyone took a seat. "Your purpose," he warbled, looking at his officers with beady bloodshot eyes, "is to carry out a successful strike against the Global Freedom Party's New Chicago Office tomorrow at O eight-hundred hours."

As his commanders, in unison, shouted, "Yes sir." He turned his attention to Elvira and me, "You people need to take notes as invigilated reporters. Any questions?" He gazed around the room.

"No, sir," Elvira barked.

"Good, I will leave you to your briefings," Commander Alexander slouched into a lackluster about-face, stepped toward the door, stopped, turned his head, and asked, "Are red *too-tight* calmovers the trend now in the islands?"

"No, sir," I replied, "they were the only clothes available at the time of our departure." He shook his finger at me and clucked like a mother hen. Then, strutting with long, thin legs surprisingly agape, he exited the room. Elvira and I, guided by a custodian's hand sat down on a white plastic bench beneath a small window.

"Ahem," the man at the podium coughed. "Hello, my name is Miguel Martinez. I am one of four speakers today. I will be discussing the Corporation's economic warfare against working-class people, Pattie O'Doul will speak about their military operations as a method of enslavement. Tom Brock will discuss the corporation's political agenda and Senior Leader Robert Onion will discuss our planned attack on the GFP's Office. So let me begin by saying welcome to our reporters," he paused, glanced at us, "would the reporter's please introduce themselves?"

Elvira stood, "My name is Ms. Elvira Evers reporter for the *American Island News* and this is my associate, Mr. Jimmie Linguine."

"I'm not your associate. You are my associate," I said.

Miguel interrupted, "Thank you both, and a special greeting to our seven-hundred-fifty-thousand military men and women watching from their programmed monitors. Applause, please." Miguel initiated the hand clapping and resumed his speech as the applause died down. "Since the early two-thousands, there has been a decline in the-" Miguel paused briefly and glanced at his visualization monitor, a chart appeared, "Uh, a dramatic shift in the…"

I took advantage of Martinez's program lapse, and whispered to Elvira, "What are we doing here?"

"Shush," she whispered, watching Martinez

The Perfect Plan

intently. As she gawked at Martinez, I detected a faint fragrance of decaying pheromones wafting from her skin. The cigars, I deduced were laced with pinnacle stimuli. An undetectable pheromone until it begins to deteriorate. That is why I had been so attracted to her; even now, her sexual magnetism affects me, which is embarrassingly evident in my tight calmover.

"Let me begin again," Martinez said clearly embarrassed about his organizational gaffe, "The Corporation (NIC) consisting of less than one, one-thousandth of a percent of the world population owns over ninety-eight point nine percent of the world's wealth!"

Martinez's speech droned on and on, and quite naturally, considering my lack of sleep, I dozed off. My nap ended abruptly when Elvira delivered a sharp elbow to my sternum at the conclusion of the meeting. She glowered at me in disgust, "How could you?" she demanded.

"It's been a long night, I didn't get much sleep," I said.

Elvira and I stood as the commanders marched past in single file, introducing themselves with a short personal blurb, an impersonal nod, and a two-pump handshake, "Pompous bastards," I whispered to Elvira as the last commander shook our hand and left, leaving only Elvira and me in the room. "Let's grab something to eat," I suggested.

"The cafeteria is down the hall on your left,"

an invisible melancholic voice said from the surround-sound speakers. I looked at Elvira clearly angered by the corporation's eavesdropping.

She put her finger to her lips, "Thank you," Elvira said politely. She grabbed my hand and dragged me toward the exit before I could voice my complaint.

The cafeteria was bustling with military officers. Elvira and I went through the service line. She selected lamb over rice, and I picked fillet minion with a side of raspberry pudding. An arm shot up in the crowded room as we searched for a table. It was Commander Martinez. He waved us over to his nourishment panel and politely stood as we sat.

Within an instant of taking our seats, an amputee approached. He balanced precariously on one leg with a waiter's rag draped across his left arm, "What shall we be drinking today?" he said with a syrupy Ofu accent. He took our order and hopped laboriously toward the bar on the far side of the cafeteria. I watched as he disappeared in a mass of tightly packed soldiers surrounding the intoxicant-dispensing center.

A gunshot suddenly and unexpectedly rang out quieting the blended discourse of the officers and enlisted men. "Traitor," someone yelled, and instantly the conversations returned to a nondescript drone. A slender young blonde girl, who appeared to be in her early teens, returned with our beverages, "Here you are sirs, madam," she

The Perfect Plan

said and calmly poured the alcoholic beverage.

"Where's the one-legged waiter?" I asked.

"Oh, the traitor, he's dead," she replied in a calm, unemotional, whisper.

"How did you like the presentation," Martinez interrupted.

"It was wonderful," Elvira replied, and paused thoughtfully before resuming her rhetoric, "I had an idea that the corporation paid off our politicians for personal gain."

Martinez nodded as he sliced his steak, "We have a plan," Martinez mumbled after taking a bite of the rarified meat.

"Do you mind if I smoke?" Elvira asked, upon finishing her meal.

"No go right ahead," Commander Martinez replied.

Elvira lit-up a pheromone-laced cigar. The smoke had an uncomfortable effect on Martinez and me. "I must go," Martinez said, rising from his unfinished meal with his briefcase pressed firmly against his groin.

"Our rooms?" Elvira inquired while gazing at the briefcase.

"Sally," Martinez yelled. The blonde girl appeared out of the galley, "Would you show our guests to their rooms?"

"Yes, sir,"

Martinez, hampered by his arousal, waddled slowly away.

"Whenever you're ready," Sally said.

"Let's go," I said, intentionally walking behind Sally and Elvira to hide my obvious erection. Sally guided us to our chambers located on the tenth floor of the chrome castle. She opened the door for Elvira and put me in the adjoining room. I was tired and immediately collapsed on a dirigible bed, but before I had a chance to sleep, I heard a rapping on the adjacent wall.

It was Elvira, "We have a connecting door," she said, "May I come in?"

I sat up and gazed at the wall. The door was between the bathroom and the alabaster nightstand, "Come in," I said, covering my lap with a pillow. She gracefully slipped through the door and sat on the corner of the bed, "Isn't this exciting?" she whispered.

"I guess," I said, "but I don't feel comfortable here, I'm not a member of the NIC."

"Exactly," Elvira glowed with enthusiasm. "You are an unbiased reporter." She moved closer to me and touched my face with the back of her hand. The lemon smell of pheromones was overwhelming. She touched my lips, "Jimmie," she said in a nurturing voice. I squirmed uncomfortably with the primal urge to breed.

"Jesus, Elvira," I whispered, "either get naked or get out." Elvira sat back and smiled. I counted each button as they slipped through the confining holes of her blouse, and slowly, erotically, inch by sufferable inch, she opened her shirt to expose her sagging breasts and pale yellow nipples. As I reached for the golden treasure, she pulled away, "Not yet," she giggled, "not just yet."

"Those pheromones will be your undoing," I whispered.

"In that case, I'll be going," she said flippantly, "don't forget, the war begins tomorrow," she paused at the door, "Toodle-oo," she said and entered her room with the grace of a swan.

Interjection: Audiovisual evidence of Scripter 1's alteration request concerning this episodes decency rating.

The executive in charge, "An alteration request has been submitted by Scripter 1."

Scripter 1, "My *Manual of Practical, Legal, and Theatrical Assumptions-* pg. 77, paragraph 2 requires ratings based on sexual and violent content. My question is should the boob scene be omitted?"

Scripter 2, rising from his prie-dieu, stated in a ghoulish manner, "I believe the nudity of an eighty-year-old woman is definitely obscene and the scene should be X-rated."

Scripter 3: "Is it the ever perishing youth of one's body that you are referring too? Is that what offends you?" 3 looked down at the floor before continuing. "It is a scientific inquiry." 3 glanced briefly at 2 before averting her eyes to the inanimate object (a spiral goat's horn) in her hand. 3 continued her dissertation; "The human body is too ephemeral a vessel to warrant other than superficial investigation. There is no obscenity in that."

Scripter 1: "What?"

Scripter 2, "Call the Priest."

Scripter 3, "Call the Attorney."

Scripter 4, "The attorney is in the Producer's office. I will get him."

The Attorney, Mr. Sage, entered wearing slippers and a bathrobe.

2, stridently remarked, "Odd to be dressed thusly at two in the afternoon."

The executive in charge handed the script to the attorney and pointed a shaky finger at the sentence containing 'sagging breast and yellow nipples'. What is your opinion concerning rating?

Mr. Sage answered without emotion, "No implied or specific penetration. At this point, the script is considered PG."

2, returning to his prie-dieu replied, "Bullshit."

The executive in charge, "Alteration request denied. Begin 3 at- I slept..."

— I slept fitfully that night, dreaming sporadically about Elvira and her pale breast. It was during one of those climactic moments in a dream sequence that I heard a volley of gunfire. My first thought was that the war had begun. I sat upright, blinked until my dream dissipated and saw to my amazement that my red too-tight calmover and checkered skullcap were missing from

The Perfect Plan

the dresser's gilded crown. I spied in their stead, a clown suit with a light blue ruffled collar and purplish wig. I was fuming about the wardrobe selected for me. It was disrespectful and humiliating. I dressed while in a rage intent on finding out who decided to make a mockery of me. While I viewed myself in the mirror, I noticed a foot thick continuously cascading wall of water had supplanted the door between Elvira's room and my own. "Elvira," I yelled into the falling stream, "Elvira," I repeated. A silhouette appeared behind the water screen, "is that you?" To my surprise, a large sparsely haired hand reached through the waterfall. I stepped back in shock and noticed an onyx ring resting behind the bald knuckle of the second finger. "Elvira," I yelled even louder. The man, presumably concerned about potential aggression, hastily withdrew his hand.

I ran to the exit and opened the door to find Elvira standing there with her fist raised ready to knock, "Wow you look fabulous," she said with a smile; then noticed the concern on my face, "What is it?"

"The waterfall," I exclaimed. She peered into my room.

"What about it?"

"Where's the door?"

"The waterfall replaces the door every night at ten. It is a soothing screen. It helps you sleep—psychologists have used it for years to fight insomnia. Oh, and there is a button on the wall to turn the water feature on or off," she said, "come on we have a war to cover." Elvira grabbed my arm before I could mention the man's hand that had protruded through the waterfall. She continuously shushed my attempt to speak as she towed me (as if I were a child) down the hall. Determined not to speak, I clammed up—I mean mum, not a word.

We sat without conversing and watched the combat on a giant screen. Elvira was taking copious notes on her computablet as I penciled a few lines on a napkin. We took a lunch break at halftime. As we entered the Nutritional Hall servers and patrons alike pointed at me in my ridiculous costume and bombarded my fragile ego with inappropriate cajoles, hisses, and snickers. The hat just so happened to be leaning against an adjoining nourishment panel. I paced to his location and voiced my objections about my hideous wardrobe. He laughed within the confines of his hat, and said, "What do you expect?" and waved his arms around his torso as a sartorial comparison. I became even more frustrated due to the hats snubbing of my complaint. Our meal was quick. I ate little and left a note in the suggestion box that my dining experience was exceedingly uncomfortable.

The war was raging when we returned to the theater. I was shocked at the devastation. The GFP fighters were out-gunned but had the advantage of numbers. There was an almost even ebb and flow to the killing until it ended at dusk and the troops on both sides returned to their respective camps for the night.

After the conflict ended, Elvira excused herself and went to the multi-gender powder room. When she returned, I detected the faint sensual smell of lemons. "Come with me. Martinez wants us to meet him in the Café de Tudor for dinner." I objected of course, but the irresistible smell of pheromones made it impossible for me to leave Elvira. Martinez stood up as we approached. "You look lovely tonight," he whispered to Elvira. He glanced at me in my clown suit placed the palm of his hand over his mouth and giggled.

"Why thank you. That's nice of you to say," Elvira said.

Martinez picked up Elvira's hand and kissed her knuckles. I noticed the onyx ring on his finger, but not wanting to create problems, I refrained from commenting about the waterfall, instead, I asked about the gunfire that I had heard earlier that morning.

"Oh that," Martinez replied caustically, "that was the firing squad. General Alexander captured more spies or traitors—whatever he calls them now—anyway he had them shot."

Martinez turned his attention to Elvira, and they chatted about the corporate cause throughout the meal, leaving me quite frankly out of the discussion. "I must be going," I said fed up with the chuckling and cooing that had evolved throughout the conversation.

"Wait," Elvira said as she lit her cigar.

"No, really, I must go," I said, knowing the stimulating effects of the smoke.

She kissed me on my cheek and whispered, "Later, then... tonight."

"Goodnight," I said sarcastically, to both my comrades.

"Pleasant dreams," Martinez replied with eyes focused intently on Elvira.

Later that evening Elvira knocked on the interconnecting door, "May I come in?" she said.

"Come on in," I grumbled intent on lecturing her about Martinez. She stuck her thin, varicose leg through the portal first; then seductively moved her scantily clad body through the opening. Once inside the room, she leaned as if in a swoon on the doorframe and with the back of her hand pressed softly against her forehead, she said, "Oh baby."

"What are you doing?" I asked in an angry falsetto.

"Shhhh," she murmured, and with a wild shake of her matted hair, and an equally dramatic rotation of her pelvis. She sent a provocative glance my way. I watched intently, and I must admit with growing desire as she provided for my consideration a decadent single finger no-no wave. With eyes fixed on my face and lavender wig, she vexingly moved her arthritic appendage to the doors brass dome and pushed.

"Ah!" I exclaimed.

The Perfect Plan

With a gush, the water screen began to sing in gurgles and splashes.

I bit my nether lip and regained my anger.

"Don't be mad," she whispered as she sat at the foot of the bed. I recognized the lemon smell of pheromones seeping through her skin.

"Why was Martinez in your room last night?" I asked placing my finger inches from her flaring nostrils.

"I was interviewing him about the war," she said indifferent to my antipathy.

"His hand," I said, "he stuck his hand through the water screen."

"He slipped on the way to the lavatory—lost his balance," she said, then continued with a puzzled looked, "what's wrong with you Jimmie?" She looked into my eyes, "are you jealous."

"Of course not, I was just concerned, that's all."

"I like you, Jimmie," she said, and nuzzled up against my shoulder; then she stood, abruptly dropped her nightgown, and slid beneath the covers.

Neither of us got much sleep that night and though exhausted from our intimate exercises we made it to the Theatre Room on time. Martinez was waiting for us or rather for Elvira, and before we had a chance to sit, he angrily garbed her by the elbow and pulled her unceremoniously into the hall. She complained but did not resist. I was nonchalant about it at first; then as time passed, became increasingly concerned. The war had resumed, and I used the on-screen violence to take my mind off Martinez's abduction of Elvira. The fighting was more violent and gruesome than yesterday. It was as if the Generals wanted to end the war quickly without forethought or concern about their men's ultimate sacrifice.

Martinez returned just as the rebel army took a direct hit from the Corporation's quasar laser. Elvira was not with him. "Where's Elvira?" I asked through clenched teeth.

"She went back to her room."

"What happened?"

"Nothing, she's just being a bitch," he said.

"If you've done anything to her, I will kill you."

Martinez smiled and said, "You too huh," before turning his eyes to the horror on the screen. The chair complained with a squeak as I pushed back to rise from the table, and without further words left to check on Elvira.

She was in her room. I could hear her sobbing, "Elvira," I whispered, "Are you alright? Open the door, honey." I heard the slide of the bolt, the door creaked eerily open; blood was flowing from Elvira's nose and mouth. "What happened," I whispered as I stepped inside. She quickly shut the door behind me.

"Martinez tried to… to."

"To what?"

"Look," she said opening a pendant that hung

around her neck. It was a mini video capture camera. The recorder showed Martinez drop his pants. A bush, suitable for display in the Rochester Botanical Garden sprung out of the waistband, pecker portal, and leggings of his modus vivendi briefs. I gasped. He approached the camera slowly through a cloud of lemon-colored smoke. The video quickly blurred into a tangle of arms and legs. There was a transitory glimpse of the ceiling; then a partial glimpse of Martinez's ear before his face appeared like a gigantic puff fish in the viewfinder. I jerked back from the screen as he puckered his misshapen pale lips into an attempted kiss. Elvira slapped him. He slapped her back. Suddenly, a knife appeared in her hand, the blade, captured on video, weaved before her like a serpent. Martinez, with an ashen face and broken will, backed slowly out of the room.

Elvira snapped the capture camera off and sat down on the side of her bed, sobbing.

"Elvira, what can I do?"

She took a deep breath, sighed, and wiped away her tears with the bedsheet. "Nothing," she said, and with shaking hands lit a cigar. I took Elvira into my arms. "Jimmie," her voice sounded as if she were in a tunnel, "Jimmie," she said again. There was the smell of old books. I passed out.

The next thing I knew, I was in the Theatre Room, standing over Martinez with a knife in my hand. My clown suit was soaked with blood. I looked around in confusion and saw Elvira and her commanders filming me with video cameras. The hat immediately ordered my arrest. Two burly guards handcuffed me and whisked me away into a padded cell. I remained in the tiny cage with little food or water for two days. The hat appeared at the end of the second day and escorted me to General Alexander's Office. He was sitting at his desk, with Elvira by his side. "Ah, Jimmie, good to see you come have a seat." The hat shoved me toward the leather chair and pushed me down into its wooden arms. "I would like to thank you for eliminating Mr. Martinez. Unfortunately, we cannot reward you for the deed."

Elvira giggled, "Do you mind if I smoke?"

"Go right ahead my dear," Alexander said gleefully clapping his white palms together. She lit her cigar and deliberately blew the smoke in my face.

"Be careful with that sweetie or he will go mad," Alexander said; then broke out into uproarious laughter. "Chemicals are wonderful if used properly," he chuckled, "these," he picked up a hand full of orange banded cigars, "are DNA imprinted, adrenaline-laced; serotonin suppressant cigars. ASS for short, but more commonly called kickers. They only interact with your DNA, no one else's." Elvira sent another puff of smoke my way.

"What's going on?" I asked angrily. I could feel my rage growing and began to struggle against the cuffs.

"That's enough sweetie," Alexander said,

The Perfect Plan

"would you kindly put out your cigar," Elvira smiled and stabbed the end of her cigar against the sole of her shoe. My anger slowly subsided.

"What's happening to me?"

"You've been under the influence son, first with pheromones, then with the kickers."

"Why?"

"We needed you to kill Martinez," Elvira said, "he's a GFP spy, and we needed a neutral, like yourself to do it," she paused, "Martinez, by the way, is the illegitimate son of, Mr. Dallas Delphi. He is a rebel who with the help of his father infiltrated our ranks. He knew too much, but we couldn't kill him—politics you know. Anyway, we needed a neutral to kill his son—a jealous neutral. So, here you are Jimmie, and may I say it was a job well done."

"Why did you fake your death commander?" I asked, trying to make sense of Alexander's rhetoric.

"To draw Martinez out," Alexander said with a smile. "As soon as the bastard heard I was dead, he leaped into action; sent secret memos to rally his allies."

"What now, are you going to kill me?"

"No son we don't kill, even the war is fake. Those soldiers you saw on the screen were just a bunch of actors performing in front of cameras."

"You're mad," I said studying his glazed eyes and intrepid smile, "that doesn't make any sense at all, why fake a war?"

Alexander chuckled, clearly enjoying his exposition, "Why," he snorted, "to bleed the population of their money that's why. The corporation can raise taxes for war you know." Alexander quieted his gaiety. "Weapon sales have lost their profitability for the corporation and are dangerous in the wrong hands. I mean if the GFP were to get real weapons—that would be serious, very serious."

"Like the Gulf Wars from 1990 to 2070, damn near obliterated the world," the hat interjected.

My head was spinning from all the ludicrous information. I was convinced it was all a lie, a game, so I pressed on to see where this SOB was going with such an asinine story, "How can you have a war without casualties? People would be suspicious."

To my surprise, Elvira spoke up, "We," she swept her arm around the room indicating all commanders, "on behalf of the National Islands Corporation, take the poor, the uneducated; the criminals, all the unproductive scum of the world, and draft them into the army. They die eventually most of them starve to death."

"And we send the ashes back to some poor schmuck's family as a son or daughter killed in action," the hat injected, as he administered a celebratory slap to his knee.

I frowned at the hat's exuberance and said with disdain guiding my speech, "Alexander just said the corporation doesn't kill people!" I shouted, "Now you're telling me that they do."

"Let me clarify," General Alexander interrupted, "The Corporation doesn't kill the employed, productive citizens of our great Island Nations."

I thought of Lola, her termination party, my unforgivable apathy. One commander, a female, interrupted my growing self-animus with her piggish squeals, "They never know whose ashes they get." She covered her mouth and snickered.

"Ignorant bastards," Hat proclaimed.

"Perfect plan," the general said as he cleaned his fingernails with a penknife. Then attacked his teeth with the same blade wiping globules of plaque off his teeth and onto the soles of his Mallard shoes.

After the cusped and keratin cleansing Alexander said, "Now, we are going to send our little video of you murdering Mr. Martinez to Delphi's supporters and drop you off among them. They will kill you," he chuckled, "for the Global Freedom Party, ironic, huh." Alexander displayed his teeth through an expansive grin, "give him a handful of kicker cigars, the orange ones, and the murder weapon; then send him on his way."

Hat pulled out a syringe and stabbed the needle into my arm. I awoke on the Isle of Colorado, in Denver, one of the southern-most cities lying within the Isles of America. It had rained and the pavement beneath the video billboard was flowing with water. The Martinez murder was on a

Donald D'lo

seven-minute recurring feed, and a rag-tag crowd of rebel sympathizers, having repeatedly viewed the video, circled me chanting death to the traitor. I crouched tiger-like, lit a kicker, and with my knife in hand, waited for the chemical reaction, and the inevitable fight.

CHAPTER 37

Saved by Elvira

"Hey," a familiar voice elevated above the mob, "That's not the clown that killed Martinez. That is Jimmie Linguine. He tried to stop his identical twin from murdering Martinez. Step aside. I said step aside —get out of the way, let me through." The rebel mob dumbfounded by Elvira's antics parted like the red sea and the super-soldier stepped boldly through the water. I say super-soldier because Elvira was wearing combat boots, camouflaged mini-denim, (worn well below her navel,) shorts, with coordinated shirt displaying her rank as GFP commander first class. A pink beret accentuated the fluttering mauve scarf looped around her neck.

She knelt beside me, and growled in a low whisper, "Put that cigar out you fool, it's a tranquilizer."

It was too late, my eyelids dropped like cheap Venetian blinds. I was out and did not come too until we were back at my apartment. Elvira was on the sofa smoking a cigar. "Don't worry," she said, "No pheromones."

"How did I get here?"

"Friends with speeders."

"What friends?" I asked trying to rub the pain away from my temples.

"Never mind what friends," she said with a sideways smile. "I want you to join us, Jimmie."

"Join who, exactly?"

"The National Islands Corporation," she said.

"I'm not a fighter."

"No, but you are a writer, a good reporter. We want you to report what happened in Poland." She paused, "Martinez must be exposed as a traitor."

"That would be a lie. He wasn't a traitor," I mumbled.

"Everyone is a traitor in some respect. Even you as a neutral have betrayed a cause. The question is which one."

I looked at Elvira, who sat quietly smoking her cigar. "Why do you do it, why deceive the people, the ninety-nine percent of impoverished humanity?" I asked.

She smiled, "Simply put, I enjoy the money and of course the power. You can share our wealth, Jimmie. This is how the world has been for centuries. Join us; write the propaganda for our cause."

"What if I refuse?"

"You're a smart boy. Do what smart boys do and survive. You have until noon tomorrow, I'll be back, and don't make me have to look for you," she chuckled, "capisce?" Elvira arose from the chair, opened the top button of her shirt, and reached down her collar, "I am fond of you Jimmie that's why you're still alive." She pulled her bra strap over her narrow shoulder, looked at me playfully, and winked, "We had a special—dare I say a rather perverse and invigorating relationship in Poland, and I would like that liaison to continue." She unbuttoned her mini-demi shorts and provocatively guided the pants with a seesaw motion past her belly wrinkles to her panty line, I presume for my pleasure, but instead of the pheromone-influenced beauty I perceived earlier, she now looked old, militaristic, and horribly obnoxious.

Elvira smiled as she tugged up and re-buttoned her shorts. She gently touched my cheek. She kissed the air before my face and finally left, with her lyrical "toodle-oo" echoing in the hallway.

I felt suddenly ill, and maneuvered, on hands and knees, to the toilet where I hoisted myself up and sat on the cold doughnut-shaped lid. With elbow resting on my knee and chin cradled in the flat of my palm, I sat contemplating my situation with gastric clarity. After an hour of meditation, and two nights of attempted sleep I made my choice and decided a drink was an adequate though temporary remedy for my woes, and so resolute in my belief, I walked somberly to Skelly's. The joint was empty. I waded through the buoyant light to the bar where Jacob was washing glass goblets.

"Hey, Jimmie, where you been?"

"Poland," I replied.

"Poland, huh, what are you having?"

"Give me a glass of Dirty Water, the hundred-year-old stuff."

"Wow, must have been interesting—"

"I am no longer a neutral," I interrupted.

"What?"

"I'm no longer neutral. I want to join the Global Freedom Party and become a true rebel, you know, do what's right?"

"Are you sure?"

"Yes, I want to join the GFP as a writer, I have a story to tell."

Jacob waded through the banded light scanning the room for NIC spies. Certain we were unobserved he said, "Follow me," I shadowed him to the end of the bar. A door yawned open as he pulled a hidden lever, and we stepped through the portal onto a small staircase that led downward into a dark basement. A single forty-watt microbial light glowed above kegs of beer, and crates of whiskey, "Welcome aboard," Jacob said as an obscure figure moved in the corner of the room. Suddenly, a match flared and the glow of a cigar smoldered briefly as the shadowy figure inhaled. Instinctively my fight-or-flight mechanism engaged. I was ready to dash for the staircase when Jacob spoke, "Let me introduce you to our Supreme Commander Mr. Dallas Delphi."

Commander Delphi stepped out of the darkness. He was a large man sporting an expensive columbine suit. His face was gaunt, his eyes small, and his ears, well, his ears were elephantine. "Are you the man who killed my son?" Delphi asked. His voice was deep, authoritarian.

"No, sir," I muttered.

"It was on video."

"Yes sir, but I was framed, General Alexander framed me..." Before I could further my explanation, a white beam of radiated light flashed from the laser-blade he had concealed in his hand.

"Traitor," he yelled as the light expurgated my left ear. "Murder," he screamed as he sliced through my chest.

Then in the brief silence before imminent death, I heard, "Stupid Ass," echoing along the damp basement walls. It was Elvira. She was standing on the stairway holding a PP-497 close-combat laser-pistol. The first shot hit Delphi in his chest, the second shot ripped through his head, propelling brain, and bone fragments over the basement walls. The third and fourth shots hit Jacob in his stomach and chest. Both men died instantly. As I lay bleeding my perception blurred into darkness.

___O___

I awoke in the NIC's Second Elected Confederacy Headquarters Infirmary with the smell of lemons in the air. My geriatric cherub, Elvira, sat on the side of the bed smoking. I could hear the war raging on the big screen in the Theatre room. "We got him," she exclaimed with great pride. "I knew you would choose the GFP Rebels, and Delphi would fall into our trap."

"Perfect plan." I heard Alexander say from the shadows.

"You used me," I howled plaintively and struggled to rise, but hampered by my injuries, I fell clumsily back into the mattress. "Will you join us?" Elvira asked from a cloud of yellow smoke. I muddled through the available options while studying her angelic face, and confidently said with a slight slur, "I am all yours."

Sleep-sweet-sleep took me to the void, and I dreamed, "Stupid Ass." It was my mother, "why aren't you ready for school?" I was in bed asleep, now half-asleep. "Get up and get dressed, now!" she said. I rolled out of bed. The floor was cold. "And get rid of that clown pajama thing you're wearing. It makes you look stupid." I slipped out of my clown pajamas and left them lying on the floor. "Go wash up," Mom said. "Breakfast will be ready in ten minutes." I rushed to the bathroom, brushed my teeth, and jumped into the shower. Breakfast was ready by the time I made it downstairs. "The bus will be here in five minutes, eat." Mother said. I ate the oatmeal saturated with butter, grabbed two pieces of toast, a pack of licorice sticks and my backpack and ran out the door.

"Toodle-oo," Mother said from behind the screen door. The buses double door squeaked open. I entered the yellow capsule and sat beside Veronica. She smiled, wet her finger with her sultry tongue, and with that damp digit wiped her left eyebrow.

Veronica died. I received serious internal injuries, and lost part of my skull, and left ear. Out of thirty-four children, I was the only survivor. A paramedic, I can't remember his name, saved me.

CHAPTER 38

The Explosion

A familiar voice said, "Wakeup." I opened my eyes. My head was throbbing. "Mama?"

"No sugar it's Elvira." she moved closer and peered into my eyes. "It's the drugs."

I looked at my body. Bandages covered my chest. I remembered Delphi and the laser, Elvira, and her pistol.

"Don't worry sugar you are fine the cauterization was successful."

"Where am I?"

"We are still at the NIC's Second Elected Confederacy Headquarters of Poland," she said, "but we have to move, and move fast."

"Why?"

"I will explain later. In the meantime, Bemire will prepare you for the trip. He is a Nurture Nurse."

Lying flat on the bed, I saw the top of the Hat's

hat. "Good to have you back Jimmie," the hat said. He marched toward the door, turned abruptly, and patted the top of his hat, "This Jimmie is going to be an adventure. Good luck." With a click of his heels and a formal salute, the hat turned and disappeared through the door. I could hear his metrical footsteps echoing down the hall.

"Hurry and prep him Bemire," Elvira said.

"What about the side effects?"

"Oh, he will be fine."

"Elvira, he just came out of an induced coma. Putting him under so soon after awakening is dangerous."

"I said he will be fine."

Bemire looked at me, hesitated for a second, before injecting me with Neo-Nap. I lost consciousness. An explosion woke me. I was on a stretcher. I could see Bemire's broad back and massive shoulders rise and fall. He was running and yelling, "The Global Freedom Party has breached our line, fall back." Another explosion ripped the ground five yards away. Bemire's body disintegrated before me. I fainted.

I do not know how long I was out, but when I awoke, someone was slapping my cheeks and lights were hovering above me. I tried to move, but leather restraints held me fast. Suddenly, an enormous light brightened the area. I was on a movie set. Bemire's head was lying beside me. "That's a wrap." A woman said. Two stagehands walked over and retrieved Bemire's head by grasping tightly his thick hair. I could see the face was a plasticized fake. A slender man loosened my restraints and helped me off the stretcher. His nametag read Porgy Bessel. Other than feeling groggy, I felt good. I gingerly touched my chest and found a swaddling of bandages but I felt no pain.

"Come with me," Porgy said. I followed Porgy and another man into a well-lit building. Image finders, stereopticons, and semblance reactors surrounded a laminated stage. A chair sat center stage. Porgy pointed at the chair. I sat down. A woman, illuminated by an overhead spotlight wobbled in on eight-inch spiked heels. She approached me casually and extended her hand, "Hello, I'm Donna Darling, the producer."

"Producer of what?" I asked.

She leaned forward, "Why the greatest myth on Earth," she replied. Her hand went immediately to her mouth, "Oh, it was supposed to be a surprise." She fanned her face with her delicate hand and with an exaggerated wink, extended her palm. "I am sorry this is all I can do. Fraternizing with lower-level employees is forbidden here at the National Island Corporation Studio."

"But I'm not a lower-level employee, I am a reporter."

"Really, may I see your W-2?"

"I... I don't have it with me."

"I was told you were an actor." She glanced at my purple wig, my missing ear, and bandaged chest, "All you can be is a victim," she paused, tapped her finger on her chin. "Can you read?"

"Of course, I can read I'm a reporter."

"Read that!" Donna pointed at a teleprompter. She stepped off the stage.

I watched the sentences roll by, "I'm not reading that—that is bull-shit, all lies—all of it, pure lies," I said.

"Very well, seat him off-stage and bring out the endorsed reporter." Porgy grabbed my clown collar and pulled me past Elvira into a dark conclave. Elvira smiled as Porgy escorted me to a bench. I watched Elvira lift her skirt and take a seat in front of the teleprompter. She crossed her legs and began to read the rolling script, "Hello, my name is Elvira Evers. I am an embedded correspondent for the *American Island News*. I will be providing unbiased news of the conflict in the Poland region. Wait," she placed her finger to her ear, "Just in, The NIC has handed the Global Freedom Party another defeat in last night's Portobello conflict. The National Islands Corporation killed seven hundred and eleven rebel soldiers in the skirmish. Less than one-hundred NIC troops were wounded, with—Oh my, this is amazing, no fatalities. Here is the video… Warning, the images are graphic, and may not be suitable viewing for young children."

As the fake war raged on the big screen, Elvira waved Donna over. "Jimmie is a good reporter. Let me talk to him after the newscast."

"He doesn't look like a reporter. He doesn't

even look normal," Donna said.

"That's why we need him. We can claim he is an injured, perhaps deranged corporate war hero. We have the footage right?"

"Yes we do," Donna paused to establish a lengthy gawk at me. "Hum a weird dystopian hero."

"Yes, weird," Elvira interrupted.

"Okay!" Donna glanced at her watch and stepped off camera, "Get ready."

Mr. Black, the auteur, pointed his finger at Donna, who in turn pointed her finger at Elvira.

"That's it, folks," Elvira said. "Thanks for watching and stay tuned for the Corporate Gospel Hour where prayer requests and donations will be taken for our fallen comrades. We will be back at ten until then be brave, be confident and please donate to the NIC cause. God bless the Islands."

Mr. Black walked past Donna without speaking and approached Elvira. "Good Job, but work on your enunciation, and do something about your face, the wrinkles, makeup perhaps will help." He smiled, patted her on the shoulder. When he turned, his abnormally large head appeared to wobble unsteadily on his thin peckerish neck.

"Ass," Elvira said. She watched him leave the stage then turned and smiled at me. I was sitting on the bench with my right arm wedged between my legs. "Hi Jimmie," she said.

"Elvira."

"Can we talk?"

"Sure," I scooted over and she sat down beside me.

"You look wonderful," she said, touching my cheek with her rough wrinkled hand.

"Thank you."

There was a long pause before she spoke, "We need your help," Elvira said. "We, the Corporation want you to report-"

"You mean the NIC wants me to lie," I interrupted. I turned away from my interrogator and unexpectedly spied in the audience a rat eating popcorn.

"Jimmie, you know that you are currently unemployed. You know what happens to the unemployed. They are terminated! Jimmie, look at me," She placed her finger on my jaw and turned my head away from the rat. Elvira starred at me briefly without speaking. She looked sad. "All you have is the clothes on your back. I mean the clown suit you are wearing. That's it Jimmie, please save yourself; work for us."

"No," I said.

"You promised."

"I was under the influence of your damn pheromones," I said.

"Okay, okay, Porgy take him to the medical oubliette."

Porgy once again grabbed me by the cuff and escorted me through yellow and blue flashing lights to an air-ambulance parked outside the door. Porgy unlocked the side door of the ship.

Five people glanced at me simultaneously when the door opened. Their faces were ashen, and their eyes were twice their normal size. It frightened me. I tried to escape. It was a futile attempt. Porgy's grip was too strong. He pushed me into the back of the ambulance and chained my feet to the floor alongside a young woman. Porgy slammed the double doors shut. I heard the engine start, felt the conduction slip into progressively higher gears. The flight was rough. The interior, dark. My fear morphed into panic. I screamed for help.

"It will be okay, just breathe." I heard a voice in the darkness and then I heard the pump and hiss of a breathalyzer. A light came on. Bemire was hovering over me. He placed a mask on my face and started an intravenous drip. "You are hyperventilating and dehydrated." We deplaned. Bemire assisted me to a wheelchair and pushed me down the dark tarmac and through the steel door of a drab building.

The buildings main hall had subdued floor lights, which was odd. They hadn't made buildings with floor lights in many years. Bemire took me to a large crowded room and removed my breathalyzer and the intravenous drip. He then strapped me to a hospital bed and left. I saw in front of me, a pastel wall where people medically and militarily clad, milled around a large coffee maker. I turned my head to the right. Bemire was sitting in a cerulean couch reading his tablet and chuckling. A shadow crossed my face.

The Perfect Plan

I turned to see a monstrous looking man dressed in a National Island Uniform. His head was small and horribly disfigured. Fresh wounds still oozing blood covered his entire face. His red hair, long for a military man, was matted and extended down his jawline. He spoke softly, "Are you awake?"

"Obviously," I replied.

"Coffee?" He pointed to the coffee maker. I tried to sit up. He put his large hand on my chest, "You cannot rise. They have you bound to the bed."

"Where am I?"

"You have been abducted and are in the hospital," he said.

"Who abducted me?"

"Opposition actors of the GFP. Bemire saved your life, Jimmie."

"Who are you?"

"I am Captain Sam Sarton of the Forty-Second Actor's Division." he looked at me quizzically, "no coffee."

"No," I said, "no coffee."

He delivered an affirmative nod, and said, "Okay."

"Why am I here?"

He glanced at Bemire who was still reading his tablet, "Mind alteration." He said while tapping his head with his index finger. "I like your clown suit," he said. "It sends a message."

"It does?"

"Yes."

He looked at me closely, "You look familiar. Do I know you from somewhere?"

"I used to be a reporter in New Chicago," I said.

"Oh yeah, you worked for the *American Island News*. You did a piece on the New Chicago Theatre Guild."

"Please move away from the patient." Sarton turned to find Bemire standing beside him. "Move," Bemire commanded. Capitan Sarton stepped back, smiled at me, and joined the soldiers and medical personnel surrounding the coffee maker. A lizard darted across the ceilings textured wall and disappeared in a crack of the cornice. Odd for a hospital, I thought. Bemire sat on the bed and patted my leg. "I like you," he said. "Is there anything I can do for you?"

"Yes," I replied, "you can undo my restraints."

"Sorry, I cannot," he said, "I'll be here all night let me know if you need anything."

"Give me something to make me sleep," I said. He disappeared and returned with a plastic cup with two capsules rattling inside. He lifted my head slightly poured the contents of the cup into my mouth and gave me small sips of water to wash the medication down. I fell asleep and slept soundly.

I awoke abruptly. The smell of fried bacon permeated the air, and I was hungry. I did not see Bemire, nor Captain Sarton anywhere within the group of people gathered at the far end of the

The Perfect Plan

room. The room was massive, "Captain Sarton," I yelled, "Has anyone seen Captain Sarton?"

A handsome middle-aged man approached, "Hello Jimmie," the man said in a familiar voice.

"I am looking for Captain Sarton."

"That's me, what can I do for you Mr. Linguine."

"Wow, I didn't recognize you."

"I was in costume last night. We were shooting *Damn Them Rebel Zombies* for the ten o: clock news."

"What can I do for you?"

"Food, I need food."

"Can't, your scheduled for mind alteration in a few minutes."

"I've got to pee," I said. "Can you remove the restraints so I can go to the restroom?"

"Sorry, only Bemire is authorized to do that."

"Where is Bemire?"

Sarton shrugged his shoulders, "Haven't seen him." Captain Sarton turned as if on cue, "Oh, here comes your gurney. Good luck Jimmie."

CHAPTER 39

The Slaughter House

A bright red miniaturized gurney-cart approached. Bemire was driving the gurney and smiling. The cart I must say was impressive. Decorative flames rose from the vehicle's step panel and chrome wind blades spun on the wheels of the cart as it approached. Bemire stopped the gurney-cart, retracted the flaming roof, climbed out of the vehicle, and shuffled over to my bed. "How are you feeling Jimmie?"

"Fine," I said, "couldn't be better." Bemire laughed and began to remove the restraints. "I like you, Jimmie."

"Where are we going?"

"Visual Therapy Theatre," Bemire replied.

He removed the last restraint, opened the door of the cart. I got in and he handcuffed my hand to the gurney's rack. "Why?" I asked. He grinned, without speaking, and drove the motor-

The Perfect Plan

ized gurney out of the building, through the paved parking lot, to an old clapboard building. He stopped at the entrance. "What is this place?"

"This," Bemire said, "Is the Slaughter House."

"I'm not going in there?"

"You have no choice," Bemire said as he put the cart in gear. I protested vehemently as we entered the building. My screams intensified as the vehicle, under Bemire's insouciant control turned abruptly down a hall where bearded men and heavily whiskered women adorned the walls. I continued to panic, "Where are you taking me?" My terror driven question echoed down the gallery.

Bemire responded with a chuckle, "You'll see."

We entered a double door. The room was dark. Bemire turned on the cart's headlights pulled forward a short distance and stopped. He got out, stepped into the darkness surrounding the cart, and returned with an ancient folding chair. He placed the chair in front of the cart directly in the oculus of light. "What are you doing?" I yelled. Bemire did not respond. I struggled against my restraints.

Bemire touched my shoulder, "Be still," he whispered.

"Turn me loose," I screamed. He removed my wig, placed it in my lap, and patted me on my bald head. I felt him remove the bonds from my hands and feet. He lifted me, with little effort, out of the cart and sat me in the chair. I could not see anything, but I knew we were not alone. There was this smell. I could not recognize it at first then it dawned on me. It was the smell of death, old and stale-tomb death. Once again, Bemire stepped out of the light. A man coughed breaking the eerie silence. I felt another panic attack coming on, "What do you want?" I shouted. Silence, then click, and an outbreak of lights blinded me. I squinted, only gradually could I fully open my eyes. I saw through blurred vision, bleachers full of bearded men and women. I was on a basketball court. "What do you want from me?" I screamed. Spittle spewed from my lips like mist from a pressurized mope bottle.

A man sitting on the first bleacher advanced, "Do you play basketball?"

Even though his face was covered with a beard, I recognized the voice, "Coach Linen, is that you?" He strode over and placed his huge hand on my bald head. His hand was cold.

"Do you play basketball?" he asked again.

"Not since high school," I replied. He returned to his seat, and another man stood and walked with a limp toward me.

"Jimmie, do you remember the explosion?" It was not a man's voice, but a woman who spoke. "The explosion Jimmie—the school bus, the explosion, do you remember it?"

"Yes," I replied, "I remember."

"Who blew up the bus Jimmie, who killed all

The Perfect Plan

those children?"

"The Corporation," I said.

"Why did the NIC blow up the school bus?"

"I don't know."

"Why Jimmie?"

"Our community was GFP supporters," I said tearfully, "Our city supported the GFP rebels."

The crowd muttered something unintelligible. It was as if they suffered in unison.

"Yes," the woman said. She removed her bogus beard. "Do you remember me?"

"Mrs. Steadman?"

"Yes," She turned and motioned to someone high-up in the bleachers, "Come down," she said.

I watched another bearded person step down the bleachers and walk to me. It was a young girl. "Do you remember her?" Mrs. Steadman asked.

The girl removed her fake beard.

"Veronica?"

"Hi, Jimmie."

"What is going on here? You are dead."

She looked into my eyes, "We are all dead Jimmie. The people in our town were purged."

I gazed at the people in the bleachers. Everyone removed their beards, except Sam Fortney, his beard was real. I recognized everyone. They were all from Madison Ohio. The town where I grew up. Out of the corner of my eye, partially hidden by Mr. Zeno Barge's large frame, I spied a turkey. The gobbler extended his bearded head from behind Zeno's torso and then quickly ducked back behind the large man. The turkey was smoking a cigarette-

"Jimmie," Veronica said, drawing my attention away from the turkey, "you need to see this." She took a deep breath and said, "Begin!"

The lights went off. A flickering 3-D image appeared a few yards away. The image wavered, disappeared. "Adjust the stereopticon to the phase four monitor," Bemire said. The image snapped back into view.

"Excuse me, sir," the voice was surly, unexpected.

"Yes?"

A man in the stereopticon's golden orb of light turned. I recognized his face immediately. It was Mr. Delphi. I looked at Veronica then at Bemire. "What is this about?" I whispered. Bemire shushed me and put his finger to his lips for silence. "But he's the man that sliced my off my ear and opened my chest." I tried to get out of the chair, but Bemired placed his huge hand on my shoulder and squeezed the Brachial Plexus nerve that ran along the back of my neck and shoulder. I froze.

The image flickered, and a woman appeared beside Delphi, "Are you ready for the meeting?" she asked.

"Yes Mary, I am," Delphi replied.

Mary reached for Delphi's hand, and squeezed tightly, "Good luck," she said.

"Thank you, Mary, for all the work you have

done on the campaign."

"Have you thought of a name for the new Venture?"

"I think I will call it the Independent Freedom Fighters (IFF) Campaign," Delphi said. "Will I see you tonight at the Buzz Bar?" It was more of a statement than a question.

"Of course," she said.

Mr. Delphi's image wavered as he lifted himself from the chair and moved within the orb of light towards a meeting room.

The double doors to the meeting room were massive. His image disappeared as he entered the boardroom and reappeared as he arrived in the communication chamber. Seven of Delphi's top liberal allies sat at the table. He looked around before taking a seat, "Thank you for coming," Delphi said. "As you know there are numerous outposts like the Second Elected Confederacy of Poland and the Gulf Coast port city of Memphis that have been taken over by the National Islands Corporation." Delphi paused and scanned the faces of his audience. "I have spoken against the corporate bureaucracy and their uses of lies to placate, nay, deceive the populace about the ongoing 'fake' war, and I have fought against the systematic killing, the purging, of innocent civilians." Delphi moved closer to the voice amplifier, "Because of my efforts to assist the Global Freedom Party, I was forcibly removed from the corporate board, and the NIC has confiscated my assets. However, I can assure you, I will not stop, I will not roll over and quit. I plan to take over the National Islands Corporation by any means necessary, including instigating a real war."

"Hold on,"

Bemire with his hand still resting on my shoulder leaned toward me and whispered, "That's Suzie Semester, the Dallas Regional Director."

Miss Semester was a light complexed, mid-fortyish, woman with black circles painted around her eyes. When she became excited, her eyes would expand making her look like a Halloween skull. She watched Delphi with wide-eyed disdain. "We cannot, and will not start a real war. That is insane." The rest of the directors nodded in agreement. "Our people do not have the will nor the funds to fight." Miss. Semester bent forward glaring at the Mr. Delphi, "Nor do you." Miss Semester took her seat.

Bemire pointed to the image of a man who spoke without standing, "That is the New America Regional Director Charles Shooter," Bemire said. The image flickered, dissolved, and reappeared.

"... Even if they did rise to the occasion how could they fight? All firearms were outlawed in the National Islands over two hundred years ago," Shooter said. His image began to fade as did his voice.

"Stop the stereopticon," Bemire said, "and ad-

The Perfect Plan

just the reactor."

The stereopticon snapped off and the gymnasium lights flickered on. Bemire leaned against the hood of the cart and rolled a rum-crum. He scratched a fuego stick against his fake sharkskin boots and a flame bloomed on its tip. The dead gasped as Bemire lit his rum-crum, inhaled, and pushed the smoking device toward me. I shook my head, and he returned the organic device to his lips. The stereopticon's golden light began to flicker on. The light stabilized, and the gymnasium lights went off.

"... Besides, regions are independent entities, most are unorganized, and lack discipline," Shooter said with a condescending smirk.

Delphi appeared agitated, "Alright, alright. Let's concentrate on the election then."

"If I may speak for everyone at the table," Miss Semester stood. Delphi nodded his approval. "Our candidate, E. W. Pile, is a history professor. He is as boring as a cuttlefish and changes his policies just as easily as the sepiida changes color. Whereas our opponent George A. Lucas President of the National Island Corporation is dominating the election."

"That may be true... but, look people our constituents are being purged because of the lack of jobs—Why? Because we failed to act," Delphi said.

"It is the times we live in. The corporation does not need employees. They have robots to work for them. What are we going to do, regress to the age of automobiles and frame houses?" Semester said. Several members laughed. Semester continued, "And the NIC has Super PACs and owns ninety-nine percent of the world's wealth. How can we win an election or overthrow the corporation without funds?"

"Our people, our friends, and families will die unless we do something!" Delphi replied. The room grew quiet. "Any Ideas?"

Bemire looked at me and raised his eyebrows as if seeking an answer from me. I ignored him and concentrated on the shimmering image of a man I recognized. It was Tom Brock, the NIC's Political strategist, and apparently a GFP spy. He along with Martinez was at the Second Elected Confederacy Headquarters of Poland, "I have an idea," he said raising his hand.

"Well, what is it?" Delphi waved his arm urging the strategist to speak.

"The truth. We need someone, to tell the truth about what is going on. Once the populace knows the truth about the purges and the corporation's hoarding of the world's wealth they will revolt, I am sure of it!"

"But who could do this?"

"I know a man. He is not a typical reporter, he is different but reliable," Tom said.

"Who?"

"His name is Jimmie Linguine."

My eyes bulged. Bells began ringing in my

ear—the ear Delphi cut from my head, "Son-of-a-bitch." I said.

"Linguine, the man who had my son, and I, and Jacob killed by that elderly bitch, Elvira?"

"Yes," Tom said, "that is the man I am referring to."

A stream of curses immediately erupted from Delphi after Tom's exposé and Bemire had the stereopticon turned off in an effort to protect the dead men and women from profanity so vile it could only have come from Hell.

My face twisted into a washboard of anger, "Are you trying to hook me up with the man that mutilated me?" I shouted.

"Delphi didn't mutilate you. It was a NIC terrorist who did that to you," Bemire said.

"Bull shit, I was there. I saw it. I felt it. He pulled out a laser blade and whacked off my ear and sliced open my chest." I took a breath and continued, "Elvira witnessed it," I sounded whiney, "She was there, she shot Delphi, killed the son-of-a-bitch." My voice dropped from a whine to an imploring sob.

"You are confused," Bemire said, "It was the bomb."

I slumped forward, shoulders squeezed in at a contorted angle, "Whatever," I replied.

"Look, Jimmie, Delphi experienced the same thing that you did. It was all theatrical, a show put on by Alexander. C'mon, just talk to him Jimmie," Bemire put his hand on my slanted shoulder, "I'll get with Tom he can set the whole thing up if you will just agree to meet with Delphi."

I was defiant, "Why, why should I help?"

"The world needs you Jimmie—needs you to report the truth. Tell the people about corporate stealing and bribery, the inequality of class brought on by greed. Expound about the murders and purging of the unemployed. You can do it, Jimmie you have a gift, use it." Bemire swept his hand in the direction of the bleachers acknowledging the dead bearded people in the room. "These were your friends gone now because of Alexander and the National Islands Corporation. Say yes Jimmie."

I looked at the bearded people. Pondered if this was real or not, wondered if I was sane, "Alright," I said. "I will try." The bleachers erupted with joy. Fake beards were tossed and captured, (within my mind's eye) in slow motion like flying headless-tailless possums. The atmosphere in the Slaughter-House was electric and static, making my wig-hair rise a full two fingers. The enthusiasm was contagious. I was overwhelmed—excited about saving the world.

Bemire said, "Okay, shut her down." The projector lights slowly faded. Only the track lights remained on. The doors of the Surgery Theatre opened automatically and Bemire guided me through the double entry doors. Bemire whistled a tune as I motored down the hall of bearded men and women the melody *Jimmy Crack Corn*,

The Perfect Plan

(our high-school fight song), accompanied by kettle drums, and bagpipes, reverberated against the narrow walls. It was beautiful. "Here we go," Bemire said, as we exited the Slaughter-House.

The gurney wobbled on the asphalt as Bemire drove me to the Discharge Office located by the electro-petrol tank on the west end of the tarmac. The discharge officer was wearing an in-fashion tensile pen suit made of, a transparent fabric used to activate the oxytocin hormone of the opposite sex. I was not impressed. Bemire handed his tracer tablet to the clerk. The transparently dressed clerk plugged the tablet into a portal to his right and downloaded my information. "Very well Mr. Linguine, here is your discharge tablet, your location tracker, a room for three days at the Broadmoor House Hotel. I think you will find it suitable and finally, your clothes, which will be in the dressing room." He pointed to a door labeled Unisex.

I entered the dressing chamber, "Thank you," I said and closed the door behind me. I slipped out of the hospital gown. A scanner flashed on, rotated around my body, and stopped. A twine bound paper package dropped out of a rectangular opening labeled Men's Clothing. I opened the package and to my delight, found a clown suit. The suit was an exact replica of the pajama's I wore as a kid. I was excited, the suit was lemon yellow and had orange rings that laddered the right arm. The collar was light blue and heavily ruffled. My large toed boots had a vivid red tongue, green body, and deep blue laces. Inside the right boot, nestled in the swollen toe I found a black undergarment, (with the crotch modified for a perfect fit), and in the modified crotch, the single eye of a gold chained monocle lay as an unexpected treasure. A poppy flower poked its cadmium head out of the left boots blue laces, and buried deep within the vamp of the right boot, I found a purplish wig. *Childish, but radical* I thought.

I dressed quickly, "I like it," I said to the clown in the mirror. I pressed the exit button and pranced out of the dressing chamber as a consummate entertainer.

"Nice," the Discharge Officer said.

"Yes, it is," I replied.

"Your floater has arrived. It will take you to the Broadmoor House Hotel. Enjoy your stay."

"Thanks," I said. The floater drifted to the connection gate, which opened as I approached. There were, I noticed, four or five passengers on board, all of whom laughed as I sat close to the automatic pilot, and buckled up. We were at the hotel in less than five minutes. Bemire was in the Lobby. He smiled when he saw me, "You look fantastic," he said, "You are in room 19 on the seventh floor, any luggage?"

I said, "No." He smiled, wrapped his arm around my shoulder and we caught the levitator to the seventh floor. I walked to room 19, placed my thumb on the lock and the door swung open.

The Perfect Plan

"Beautiful," I said.

Bemire gave me seven hundred coupons, "For expenses," he said, and promised to return tomorrow, "hopefully with good news about meeting Delphi."

"Bemire," I said.

Bemire pirouetted to his right—planted his feet at a sideways angle during the third revolution, rested his chin upon the blade of his shoulder and smiled displaying his huge horse teeth. "Yes?"

"What just happened? I mean why, how did I get here?"

"The NCI as you know had you on the unemployed purge list. I bribed a certain NCI person of high rank to falsify documents for your release. That person was an agent of the Global Freedom Party and an ally to Delphi. You owe Commander Delphi, Jimmie."

"What about the Slaughter House?" I asked.

Bemire laughed, and stepped directly in front of me, "We rented a studio, a communication center that was filming Bearded Zombies."

He patted me on my shoulder. "See you in a few hours."

Bemire walked to the door and turned. I waved. He returned my wave and shut the door behind him.

CHAPTER 40

Bemire and Elvira

Elvira was soaking in the bubble tub when her cubicle phone rang, "Martha, can you get that?"

"Yes Mum," Martha said in a thick British accent. Martha, a young student at Bib University was studying ancient languages and was practicing her Old English for next week finals. "Oloo," Martha said.

"Who is it?" Elvira asked.

"Some bloke named Bemire," Martha said.

Elvira eagerly accepted the phone and turned on the transmission secure code at the base of the receptor

Elvira met Bemire at his home on Lancaster Street in New Chicago. She was smoking a cigar. He studied her carefully—noticed she was wearing a transparent Pandora skirt and an irradiant fish scale blouse. All the hair on her lower torso was visible. Bemire considered her attractive des-

The Perfect Plan

pite the pendulous breasts and a dark mole on her left ear. A single hair, like an antenna, extended from her mole. The protuberance swayed as he whispered sweet disobediences in her ear. She smiled and removed her blouse. He removed his trousers. She removed her skirt. He removed his shirt. She retained the cigar as she fondled him. The smoke, like exhaust from a cutter's dual tailpipes, billowed through her nose. Bemire's senses heightened into a virile torrent of actions, (specific actions have been redacted.) A shudder so ecstatic that it forever claimed her soul. Every hair stood erect—a porcupine, he imagined. He gingerly rolled off her body.

A turkey gobbled. Bemire smiled. Elvira pulled the sheets up to her neck and asked alarmed about what could have possibly made that noise. Bemire explained the sound she had heard came from a visiting friend. The friend, he said was an admirer of his from back in the day when he worked as an animal trainer for the cinema. That was before the industry brought in robot labors.

CHAPTER 41

The Turkey Head Tavern

I was in the Turkey Head Tavern, sipping on a glass of Dirty Water (a stout alcoholic beverage), and feeling slightly buzzed when Elvira entered through the back door, gave a nervous glance around, and sat down next to me. She was old, thank God, and smelled clean, or I should say, odorless in the sense she was pheromone free. She smiled and patted my shoulder. I must say I was surprised to see her, especially after our conversation at the theater. I tried to ignore her and gazed awkwardly around. I was suspicious of her and felt uncomfortable being in her presence. I heard a faint noise and glanced upward. I saw, to my surprise, a turkey-head trophy hanging above the solace mirror. Its eyes blinked. He moved his innocuous head. It was some kind of illusion, I was sure of it. My mental state lately had deteriorated into a post-traumatic mental impairment. The turkey stared unblinkingly at the

The Perfect Plan

far wall. I followed his gaze and found the turkey's ass displayed upon the opposing wall. His derrière spoke with rectal ease, "I know where you have been." The turkey-ass emitted foul (fowl?) breath as he spoke.

"You talking to me?" I asked.

"No," the cesspit said, "I'm talking to your date."

I envisioned the mechanics of a talking rectum, and muttered, "Doubtless, the nerve arrangement for this kind of pulsation is similar to that involved in the locomotion of the urchin, Echinus."

Elvira looked at me irreverently; then turned to the turkey-ass, "Me? I'm not his date."

"What be—the—be," the turkey said.

"Bartender, can you shut this turkey-ass up?" Elvira said with a calmness that surprised me.

The multi-talented table tender and liquor server looked at Elvira, "Do you want him to sing instead of talk?"

"No." Elvira said, "Shut his ass up."

The Bartender retrieved a small stepladder from the storage room and pulled a cork from a bottle of Serpent Head Wine. The turkey head watched his ass wriggle in self-defense, "Hold still," the bartender said.

"But," the turkey-ass muttered, "It's about her, that woman..." The bartender slammed the cork up the turkeys' sphincter before he could finish speaking.

"So, what does this turkey-ass know about you?" I asked

Elvira squirmed, took a sip of tulip soup, and said, "It's about my reputation."

"Sex?"

"Kind of, but, it is more about someone you know."

"Me?"

"Yes, I have been labeled as a familiar."

"What did you do?"

"Well, first there was you… and now Bemire," Elvira dabbed her eyes with a tissue extracted from between her two flaccid gourds.

"Pheromones?"

She gave an affirmative nod. "Sweet Ignacio Elvira, how could you?"

"I was lonely," she said.

"How did the turkey find out?"

"Bemire has a turkey friend. He was there with us at the time of-of fornication," Elvira whispered, "You know how turkeys' love to talk."

"You were with Bemire?"

"Yes."

A loud noise rattled the glasses behind the bar. The turkey-ass, due to abnormal gastric compression exploded and green turkey poop went everywhere.

"Aw shit," Elvira said.

CHAPTER 42

Urdu's Strange Request

The narrative returns to Jimmie in the Broadmoor House Hotel.

I turned on the wall screen as soon as Bemire left. The National Island Corporation was running a proselytizing advertisement. In the ad, a beautiful young, scantily clad, woman was asking volunteers to participate in corporate-sponsored sex research to test an experimental drug that claims to provide sexual arousal for five days. If the participant survives five days of continuous sex, which is part of the endurance training, He or she (the program is available for women also) is required to sign up for an obligatory five-year military assignment. Oh, and this is the kick-ass artifice, the applicant must pay to participate.

Bored with the enlistment commercial, yet excited about the libidinous imagery, I was in need of a drink and company perhaps with someone from the female persuasion. There was a gaming bar across the street and a cross light from my room to the gambling tavern below. I stepped on the buoyant conveyor and rode the beam into the William E. Nelson Casino Bar and Grill. The tavern had an urban atmosphere. Chrome glistened on the beer and wine dispensers. It was a noisy place. The slots, roulette wheels, and video games programmed by gaming psychologists got the maxim participation from the 'losers', and the repeat and reward glockenspiels and flashing lights created a nonstop dopamine rush. It was too much for me and I stepped outside to survey the area for a quieter, more relaxing atmosphere.

Down the street, I noticed a giant neon sign. The signboard flashed red and blue, Pet Shop, (red,) Pet Store, (blue,)... Pet Stop, (red,) Pet Store, (blue.) It was hypnotic. I felt drawn to the store as if beckoned by an unknown force. I walked over and peered through the window. What I saw was astonishing. It was Mother Urdu engaged in a boastful swagger. She was selling goldfish to a half-minibike-half human android. She looked up briefly saw me and smiled, "Jimmie," she said, "You have your clown outfit, it looks suburb on you. Come here boy and give me a hug." Urdu gave the android its change. The human part of the mini-bike took the remaining coupons and its package of fish and left the shop, saying, "Thank you," on her way out.

I approached Urdu cautiously, and embraced her with trepidation, "What are you doing here?" I asked, "Where are the little ones, your little reincarnates?"

"They are in daycare until I return," she said.

"Why are you here?"

"I wanted to speak to you secretly. I want you to help retrieve a lost soul, a soul that was due to return for re-birthing, and didn't show up," she said.

"Whose soul?"

Urdu hung her head. Her ears fell like pigtails, "Izabelle's soul," she said, "Last known to be in Blind Betty Brangan's body. The Expiry Corporation, a subsidiary of the National Island Corporation purged Blind Betty yesterday. No one knows how Izabelle's soul escaped. She may have learned how to transfer her soul without me."

I looked at Mother Urdu. She wet her toe with the tip of her tongue and with her stumpy digit brushed back her eyelashes.

"It is not unheard of—the last time it happened was when G. D. Hatton and Spot did it back 1968. That was my fault, I should have known better." Tears began to flow down her short snout; she licked the tears away with her long elastic tongue, "Will you help?"

"What can I do?"

"I want you to find out how Chacho's soul got transferred to Hatton. The exchange happened August 28^{th,} 1968 to be exact."

"Who is Spot?"

"He is a dog." I looked at her quizzically. "It is

a long story, and I have little time." She said.

Urdu put on a trench coat, turned the lights off, stepped outside, and locked the door. I followed her out to the sidewalk. The fog had settled over the city and the streetlights cast an eerie glow. "The corporation will shut off the lights soon. I have to go," she said as she pulled the trench coat close to her body dropped down on all fours and disappeared into the gray swirling mist.

CHAPTER 43

Jimmie speaks to God

The corporation shut-off the streetlights just as I reached the hotel room. Curfew had begun. I pressed the bed button on the wall and an airbed drifted down from the ceiling and hovered above the floor. I slipped out of my clown suit, brushed my teeth, showered, and slipped beneath the translucent covers. Bemire had rented the honeymoon suite. A Kama Sutra stereopticon presenting sexual positions began playing. I watched the couple maneuver through all sixty-nine positions before my voice request turned the program off. I did not fully realize until now how lonely I was and how much I needed a woman.

Bemire and I, had breakfast at the Broadmoor Breakfast Club. The club was conveniently located in a granite vestibule on the hotel's first floor. We ate synthetic eggs, lovingly displayed over a bed of hydroponically grown vegetables, broccoli, I think. Bemire wiped a yellow stream of egg yolk from his lips, and said, "Did you like your room?"

"Yes, It is nice," I replied recalling the images of the Kama Sutra couple. We continued to eat in silence. "Have you seen Elvira?" I blurted the question out and immediately regretted the outburst.

"No," Bemire replied. He took a bite of broccoli and chewed slowly. "Why do you ask?"

"Just curious," I said. "What time are we to meet Delphi?"

"I have scheduled a conference niche here at the hotel. The teleconference will begin at ten." I looked at my cellular. It was 9:37 a.m. We finished our meal, tipped the mechanical waiter, and headed for the lobby. Bemire found the conference niche at the southwest corner by the women's restroom. The niche was a glass cubicle with a table and two chairs centered in the small area. The tele-viewer was on the table. Bemire and I sat down and waited. The call arrived at exactly ten o: clock. Delphi's face appeared on the screen as a digital image. "Good morning Mr. Delphi," Bemire said.

"Morning," Delphi replied.

I noticed a half-naked woman casually lurking in the background, behind Delphi's chair. She had a finger bone in her nose. Kinky! I thought.

Bemire spoke in a placid tone interrupting my thoughts of the primitive woman and Delphi.

"Let me start off by saying that we, Jimmie

and I appreciate your meeting with us," Bemire said, "and in a way of disclosure, I want both of you to know that what you experienced back at Skelly's was an illusion brought on by a mind-altering aerosol that Elvira prior to your arrival sprayed in the basement. Both of you were led to believe what happened was true. Your son, Miguel Martinez is still alive, Mr. Delphi, but remains a captive of the National Island Corporation, and, of course, you are still alive."

"I survived Elvira's attempt to kill me. Look at the scars." He pointed to a pimple on his forehead and a two-inch scar on his wrist.

"Jimmie, did Mr. Delphi look wounded or dead?" Bemire asked.

"He looked dead to me his brains were splattered all over the basement walls. He couldn't have survived."

Delphi looked as if he was still uncertain about the events surrounding his fake death, "What is the plan?" He murmured.

"We need Jimmie to report the truth about the National Island Corporation's purges and the hoarding of the world's wealth. We need the people to revolt!" Bemire studied Delphi's blank face, "Do you understand?"

"You said my son is still alive?" Delphi asked.

"Yes, he is still alive," Bemire said.

"Do you have proof?"

"I have a stereopticon image of him being tortured."

"Let me see it?" Delphi said.

"I must warn you it is brutal."

"Let me see it," Delphi said in a low guttural voice.

Bemire plugged in the digital transfer of his handheld stereopticon and turned it on. Delphi watched the closed-circuit viewer without speaking. After the viewing, Delphi said, "Okay, let's do this, and Bemire, I want you to figure out a way to get my boy back."

"I will get with Tom Brock and put both plans into motion."

"Jimmie, welcome on board," Delphi said; then paused and gazed at me with cynicism, "The clown suit—what is the purpose of the clown suit—you want people to laugh at you-you doing this for attention?"

"No sir," I said, "I'm doing it because all superheroes have a costume."

I heard Bemire chuckle.

"I'll be in touch," Delphi said.

Bemire turned the tele-viewer off, "Well done" he said, and patted me on the shoulder, "Now let's go to work. I will contact Tom Brock and let him know that you are on board; then we will meet and work out a plan. Okay?"

"Sure," I said; then fell into a self-indulgent, fear-based analysis, of my future. I must admit, I am not totally convinced this will work. In all probability, I will be captured and held prisoner in a revolting dungeon by corporate statisticians, and I will die of boredom. The thought lingered even after Bemire said, "Let's meet tonight for super. I'll pick you up at seven."

I nodded, and said, "Okay."

Bemire turned abruptly and was outside the building before I could mention my current state of fear-induced nausea. I managed, in ever hastening steps, to make it to my room before the contents of my stomach i.e. syntactic eggs and broccoli spewed into the bowl of poop. Which, of course, intensified the retching. Sorry, I forgot to flush. Aware of the seriousness of my 'imagined' capture and torture, I decided to pray. I strapped on synthetic kneepads I had found in the dresser beside the Bible and genuflected. I clasped my hands firmly together, and said, "Dear God." No answer, I forgot to turn on the neural receptor behind my left ear.

A crackling noise ensued when I flipped the switch a voice registered in my mind and the Bright Light of God spoke, "Hello." It said

—Silence.

I said, "Look God."

"Call me Ralph Jenkins, Doctor of Theology, and Demonology." A soothing voice said. I heard a chorus in the background singing Hallelujah. Angels, I assumed.

"Okay, Ralph Jenkins, Doctor of Theology, and Demonology. I seek guidance about the impending uprising against the National Island's Corporation and all of its subsidiaries."

"Woah, brother you've got the wrong God, The National Islands Corporation is one of our biggest supporters. You need to contact an unaffiliated link. Hold on let me get it for you. Okay, ready? You can find that link at Seventh Heaven/ uninsured/ uninspired/and unemployed.com. Let them know it is for an imminent purging. Goodbye, and God bless."

"Son-of-a-bitch," I said.

"I heard that," it said.

"Fuck you," I screamed.

"Fuck you too," it said with a calmness that disturbed my inner-self. The light within my mind faded slowly with a crackle and buzz; then snapped off with what sounded like a finger-in-cheek, pop.

I went to bed frustrated, slept fitfully, and suddenly without a rational reason, began to tremble. I opened my eyes. Bemire was shaking me. I felt the need to throw up "It's time to go," Bemire said, "I have arranged the meeting with Tom Brock. Hurry up, get dressed, we have to be at his office in an hour." I ran to the bathroom and puked once again in the still unflushed toilet; then flushed.

Bemire and I boarded the public floater and headed via the orbicular flyer to the Free for All Campaign Building. I must confess I was nervous and a little shaky about my recent hallucination, brought on, I believed by a self-diagnosed allergic reaction to synthetic eggs, but Bemire had a

The Perfect Plan

calming effect on me—that and the little blue pill he administered via rectum injection with an ungloved hand. Midflight, Bemire straightened the neck frills (with unwashed hands) on my clown suit and after a fifteen-minute delay (security check), we debarked the floater at 101 Reign Street, South Side in New Chicago.

We entered huge double doors Tom Brock was sitting behind an enormous plasta-mold desk. "Thank you for coming," Brock said. He switched the coder on and the electromagnetic field sizzled and crackled down the walls, completely sealing the room from outside listening devices.

"I don't think the coder will be necessary," I exclaimed.

Brock said, "Why not?"

"I, umm," I said nervously, "uh wishing to speak to God, I umm, disclosed our intention to revolt against the National Island's Corporation."

Tom Brocks face turned red, his voice quivered in anger, "To whom did you disclose the information?"

"Umm, to Ralph Jenkins, Doctor of Theology, and Demonology," I paused for a moment. "I thought he was God."

"Holy Shit," Brock yelled, "Ralph Jenkins is the National Island Corporation's Director of Purges."

"Let's stay calm," Bemire advised.

"Calm?" Brock yelled.

"I can fix it," Bemire said before rolling a rum-crum.

"How can you fix it?" Brock asked.

"Mr. Linguine will allow himself to be captured by the National Island Corporation. He will locate Delphi's son Miguel Martinez and extract him from the National Island Corporation's Prison. Simple, problem solved."

"That's preposterous," Brock said.

Bemire took a long drag on his rum-crum and excelled, "I promised Delphi that I would find his son."

"The election is in four days. We need to establish our presence before the first primary, or else all is lost." Brock said.

"Our candidate, E. W. Pile is on the ticket is he not?" Bemire said.

"Yes."

"Then it does not matter, our opposition will come after the nomination. Trust me on this Tom with Linguine's help we can defeat the Nation Island's stronghold on our people. We can reverse the course; put our people back to work. We Can Win!" Bemire slammed his fist down to the slick desktop.

Brock flinched and gazed with worried eyes at Bemire; then capitulated, "I guess there is no other choice. Implement your plan."

CHAPTER 44

The Rescue

Concordia, the Second State of New Hampshire, February 7th, four days before the Regional Primary.

I was at the Turkey Head Tavern, by design. I had learned from Bemire that the NIC was engaging in an effort to disenfranchise the turkey population who were politically leaning to the left in support of Delphi and the GFP.

I was standing at the bar enjoying a Lime-Lilly with several party members when the explosion and scattering turkey poop occurred. I instinctively ducked, but too late, layers of fetid guano covered me.

Elvira stepped out of the lady's room and said, "That was the sign."

"What sign, what are you talking about?" I asked wiping pea-green goo from my face.

"Jimmie, you know I love you, baby. I really do, but... I'm going to have to take you back to the

Second Elected Confederacy Headquarters."

There was this ticking sound, "Aw shit," Elvira said, "That's the other sign."

"What other sign?" I asked as she ducked back into the restroom.

A second explosion rocked the building. I awoke in a hospital bed. My pinkie finger was bruised and my clown suit was covered in a mixture of blood and excrement. "Not again," I whined.

"Will you join us?" Elvira said amidst a cloud of yellow smoke.

I thought about the perfect plan Bemire had devised and confidently replied, "I am all yours." I could hear the fake war raging on the big screen in the Theatre room. "We got him," she exclaimed.

Hat stood by my bed, his belly bulged with pride, "Fantastic," he shouted, "good to have you back Jimmie." The Hat marched toward the door, turned abruptly, and patted the top of his hat. With a click of his heels and a formal salute, he turned, and I saw, through admittedly blurred vision, a butt-crack wedge in Hat's skin-tight pantaloons. He must have been playing with the boys, I thought as the tranquilizer took effect and I fell asleep.

I awoke in the recovery room. A fresh clown suit was lying at the foot of my bed.

"Pardon me," said a sumptuous redhead who had just entered the room carrying my bulbous-toed shoes, "are these yours?"

The Perfect Plan

"Yes my dear, they are in fact mine." I could not glance away her beauty was so stunning, so with a lingering gaze, I asked, "Are you from around here?"

"No silly," Her freckled smile drove me mad. Her polished teeth, her deep blue eyes, all parts of her anatomy made one part of my anatomy rise to the challenge of speech. "Are you available?"

"I was asked to tend to your needs," the redhead said.

I wriggled with glee, "Your name?"

"Beatrice," she said.

"Ah Beatrice," I rejoined with a different enunciation than she. I pronounced her name as Be-at-truss.

"No silly, pronounce it like this, Be-a-trees."

"Oh, Be-a-trees."

"Yes, that is it. Where shall I put your shoes?"

I replied, "On the floor right below my clown suit." I could not help but ogle at her cleavage as she stooped to place my shoes on the floor.

"Where would you like your proton gun?"

"You have a proton gun?" I exclaimed.

"Why yes, it is yours, where would you like it?"

"Here in my bed," I said with a stiffness of voice and pecker. She placed the gun by my side and I quickly slipped the murderous machine beneath the covers. The cold metal felt good on my thigh.

"Anything else?" she asked.

"When shall I see you again?"

"Ring the bell," she pointed to a small button on the rail of my hospital bed, "and I will come," she replied.

Oh, my God, I thought, this shall be a marvelous experiment in stoic duplicity. "Thank you, Beatrice."

"You are welcome," she smiled again. Her smile caused the accident. It, the accident, had been building. An explosion similar to the Mount Vesuvius eruption thrust my bed covers the height of the plaster ceiling. Beatrice blushed, put her tiny hand to her lips, and skirted down the hall with parroting giggles similar, in my mind, to a child's display of merriment at a circus or other clownish event.

So enraptured by Beatrice was I that my memory about the proton gun and my mission here at the Second Elected Confederacy Headquarters was temporarily lost. The wetting sensors on my bed noticed my, (how should I put it,) my indiscretion, and began to clean the large wet spot.

I recalled a recent report from the magazine *Mans Man*, which stated the typical volume of a man's sperm during a single ejaculation, is approximately one teaspoon. My semen, I am proud to convey, was more like a teacup in volume.

Soon after the cleansing, I was back on track. I extracted myself out of bed and dressed. It was difficult due to my bruised pinky finger, but I per-

The Perfect Plan

severed. There was a moment, I must admit when I panicked. I could not find my monocle and purple hairpiece, but after steady concentration, which allowed a focused and thorough search, I found both items within the confines of my red and blue two-tone shoes.

"You can take a breath now," Beatrice said. She was standing in the doorway with her hand lounging seductively on her hip. A Seraphic malady or luxury? I thought hoping for the latter. "Here is the key to Miguel Martinez's cell." Said Beatrice dropping the keys on the floor with a clatter. My approach was casual, confident. "Key's," I said, "in this day and age?" I reached down to pick up the security tool; she placed her hand firmly on my back and pushed. It was an easy task. Weakened by the blast, I had little strength. She continued to push until my eyes dropped below the hem of her skirt. Naturally, I looked up. She was mechanically sexed, a replica with a huge bush.

"I have been purchased to assist you." She said.

I continued to gaze up her skirt and focused in a delirious malady at that elusive flower I so desired. "By Whom?" I replied. My voice echoed within the fabric of her skirt.

She removed her hand allowing me to withdraw my head and rise, "The GFP silly." She replied in a sincere and seductive voice. Beatrice dropped on all fours so sudden it startled me. A sexual strategy? Doggy style, I assumed there was a longing somewhere within her body that would appear once aroused, but no, she was a cold dedicated combatant intent on completing the mission. "Get on, let's go get Martinez," She said, in a commanding tone. I raised her dress. She reached back and slapped my hand, "Not that silly," she said. I placed myself in the cradle of Beatrice's lower back, and with my good hand, grabbed the long braids of her beautiful red hair. I observed with considerable passion, the back of her head, the parted hair a few fickle strands swaying by my breath. Even the back of her pale semi-lucent ears and the freckles on her neck were gorgeous. "Ready?" she said.

"Yes," I replied. She bolted like a thoroughbred in a heavily wagered race. I leaned forward across her shoulders and felt with casual awareness the metal muscles working beneath her skin. The wind whistling past my ears. My legs, more specifically my shoes, however, were a problem. The bulbous toes of my clodhoppers kept bouncing on the floor.

"Pick up your feet, lie prone against on my back," she said. I lifted my legs and stretched my body on her back the rocking motion of her gallop was stimulating. I felt myself reacting. I came without warning. The pleasure, the spasms were so intense. She stopped suddenly. I fell off; slid uncontrollably along the floor and banged headfirst into the wall. The crotch of my clown suit was soaked. When I stood, rivulets of semen wriggled down my legs. Beatrice stood erect, combative, like a legendary Amazon. I cowered below her, with hands spread over my groin to conceal the wet spot "What is your problem?" she screamed.

I shrugged my shoulder, "It was an accident. Humans have accidents you know."

She scanned my body with angry unblinking eyes. Her gaze rested, (it was an awkward and lengthy repose), on my wet spot. She shook her head as a bear might when annoyed, "You are going to walk from now on," her voice was menacing. We began to walk at a fast pace, She seemed to realize my vulnerability, my weakness of mind and body, and slowed down. I reached out my hand. She reluctantly accepted my palm. Her grasp was unusually warm and comforting. Once again, I felt the rocket rise. Beatrice, noticing the tightening of my grip, looked at me, and saw the bloom of my cheeks, the gratifying smile; the bulge in my pants and immediately dropped my clammy mitt. She walked ahead of me. I watched her cloth covered mechanical ass sway with each rhythmic step.

A thought, surprisingly unrelated to sex, came to me suddenly, and I asked, "Why are there no guards? Where are all the people?"

She turned and checked my pants before replying, "I killed most of them, even the actors, the fake soldiers, the bureaucrats, politicians, and creeps. The rest fled on a shuttle." I noticed that she put a bit of emphasis on creeps. "We need to hurry before they return with reinforcements," she said.

I picked up the pace. We reached Martinez's cell. He was sitting on the crapper when we arrived. I noticed he was reading the *American Island News*. "What's the latest?" I asked.

"Same old shit," he replied. He looked up and recognized me, "Jimmie Linguine, what are you doing here. I thought you were dead."

"Same here," I replied, "you were supposed to be dead too."

"We've come to take you home," Beatrice interrupted.

Martinez wiped his ass and flushed without standing, "Do you mind," he said, "I need to pull up my pants." Beatrice and I turned our heads. A few seconds later he said, "Okay, let's go." I unlocked the cell door.

"How are we going to get out of here?" I asked.

"I have a skidder tethered to the rear portal," Beatrice said. Miguel Martinez followed Beatrice. I concentrated on her ass while Martinez packed his belongings.

"Have you seen Elvira?" Martinez asked.

"Yes," I said, "she hasn't changed—still the reckless cigar smoking bitch she's always been."

"Be careful how you speak of her," Beatrice warned.

We reached the skidder without incident. It was a relatively short ride to the New Chicago

Port of Airships. A floater was waiting for us at the gate.

CHAPTER 45

One day before the Primaries

Bemire and I, met with Delphi and Miguel Martinez a day before the primary. There were three candidates, Charles Monroe, Cremorne Allen Udder, and an unlikely candidate from Texas, Ernest William Pile. "Once we have a candidate," Delphi said, "we can start our exposure campaign."

"I think we should start now. I need investigators and time. The more time and the more investigators we have, the better."

"I agree with Jimmie," Bemire said.

Delphi looked and Bemire, and then at me, "Where are you going to start?"

"Second Elected Confederacy Headquarters of Poland," I said.

"Why?"

"There is plenty of evidence of the fake war. We can use that information in our campaign against the NIC Presidential Incumbent George

The Perfect Plan

Lucas,"

"I'll set it up," Delphi said.

"Keep us posted about the election," Bemire replied.

Delphi shook my hand, and then Bemire's hand and gave his son a gentle pat on the back, "I will," he says with a smile, "good luck boys."

Martinez escorted us to the door, "I never got a chance to thank you for rescuing me, Jimmie." Martinez said.

"Glad I could pull it off—that gal Beatrice was fantastic—couldn't have done it without her," I replied. Martinez smiled and shut the door behind us.

Bemire turned down the narrow hallway. I followed close behind. We walked to the closest transport station and caught a Hummer (named for the sound of its rotating blades), to the airport. The long-range Speeder, piloted by Larry Incarnate III was waiting for us on the tarmac. "Load up boys," Larry yelled from the portal. We stowed our bags and entered the speeder anxious to be on our way.

"Did you pack your suit?" Bemire asked.

The speeder jumped vertically four or five thousand feet, then shot forward jerking our heads back, "Ye..ee..ep," I said. My fleshy cheeks shilly shallied by gravity distorted the sound of my voice. Bemire's smile exposed rows of glistening white teeth as his jowls wobbled from the ships accelerated speed. We finally settled into slower cruising speed and our faces and speech returned to their normal placidity.

Before we deplaned, I took the liberty to remove my clown outfit, dressed in a business suit and stuck a microscopic camera up my nose for the purpose of videoing any and all evidence. Elvira met us at the gate. Hat soon followed. He had grown a mustache, the ends of which hung well below his hat. "I heard you were coming," Elvira said. Her rather thin mustache had gotten longer too. She embraced Bemire with the strength of a bull snake. Bemire blushed. Elvira looked at me and winked. I could smell lemons on her breath. The Hat saddled up to me and said, "Where is the Comanche killer?" He turned his hat slightly, "Oh, I have read about you and your *Teaspoon Hays Man of the Day.*"

"That wasn't me you fool," I said, "that was President Hays's political slogan back before the weather changed. My slogan is, *Expose the Lying Bastard's.*"

Hat shook his hat covered head in disbelief, "Come with me," he said. His words flowed from under the brim of his hat and fluttered past his mustache. I stepped behind Hat. Bemire and Elvira linked arms and strolled casually behind me. Hat knocked on General Alexander's door. A frail, high-pitched inaudible word seeped through the metal frame. "What?" Hat yelled.

"I said, Enter, you moron." Hat clicked his heels together and saluted the metal frame before

The Perfect Plan

reaching for the door handle a good two feet above his head. He stood on his toes to reach the doorknob; stretched and balancing painfully on his ten stumpy digits he managed to turn the knob. The door swung open. Everyone gasped. Sitting in Alexander's desk was George A. Lucas, the Incumbent President of the National Island Corporation. "Arrest them all," the president screamed. The stereopticon image of the president flickered and blinked off. Hat looked confused. Bemire and I uttered a communal sigh and then we scattered like sparrows below a hawk.

The nose camera did complicate my breathing, especially while racing for my life in an attempt to escape Hat who had pulled the biggest gun I had ever seen out of his waistband, shot at me. The bullet whizzed by my head. Fortunately, the theater room was just a few feet away, and I, without thinking, dashed into the amphitheater and started filming through my nose. It came naturally to me. I guess I have always had a knack for sticking my nose where it doesn't belong. I remember sticking my nose up a tortoise ass once! Ah, but that is another story... in another life...

The pictures I took were scenes of fake military casualties as well as fake skirmishes taking place on the stage. The best video, however, taken from neighboring studio B was of the two opposing sides having lunch together on the fake battlefield. As I was filming the meal, I received a message on my coder. It was from Bemire, he said, "Elvira and I have found purging documents for actors, both men, and women, over the age of forty. The actors were too old, the document stated, to represent the typical age of our current military men and women." My coder malfunctioned, and sections of Bemires message were lost… "Meet at the hospital ward"… static… "Hat is currently indisposed." I did not know what Bemire meant by indisposed—speculation of Hats circumstance would, of course, have been absurd even in this environment. I tiptoed down the hall and entered the ward with a certain amount of trepidation.

The hospital ward had the familiar smell of lemons. The room was empty except for Bemire and Elvira who had claimed one of the beds for a passionate timeshare. "Uh-um," I said.

Elvira sprawled on the bed with Bemire on top raised her thin arm and waved, "We'll be done in a moment, Hun." Bemire grunted like a hog, a progressively vocal hog. The grunts escalated into a series of short quick snorts until suddenly one gasp and a shudder and the ordeal was over. Bemire rolled off Elvira's thin frame. "Hand me that robe," Elvira said, pointing to a maroon robe hanging on the far wall. She lit a cigar as I fetched the garment. My reaction to the smell of the cigar was immediate. It was an instantaneous and awkward walk. She looked beautiful. My hands trembled as I handed her the kimono. Elvira administered a stinging slap to my face, "Back to business," she

The Perfect Plan

said while extinguishing the cigar in the palm of her hand.

"Here are the documents," Bemire said. He handed the papers to me.

I had not noticed the cuckoo clock hanging on the hospital rooms pale yellow walls until the wooden bird erupted and chirped seven times. For some reason, the singing bird sounded alarming. I had a strange feeling. Perhaps it was the naissance of caution. I paused, tapped my right index finger on the cleft of my chin and thought, this is too easy; when I said, "This is too easy." My voice sounded hollow.

Bemire was sliding into his jumpsuit, "What do you mean?" he said.

"Where is the resistance? What was the pretense for our arrival? Why do we have access to all these files? Where is everyone?"

Suddenly Hat walked into the room with his big-ass gun and ten big-ass men. He pointed his cannon at my crotch, and said, "All has been arranged. George A. Lucas has circumvented Delphi's intentions. You and Bemire are his captives."

"Shit," I said.

"Dido," Bemire said.

"Double dido," Beatrice said. She held a fingernail file in one hand, and my clown suit in the other. "I'm here to rescue you, boys." Beatrice was standing in the doorway behind Hat and his men. She threw the clown suit to me, "Here put this on," she said.

Hat and his men gawked at my erection in disbelief as I stripped and slipped into my suit. I must admit Elvira eyed me carefully as I undressed. The effects of the cigar smoke had not subsided. "Bemire," I said, "film this for posterity."

"Your erection?"

"No silly the assault," I said.

Bemire reached for the video camera on the vanity beside the bed. He had been videoing the sex-act with Elvira, and the camera was within easy reach. Hat pointed his gun and pulled the trigger. He missed Bemire but hit the camera. Beatrice reacted stabbing five of the ten big men with her fingernail file. Elvira ran, as did Hat.

That left Beatrice, Bemire, and me to take on the remaining five big-ass men. I selected the smallest of the big men. I kicked him in the groin. Once on the floor I bitch-slapped him unmercifully. Beatrice grabbed the two biggest of the big men, one under each arm she banged their heads together.

Bemire went into his Kung Fu stork stance one leg grounded the other cocked to deliver a deadly blow. Unfortunately, while Bemire was waiting for the man to attack,

Beatrice shoved the fingernail file through the back of his neck and then finished off my man lying on the floor by stabbing him in his cranium. She wiped the blood from her utensil using the most recent dead man's clothing—that would be my man—and said, "Let's go."

The Perfect Plan

Larry Incarnate III was waiting for us in the speeder. As soon as we boarded the missile, Larry forced the throttle up and zoom we were gone.

Section III

Urdu, Izabelle, Loki, Blind Betty Brangan, Beelzebub, Alice, and Beatrice's Connections and Backstories.

CHAPTER 46

Loki also interfered with Blind Betty's baby soul transfer

Loki hitched a ride as a flea on the back of Izabelle' soul. He and Izabelle were headed to a remote location (Latitude 34° 51' 35.81" North, and Longitude 106° 1' 35.81" West) in the Western American Islands. He thought about Urdu as he traveled. He despised his ex-wife, the authoritarian Urdu. He believed that she was sloppy in bed; had very poor personal hygiene, (smelled like a wet dog), and was unappreciative of the coins he provided. He sincerely believed that sex should be free.

His marriage to Mother Urdu had, in his mind failed. He was tired of paying the bitch (his words) for sex. Urdu' accountant, however, claims that Loki had not paid Urdu in three years.

Urdu's reaction.

Mother Urdu for coin and company allowed

her X-husband, Fyodor the Epistler to move back into her cave. He was not the animal that Loki had been in bed, especially during estrus, but Fyodor had money, served a purpose, and he was loyal.

Mother Urdu did not concern herself with Loki's disappearance. She was saddened, of course, but not overwhelmed by his absence, and within a decade... or two, she had forgotten about him completely. Only when he started interfering with the re-birthing of souls, did she become angry.

Loki did the soul disturbance gig for two reasons, to spite Urdu, and to improve his self-respect. He felt Urdu had robbed him of his intrinsic benevolence, his macho manhood, and his sterling virility. He even took a seminar on Self-Actualization and Responsive Generosity, and according to Loki's SARG Instructor Charlie Marmoset Ph.D., there was a good side to Loki not frequently revealed. Despite most opinions, vision, and views, Loki was a caring person and concerned about humanity.

Take, for instance, Loki's giving Chacho's slimy slug soul via Spot to Hatton. Loki surmised logically that Chacho's soul must possess virtuous powers and armed with that assumption—

Nature of Loki's assumption.

Urdu did not inform Loki that Chacho was Jimmie Linguine's first father and a drug addict. Loki's assumption of Chacho's virtue came from

The Perfect Plan

His concern for humanity—that and his insatiable cravings for magic mushrooms, which arguably may have distorted his logic and reasoning. The point is Loki wanted to impress Urdu with his good deeds. The greater objective is that he wanted to have free sex with Urdu, and he wanted to do it doggy style.

— Loki made the transfer to Hatton because he (Hatton) was a verifiably evil man. What Loki failed to understand was that Suzan was a bad mother. You see, Suzan loved Spot more than she did her own child, an unforgivable sin, an Izabelle sin... just saying... Loki's intention, regardless of the outcome, was virtuous. Now, about the Blind Betty Brangan incident.

Blind Betty Brangan had two strikes against her, one, she was blind, and two, she was pregnant. The Expiry Corporation placed Betty on the purge list. It did not matter to the company if she was pregnant. They had no need for additional people especially with the increased production capabilities of the androids.

After Loki purged Blind Betty, he, with nimble fingers and tempered pleasure extracted the infant's soul, Izabelle's soul—and gave it to the redheaded Replica, Beatrice. Loki met and fell in love with Beatrice while working in the corporate-owned Semen's Pleasure House—currently closed for renovation. She needed a soul. He needed love. They seemed compatible.

CHAPTER 47

Dirty Details on how Beatrice got Izabelle's Soul
Or
Loki's confusing opus on sex

As previously reported, Mother Urdu sent Izabelle's soul to a remote location (Latitude 34° 51' 35.81" North, and Longitude 106° 1' 35.81" West) in the Western American Islands to Blind Betty who, unfortunately, was held by the West Target Holding Compound for immediate purging. It is unclear if Urdu was aware of that fact.

___O___

Beelzebub agitated and glowing red, stated in a hostile tone, and trembling voice, "Why did Urdu send my daughter's soul to a woman sentenced to be purged and why in Hell did you steal my daughter's soul, Dog-Man?"

Loki lay upon the rooms rough plank floor-

The Perfect Plan

ing. He had a broom straw in his mouth and held a book of poetry *Eidolon Bogey Remember Me* in his hand, "Dog-Man, hey?" In an obscure method to advance his cause, Loki spoke. "Let me expound upon my ideas about ethereal psyches, the making of individuals, and the soul's placement in beings." Loki took a deep breath and continued, "It has been a communal fact for fully fifty centuries in all parts of the world that epileptic visionaries like Saint Duebe, Mother Urdu, and others, have sought a justification for fecundity in order to produce offspring, and I not only approve but participate as well. The preservation of conception and pregnancy and the increase of these processes is not a mysterious abstraction. The paternal factor is most certainly required, as any male such as yourself, Beelzebub, fully understands. I mean you do enjoy sex, do you not?"

"What does the placement of souls have to do with sex?" Beelzebub shouted. He raised his hands in a spiteful gesture and exposed the red hair of his armpits.

"Just pay attention," Loki said, "You'll figure it out. Now as far as the souls (ethereal psyches) are concerned, I refer to Dr. Wisden Leaven's opus on the soul, he envisaged the soul as a sexless bird on mind-altering medication. It is a wraith-like and fragile essence placed in a fetus, (as a result of fecundity mind-you,) to complete its purpose within a living being." Loki arose from his prone position and stood before Beelzebub, "By changing the recipient body, the soul's purpose is lost, and you Beelzebub deals in lost souls, do you not?" Loki chuckled... "I have just sent you some business son."

"But it was my daughter," Beelzebub said.

"Listen, brother Bee, it had to be chronicled that way. The father of your daughter's soul was Faience Comings III aka Trey dressed up as a dirty cop. If the recipient's mother Blind Betty gave birth to that baby, it would have changed the direction and complexity of the story perhaps even altered the drift of the war."

Beelzebub wrinkled his brow, "Because?"

"Because Izabelle's soul was destined to be General Alexander."

Beelzebub raised his shaggy eyebrows and queried with a slight turn of his neck, "The General Alexander leader of the NIC forces?"

"Yes that General Alexander, I had to take Izabelle's soul before it appeared out of Blind Betty's womb, and became General Alexander."

"What's wrong with General Alexander?" Beelzebub cried. "He was a great man."

"He's going to Hell! Is that where you want your daughter?"

Beelzebub's eyes drifted upward in an expression of the thought process.

Silence.

Loki combed the hair on his chin with his fingers, "Look Blind Betty Brangan and her child carrying Izabelle's soul by the anointing of fate was going to die anyway. Now at least the child can live on, temporarily, in someone else's body."

"Yeah your girlfriend's body," Beelzebub shouted in a fit of explicable rage which included chest thumping, head banging, booty-wagging hip-thrusting, and obscene hand gestures.

CHAPTER 48

How Loki met Beatrice

I had just arrived in Concordia for the Primaries. Beatrice invited me to go to the Semen's Pleasure House, a corporate subsidiary of Alexander's company Fairies Gadgets, and Goo. She was the maître d.

Thirty or more tables accompanied by four satellite chairs orbited a center stage. Four bars located in each of the corners served as a docking station for boozers and bandits. Mollie the Muskeg was performing. It was a rotational routine, i.e. the dancer moved counterclockwise for seven steps, rotated her hips, turned, and took seven steps in the opposite direction which allowed the customers both front and back views of the performance. Molly, to arouse interest used a turkey tail fan as her prop. As she seductively lowered the fan, a turkey in the audience became aggressive and jumped on the stage with intent to "Reclaim his sister's tail." Mollie frightened as a cricket in a grass fire, dropped the turkey tail fan and sought refuge in my outstretched arms. In an effort to safeguard Molly from the irate turkey, I embraced her tightly around her waist and to comfort the hyperventilating stripper I slipped her a coupon. Meanwhile, a Melon-headed-hairy-man with a net of braided hog hide captured the turkey and escorted the bird out of the building.

Molly thanked me while administering soft kisses to my cheek, neck, and lips and then returned to the stage where she bent over provocatively—Oh my God, the site of that—and gathered her feathers.

As the audience watched Mollie gather her plumage, the recently ousted turkey re-entered the establishment and lambasted Molly with a series of inappropriate gobbles. Melon-head immediately grabbed the turkey by the neck and once again escorted him out of the building. This time with extreme force.

An attorney sitting in the first RSVP seat noticed the brutal way in which Melon-head abused the turkey and immediately filed a complaint with management. The floor supervisor summoned the bouncer to the manager's office. I overheard the supervisor say something about a lawsuit.

During intermission, I took the opportunity to talk to Beatrice. I affectionately call her Bea. "I want to thank you for rescuing me," I said.

"You don't have to thank me," Beatrice replied.

"And apologize."

"For what?" Bea said with a look of amusement.

"My lack of control, my inadequacies as a man. I acted like a juvenile when you rescued me and Martinez." I said with a slight blush.

"Forget it," Bea said.

I extended my finger to scratch an itch that had manifested itself on my cheek, "How did you get a job so quick?"

Interjection: The muskegs

The muskegs are a violent race of light-skinned people who inhabit the swamps and coastal areas. Their territory has grown due to dramatic global warming and unusual weather patterns in recent centuries. Capitalist corporations have tried to domesticate these uncommon people but without success. They are descendants of water monkeys. They abhor theater, and the military and they are immune to all purging techniques used by the National Islands Corporation, or any corporation for that matter.

— She gave me a radiant smile, "I had help. A month ago, that funny looking guy, the melonhead—you know, the one that grabbed the turkey, his name is Loki."

I did not recognize Loki. He had shape-shifted and looked nothing like the man I saw at Hatton's bedside in New Chicago. "I know Loki, he doesn't look like that."

"That's what he calls himself Jimmie, anyway Loki managed to manipulate Bab's; she is the boss's girlfriend who was a server at the time. He talked her into getting him a job interview. During the interview—now get this; he used a weird philosophy on the boss, Dave." Bea turned her head to eye a complaining customer and then returned her gaze to me. "His strange story worked. Loki got the job. A week later, I met him at a dance club down the road. He was an impressive dancer. We danced, talked, connected romantically, and using the same canard, he got me a job here as a bartender at first, then management promoted me to maître d."

"What about your career with the GFP"

"What about it?"

"Are you still a service member?"

"Sorry, I cannot respond. That information is confidential."

"You and Loki are a thing?"

"Yes."

"Does he know that you are a replica?"

Beatrice smiled, "well he does now." She paused and looked woefully at me. "He said he was going to give me something special."

I felt betrayed, I was jealous, yet I found the presence of mind to say, "Nice."

A chorus of shouts from the surrounding clientele interrupted our conversation. A scantily clad woman strode upon the stage. The stage lights flashed an annoying red and green. She started to sing, *Lester Come Over*.

"Would you like a drink?" Bea said.

"No thanks," I replied.

"How is Martinez?" Beatrice asked as she wrote a reminder note for one of the servers concerning allowing patrons too close to the stage.

"He is back with his father, they are working on a plan, election stuff, you know."

Beatrice nodded her head. A lock or red hair fell in front of her face. She puckered her lips and puffed the errant strands away. As soon as the song ended, Molly returned to the stage, "Catch you later Bea," I said as I rushed to my table, sat down quickly, and waved a coupon at the amatory dancer. She stuck the voucher in her G-string and rumbaed away holding the turkey fan over her breasts. I left my phone number on the back of the coupon. Mollie called later that night. We had breakfast the next morning.

Loki returned to the entertainment lounge unscathed. He had managed to defend himself with Jihad J. Ready's manifesto embracing neutrality in which he claims inaction is the prerequisite for accomplishment.

CHAPTER 49

Blind Betty's Story

Loki's not so distant past

Semen's Pleasure House closed for renovations. Loki and Beatrice went to work for the West Target Holding Company as guards.

Blind Betty's distant past:

Eight and a half months prior to Blind Betty's arrest for vagrancy, ardency, prolificacy, and motility, she became pregnant. An off-duty policeman raped her.

Mother Urdu after a night of profanation against Loki unknowingly provided Blind Betty's embryo with Izabelle's soul. The sexless bird on mind-altering medication entered the womb at the time of the cop's pecker insertion, and subsequent embryo fertilization. The father, known only to Blind Betty as a dirty cop and sorry-ass-bastard was indeed a sorry-ass-bastard as well as a pervert.

Blind Betty and Loki's recent past:

Debbie and Alice shared the same cell with Blind Betty in the West Target Holding Compound. Betty was lying on one of the two available cots. Betty's large belly was a sign that the baby was soon to come. Susan greeted Betty tearfully, "Hello," Debbie said. Betty turned her head toward the speaker.

"Hello," Betty replied as she touched the curve of her swollen belly.

"When is your baby due?" Debbie asked.

"Soon."

There was a calm silence in Betty's cell. The noisy inmates surrounding the cubicle created a dull buzz, much like furious bees within a hive.

"How long have you been here?" Debbie asked.

"Six months or more," Betty replied, and sensing someone else in the cell asked, "Who is that with you?"

"This is my daughter Alice," Debbie said.

"I am Betty."

Alice extended her hand, but let it drop after she realized Betty was blind and could not reciprocate, "Nice to meet you," Alice said somewhat embarrassed about the attempted handshake.

With a beckoning wave of her hand, Betty summoned the mother and daughter to her side.

"It is not safe here," she whispered.

"We know," Debbie said.

"I must escape."

"You cannot escape this place," Alice replied.

"I must save the baby." Betty cried, "I must."

"Perhaps I can help," a clear voice came from the surrounding buzz of inmates.

"Who said that?" Betty asked, turning her head in an attempt to locate the speaker.

"I am an employee." The stranger replied.

Alice and Debbie fell to their knees in despair as a wolf-like man stepped to the edge of the cage. He tapped on the glass with his long claw-like fingers. His eyes seemed to be red coals in the dark brown fur on his face. Debbie and Alice were clearly startled.

"It's just reflected light," Loki said. He searched the women's faces for understanding. "My eyes reflect light," he repeated. "Do you want my help or not?"

"Yes, please," Betty, replied.

Three men and a woman stepped out of the shadows and into the light. "I'm afraid I must cuff you." The hairy man said. His four colleagues stepped forward with plastic ties and bound the three women. The guards led the captives to a gas chamber and forced them to kneel down on the floor. All three women were crying, Betty sensing that something was wrong asked between sobs, "Who are you?"

Loki considered lying but decided against it.

Lies are much too messy—honesty is the best strategy, no reason to build up the blind woman's hope. She would rather want to know the truth, not that it would be less painful; it would not. Loki scratched his hairy cheek with a long black finger. He was wearing an imaginary ring. One of the late Lord Ether's favorites. "I am your executioner and you are in the gas chamber." His captives in unison began to cry. Loki immediately felt sad about telling the truth.

His sadness was brief, he regained his hardline sensibilities and nodded to one of his assistants, "Take those two place them in body bags and carry them to the cruiser." Loki said. The men took Debbie and Alice out of the gas chamber. Betty was alone in the chamber. She was sobbing, "You said you would help." She screamed. "I will help the child. There is nothing I can do for you." Loki said from behind the chamber door. He nodded at the redhead who had positioned herself at the control panel. The panel light turned red as she hit the button marked gas. Betty and her unborn baby were dead in minutes. "Clear it," Loki said. The redhead flipped the vacuum switch to an upright position. They watched through the viewing window as the vacuum siphoned the poisonous gas out of the chamber.

A green light flashed indicating the room was safe to enter. Loki and the redhead sauntered in and Loki began to pry into Betty's vagina. "Sit down here beside her," Loki said. The redhead sat down beside Betty's body, "Closer," Loki said. "Place your hand on her belly." As soon as the redhead touched Betty's bloated belly, Loki pulled a pistol full of a foul-smelling liquid from his hidden underarm holster and filled Betty's vagina with the fluid. The wisp of soul that oozed out of Betty's vagina started slowly. Then ramped up as her belly deflated to a thin flat surface. Loki had seen this kind of fleshy surface before, The Unary people used it as a platform for premarital ceremonies—what he considered sex education classes. As Loki reflected upon the Unary Tribes marital ceremonies, the soul swirled and twisted around Beatrice's hand. She flinched at the sting of the soul being absorbed into her rubbery flesh. Beatrice the Replica, now has a soul, Izabelle's soul. Loki thought it wonderful. Boy oh boy was he wrong!

CHAPTER 50

Missing Souls

"It wasn't really his fault," Urdu explained to Fyodor the Epistler. "Loki was just trying to help a friend who had no soul." Mother Urdu sighed as Fyodor touched her brow with his pencil-thin clammy finger. She sighed, sniffled, and verbalized her thoughts about Loki's unauthorized actions, "He was wrong to do that… What shall I do?" Urdu asked.

Fyodor, dressed in his finest sculpted contour brief responded with a thick Latin accent (he was Swedish), "Actually," Fyodor said, "Izabella's soul is not lost it is in Beatrice, the replica, and the replica will never die. Therefore," Fyodor scratched an area just below the pressurized nut sack of his extended brief. Urdu's eyes followed his finger. She watched the digits rhythmic movement. Fyodor continued, "Izabella's soul will never be reborn." Mother Urdu thought for a moment. Her eyes remained focused on his fingers movement.

The Perfect Plan

"What shall I do?" she said.

Fyodor stretched out on a blanket at Mother Urdu's feet, "Do me," Fyodor said in his fake Latino accent. She gazed at his thin, skeletal body and shuddered as if suddenly awakened from a dream or nightmare. How appropriate she thought as she gazed at Fyodor's frail body. "Leave me," Urdu commanded. She watched Fyodor slink off into the dark recesses of her cave and smiled as an idea came to her mind. She gathered the small souls she had placed in a wicker basket. It was a preventive measure, the children did not need to see the antics of Fyodor, and the souls began to suckle. Jimmie Linguine was especially hungry.

"I must ask a favor," Mother Urdu said, to the slurping Jimmie Linguine. She stroked his bald head affectionately and cooed. Young Linguine rolled his eyes up and gazed into Mother Urdu's whiskered face. "You must find Loki when you return to life and give him a message. It is important." Linguine, still attached to Urdu teat nodded his little softball size head. He fell asleep and awoke clinging to the breast of his new mother Ursula, a Komatiite from Tampa Florida. It just so happened that Loki and Beatrice, fleeing the eyes of the National Islands Corporation, settled in the small, remote fishing village of Tampa. The same small village where Ursula and Jimmie lived.

Jimmie's mother was a house cleaner by profession. She had a small army of robots that did the work. His mother was a happy person, and she loved her work. She would turn her small mechanical army of cleaners loose and they would scurry around doing their programmed task. First, the dusters, then sweepers, mop robots, and polishers would work. Then the automata washers and dryers would clean and dry the clothes, finally, the servant drones would make the beds and review the robots work to make sure everything was done properly. The business thrived until sadly, Jimmie's mother had a debilitating stroke. Jimmie was fifteen years old, and he had to drop out of school to take over her business. His mother died when he was twenty. Soon after his mother's death, Jimmie met Janice. She was the meter-reader for the village of Tampa. They were married two days later.

On June 5th, at 1:57 pm, Western Standard Time Mother Urdu sent a message to Jimmie via the reborn clairvoyant Evan. Urdu said, to Evan who relayed the message to Jimmie, "Convince Loki to return Isabella's soul to me." In that instant, it became clear to Jimmie (I am sure it was Evans doing), that Loki and Beatrice, aka, Mr. Harry James, and, his ill-mannered and despicable wife, Bea James were his clients. That was, of course, convenient, he had access, via his cleaning service but, what made Jimmie's task difficult was that Mr. James was the Mayor of Tampa and his wife Bea was the diabolical Sheriff.

One would assume Jimmie would or could

The Perfect Plan

recognize Bea. They were, after all, intimate at one time, but alas, she had changed skin. Bea wanted an exterior that portrayed the true nature of Izabelle's soul. Now, Bea looked like a sixty-year-old hooker, and, she had the temperament of a wolverine.

Evan's change of heart.

Evan, in his communique with Jimmie, said that after he was murdered, his little turkey soul went straight to Mother Urdu. She explained to him how all souls have a purpose. His soul's purpose, she said, was to use his clairvoyant skills to assist other beings, both human and animal to overcome the atrocities in ones' life. She rationalized that his good deeds would ultimately win the hearts and minds of rich, white, liberals, and they —the liberals, would eventually pass civil rights laws, and put an end to the genocide of turkeys. Moreover, she said turkeys would have the right to vote.

CHAPTER 51

Izabelle's Soul

Bea's change from a personable replica to a murderous bitch was quick. As soon as Beatrice received Izabelle's soul, changes for the worst became dramatic, and naturally, Loki became apprehensive about her devilish ways. He did not share his anxiety with friends, Chaplin, or Psychologist, because he was, in his mind, at least partially to blame for placing the wrong soul into the women he loved. He attempted to fix his mistake, but none of his endeavors, including exorcism, was successful. In addition, as many of his close friends new, in many ways, Loki aka Mayor Harry James was afraid of his wife Sheriff Bea James.

Interjection: Bea went into law enforcement with the same zeal she had as a shoulder. Sheriff Bea used trumped speeding tickets to arrest and imprison out of state visitors. She held these in-

The Perfect Plan

nocent passers-by until their families could raise an outrageous amount of money for bail. Many of those rocketeers who could not pay simply disappeared. Bea impounded their aerial vehicles and sold them, in an illicit manner, to fill her personal coffers.

— Bea got her reputation as a homicidal bitch, during the war (it was a local conflict) between the Tampa Pirates, and the Lessor Company a subsidiary of the National Islands Corporation. The war only lasted twenty-seven days. The inexperienced actors and playwrights employed by the Lessor Company were just no match for the equally inexperienced but highly motivated Tampa Pirates. The only competitive force the Lessor Company had were the wrestlers, and as soon as the money stopped, the wrestlers deserted the Company to fight with the Tampa Pirates. Bea, as a Tampa Pirate, was a ruthless killer. Once her opponent was slain, She would take the man's' testicles or the women's nipples as trophies. There were even rumors of her eating the flesh of the younger actors. She claimed the charges were unfounded. An investigation conducted by the (NCoP) National Conference of Police, resulted in the dismissal of the charges based on the lack of credible evidence, or as she jokingly stated, "Edible," evidence.

I contacted Mr. Henry James at his office to schedule an appointment to clean his house, and in our conversation, I suggested we meet for tea at the Runaway Café. He accepted my invitation, and we met on the veranda. Mr. James was nothing like the Loki I remembered. He was smaller, paler, and his speech was quieter, almost a whisper. We shook hands and sat down beneath two umbrellas that looked like two enormous (size 48V) teat-cups. Henry and I sat beneath the teat-cups and enjoyed the shade. It was a blistering hot day. Henry ordered a blank sippy. I ordered a dark Morgana. My drink was refreshing. Henry rarely sipped his sippy. He seemed miserable.

"Are you okay?" I asked.

"Yes," he whispered.

"We have a common acquaintance," I said.

"Really who?"

"Mother Urdu," I said. Henry's pale face seemed to blend in with his surroundings as if he were a chameleon hiding under a canopy of leaves, or in this case teat-cups. "She has a message for you."

"What is it, the message, what does she want?" He tapped his pale fingers irritably on the table.

"Henry, she wants you to return Izabelle's soul to her," I said with more compassion than he deserved.

"Call me Loki."

"What?"

"I am Loki the trickster. Call me Loki when we speak in private."

The Perfect Plan

"Okay," I said taken aback by his candor.

"Anyway, I can't, I have tried to remove Izabelle's soul from Beatrice. To make things worse, Beatrice is a replica she will never die." I could hear the strain in the poor man's voice.

"What if we shut her down? She is a computerized replica can't you shut her down and remove her soul?"

"I do not have the expertise. I am a trickster, not an engineer," he replied.

"Then trick her," I said.

"I've never thought about that," says Loki with a pleased expression on his face.

He gazed intently at me, "Do I know you from the past?"

I did not reply.

Loki shrugged, "I will see what I can do," Loki said.

I received a call from Loki two days later. He had a plan, and it involved my assistance.

We met Wednesday night at the bowling alley. It was raining. I was soaked and frankly in a bad mood. My wife Janice had just left me for Tampa's only garbage collector, and my trash was piling up, literally and metaphorically. Loki's plan, simply put was to change himself into a bear and attack Beatrice. I would come to Bea's rescue. She, of course, would be grateful and seduce me. "I was," he said, "a handsome fellow. She has a weakness for young handsome men." He pulled on his earlobe with his left hand and continued, "And druggies, bums, sadist, and drunks, especially drunks. So be drunk when you rescue her, okay?"

"Alright," I said, "I have an urge to drink anyway."

"Tomorrow night then?" Loki said.

"Tomorrow night," I replied over the boom and bang of bowling balls and scattering pens. I left the bowling alley, which was only two blocks from my home. The rain had subsided, but the wind picked up to pre-hurricane speed. I was exhausted when I reached home and troubled. The idea of seducing Sheriff Beatrice James containing my original mother's soul disgusted me.

The next morning I called and canceled all appointments. Instead of working, I went online to study the anatomy of a Series 274 Replica. My hope of finding an easy solution crashed down upon me like a rockslide. There were three steps in shutting down a replica. First, you must probe the machines mouthparts. There is a blue button beneath the Replica's tongue. That button shuts off the electrical system. Second, there is a muff between the machine's legs. Hidden deep within the muff is a small lever that shuts down the mechanical system. The instructions said to lift the lever until the replica arches its back. Third, one must shut off the senses, i.e. sight, smell, and touch. The senses button is located in a chamber beneath the Replica's big toe. To disable the machines sensations, lift the toenail located on the right foot,

The Perfect Plan

and presses the red button. You must hold the button down for five seconds. My God I thought, this would be impossible to pull off and with that thought in mind, I began to drink.

The buzz of my communicator woke me. I had passed out and was lying on the bathroom floor. My pants were soaked. I smelled like urine. A beep sounded, and the message cracked on, "Loki here, it is time."

"Shit," I said. There was no time to clean up. I stumbled to my floater, thought about driving while intoxicated, and decided not to float. I walked or should say staggered the five blocks to Henry and Bea's residence.

I searched for the doorbell, gave up the hunt, and lifted my fist to knock. The sound of a scream startled me. I opened the door and saw Bea wrestling with a bear.

Beatrice had the bear in a chokehold. The bear's eyes were bulging. He was gasping for breath. My inebriated brain tried to think. No time, I approached Bea and the bear and swung. My fist landed squarely on the bear's nose with supreme results, I knocked his ass out. Bea immediately dropped the bear and raised her arms in a triumphant dance. It was an amazing mixture of rumba, tango, and neo-classical ballet.

With arms extended above her head, she pirouetted to me, draped her arms over my shoulders, and embraced me. Her hug was breathtaking, literally. My breath left my chest with a snakelike hiss. She maintained, nay, increased her embrace until I stopped struggling. She then planted a kiss on my bald head and released me. I collapsed on the floor along with the bear. She seized the pivotal moment and reached for the large animal. I could see, granted through blurred vision, the Replica grab one of the bear's hairy paws and with little effort, she pulled the three hundred pound monster through the door, onto the front porch, and kicked him off the precipice. He landed with a grunt on the ground and palsied there a good ten feet away.

    I passed out due to an excess of fear, or beer, or both, and awoke in Bea's muscular arms. She had exchanged her Sheriff's uniform for a see-through negligee. "There is a piss smell about you," Bea said, "I find it charming, I really do, but for the sake of sex, I would like you to be clean." Bea left for a moment. I could hear water splashing in the bathroom. She lifted me out of the bed as if I were an infant, carried me into the bathroom, disrobed me, and gently placed me in the tub. Bea scrubbed indiscriminately and harshly and paid no heed, none at all, at my pleas for mercy. Throughout the painful bath, I noticed she spent a lot of time scouring my lower torso. If it wasn't for the pain, I think I might have enjoyed the burnishing of the nub, as they say in Tampaneese.

    Back in bed, while nude, I meditated; briefly, on how in the hell I was going to pull off my mission to turn Bea off before she turns me on.

The Perfect Plan

Beatrice stiffened and stared intensely at my manhood. "Do I know you?"

"No" I quickly stated.

She smiled and said, "Sugar, I'm going to undress now."

She undressed slowly, seductively, and I noticed her searchlight nipples. I began to think of the old Bea, my friend, and at one time an aspirant lover, that Bea. Too late, too complicated, I thought and began to panic. My brain froze no ideas came to my mind. My plans of shutting down the replica became nonexistent.

"Relax sugar," she whispered.

I tried to relax, my body stiffened. "I need to pee," I said while cupping my pecker.

"Don't you be gone long sugar," Bea said.

I dashed to the bathroom and closed the door. I glanced in the mirror and found my inebriated reflection sandwiched between two Jewish characters with long sideburns and beards. I also noticed in my drunken discord, a large flat-brimmed hat that sat upon their locks of black braided hair.

One Jew, the right one, said into my right ear, "Leech infestation."

The other left Jew, said into the opposing ear, "Here in Tampa."

Both said simultaneously, "Now go."

I stumbled out of the bathroom and fell into bed with a gracious, "Sorry."

"It's okay sugar. Did you wash your hands?"

I ignored her, and said, "Do you mind if I check

your mouth, for a possible leech infestation? They have arrived in epic proportions from the west coast of Venezuela." I took a deep breath and forced a smile to appear upon my pasty face before I continued, "Nearly eighty percent of Tampa is infected," I said, almost too casually, and immediately regretted it- How insane, I thought, who would believe that load of crap?

"Sure, I would like that. Are you a Doctor?"

"Uh, why yes I am. How did you know? I..."

"Shhh," she said, "just do it." She opened her mouth wide.

"I think I see one, lift your tongue please." Bea lifted her tongue. I saw the button, a blue pearl in a clammy oyster. "Hold still," I said, reaching into her mouth, "Almost there." My finger shook as bad as an amateur magician's wand at his first magic show. I touched the top of the button and pushed, simple enough, I thought, but before I could extract my finger, Bea's mouth snapped shut. I could hear the bone crack, blood streamed down my broken finger. I saw the light go out in her eyes. The pain was horrendous. I took a breath and meditated on the remediation of my worsening predicament.

I decided to keep it positive—first step completed, now for the muff lever. I stretched my left hand, lifted her negligee, and felt for the muff. My God, I thought, thoroughly impressed by the size of her bearded mound. My second thought was the depth of this woolly mam-

The Perfect Plan

moth. If the width and breadth of her pelt was any indication of the depth, I was in trouble. My concentration changed from muff exploration to electricity when a crackling sound erupted from within Bea's head. Her eyes started to flicker. She had a backup generator located somewhere in her system. I had to hurry before she came back online. With my broken and bleeding finger still lodged in her mouth, I probed her muff with my left hand for an opening—found it! It was a little moist and frankly, I became concerned about electrocution but I decided it was too late to worry now and drove my index finger down and wagged my appendage blindly for the lever. I felt something metallic. Bea moaned, I must be close, I thought... There, there it is! I could barely reach it. I withdrew my index finger and inserted my longer middle finger. Bea's moans became repetitious. Her breathing accelerated. I knew it was now or never and with a deep extended stroke, I submerged my hand entirely into the slippery cavern, found the switch, and fiddled the lever up. Bea screamed "Ohhhh," arched her back and collapsed; then sighed as if relieved. Once again, however, I realized I had a problem. My dilemma? I could not withdraw my hand from the Venus flytrap between her legs. I began to panic and jerked my hand repeatedly, but to no avail. My hand remained wedged deep within her furry fissure.

To be honest, at that moment, I lost all hope of completing Beas shut down. How could I, with both hands trapped reach her big toe? I was flexible as a kid. I remember how I used that flexibility, especially with my feet. I would walk among the boys playing marbles and steal their marbles by grasping the spherical gems with my toes. Now, however, at my age, impossible. But wait, would it be possible for me to open Bea's toenail with my toe, press the button within, and hold the knurl for five seconds? It was worth a try. I thought with increasing confidence. I extended my foot and felt for her toes, I tried, but could not pry open her toenail. Then it dawned on me the lever according to the diagram was in the right toenail. I had been working on her left foot. With both of my hands still trapped, I began to rock back and forth until I had enough momentum to roll Bea's body over, exposing her right foot. Using my left foot, I grasped her toenail with my toes and managed to pry open her toenail, But I could not place my toe inside her toe chamber and push the button. It was futile. I began to lose hope. While pondering on the situation, I noticed Bea was wearing bobby pins, outdated. Yes, but currently the rage with older women. I managed to grab a bobby pin with my teeth and using moves not yet dreamed of by the Contortionist Willie the Rubber Man, I managed to extract, with my toes, the bobby pin I held in my mouth. I stretched my leg fully and with the pin wedged between two of my toes, I attempted to press the knob. The pin slipped off. I tried once again with the same results. I just could not man-

The Perfect Plan

age to manipulate the metal hair harnesses. I was defeated. I knew it, and I was exhausted.

"Can I help?" Loki asked. He was sitting in a dark corner on a cushioned chair. I could see the glint of his teeth. He was smiling.

"How long have you been here?" I asked.

"I arrived during the muff exploration," Loki said, and continued, "You are good."

"Press the button in her toe chamber, hold it for five seconds, and get me the Hell out of here," I said. Loki walked over to Bea's exposed toe and pushed the button. The replica shuddered and released her hold on both my hands, "Damn it Loki, I should kill you." I said. My broken finger was throbbing.

Loki found a pair of Bea's discarded panties. He spoke as he wrapped my finger, "Yes, you probably should, but we have, at this moment, the matter of extracting Izabelle's soul and releasing her to Urdu. Then we can get you to a doctor." Loki pulled out his liquid dispenser pistol, pried Bea's jaw open, and filled Bea's mouth with cocky serum. It smelled like rotten broccoli and sulfur. Izabelle's soul oozed out of Bea's ears, Loki quickly pulled a rat out of his pocket. A fitting transport for Izabelle; he thought as he lifted the rat's tail and guided the smoky substance into the rodent's ears. Loki turned himself into a flea hopped onto the rat's fur, and notified Mother Urdu with some type of electronic signal that he was ready to come home.

The rat died suddenly from hepatitis B+, and the rat's body carrying Izabelle, and Loki made its way to Urdu's Cave and Cosmic-Kinder Care Center. Urdu was standing with arms folded across her chest. She tapped her clawed toe on the stone floor angrily as Izabelle's soul arrived. Urdu immediately directed Izabelle to the wicker basket and confronted Loki who had morphed back into his original wolfish self. The two stood eyeball to eyeball, nose to nose, chest to chest. They were close, too close, old feelings started to emerge, insatiable longings, unsatisfied desires. Urdu stepped back before swooning and took a breath.

"What am I going to do with you?" Mother Urdu asked.

Loki self-directed his finger to his hairy chest. "Me?"

"Yes, you." Urdu roared

"I think forgiveness would be appropriate," he said. Urdu frowned.

"And Izabelle, such a stubborn child, what am I to do with you?" Urdu asked.

Izabelle formed a mouth within her soft dark cloud of a soul, "This is my purpose, is it not" Izabelle replied, "To create problems so other souls, the souls with a righteous purpose can succeed. If all souls were good, we would not need a purpose. We would not need to be reborn or renewed. You would prefer, Urdu, not to deal with problem children, huh. It is hard to love the bad,

The Perfect Plan

the evil, the immoral, the revolting. I can see it in your eyes every time I come back you have a sad look."

Breathe.

Mother Urdu's eyes became a fountainhead for the sadness she felt. It was true. It was difficult to love evil. Urdu understood Izabelle's dilemma.

"I did not ask for this purpose." Izabelle continued, "It was not my choice."

Tears came to Mother Urdu. She shuddered as the tears surged down her hairy jowls and splashed over the reincarnates at her feet. The great mother reached down and picked up Izabelle's small soul, embraced the darkling; then placed the nefarious essence of anger on a teat—the small one the one farthest from Urdu's heart.

"I am reminded," Loki says, "of a thesis written by the Theologian Dr. Peter Bellhad, in it, he states, 'Doing is the process of digesting life, and suffering is the malady of life's constipation,'" Loki placed his hand over his heart, and pointed toward the ceiling, "And happiness is like a bowel movement—a release, if you will." Urdu sustained a puzzled look on her face long after Loki had retired to the kitchen. He had hatched a plan for rewinning Urdu's heart with an extravagant meal.

Mother Urdu went to the wicker basket retrieved all the little souls and began to nurse. Urdu found comfort in nursing as many women do.

Donald D'lo

Interjection: Relevant research.

The following information, recorded in the NIC awareness room claims the NIC is no longer involved in a theatrical war. General Alexander has declared *actual war* on the GFP.

Section IV

Back to the Campaign

CHAPTER 52

Alice and the NIC Purges

Roughly, seven thousand people participated in the (GFP) Global Freedom Party's Primary; almost all voters were from the state of New Hampshire. Whereas George A. Lucas the incumbent President of the National Island Corporation had one hundred thousand, (more or less), people brought in from purge camps outside New Hampshire and forced them to vote for the NIC. The corporation purged many of the voters as soon as they cast their ballot.

E.W. Pile, the Texas history professor became the GFP candidate. Martinez commented to me as we sat in the mechanical closet playing Pernude on a computerized tee ball screen. "George A. Lucas has a dominating persona. It will be difficult to win the election with a shy candidate like Mr. Pile."

I agreed with a nod and threw a Hail Marry.

The Perfect Plan

Miguel intercepted the pass, "Damn," I said, "let's get back to work."

"You go first," Miguel said. "It will look funny if we leave together."

I opened the closet door, looked around the office, it was empty and stepped out into the light. Miguel followed a few minutes later. He sat at his desk. I sat at mine, and together over a secure cognizance device, we planned our strategy. I was going to disclose the Purges. Miguel was going after the NIC's wealth.

I arrived in Stanford dressed in my now famous clown suit. I obtained a pass as a political organizer to meet the NIC's Regional Director and General of the NIC military forces. His name was Faience Comings IV (nicknamed Alexander). He was sitting at his desk reviewing the latest election schematic. "How is the election going?" I asked while striding to his desk. Alexander smiled. I noticed part of his ear was missing, "The incumbent President George A. Lucas is ahead by three thousand six hundred cities." He stood, and we shook hands. "How can I help you Mr.?"

"Linguine," I said

"What can I do for you Mr. Linguine?"

"I would like to work, as a volunteer for Mr. Lucas," I said.

Alexander looked at my costume, "Why the clown suit?"

"It is a way-umm—how should I put this, a way to get noticed. I want people to remember me, and, uh, of course, the NIC's candidate Mr. Lucas."

"Oh, I see," Alexander, said, "what position are you interested in?"

"Well, I am a reporter by trade. I would like to document the life and times of George A. Lucas. Perhaps make a commercial or documentary—you know something like that."

"Sounds interesting," Alexander said, "I'll talk it over with George and get back to you."

"Great," I said. I removed a personal identifier card out of my wallet and handed it to Alexander. As he was scrutinizing the card, I glanced at a paper lying on his desk. The paper appeared to be from Alexander written for a military officer named Major Joe Cabinet, it read,

— Certain that President Lucas will win the election, our largest city, Washington, DC hired six-hundred Purge Masters. The homeless and underemployed population in Washington is well over eighty percent and growing, and—

I could not read the remainder of the text, due to the placement of Alexander's hand.

"Okay, I'll do a background check and give you a call," Alexander said.

"Great," I replied.

With the consent and financial backing of the GFP, I boarded the first available flight to Washington D.C. The purpose of my trip was to find my contact and record the purging. It began to rain

The Perfect Plan

mid-flight. I fell asleep and began to dream. My dreams, labeled by the renowned psychologist Dr. Cat Divan's were reminiscence dreams of my numerous deaths. The first dream took place during what I call the primitive period, 0 through 1100 BC. It was November 27, 1095, and the Seljuk Turks had taken control of Jerusalem. Pope Urban II had just given his rousing speech calling on all Europeans wishing to cleanse their sins to march on the infidels and retake Jerusalem. I of course at the age of twenty-nine was loaded with guilt. There were among many raucous situations the infamous virgin incident and brothel incident as well. Not wishing to die at the hands of her, (the so-called virgins,) father, I volunteered to fight the infidels. My services due to a neck injury lasted only a year. I will not speak of the neck injury as it is a sensitive matter involving seven women and two stray cats. Anyway, I was sailing home on a ship full of injured soldiers when a great storm came from the east and sunk the ship. Coincidently, I also died, due to bad weather, on the same month and day in 1703. A great storm hit England killing ten to twenty thousand people. I was bedding an African woman at the time. I was on my back cushioned by a grass mat. She astride me, doing the pogo on my pecker when a thunderbolt struck. The lightning hit her, traveled down her body, and fried my ass; left me a smoking pool of goo. As my soul departed my body, I noticed my African friend had survived. I guess my body was a ground for the electrical current. The shock, however, had frizzed her hair into a magnificent afro. She was so beautiful.

A brilliant flash of lightning followed by a boom of thunder woke me from my dream. I was startled, and yelled, "Japura." My fellow passengers disquieted by my outcry mumbled obscenities, nevertheless, I ignored them and thought only of my lovely African lover, Japura.

The rain dwindled to a fine mist as we landed at the D.C. Airport. A porter-bot met me at the terminal and drove me to a cheap hotel across the street from the west side purging station. I lay in bed for an hour or so listening to the purging pumps squash and grind bodies until exhausted, I drifted off to sleep. A loud whistle woke me the next morning. The blast indicated an end of the night shift and the beginning of the day shift. I watched from my second-story window as the workers, wild as ants and ostensibly mad pushed and shoved each other through a narrow corridor, some going to work while others were getting off work, those leaving scurried quickly away. Those arriving were as stiff as Zombies. I left the apartment at 9 a.m. and went casually to the candy store where I purchased a stock of licorice. From there I went to the theater and witnessed the premiere of Wonderland, an optimist movie about the future. I arrived back at my apartment at 3:43 and polished my monocle for a little less than an hour. It was getting late, and I turned my

The Perfect Plan

attention to the matter at hand. The GFP provided me with a picture of my contact. She worked the day shift. Her name was Alice. I left my room and waited at the gate of the purge building for the day shift to exit. Soon after the metal mouth screamed a high gas filled falsetto, the workers started to jostle their way out. I recognized a young woman from the photo and grabbed her arm as she rounded the corner. "Pardon me," I said.

She pulled away and asked in an angry tone, "What do you want?"

I fluffed the purple collar of my clown suit, smiled, and said, "I want to talk to you about work."

"No," she said emphatically, and turned quickly to leave,

"I'll give you a coupon," I said.

She turned to face me, "Let me see it."

I pulled the bill out of my pocket. A slight breeze made the paper flutter enticingly. "Are you hungry?" I asked.

She glanced around for anything suspicious; then focused on me, "I like your outfit," she graciously said. Alice paused for a moment before continuing. "And, yes, I am hungry."

"Great, I know a nice little restaurant down the street," I said. "Would you like to join me?"

"Sure," she said. We began to walk, "My name is Alice," she said.

"Linguine," I said and extended my hand. She glanced briefly at my powdered hand without extending her own. She remained silent until we reached the Born-Again Restaurant. I opened the door and followed her inside. She picked a table beside the front window. I pulled out the chair for her. She sat.

I sat across from her, and said, "Where are you from?"

"I grew up in Spud Idaho," she replied.

I turned my head to search for the waiter, and said through the corner of my mouth, "Any family?"

"No," she said, "My mother, and I were caught by the NIC employment detectives... We escaped once, but my mother was caught again and," Alice began to cry. "She was purged a few years ago."

"Sorry..."

The waiter interrupted our conversation, "What'll you have?"

"Better Burger, spuds, and a chocolate," I said.

"Make that two," Alice injected. She smiled at the server, a slim muscular man with huge ears and a sharp angular nose. He returned her smile displaying dingy rodent-like teeth. She turned at the site of them, surrounded her mouth with her hands and whispered, "Holly crap, its Rat Man."

I chuckled and glanced out the window at the people passing on the sidewalk. "What's it like in there?" I asked still focused on the pedestrians.

"Horrible," she said, "just horrible. They murdered one-hundred-fifty-six people during my shift today."

The Perfect Plan

"Why do you work at a Purge Factory?"

"It is better to work there than to be there." Her eyes enlarged. I could see her green irises beneath the umbrella of her eyelashes. A blush surfaced from the capillaries in her cheeks, and I suddenly had the urge to kiss her.

The food arrived. I raised my monocle to inspect the meal. She did not hesitate and ate the burger and fries with the gusto of a Tibetan Monk after a seven-day fast. I ate my burger and a few fries. She finished well before I did, but did not seem satiated. I gave her the remainder of my fries and she wolfed them down without pausing to speak or even breathe properly. When she had finished and began to breathe normally I said, "Alice, I am a reporter. I want to learn as much about purging as I can. I want to find a way to stop this murderous process. I want to stop the National Island Corporation from killing people. Can you help?"

"You are ambitious for a clown," she said.

"Not really," I said and fixed my gaze firmly on my guest. "Alice, was your mother Brenda Lee Leigh?"

The rosy blush drained leaving a pasty white on her face. "How did you know?"

"Our investigators learned of you and your mother from a source in Spud Idaho. I cannot reveal the person's name. We do not know any details about your escape from the West Target Holding Compound, nor do we know how you got to Washington D.C. Can you tell me?"

Alice sighed, "A man named Loki, his two assassins, and a red-headed woman purged Blind Betty and her unborn child. Instead of killing us, the two men placed Mother and me in body bags and put us on a cruiser. We were flown to D.C. and released in the Portabella Slums."

"Why didn't they kill you and your mother too?" I asked.

"I don't know. I think they got what they wanted from Betty, and did not need us, but I do not know for sure. We were here for a month when the NIC took my mother." Alice began to cry. "I had to go to work or starve—or worse, be purged." She said.

I wiped tears from her cheek, "Alice, the NIC is sending more Purgers to Washington I need to stop them. I need to get inside the factory and film the murders of these poor people. I need to let the world know what is going on here. Can you help?"

"I can slip you in the back door if you can climb the fence unnoticed." She said.

"What time?"

"Seven."

"Okay, I'll be there. May I walk you home?"

"No, thank you," she said.

"Okay, see you tomorrow," I said.

I notified the office of our plans to film the purging process; then attempted to connect with the reincarnated turkey, and converted liberal, my friend, Evan. He did not answer, so I left a message.

The Perfect Plan

He replied thusly, in antiquated Morris Code. *I am on the crapper. Stop... Cannot talk now. Stop... Will talk later. Stop...* I waited patiently at the café for his return message. It never came.

The next day I decided to leave my clown suit behind. My shoes would hinder my fence scaling abilities, and I must admit purple and pink colors are not advantageous blends in today's popular camouflage schemes. I arrived at the back door of the building carrying my lunch, (summer sausage sandwich), nose camera, and Taser. The time? Exactly seven o: clock. The door opened slightly, Alice stuck her head out of the back door and looked both ways. "All clear," She said and fully opened the door. I entered the dark interior. She provided me with a red and white striped company uniform. I watched her watch me undress. She seemed fixated on my sausage. I stored the information in my memory banks for other possible adventures; placed the taser in my pocket and with Alice by my side, slipped off into the bowels of the wretched building.

We passed the cafeteria and rounded the corner to the killing room. Alice whispered, "The NIC at one point used gas to kill its clients. Now, due to cost-saving measures, and Loki's illegal use of the gas chamber, asphyxiation via plastic bag is the current modus operandi." We stopped at the viewing window, "Once dead," she said, "the body is placed on the conveyor." She pointed to a canvas conveyor belt. "The dead stop at the hair removal department. That is where I work. After we clip the hair, the body travels by conveyor to the protein department where the cadaver is liquefied and its protein is extracted. The hair goes to the clothing factory, and the protein goes to the food factory."

As I was filming through my nose camera, I saw, to my horror, Beatrice the replica. She was folding affixation bags and neatly stacking them in a closet. I was in the open. I turned my back on Beatrice closed my eyes and hoped for the best. I felt her cold breath on my neck, I heard her whisper, "Jimmie is that you?" I turned to face her. She was smiling. "It is you. They told me you would be here?" She must have seen the terror on my face. She grabbed my elbow leaving Alice standing in front of the liquefaction chamber and pulled me into a quiet alcove. It smelled like excrement. I think it was mine. "Didn't they tell you?" she asked.

"Tell me what?" I said. "What the Hell are you doing here?"

She rolled her eyes, "Loki insisted the GFP reactivate and reprogram me to be a guardian—your guardian."

"My guardian, no one told me, besides, I don't need a guardian," I said.

Someone screamed. I recognized the voice it was Alice. I dashed toward the sound of her scream. A large man had her in a bear hug.

"What do you want? ... Stop." It was Evan.

The Perfect Plan

"Not now Evan, I'm busy," I said.

"Well, you called me... Stop."

"Will you please stop with the stop," I said.

"Jimmie?"

"Yes?"

"Call me back when you feel the time is right. Oh, by the way, the Lemmings are on their suicide run in Alaska, would you like to see them commit suicide? Stop."

"Not now," I yelled and turned in time to see a huge hairy knuckled fist headed straight for my nose. Beatrice interceded. She grabbed the man's arm and slung him across the room.

"Well, you don't have to be rude... Stop"

"Stop," I screamed.

Beatrice looked at me queerly, "Seriously?"

"Not you," I said.

She shook her head in disbelief, and said, "Okay Jimmie, you go rescue, Alice." I danced toward the attacker and positioned myself before him in a boxer stance. He released Alice and began his approach with murderous intent. Sirens were going off. I knew I had little time. He swung. I ducked and turned my body aggressively to the right. I threw an uppercut. The punch landed solidly on his testicles. I could fill them enter his belly cavity. They did not come out. He was done. Beatrice, with me and Alice in tow, made it to the back door. She broke through the door, ripped a hole in the perimeter fence and we escaped.

"Jimmie," Evan said. "Are you mad at me? ...

Stop."

"I'll get back with you Evan. I am really busy right now."

"Who are you talking too?" Bea asked. I shrugged my shoulders and did not answer her question. "Follow me," she commanded. We dashed, ducked, and darted to 110 N. Birmingham Street. The door was open when we got there. The door closed as soon as we entered. It was dark. We waited. No one spoke, not even Evan.

CHAPTER 53

The Decision to Attack

It was dark. We waited. The silence, I believe was appropriate, but when taciturnity is maintained, especially during periods of stress, it can be nerve-racking. "No one move, they are here," Bea whispered from the darkness. Then I heard the sound of footsteps retreating. I was on the verge of a nervous breakdown. I clasped my hand over my mouth to keep from calling out. Suddenly, the front door opened, and I saw before me a muscular semi-clad, light-skinned woman with a large finger bone inserted into her nose. She looked strangely familiar, but I could not due to my fragile mental condition, place her, perhaps Lebanon or Dallas, definitely not Chicago, I thought.

She moved like a cat. A loincloth girded her hips, and stuck within her diaper, something as long as... well at first glance, I thought it was a pecker, but upon second glance, I saw the sharpened edge of a knife. A few stray pubic hairs skirted the bloody blade. I was intrigued and aroused by the site of her felinity. So much so that I failed to notice the bloody bodies of several men lying behind her, "Come," she said. We followed the young woman to the edge of an overgrown lot where the skeleton of a five-story building leaned dangerously over an ancient highway. She made us squat behind an abandoned buss-mobile and wait. It was not long before a floater arrived, and we boarded the craft. We departed hastily from Washington and arrived at Delphi's headquarters in the Second State of New Hampshire. Our hero, I learned mid-flight was a Muskeg warrior named Comica.

After we landed, a guard took Alice and Beatrice to a winery where they were debriefed. Comica escorted me to the Theatre Room where I downloaded my nose camera into a secure computablet. Delphi viewed the film personally. I sat on his left, Comica sat on his right. I could not help but stare at her then it came to me, (I recognized the finger bone in her nose). She was in Delphi's office when we had the teleconference. She— Delphi interrupted my thoughts-

"It has begun," Delphi, said, "We will attack the NIC Purge Building, and free the people. We will shut down their clothing manufacturing system as well as their food production. Most importantly, we will stop the killing." We left the theater room, Alice and Beatrice sat quietly in the winery room.

"What's going on?" Alice asked as we entered.

"We will fly back to Washington D. C. tomorrow. Alexander must be removed, and the Purge Building destroyed," I said, "but for now we rest."

A robotic orderly entered the waiting room, "Follow me," it said, "I will take you to your bedchambers."

We followed the robot to the elevators and entered the sliding doors. After a second or two we jerked to a stop. The robot led us to room 710. "This is your room, Jimmie." The robot gave me a card. I opened the door and stepped inside. Beatrice stepped with me.

"Whoa," I said, "This is my room."

"I am your guardian, we go together," she said.

I shrugged, and docilely said, "Okay."

The robot led Alice to the adjoining room. I watched as Alice entered her room.

Beatrice giggled and flung her red hair aside, "I have competition," she said.

I had a sudden and immediate flashback to Tampa. There I was sprawled naked on the bed, with one hand in Bea's mouth and the other hand lodged in her warm wet muff. I wonder... (The thought buzzed in my head like a ravenous insect), if she, as a guardian served her master in both security and pleasure. The thought was, I must admit, appealing. Oh, forget it I said to myself, I prefer Alice. It was not, however, a convincing statement. For some odd, reason my finger, now healed from the break, ached, not from pain, as I had imagined, but from longing.

An announcement blasted over the intercom, "Lights out at 9 p.m." It was 8:52. I climbed into bed the lights went out. Bea giggled as she snuggled next to me. I must have fallen asleep. The intercom voice reverberated through the building "Rise and shine. Chow in thirty, don't be late." I stretched. Bea stretched. I yawned, and she yawned, I scratched my balls, she scratched my balls. We smiled. I was surprised to find my clown suit folded neatly on the dresser. I donned my outfit and admired myself in the mirror. Bea dressed in combat fatigues and boots looked threatening. The two of us marched to the elevators and went to the basement where the mess hall was located. After breakfast, we went to the Theater Room and watched a motivational video.

Commander Don David Dusseldorf, a man of average intelligence, height, weight and shoe size, assigned Bea and me to the Section One 7th Air Calvary. We were to storm the Purge Building and free the employees. My specific job was to report on the action and provide a video feed to headquarters.

After the employees were free, Section 2 and 3 were responsible for the destruction of the food and clothing factories. Section 5 and 6 were assigned the difficult task of destroying General Alexander's Headquarters and capturing Alexan-

The Perfect Plan

der, if possible

We arrived at the D. C. Purge Building at seven a.m. propelled out of our floaters with mini-guides and entered the building with little resistance. There were a few robotic snipers scattered throughout the building, but nothing of great concern.

What we found in the gymnasium was horrifying. The remaining employees had plastic bags over their heads. Their grisly blue faces, with bulging eyes, and mouths open in silent screams were horrifying. I filmed as much as I could, but honestly, it was too much. I puked.

Bea sat me down in a dark corner, massaged my neck with a warm wet wobbler, and provided me with a vile of water. Her treatment relieved the symptoms, but the cause of my illness, the horrible visions, remained.

As Bea and I sat in the corner, an announcement came over our military communicator that the building had been secured but Alexander had escaped. The communicator also reported the National Island Corporation's airships were missing which led me to believe General Alexander and his men left for the Second Elected Confederacy Headquarters of Poland.

CHAPTER 54

The Black Ops Corporation Becomes Involved in the Conflict

Sam Merchant ate an under-cooked Chicago Dog prepared by the dirty-handed, cook, Ralph. An investigation of Mr. Merchant's death by a member of the state board of health found a hybrid parasitic protozoan Toxoplasma Gondi in Sam's partially eaten hot dog. Ralph's cat, Peach Fuzz was determined, to be the cause of the contamination. It was the cat's caca, shit, or poop—whatever the current politically correct term for shit is that contaminated the weeny. A week before he died, Sam got on the horn with General Alexander and offered his services as a weapons provider. For the modest sum of a billion coupons, Sam was willing to increase Alexander's arsenal by an astonishing 100%.

Alexander purchased the majority of the Black Ops stocks, took out a life insurance pol-

The Perfect Plan

icy on Sam Merchant for the negotiated price of seven-hundred-million coupons for the armaments. It was a done deal. Transportation of the equipment began immediately. The Second Elected Confederacy Headquarters of Poland received all the armaments within a week. Sam Merchant died from complications of the Toxoplasma Gondi protozoa. His bowels ruptured while he was on the skip (an audio-visual medical device) with his Doctor.

Ralph the cook somehow became a very wealthy man. The first hundred coupons he spent on Peach Fuzz. He purchased a fast food franchise with the remaining, two-hundred-seven coupons.

Interjection: Sam Merchant is the great, great grandson of David Dennison Merchant, a billionaire arms manufacturer who rose to fame in the Turkey Crises by selling weapons to underage hunters. Sam, a self-proclaimed profiteer, went on to expand his great, great grandfather's empire by manufacturing military grade traditional, and nuclear weapons.

Interjection: Stereopticon evidence:

Scripter 1 provided the research to determine the source of Ralph's wealth:

First, Scripter 1 sprinkled tea-leaves in her tea and read the floating arrangement. She surmised the leaves suggested she should use her investigative skills to obtain the desired information. She in the guise of a whore went undercover with Ralph's bookkeeper and coaxed him with manipulative fingers and lips into spewing among other things a wealth of information

— Delphi, aware of the transaction, unfortunately, lacked the resources or manpower to stop, or even impede, delivery of the weaponry. His only option was stealth, which meant utilizing the Muskeg.

CHAPTER 55

Mother Urdu returns Izabelle's soul to the world

Whether Mother Urdu intentionally placed Izabelle's soul in this particular child, will possibly, remain a mystery. Some people, who knew Urdu well, claimed that placing Izabelle's soul in the Muskeg infant was deliberate. Others believed it was coincidental. The majority of those who thought Mother Urdu did it intentionally also believed Loki played a significant part in her decision. Perhaps Mother Urdu or Loki, or both, thought that the influence of culture, especially the Muskeg's stringent tribal culture, could transform a rotten soul. At any rate, it was a gamble, a very large gamble.

Regardless of intent, the woman, Aria, a Muskeg priestess, gave birth to Comica, the proprietor of Izabelle's soul. The muskegs were a matriarchal society, descended according to current mythology from Burdon, Urdu's half-sister.

Men in this society were the homemakers. They rarely left the village and only took on the role of providers when their wives were in the last trimester of pregnancy. The Muskeg women were Fishermen primarily but had to learn new skills when the polluted oceans began to die. Their first adaptation was as recyclers of plastic. The women harvested plastic from the oceans instead of fish, reformed the plastic, and used it as a building material. The entire village, including the streets of Torreon, Comica's birthplace, was made of plastic. It was not long, however before the large, greedy Corporations, saw the potential for wealth in the recycling industry, and began to compete with the Muskegs. The corporations sold their harvested plastic below market and effectively shut down the Muskegs economy.

Due to the disastrous effect of corporate induced starvation, Aria took the initiative to learn another trade, one that would allow her tribe to retaliate against the corporations and still earn income. She wanted to learn the art of war under Hesper, the ancient Muskeg God of Combat. Aria believed Hesper lived in the Malanda Jungle on the banks of the Pigeon River. She left her child Comica with her husband Steve, trekked seven-hundred miles to the mouth of the Pigeon River, built a plastic canoe from the discarded plastic bottles trapped in an inland sea, and began her trip upstream. Ten days later, she found evidence of life. A single building sat on top of a lofty hill. The structure, constructed from wood was approximately ten meters long and ten meters wide. The roof, unlike Torreon's domed roofs, was pitched and covered with wood shingles. The residence painted red stood in stark contrast to the lush green forest surrounding it. No windows were visible and only a single opening allowed access to the buildings dark interior.

Aria heard an unfamiliar noise and briskly stopped at the buildings shadowed entrance. A large bird rushed out to meet her. It was a turkey. The turkey spread its massive tail, wobbled its blue-red head, shook its beard, inflated its chest, gobbled, and began to dance. "My name is Evan," the turkey said telepathically.

"I'm looking for Hesper, the God of War," Aria replied.

"Hesper is gone."

"Gone where?"

"A woman claimed Hesper some time back —forced him to marry her; got her pregnant you know, beautiful ceremony, I was his best friend. Hesper is a domestic now, no more fighting. He only cooks and cleans."

"Oh my," said Aria, "What is your name?"

"Evan."

"Tell me where he is Evan."

"I cannot. I do not know."

"Can you communicate with him? If so, tell him the Muskegs of Torreon needs his help. We need to learn how to fight the Corporations."

Evan paused his dance routine and silently communicated with Hesper. He shook his head as if in agreement with his friend, looked optimistically at the sky, and said, "Hesper said no."

"Oh, what shall I do?" Aria said, pretending to wipe a tear from her eye.

Evan gobbled gleefully, and communicated once again via thought waves to Aria, "I know a thing or two about war. Fought in the Thanksgiving Revolts of 1972 and 2025 among other small and large conflicts. I confess, I disavowed war in favor of the liberal pacifist movement, but no more, I see a radiant future in conflict. I will help you, but you must agree to bring me your child Comica. I will personally train her in the strategies of warfare."

"How do you know about Comica?" Aria asked.

"A little bird told me." Evan shuffled his feet. He stopped abruptly and said, "Actually Mr. Stork told me." Evan chuckled, as he imagined his drinking buddy the stork carrying a diapered baby in his lance-like beak.

Aria thought for a moment, "First you must prove to me you are qualified. Tell me how we can fight the corporations."

Evan ruffled his feathers and perched beside Aria who had sat down on a fallen log. He crossed his thin legs. Aria noticed his dirty toenails. "You must become assassins," Evan said, "Hesper will train you, and you can train your people."

"But," Aria interrupted, "You said he would not help."

"Leave Hesper to me. I will convince him of your urgent need to kill the greedy Corporations. Comica will remain with me and I will train her in tactics used by myself, and others in surreptitious warfare. We call this type of fighting Soft Target Intrusion."

Aria, without other options, reluctantly agreed and returned to Torreon to retrieve Comica, now four months old, She returned to Malanda with the child strapped to her back in a plastic five-gallon bucket.

Evan sat on his front porch swing. He was swinging and telepathically singing the song *I Met Her at the Library* to an old hen friend in Paxton New Jersey when he spied Aria approaching down the worn path. Evan stopped singing and placed his splayed toes on the ground to stop swinging, "Let me see the child." Aria placed the bucket containing Comica at Evan's feet. Evan twisted his neck and gawked at the baby first with his left eye then with his right eye. He chuckled and said, "Coochie Coo," as he tickled the child with his wing feathers. Evan looked at Aria, "I took the liberty to barter with Hesper on your behalf. He has agreed to train you if you take over the domestic chores. He needs to feel manly, you know," Evan said.

Aria wagged her finger in front of Evan, grabbed the bucket and baby, backed slowly off the porch, and spat upon the ground. "I will be no one's domestic," she said.

Evan cocked his blue-red face sideways. His finger long red snood fell over his right eye as he eyed the phlegm. The wad of spit reminded him of watery goose shit, "Fine leave. Be on your way woman." He shuffled his feet (being careful not to step on the spit), threw out his chest, and gobbled. It was a mocking sort of chuckle. Aria pulled a knife out of the scabbard attached to her loincloth. Evan pulled a gun from a shoulder holster beneath his wing. "Do you want help or not?" Evan waved the gun unsteadily. He had put on weight and he found it difficult to balance his rotund body on one foot while aiming the pistol with his other long-toed foot.

Aria considered her options carefully and returned her knife to its sheath. She was upset. "So I will be a servant to Hesper?"

"You could say that," Evan paused as if he was communicating with someone else. "Just while you are in training," he continued.

"Okay, I'll do it, she said."

Evan returned his gun to its holster and shook his leg to remove the cramp that had seized his thigh. A man dressed in camouflage green stepped out of the red house carrying a mop and broom. "You can start by cleaning the floor." Hesper laughed. "Then you can cook breakfast."

"Where's your wife?" Aria asked.

"Oh, she left me. She said I couldn't cook or

clean imagine that me failing as a domestic." Hesper chuckled.

Evan gobbled in turkey laughter.

Aria's schedule was rigorous. She was up at four a.m., chopped firewood until five, made breakfast, and was in the field training by six. She remained in the combat arena studying martial arts until three in the afternoon, ate a small meal of potato skins and water, and then studied weaponry. Aria spent her nights practicing stealth. She slept for six hours and resumed the same schedule at four the next morning. This went on seven days a week, for three years. On Saturday, June 1st, her birthday, Hesper gave Aria a week supply of spud- skins and sent her back to Torreon with a domestic diploma for her housework and a killing degree for her combat skills. The child, Comica, remained at Malanda studying war with Evan. On Comica's seventeenth birthday, Evan summarized his fighting philosophy before sending the teenager to her mother in Torreon.

Evans Soft Target Intrusion Philosophy

Evan realized the IFF and independent clans like the Muskegs could not face the NIC head on. He suggested every man, woman, and Muskeg child, is responsible for their own personal warfare against the corporations. He gave examples. Hit soft targets, like corporate shareholders at shopping centers, factories; especially purge buildings, even target transportation vehicles, and corporate schools and theaters, all he insisted are fair game. The premise, he stated was simple, the Muskeg people must generate enough hatred to kill anyone affiliated with the corporations and destroy them, the enemy, without remorse. This he explained, will weaken the NIC, drain it of its profits, and make it vulnerable to attack.

CHAPTER 56

Comica and Linguine, the first meeting

Roberta Flannigan was three months pregnant when she read *The Modern Writings of J. P. Lovejoy*. She was interested in his research into reincarnation. Lovejoy's discovery of the phenomenon of Cellular Memory, which, according to his findings, indicates historical data are recorded in each human being's cells and the person's body, uses these hidden codes to advance oneself on the road to rectitude.

Linguine meditated during his journey, traveling by coach, (he was three months into a nine-month journey) to meet his new mother. He deliberated on the reasons for a rebirth. He believed, deep down in his pea-sized heart, that people are reborn in a series of independent performances to achieve ascension, as Christ must have done, to be one with the universe. The developing infant's newfound knowledge lodged itself into his recently formed intellect and waited in his illuminated processing chamber for the results. Jimmie's conclusion was that each of our past lives assigns a DNA-like code during rebirth. This code, Linguine labeled, AS-MaN, upgrades with every reincarnation. It carries our past and present experiences, which, inevitably, will be the building blocks of our immediate and extended destinies. Once our purpose is complete, we will begin again and continue until we are perfectly defined, and absorbed in the cosmos... However, there was a lingering, unanswered, perhaps unanswerable contradiction in Jimmie's hypothesis. Not all people improve; some people like his first birth mother Izabelle was born evil and remained that way. He hoped his new mother would be a good person.

Roberta Flannigan, Jimmie's 'new' mother, was a street hustler, a con artist, and a thief. She avoided the purging process by becoming a mistress to a wealthy NIC shareholder named J. B. Tennyson. Roberta lived on the streets but received night privileges at Tennyson's mansion. Tennyson, a petite man accustomed to wearing an elevator shoe on his right foot and a flip-flop on his left, had a small room in the basement, made available to Roberta for the purpose of sexual favors. Once pregnant (with Jimmie), however, the room became convenient for the dramaturgy of fellatio, which Tennyson thoroughly enjoyed. However, that soon changed when Roberta developed a fear of coconuts and cucumbers. Roberta choked on a cucumber while practicing fellatio, and simultaneously juggling coconuts. Unfortunately, for her, she developed a tubular and testicular, careerending, phobia.

Twenty-one Years Later, a Prelude.

Roberta managed to stay on at the Tennyson Mansion as a house servant specializing in flagellation. She considered herself an actor playing the part of Lash Larios, a nude cowgirl whipping nude cowboys on stage in front of a handful of people, including Tennyson who sat in a reserved seat in the front row. Roberta, however, wanted to take her career in a new direction. She wanted legitimacy. She wanted to play on the big stage. That is how Jimmie got involved in acting. He was good at playing a clown and became the featured actor in the play *Up is the New Down.* His mother had a small part as a nude dancer. She, metaphorically, represented the pitfalls of being happy.

Now, here is where things get ugly. The production manager, Charles de Lessor, loathed Linguine, whose wardrobe, by the way, was fantastic. Charles with a snub of his nose said how much he despised Jimmie the Clown that night at an open mike event during the board meeting. J.B. Tennyson just happened to be there with his escort a six foot six Muskeg woman dressed in high heels and a fashionable loincloth.

Charles, having had too many sips from a bottle of Bees Beer, whistled into the speaker cone and began to mutter. "Mr. Linguine here," he shook a finger in Jimmie's direction, "Thinks himself a clown—takes pride in it, one would assume by the way he is dressed in that ridiculous costume. The clown, in my opinion, is a mixed bag of elevated hope, perishable dreams, and uncontrolled emotions." Charles took a sip of beer, wiped his mouth with the sleeve of his shirt, and continued. "The clown delights us with his exaggerated moods, embarrassing sobs, and exhilarated laughter. When given a horn to blow, he becomes an antiquated nuisance." Charles pleased with his rhetoric danced around the speaker cone. Jimmie contrariwise scratched his bald head beneath his wig and glared at the dancing toastmaster.

Charles continued to ramble, "The clown is, some would say, a toy for the conventional person to play with then discard without attachment." Jimmie blushed and squirmed on his stool.

Charles raised his voice reaching the lower scale of a soprano, "He lacks the strength of mind for serious thoughts and intellectual communication. He is the last ass of a long line of asses that sprang from, his mother, Roberta's womb."

Jimmie suddenly and unexpectedly stepped away from his stool, aimed the tulip flower pinned to the lapel of his jacket, and squirted Charles De Lessor in the face with Loki's cocky serum. No one knows how Jimmie got the serum. It smelled like rotten broccoli and sulfur. Charles' face began to form as a tiny baby-faced cloud. The cloud ascended to the ceiling and dissipated like rain upon the crowd. The remainder of De Lessor's body fell to the floor. At that moment of awe and utter silence, Comica slashed J. B. Tennyson's throat.

That is when the board members made a mad, hysterical dash for the exit. Two people were killed another seven injured during the frenzied sprint for freedom. Comica and Jimmie in self-defense, also hauled ass, each headed in a different direction.

These acts of violence premeditated by Comica, and aleatory by Jimmie, were the prelude to the Symbolist Campaign.

CHAPTER 57

The Threat

I relieved myself of two days of accumulated waste, stood with an air of disbelief, stared at the product a minute or two, and then flushed. I waddled to the entertainment chamber and sat beside Bemire. He was scanning for intruders on his spyware. He stopped, leaned into the viewer with keen interest, I mirrored his movement, we both exclaimed in unison, "Elvira!"

Elvira and Hatton were aboard a floater, "Damn you Linguine, you too Bemire, I thought we had a thing going on." Her face distorted by the spyware appeared conflated.

Hatton's voice echoed from within his hat, "Damn you, all of you."

The munchkin placed his hand on top of his stovepipe hat and jumped up and down as if he were an angry toddler. Then with an assumed facial gesticulation of anger, he posed a question to

The Perfect Plan

Elvira, "Why were you screwing those two?" She whispered something. The words were inaudible.

Then they delivered a rehearsed message, in finger sign, accompanied by a clamorous duet delivered in the flat of B major, "We are coming to get you SOB's—both of you!"

Section V

The short-lived Election, and Jimmie's Postmodern Candidacy

CHAPTER 58

The Election

There was only one Primary, in Concord. The primary, held at the Take-Down Wrestling Arena, held eighty spectators. The GFP would broadcast the event over the entire world, including the tiny island of Farrer and the swampy lands of the Muskeg. The Coliseum doors opened at one O: clock. Peewee Cotton was the promoter. The Global Freedom Party provided free food for the attendees. Possible voters filled the arena by three p.m. The speeches began at four. I in my clown suit was the moderator. There were three candidates, Charles Monroe, Cremorne Udder, and an unlikely candidate from Texas, Ernest William Pile. The speeches were brief and spectacularly boring. The event ended at five and people from around the world began to cast their ballots. The results were in by ten that night. The announcement came at seven O: clock the next morning while E.W. Pile was soaking his swollen hemorrhoids in hot bath salts. The news delivered nationally over public stereopticon confirmed E. W. Pile, was the presidential candidate for the Global Freedom Party. The broadcaster went on to say, "It was a low turnout; forty-two votes from within the Take-Down arena and only seven votes came from outside the arena. The stadium voters split their votes equally between the three candidates. All votes from outside the stadium were from Texas, and all were for E.W. Pile."

Cotton immediately went to work for the Pile campaign. Using clips from my nose cam videos, he provided images of the purges, and of our attempted murder. The videos streamed over every credible network and relayed the truth about the National Islands Corporation. The facts, at last, came to the mass of downtrodden people. The truth as if a powerful river flowed from screens, monitors, stereopticons, and video billboards all across the world. The message, we the people of the Global Freedom Party and others, are not taking this crap from the NIC anymore. The message was lurid and vibrant.

CHAPTER 59

Two months after E.W. Pile becomes a GFP Candidate, Elvira, and the Hat arrive in Concord

Needing a break from the campaign, I sat in my apartment viewing the comedy program *The Clown Clan*, on the Loadshow Network. Bea was by my side. I leaned over and sniffed her stale hair. She smiled and playfully thrust her massive shoulder into my ribcage. Robert, the ringmaster stepped to the podium with a bullhorn, "Ladies and gentlemen, I am pleased to present to you the greatest clown on earth, Elvira, and her associate, Mr. Hat."

I jumped up from the couch and screamed, "What is she doing?"

Bea grabbed my clown shirt and gave it a tug, "Sit down sugar and let's see what she is up to." I slumped down to the cushion extremely hurt by Elvira's presence on the show. I had applied several times to be on the program, but the producers rejected me. "I am the one who should be on stage," I whined. Beatrice laughed as Elvira pulled a severed hand out of her hat, and Mr. Hat pulled a severed hand out of his ass. Beatrice continued her outlandish laughter. I could no longer watch the program and went to the kitchen to satisfy my craving for licorice. I heard Beatrice in the other room scream, "Oh no she did-in't."

I exploded into the living room to see what was happening and saw to my horror E.W. Pile in an open casket. It was an expensive coffin. Satin pillows supported his misshapen head. The little imp, Hat, was standing beside Elvira holding a rack of swords and long knives. I fell on the couch in disbelief, and horror as Elvira closed the casket's lid. She eloquently took a sword (one bedecked with jewels), cradled it lovingly in the crotch of her elbow, lifted the blade above her head, briefly held the sword aloft, looked at the camera, and plunged the blade into the middle of the coffin.

The cubicle phone rang. It was Bemire, "Are you watching, *The Clown Clan*?"

"Yes," I replied.

"Where are they filming this program?" he asked.

"I think it was prerecorded, but the studio is on 4th street. I have been there several times."

"I'll meet you there," Bemire said. His voice seemed strained.

I grabbed a hand full of licorice sticks, "I am

going to the meet Bemire at the studio on 4th street."

Beatrice looked away from the monitor, "Wait," she said, "I have to pee. It will only take a moment." She dashed into the bathroom. I heard her making water, the toilet flush, the toilet paper roll, the water tap come on, and finally the rustle of the towel she removed from the shelf.

Silence.

She blew her nose, combed her hair (I heard the aerosol can hiss), put on her lipstick, (she popped her lips), Went into our combination living and sleeping area put on lavender slacks, beige blouse, and combat boots, got a pistol from beneath her pillow, and said, "Let's go."

Breathe.

She opened the door and was the first to penetrate the entry's threshold. I followed with a stick of limp licorice dangling from my mouth.

Beatrice drove an ancient 007 Floater that she massaged back to health from a significant crash. We arrived moderately vexed by anxiety. Bemire was already there parked with lights off, in the darkness. Beatrice pulled in behind him. I got out of the floater and walked to Bemire's vehicle, "Looks like the studio is closed." I said.

Bemire scratched the stubble on his chin. "I notified Delphi."

"And?"

"We need to B and E... see if we can find any

evidence that will lead us to Elvira, and we need to verify if Mr. Pile is dead. No one has been able to reach him." Bea exited the floater, "Hi Beatrice," Bemire said.

"Hello Bemire," She replied.

"You look good."

"Thanks."

"C'mon, let's go," I said. We walked side by side to the studio's front door. Bea was in the middle. She knocked. There was no answer. Bemire placed his ear to the door. Satisfied the building was empty he inserted a bump key, turned it slightly, and opened the wormwood door. The interior was dark, "I can't see a thing," I whispered. Bea removed her blouse and brazier and turned on her tit-lights. The double beams illuminated the area. We followed Beatrice's headlights into the staging room.

"Over there," Bemire said. He pointed to a casket. Bea pinched her areolas and her tit-lights changed to high beam. She scanned the coffin. We approached cautiously. The flag-draped box was riddled with holes. I watched nervously as Bemire lifted the coffin's lid. The three of us leaned forward... A noise detracted us. Beatrice turned her tits toward the sound. We saw a man. The man was sitting in a large metal birdcage. Someone had severed his hands. We approached silently, on tiptoes. I recognized the handless man. It was... A rustling noise came from the casket. We turned in unison and tiptoed back to the highly polished

The Perfect Plan

red oak coffin. The three of us, as if attached at the hip, simultaneously peered inside. A piece of paper was pinned to Candidate Piles chest. Bemire removed the paper from Piles torso. He gave me the note. I placed the monocle in the cup of my right eye. Beatrice positioned her boobs for maximum luminosity. I began to read. "To whom it may concern."

"That would be us," Bemire whispered.

I continued to read, "Come get me if you dare. I am at the Purge Building on Crescent Street. Signed Elvira."

Beatrice turned toward me, "Let's go," she said blinding me with her lactiferous duct lights.

I covered my eyes, "Wait," I said, "the man in the cage that is the Freedom Party's promoter, Peewee Cotton." Bea turned toward the cage and began to walk toward the deceased advocate. Bemire, and I furtively followed the replica. I watched Bea's rear oscillate in her tight lavender pants. I felt the urge for another licorice twist. She stopped. We stopped. "He is dead," she whispered, "bled to death." Her lights swept over Cotton's body. Not only were his hands missing, but his feet were gone too. "Let's get out of here," Beatrice said.

The three of us walked in-step, side-by-side toward the door. Beatrice illuminated the path before us. "Are we going after her?" Bemire asked with a semi-whispery lisp. He was nervous.

"It's a trap," Bea said.

"She's probably armed," I said.

"I bet she is," Bemire replied.

"Do you think you can take her down Bea?" I asked.

Bea paused, and considered the possibility, "Probably, but if it is an ambush and she has weapons, maybe not."

"I know someone who can do it?" I said.

"Who?" Bea replied.

"The Muskeg assassin, Comica." I turned to Bemire, "Call Delphi, let him know Pile and Cotton are dead—see if he can get in touch with Comica. Elvira needs to…" A laser blasted through the window, splintering the wall not more than an inch from my head. We three as one, dove to the floor, Bea landed chest-up, with her back on the floor. Her boob beams shot up and vacillated on the ceiling like two klieg spotlights searching for enemy aircraft, "Dowse your lights," I whispered. Beatrice squeezed her areolas, and the lights went off.

"What are we going to do now?" Bea said.

"Two options," Bemire replied, "hide or run." A laser shot blew a hole in the wall, another ricocheted off an improver mirror, and exited with an explosion through the opposite wall.

"Inventory our weapons," Beatrice said in a commanding voice.

"Tulip," I said.

"Handheld PP-497 close-combat laser pistol," Bemire said.

The Perfect Plan

"I have a gas propelled 707 stashed in my bag," Bea said.

"What's the plan?" I asked. My voice was trembling. I reached for a comforting licorice stick.

Bea replied, "Call Delphi, tell him about Mr. Pile—fill him in on our situation. If he can send Comica over that will be great. In the meantime, I will circle around Elvira. Perhaps I can catch the bitch by surprise. You two crawl inside the casket with Mr. Pile and wait for the all clear. Whatever you do, don't leave the casket."

"Got-yah," I said.

Beatrice reached into her medicine chamber located in the heel of her shoe, retrieved a needle, self-administered a testosterone shot, and said in a deepening voice, "On my signal." Beatrice made a move for the door, and dove through the opening, "Now," she said as laser shots lit up the dark space around her.

Bemire scrambled toward the casket. I was right behind him, "Get in first, I don't want to crush my flower." I said. Bemire turned and faced me. He looked confused, "Hurry," I said. Bemire reluctantly followed my command, stepped over the lip of the casket and stretched over Mr. Pile. I followed and closed the casket lid. It was a tight fit and infinitely dark. I with great effort and discomfort due to the snug quarters of the casket retrieved my cell phone from its leather holster strapped to the waistband of my polka dotted undies and called Delphi. Using soft whispers, I briefed him on our situation and suggested he contact Comica for assistance. He agreed. We waited. Bemire complained constantly about my weight. I was angry and began a well-deserved internal discourse...

Nag, nag, nag, I mean I only weigh one-hundred and forty-two pounds for Ignatius sake. I can't imagine how he would complain if I weighed two-hundred-plus pounds... Shit...

I felt better. An hour passed; then two before we heard the sizzling hiss of lasers. Bemire sighed, I could not discern if it was a sigh of relief that his burden would soon be lifted or a recognition that the end was near. The combatants sounded close. I heard a distant footstep then another someone was approaching. The lid squeaked open. I was blinded by the light, "Bea, is that you?"

"It is me sugar," Comica said, "Beatrice is in the floater shaving. That testosterone did a job on her," Comica laughed. It was a girlish twitter.

"Did you get Elvira and the Hat?" I said.

"No sugar, they high-tailed it out of here. She left some cronies to fight in her stead. We got all of them. They were amateurs." Comica paused. The sound of Beatrice's electric razor buzzed in the still air. "Call the Undertaker and let's split this scene," Comica said. I called the Coroner, and we left.

CHAPTER 60

If Dar didn't Blow up the School Bus, Who did?

On the day of the bombing. A school bus mechanic witnessed some suspicious looking Indians dressed up like turkeys. No one has claimed responsibility for the terrorist attack. The question, who was the perpetrators, requires resolution.

"I do not agree," replied Ellison Bogdan. He spoke to a mysterious woman behind an ornamental silkscreen. A mild vacilating breeze distorted the woman's outline. Ellison scrutinized the woman's silhouette for any signs of beauty. He found none. She looked like a stick figure to him, and he wasn't partial to thin women they reminded him of his X-Wife.

Interjection: Documents discovered by the Association of Avian Literary Artists revealed that the mysterious woman Ellison observed from a slight embrasure in the silk screen was none other than Destiny Johnson, aka Virginia Fawn.

— Bogdan rocked nervously back and forth in his mother's antique rocking chair. His graying beard, which fluttered gently in the breeze-contained streaks of yellow mustard and flecks of potato chips. He lifted a bottle of beer to his lips. The tubular top disappeared between his mustache and beard when the bottle-top reappeared the bottle was empty. Ellison let out a loud and satisfying, "Ah."

"Well?" the woman said.

"Well, what," Ellison replied.

"Find out what happened."

"I'll have Evan look into it."

"No, you cannot. He and his turkey friends may be responsible for poor Jimmie's death," she said angrily.

"Well, I can't. I've got my goats to tend to."

"What about that FBI Agent, Mr. Chung?" The woman asked.

"I don't think he likes me," Ellison said, then added, "or Evan."

"Well try. We need to do something for Jimmie."

Ellison bowed his head slightly, "Okay, I'll try."

Ellison Bogdan buzzed Evan via telepathic code. He reached Evans mental mailbox and left a message. Ellison then called Agent Chung. They had a brief hostile chat, and Chung, tired of defending his integrity, hung up the phone. Ellison felt Chung had reacted prematurely by discontinuing the conversation and tried calling again, but without success, Chung did not answer.

Two days later Evan returned Ellison's call. Evan was in Colorado hunting rich conservative Caucasians. After a few questions and answers concerning health and wellbeing, Ellison got to the point. "Evan, who blew up that school bus in Madison Ohio?"

Evan said, "Dar and his girlfriend Camden Hart did it."

"I thought they were hiding out somewhere in Texas."

"No, they never made it to Texas. Let me tell you what happened. The boys and I were protesting the slaughter of turkeys on Thanksgiving Day in the Madison Walmart parking lot. I got shot remember."

Ellison said, "Yes."

"Well before I got shot... by the way, do you know who shot me?"

"No, I don't," says Ellison.

"Barbra McCoy's husband Rob Roy McCoy. He's the one who shot me. You see, I had been messing with his daughter's pet turkey, Solicitous; she was a real beauty and good on the roost if you catch my meaning. Anyway, McCoy's daughter caught us making out up in the oak tree in their backyard. Solicitous got pregnant. She laid thirteen eggs, twenty-eight days later all of them hatched. I was a happy father. Rob Roy did not appreciate being a grandfather and being an angry human, 'such short tempers you people have,' he shot me."

Ellison said, "Sorry about that, I somehow feel responsible."

A long period of silence shrouded the airwaves, "Evan, you there… Evan?"

"I'm here—had to take a moment, and reflect on my death you know," Evan said.

"Sorry."

"It's okay," Evan replied. "Now as to the bombing of the bus. Dar slipped out of the rental car just outside Madison city limits. He sent Camden Hart to Salem, a small town, a few miles away with instructions to pick him up at the Rocky Ford Bridge where he would be hiding. Dar's first choice was to blow up the public swimming pool, but it was fenced, and guarded by protective mothers. His second choice was Lipson's Gym, but he did not have any money and could not pay the entry fees. Lipson's gym was located a block from Snyder's Elementary School, Dar saw the parked school buses and decided to blow one up. He selected Bus number TR08 because his Aunt Florence lived on Rue Tralee de Puce, house number 8 in Paris. Dar placed the bomb on the rear axil of the bus and set the timer. The rest, as they say, is history."

"What about the Indians dressed like turkeys?" Ellison asked.

"That was an attempt to distract the investigators. Point the blame, as it were, to the innocent Native Americans and equally innocent turkeys. The minorities of this world have always been the victim of lies and false accusations by the establishment."

"Was Dar affiliated with the NIC?" Ellison asked.

"Yes, he was recruited by the NIC insurgent team," Evan said.

"Thanks, Evan, enjoy your vacation."

"I will, take care, bye."

"Goodbye," said Ellison. He disconnected from Evans brainwave and took a well-deserved nap.

CHAPTER 61

Delphi Builds his Military

Jimmie Linguine Proclaims Himself the Picador of the New Army.

"What floor can you see underfoot?" asked Jimmie while pissing on a hapless Mantis, scurrying between his bulbous clown shoes. The Praying Mantis, Jimmie surmised, looked very much like Elvira.

"None Sir," Staff Sargent Morris replied. "We are in the Global Freedom Party Headquarters on 6th Street, Albuquerque, New Mexico."

"Why are we here Sargent?"

"Recruiting Sir," Morris answered.

"How do I look?"

"Fabulous Sir, the clown outfit is gorgeous, and I might add marvelously creased military style. But it is the lavender wig that I truly adore."

After a complete and thorough pecker wag, Jimmie zipped up, "Thank you," he said with his

The Perfect Plan

chin leveraged toward the domed ceiling. "Where did you say we were?"

"Balcony Sir in the Global Freedom Party Headquarters," Morris replied.

Linguine's piss flowed in small rivulets across the marble floor. The urine was at the balcony's precipice when Sargent Morris pulled a kerchief out of his back pocket and rushed to sop up the golden stream, unfortunately, he was late a dozen or more drops cascaded over the balcony's lip, hitting a few balcony-gazing bystanders below.

Linguine collapsed.

He awoke in a hospital bed. Bea was there as was Bemire. Bea's vigilant eyes meandered around the tiny room and came to rest on Jimmie's purple wig and red-ball of a nose.

"What happened?" Jimmie asked in a helium-inflated voice. He had been sucking on balloons in his dreams.

"You were poisoned." Beatrice said, "Looks like the effect of Amanita Ocreata, a poisonous mushroom."

"But why and by whom?"

"Don't know yet," Bea, said, "We're still looking into it—"

"Where am I?"

"Press Hospital," Bemire said; then leaned heavily against the wall. "Jimmie, with the death of Candidate Pile we need someone to step up and take his place. We need you, Jimmie, we think you are perfect for the job. We want you to be our candidate."

"I've just been poisoned for Ignatius sake," Jimmie whined.

"It's important Jimmie," Bemire said; cleared his throat, and continued, "We have raised a large army; most are volunteers. They need your leadership."

"Why doesn't Delphi do it? He started this whole thing." Jimmie said. Bea glanced at Bemire; then quickly averted her eyes. "What, what is it?"

"Delphi's gone missing."

Jimmie' faced paled, "No, no I won't do it. You be the candidate Bemire."

"I'm too old Jimmie, too fat, I can't do it," Bemire said jerking up his gut-draped belt.

Jimmie made an apprehensive gesture with his finger, and said, "Not me, nope, it ain't-a-gonna-happen. I am not going to be the candidate."

Bemire looked at Bea and nodded his head in an affirmative gesture. Jimmie looked at Bea and nodded his head in a negative gesture.

"It is for the good of us all, sorry," she said. Jimmie glanced quickly at Bemire. He tried to figure out what the coded nod meant when he felt the sting of a needle in his leg. Bea had given him a shot. "What was that? What did you just give me?" Jimmie shouted. Bea leaned toward Jimmie, closer still until her lips were at his ear. Jimmie was drooling. He hated her—he loved her. His desire spread to his groin, his loose clown pants be-

The Perfect Plan

came a tent. His anger went to his head. Jimmie tried to sit up, but Bea held him firmly on the bed. He growled, "What did you give me?"

"Testosterone," Bea whispered.

Jimmie came, (in a carnal way) flooding his tent-pants. It was both a relief and a curse. A relief sexually, a curse psychologically. Jimmie suddenly developed an aggressive attitude, and said, "Okay, I'll do it. I will be the candidate. I will be the Picador that makes this country great. I'll be the clown that wins this damn war."

Bea smothered Jimmie with rubbery kisses. Bemire shook Jimmie's hand, and said, "Congratulations, Mr. Candidate."

CHAPTER 62

Hooked on Testosterone

I was hooked on testosterone during my candidacy. I was aggressive and hostile toward my opponent George A. Lucas running as the incumbent candidate for the NIC party. He cringed under my barrage of personal attacks. Not only did I intimidate my opponent. I bullied my constituents and terrorized the GFP party members as well as my supporters. My greatest success, I believe is when I convinced voters through false promises, everything their little hearts desired. I convinced voters, Seventy-two-thousand men, women, and children, to vote for me and join the International Freedom Fighters. "Some must die for others to live." Became our slogan, and it resonated through the crowds, especially those on the purge lists.

I was standing on a podium during one of my rallies. My purple wig was slightly askew as I reached to adjust the hairpiece I saw Delphi appear from within the ranks of the magnificent Minneapolis Mississippi High School Marching Band. Comica was with him. "Make an announcement," he shouted, "that I have returned."

Awestruck, I mumbled incoherently, "Sweet Ignacio," and then gathered myself together for the purpose of this important announcement. "Attention, our Supreme Commander Mr. Dallas Delphi has returned. He wishes to speak."

The crowd cheered as he approached the stage. I embraced him. He carried the acrid smell of hot plastic in his clothing. I handed him the voice amplifier.

"I have been away with the Muskeg people, learning their way of warfare. I have returned to begin our campaign against the NIC, and their affiliates. We need volunteers, so sign up. Thank you."

He returned the amplifier back to me. "Let's hear it for our Supreme Leader," I said. The crowd once again cheered. "The enlistment booth is on my right." I pointed in the direction of the conscription table, and the crowd began to amble forward. "Age limit," I said, "is five years and over." I went searching for Delphi as soon as the conscription began. I found him and Comica under a large heavily leafed tree. They were making out. "Ahem," I said.

Delphi looked at me and said, "Give us a moment Linguine." I retreated a few yards and slid into the shadowy arms of a Polythorn Tree,

He promptly resumed kissing Comica, and the two soon became involved in a war of tongues. Comica's tongue-lunge caught Delphi off-guard. Her long pink mouth-muscle went straight and deep into Delphi's esophagus. She landed a direct strike on his tonsils. Delphi took the blow well, gagged slightly, but soon recovered and countered with an elaborate riposte. His tongue struck a glancing blow against the roof of his lover's mouth and sent spittle flying. The two sparred thusly for half-an-hour before advancing to a gruesome pelvic attack. I must say that due to my elevated testosterone, Larder, (I named my pecker Larder), swelled-up and extended his elevated head from my navel to my nipples. I squeezed my eyelids tight thinking that by removing the visual stimulus I could ease the terms of my erection. Unfortunately, the sound of buttressing bellies and slapping thighs excited me even further. Sadly, I succumbed to the law of nature and hosed the native garden in which I was hiding, with wasted seed.

Later that day, Delphi came to my hotel room. "Sorry about the delay," He said, "I was in a strategy conference with Comica." He sat down on the bed and patted my clown pants, just above the knee. "You have done a fine job, Jimmie, I am proud of you."

"Thank you, sir," I replied.

"What is it that you wanted to talk about?"

"I no longer want to be the candidate," I said

The Perfect Plan

clearly, despite the licorice stick hanging from my lips.

"No Jimmie you are the best man for the job. Most of the citizens like you. They consider you a straight talker, a man of character. You run for president, I will manage the war."

Delphi continued to pat my leg. "We need weapons if we are going to fight this war," I said.

"I am aware of that," Delphi replied.

"When are we going to get them? We can't train the troops without weapons."

"I am aware of that," Delphi repeated. I glared at Delphi probing him optically for more information. "Soon, Jimmie, I promise," He stood. My purple wig slipped to the right as I turned my head to watch him rise. He straightened my purple pelt, "I must be going, see you later," he said and strode briskly out of the door.

CHAPTER 63

An Intrusion provided by an unknown person or thing sympatric to the GFP

The problem.

Alexander, as the majority shareholder of the Black Ops Corporation, was in control of all world armaments. We were unarmed soldiers. The NIC had unlimited access to weapons and munitions. We had nothing, but a promise from Delphi.

An additional problem.

Professor Mostlow asked the rhetorical question, "What does one want when one has nothing?" Mostlow scanned the room full of NIC administrators. "One wants everything, but more specifically there is a pyramid of needs and the basic stuff like food and shelter comes first, then safety. My friends our enemies, by design, have none of their basic needs met in today's society." He looked at a young man sitting in the first row,

The Perfect Plan

"And that George is good. Why if the populace had their basic needs satisfied, they would have time for happiness, and the inclination, (out of boredom,) for war. So dear fellows what do we do?"

"Deny them everything," George said without raising his hand.

"Exactly!" Professor Mostlow shouted. As soon as the election is over, we will withdraw revenue from the population, cut back on their utilities and services, and resume purging the elderly and unemployed.

The response.

Delphi had a spy at the meeting. Her non-de-plume was Sugar Something. Her real name was Something Else. She briefed Delphi, and Delphi sent out a coded communique to the Global Freedom Parties Commanders. The message was brief and concise. "War is imminent. Gather all available troops and await further orders."

CHAPTER 64

History of the Hays Military Endeavors

1812 to 1815
William Harris Hays fought in the Indian War of 1812.

1835 to 1842
William Hays and his slave son, Bob fought in the Second Seminole War.

1861 to 1865
Bob Hay's son German Hays served in the Union army during the Civil War.
He also fought from 1899 to 1913 in the Moro Rebellion.

1917 to 1918
German Hays' grandson Dennis Hays served in the First World War as a Medic.

1941 to 1945
Dennis Hays son Robert Hays served in WWII as a sniper.

1950 to 1953

Robert Hays served in the Korean War.

He also served from 1962 to 1965 in the Vietnam War.

1990 to 1991

Robert Hays son Randolph served in the Persian Gulf War.

2001 to 2015

Randolph's son Peter served in the Afghanistan War and Middle Eastern Conflict.

2021 to 2027

Peter's son Bruce served in the Norwegian Campaign.

The years 2092 A.S., (after sainthood,) through 3030 A.S, are missing from the original manuscript. Research of the 'War Archives' provided information concerning the Hays Military service.

Bruce's illegitimate son Dallas Delphi (Who took his mother's name) served as commander in the Symbolist Campaign. Dallas Delphi's illegitimate son Miguel Martinez died in the NIC's Abstract Raid on New Chicago June 1st, 3042 effectively ending the Hays family (1,230 years) dedicated to war.

November 25th, 3054 the Turkey Uprising was the last day of recorded conflict. That day

Donald D'lo

lives in telekinetic memory as the rapture.

CHAPTER 65

Loki Revisits the Agreement to Access the Results of Jihad J. Ready Philosophy

Mother Urdu came to New Mexico to purchase a bag of the famous Estancia Valley pinto beans. It was dark and she was slowly peddling her handmade, tricycle (trike) down Highway 41 in downtown Estancia. The trike was a two-seater. Loki was in the back seat, holding on to Urdu's long ears. The hairy man was nude, except for a red bow tie that adorned his thick hairy neck. She was a bit erratic with the steering of the cycle. The handlebars had not been aligned correctly. It seems Loki's placement of the handlebars, (he was responsible for the vehicle's maintenance), was off center, making the tricycle veer to the right. Mother Urdu, weary of dismounting and repositioning the bars, pulled over and parked under one of the massive, half-dead, elm trees that lined the street Estancia. It happened that the elm tree-bordered the Family

Coupon Store's parking lot. Loki spread a blanket on the sidewalk and assisted Urdu off the tricycle and onto the blanket. Her voluptuous rump extended over the curb. It was uncomfortable, but she refused to move, claiming she was too exhausted from having to carry Loki's large hairy ass on the back of the trike.

Loki left his tools at home, and without coin or coupon decided to 'borrow' a brand new set of wrenches from the Family Coupon Store. He walked across the parking lot, stopped at the storefront to check out the display of bottled water, potting soil, miniature lamps, and water hoses. He was shocked to see the reflection of a hairy man sporting a pistol size penis. Not a derringer-mind you. He was packing a large piece—a self-declared magnum.

He was admiring the full frontal reflection of himself when he heard a scream. The alarming squeal came from a woman in a red pickup truck who had just pulled into the parking lot. She mistakenly thought of him as an Abominable Snowman, Sasquatch, Yeti, perhaps, or maybe even Big Foot. She had seen an identical image on the cover of The National Inquirer. His hair covered buttocks was the leading component of her mistaken indictment. The reason the woman pointed a gun at Loki, (his back was turned mind you) was simple, she at the time, feared the giant wolf-like man, and without hesitation, the wide-eyed woman pulled the trigger. The bullet, due to her trembling hand, and astigmatism missed Loki and shattered the store's plate-glass window.

"Raise your hands," the woman yelled, as the store employees and customers began fleeing the building. Loki found the woman's demands, appealing, in an odd way and he was receptive to her firm commands. "Turn around," she said, "slowly." Loki, with hands raised, pivoted allowing the woman, other customers, and employees to gaze upon his giant pistola.

Mother Urdu watched from the sidewalk as Loki extended his long loose arms, which he bent slightly at the elbows. He turned his hands inward at the wrist, (an enticing lure for young girls), wriggled his fingers, and began to twerk. For those unschooled in fashionable dance, twerking is the process whereby a person assumes a squatting position and thrusts and rolls his or her pelvis in a provocative manner. As soon as Loki dropped his arms and spread his legs to squat, brothers, and sisters, senor's and senoritas, it was on. To quote a twenty-something red headed spectator, "That ass was moving." Even Beelzebub twerking at his best would envy the hip thrust and pelvic rolls that Loki displayed. Beelzebub, by the way, saw a video of Loki's moves. The Devil's associate the controversial Reverend Dulcimer sent the video, to the Nob via cell phone. Beelzebub subsequently broke his hip trying to mimic Loki's thrusts and gyrations during a twerking contest in a popular nightclub called the La Charles, in New

Orleans Louisiana.

Loki, Urdu thought, looked like an orangutan performing for the girl-juvies at the Claremont School for Nymphos. He put himself and Urdu at risk, she surmised, just to get laid. Urdu felt the need to take action. She covered herself with her blanket and walked briskly to the woman frozen in an intense gaze. "Give me that gun," she growled. The woman mesmerized by Loki's dance ignored Urdu's command. With little effort, Urdu lifted the gun from the woman, aimed carefully at Loki, and calmly said, "Get your ass over here."

"Wait," the woman said without squandering her focus on Loki, "Excuse me, I'll pay just to see him dance."

The customers and employees, both male and female, joined in, "We'll pay too," and they began to throw money at Loki's feet.

"What about the window?" Urdu asked.

"They've got insurance," a short balding man replied.

"Go inside and get a radio from off the shelf," said one of the spectators. A large man wearing bib overalls and a cowboy hat dashed inside the store grabbed a disk-player and an assortment of h I p-h O p Disk's, plugged in the player and bam Loki's double-bubble butt cheeks gyrated into a rhythmic spasm. People used their cell phones to video and spread via the outernet Loki's dance around the world, and soon the entire population of Estancia (all 272) men women and children were at the Family Coupon parking lot to watch, live and in person, Loki twerk. He danced well into the night and in the end ... He was jailed for public nudity. Loki, even though exhausted continued to dance just to entertain the police officers. One particular officer, a blonde heavily armed female, found him most attractive, she clung to the bars as he pumped, puffed, and rattled around the cell. When he could dance no more the blonde in body armor sung country-western songs to the convict sending him safely into the land of dreams.

The next morning Urdu bailed Loki out of jail with the coupons that he had made twerking. Loki bought some tools with the excess coupons and repaired the trike. Urdu peddled out of town, at an excessive speed, without purchasing the famous Estancia Valley pinto beans.

Interjection:

A question posed by the executive concerning plot.

"Now the question proffered by Beelzebub, (presently recovering from hip surgery), is why was Loki and Urdu's trip to Estancia trip an essential part of Jimmie Linguine's story? By the way, Beelzebub has been following this narrative closely. His motives, at this time, are uncertain. Perhaps he enjoys reading a romantic thriller. I suspect, however, his intentions are to capture Linguine and place said clown in the super-hot lava flow of Hell as punishment for past felonies and misdemeanors. Regardless, of his motives, Beelzebub's question is a valid one."

CHAPTER 66

The Rest of the Story

Hotel Caledonia

Urdu and Loki were traveling on a dark Mid-Western Highway. Loki was singing a rap song he had heard while twerking. It was getting late when he spotted a row of glimmering lights. "It's a hotel," Loki said. "Let's stop for the night." Urdu was tired. She turned the tricycle into an empty parking lot, cruised to a space marked handicapped, and stopped.

With her blanket draped over her right arm and Loki clinging to her left arm, Mother Urdu entered the dilapidated hotel, approached the clerk, and asked for a room. The clerk, named, Reba, undisturbed by Loki's nudity, (she assumed he was either a costumed gay guy or a sex toy), requested payment up front and provided a form for Urdu to fill out. Since Urdu could not write with her doggish paws, Loki completed the form for her, including name, address, and the license plate number of the three-wheeled non-motorized vehicle. He made up the license number from a wellspring of mathematical formulas masturbating, (figuratively speaking), in his head. Reba collected thirty-four coupons, and change lit a candle and showed the couple to their room.

Once Loki and Urdu had settled in, Loki rang the front desk and asked for a bottle of wine.

Reba announced that the hotel was located in a dry

county in Texas and that no alcohol was available.

"Bummer," Loki said.

"Yeah," Reba replied, "but we do have something that you might like."

Loki was excited about the news, "What's that?"

"Magic mushrooms," she smiled, "I purchased them from a slug-of-a-man for my own consumption."

"I have a fondness for mushrooms," Loki said.

"That will be an additional fifty coupons."

He paused, "Okay."

"I'll bring them right up." She was at their door in five minutes. Loki gave her the money and kissed her on the cheek. She, because of her previous consumption of mushrooms or Loki's virility, (her motive at this point is uncertain), returned his kiss with prolonged exuberance, and detached

The Perfect Plan

herself with a Slurpee, "Goodnight."

Urdu witnessed this act of affection with disdain and spoke to Loki in a tone flecked with anger. "You are loathsome," she said.

"I am a kind and gentle soul," Loki replied with a shocked expression that surfaced beneath the hair on his bristly face.

"Don't give me that bunk. You actively pursue women and... and... and you treat people in a deplorable manner."

"Do not!"

"Yes, you do! You steal souls and... and... and look what you did to Linguine."

"What did I do to Jimmie?"

"Thirty years and one day of life, that's what."

Silence.

"I'm sorry. I do not mean to hurt anyone —sometimes I act without much forethought. Sometimes—"

"Shut-up!" Urdu spat out the hyphenated word with a spray of spittle and went to bed. Loki cautiously lay down beside her. He noticed the mirrored ceiling that adorned the region above their massive mattress. Loki consumed a handful of mushrooms and handed the bowl of Psilocybe Azurescens to Urdu. She ingested the uncooked mushrooms with the refined dignity of a queen. Shortly thereafter, she heard voices. Loki was speaking to Prosperous' soul in Alexander's body.

Loki said, "Look Prosperous, Jimmie Linguine has not followed Jihad J. Ready's Manifesto concerning the requirement for inaction quite the contrary, Jimmie has taken an active role in the war against the NIC. This changes everything."

"How so?" Prosperous' soul via Alexander's body replied.

"You continue to pursue capital. Yet Jimmie is no longer a passive bystander. Those two ingredients do not mix. You cannot have an angry and aggressive population and still pursue wealth. The people are, thanks to Linguine, informed about your greed. They are mad as hell, and if something is not done, they will defeat you."

"What do you suggest?" Prosperous said.

"Modify the contract," Loki said.

Mother Urdu turned her head toward Loki. He was looking at the ceiling mirrors. He smiled. Prosperous and Loki's conversation returned in her head.

Prosperous replied, "To what extent?"

"My proposal, based on the Socio-Capitalist John Rayne Rimes philosophy is to pay Jimmie off and allow him to return to a normal life."

"Jimmie is a weeping soul," Prosperous declared, "he cannot return to a normal life."

"You murdered him prematurely. You sent Dar to blow up that school bus."

"That wasn't me that was Izabelle in Dar's body."

"You asked her to do it. You broke the rules. You violated the agreement," Loki replied.

The Perfect Plan

Urdu once again turned to gaze upon Loki lying beside her. Loki's gaze remained fixated on the mirrors. She wondered if his fascination was on her reflection or his. He smiled. She returned her gaze to the mirrors.

"Your only recourse," Loki said, "is to undo what you have done. Go back and renegotiate the contract with Urdu, give Jimmie back his natural life."

"Shit," Prosperous replied.

Interjection: A video depicting a conversation between the scripters and the executive in charge that places doubt on historical events.

The executive in charge:

"I apologize for the interruption, but changing the storyline at this point is unheard of in scripter history. Bring out the scriptwriters to see how this event is going to play out?" The scriptwriters appeared from behind the breakroom door and seated themselves on a bed the executive brought in for his indispensable cogitation. Scriptwriter 4 was absent due to a severe hangover. He celebrated his sixtieth birthday with his eighty-eight-year-old mother.

"That storyline changes everything," said 3.

"5 wrote the scene," said 2, not us.

3, "What about the producer?"

1, "She has never read the script, she will never know."

3, "How does this change in the script alter

the narrative. How will it affect the ending?"

"That is unknown." Says 2, "We will have to wing it from here on out."

5, "Leave the scene in the story, let them renegotiate the contract."

2, "If we change the narrative and allow Linguine to have a normal life, he will have lost his purpose. Linguine's previous lives will mean nothing."

1 arose from her place on the bed, "Wait, It doesn't matter if Jimmie's life changes at this point in the script everything before this event remains the same. Jimmie has lived and died every thirty years and one day until now. I believe he can enhance the plot if we give him a longer life."

"Ah," said 3, "that is brilliant."

"Let's do this," says 1. "We have the power to give Jimmie a normal life, let's do it." She crossed her legs, lifted both boobs, not quite to her chin, but high enough to get everyone's attention, and giggled at 5.

5 lifted his glasses to the crown of his forehead, "Keep the scene, all of it!"

2 says, "It's up to the executive in charge whether to keep the scene or scrap it."

All eyes turn to the executive in charge. "Keep the scene. Allow Prosperous to renegotiate the contract with Jimmie."

— Urdu turned to observe with adoration, the wolf-man lying beside her. He returned her

The Perfect Plan

gaze. He kissed her, and that put an end to Loki's conversation with Prosperous. However, (this is the strange part), while Urdu was listening to the conversation between Loki and Prosperous, Loki, simultaneously, was listening to Urdu's conversation with her husband Fyodor the Epistler. Impossible right? Welcome to the world of Magic Mushrooms where nothing is impossible.

Loki listened intently as Fyodor whispered into Urdu's ear. The Epistler's voice was barely audible, "He is of no use to us, all he thinks about is getting laid that's it."

"He tries to do the right thing," Urdu said.

"Was his unapproved exchange of souls the right thing to do? Was negotiating a worthless contract with Prosperous on Jimmie's behalf a good thing. Was it acceptable that Loki stayed in the National Islands and took a nonhuman replica wife? Moreover, he gave Izabelle's soul to that same wife, was that appropriate? Especially after, he committed himself to you." Fyodor took a deep breath. "Urdu, when will you learn, you cannot trust a trickster."

"But he is fun to be with," Urdu explained.

Loki turned his head toward Urdu. She was staring at the mirrors with the covers pulled up to her chin. She had the hollow look of frustration and loss on her face. He wanted to touch her, but he dared not, not now, not when she was supporting him despite Fyodor's candid and rational argument.

"What's more," Fyodor said, "he does not love you, never has, and never will. Not like me, I've always loved you."

Loki thought that Fyodor's last comment was boastful and simply not true. He turned to gaze upon his lover and friend, Mother Urdu. Her lips were moving as she said a silent prayer. He was unsure if the prayer was intended for him or if she was praying for herself due to the misery he had created in her life. In that instant, Loki understood the fragility, the sacrifice necessary to obtain love, and the deep longing when love is absent from one's life. Loki felt bad about his actions, his carelessness with Urdu feelings. He promised himself that he would make things right. A single tear fell from Loki's furry face. The wolf-man turned to Urdu looked amorously into her eyes, and said, "I love you," she pulled the hairy man to her breast, squeezed his head between her massive paws, and replied, "Really?"

"Yes," Loki said, "I do." Urdu pulled the furball closer to her and said, "Do the Twerk for me." After Loki twerked a couple of sets, He fell into Urdu's arms, and said, "We are hostages of our own design," and they made love locked in the warm jail cell of affection.

The next morning when they tried to check out, Reba met them at the door, "How was your stay?" she asked.

"Wonderful," Urdu replied.

"Beautiful," Loki said.

The Perfect Plan

Reba chuckled and said, "You know, you can check out any time you want, but do you really want to leave?"

Urdu peered at Loki. He returned her loving gaze, "Well," Mother Urdu said, "maybe, just one more night."

"After seeing the extent of their affection, they may never leave," Reba said to her owner while sitting on the chamber pot.

Early the next morning the couple left on their tricycle, Loki was peddling. Urdu sat in the back. They were happy. Bless his soul Loki had changed. Or had he?

Interjection: This video is curiously incongruous and lacks historical relevance.

Interjection: Here is an example of humanity's use of mythological absurdity to promote the development of family values. No wonder humans have failed as a society.

— Mother Urdu practices Levitation with Loki, the Lothario from the Northlands.

A rebellious mob of Loki and Urdu fans demands a contest between Loki and Mother Urdu. The reason for this contest is unclear. The venue? A four foot by eight foot by ten foot, green plastic kiddie pool. No other props are on stage. Hat is the referee. Elvira is the orator. A voice amplifier squeals as Elvira taps the metal cone three times. She raises a kerchief to her upper lip and dabs at the accumulating perspiration. Apprehension snuffs out the noise, silence, someone coughs. The announcement is abrupt, "In the red corner stands Loki, the Lothario from the Northlands, he is a trickster, dancer, shape-shifter, negotiator, and," Elvira pauses to build tension, "and well endowed."

The crowd applauds. Dispersed within the clapping of hands are random hisses, diatribes, and boos from Urdu's supporters.

"And, in the white corner stands Mother Urdu, she is a Lovie, and a dovie, and a fun loving gal," Elvira once again pauses to allow her next comment justifiable weight, "who bears the weight of all humanity on her broad semi-furry shoulders." The crowd erupts in shouts of adulation and applauds. There are no critics, no vile expletives hurled at her. A loving fan tosses her flowers. One man slings his underwear on the stage and shouts, "We love you Urdu."

Elvira asks, "Are all wagers made?" A few final moments of conversation ensues while money passes between members of the audience. Once again, the crowd is silent. A woman farts.

Hat steps to the pool and peers over the plastic lip. "Disrobe," he commands. His high shrill voice reverberates within the tube of his hat.

Loki stands and lowers his silken speedos. The embroidered tiger on the garment's backside wafts down his hairy legs and settles silently on the floor. Gasps soar from Loki's female fan club as

The Perfect Plan

he turns and provides a view of his muscular chest and stiff erection. He throws the women in the audience multiple kisses. His rocket wobbles. His fans scream.

While Loki faces the audience, Mother Urdu slowly, seductively removes her G-string and eight cup bra. Numerous men in the audience swoon at the sight of her standing before them, naked. Loki, hearing the seductive whispers of Urdu's fans, turns to face his opponent. He is in control, unaffected by her pursed lips and pulsating breath. She maintains a steadfast gaze. His eyes are like twin elevators stopping to view every sumptuous teat before getting off at her furry basement.

"Sit," Hat says. He pauses allowing the contestants enough time to lower their bodies into a vat of bullshit, "Begin."

"Stop!"

A mousey voice rises from the peanut gallery. The irreverent orator is a woman with obvious mental problems. She stands and addresses the crowd. "What has this to do with the message that this story is trying to convey?" She places her hands on her broad hips. "And where is the reality in this offering?" Someone in the audience hurls a half-eaten sandwich. Mayonnaise and baloney splatter against the critic's bonnet. She retrieves her sunhat from the floor, gives it a curtsey brush, and places it on her gray hair. "How can a man see through a hat?" She pointed at Hat. "How can someone who looks like a dog, nurture souls?" Mother Urdu covered her breasts in response to the critique. "And how can any man have such a large... Dick?"

The old woman steps out of the maddening crowd. Loki turns to observe the annoying critic. His eyes expand. He howls, "Mom?"

CHAPTER 67

The Deal

Subtitled The Elephant's Ass

Comica became cynical with the Global Freedom Party's supreme commander Mr. Dallas Delphi and his war. She and her people had received little compensation for fighting for the GFP, and though talented, Delphi was far from the best lover she ever had. Her new lover Sampson was riotous and notorious in his lovemaking, and he was breathtakingly beautiful. He was all she ever wanted in a servant. To show his love for the Muskeg, he sequestered a canopy of bear hides and goat-pelts and provided fifteen wailing prisoners in chains on their knees, of course, begging for mercy. Sampson was also, unbeknown to Comica, a representative of General Alexander. He, with his alluring speech, convinced Comica to abandon Delphi and meet with his boss, Alexander. She agreed to contact the General on her terms, conditions, and location. The location? A plastic elephant's ass!

___O___

The elephant ass was a plastic people friendly Muskeg sculpture that opened upwards, with a pull on its synthetic tail. The interior, carpeted with the sin of amber appeared bright pink against the dark onyx colored leather loveseat centered in the soundproof booth. The elephant was located in a museum in the Slimdown community, North West of Bridgeport the largest sea terminal in the Muskeg Territory. Alexander arrived girdled in a slim suit made from pureed and plasticized milk squeezed from the breasts of pre-purged women. "I am glad that you decided to parlay," Alexander said.

"Sampson was quite convincing," Comica replied.

"He is yours to do with as you please," Alexander paused. He focused for a moment on the wart on his left knuckle; then said, "I am willing to offer you an equal partnership in the plastic industries and stock in the National Islands Corporation valued at 700,000 coupons."

Comica stretched her long legs in the cramped booth and pursed her lips. She whistled a signifying toot at the amount Alexander was willing to offer. "Hello sweetheart," she said; then gazed briefly at the wart on Alexander's knuckle, "What do you want in return?"

The Perfect Plan

"I want you and your people to protect the NIC from any and all enemies, and I want Muskegs to participate in our counterfeit wars."

"Why fake wars?"

"For propaganda purposes," Alexander replied. "We will never lose a combatant, skirmish, battle, or war. The population will eventually become discouraged and give up on the Global Freedom Party. Without the support of the people, Delphi cannot win." Alexander paused to recite from the treasury of his mind, "Plus it is far less expensive if we stage a fake war."

"And when the GFP attack? As you know they surely will..."

"I want you and your people, as mercenaries, to make a preemptive strike on the GFP and handle all combat duties both offensive and defensive," Alexander said.

"Here's my counter," Comica replied, "We want ownership of all the plastic industries from around the world, everything that supplies, gathers, process, and markets plastic. I want a binding contract and a deed to all real estate on which the manufacturing and storage plants are located." Comica tapped on her cleft chin with her index finger, "Oh, and raise the stock offering to 850,000 coupons. Finally, we want unlimited weapons and ordnance to fight the GFP, on the ground as well as in the air."

"Done," Alexander, said, "On one condition."

"What is that?"

"Have you ever screwed in an elephant's ass?" Alexander raised one eyebrow and snorted pig-like.

"Not until now," Comica replied.

CHAPTER 68

NIC Stages a Fake War

Before it rained, Alexander issued forth an advertisement for guards to provide security for his next theatrical event. Seventy-seven unemployed Muskeg warriors applied. Seven of the meanest Muskeg women warriors were hired.

While it rained, Alexander sent one-hundred and fifty troupes, (actors,) along with a handful of Muskeg warriors, (killers,) for security with instructions to Hat that the actors should immediately begin to fake an assault on District 17. "The attack," Alexander explained, "should be dramatic and clearly, show the NIC superior fighting ability over the GFP's freedom fighters." Alexander also sent along large quantities of uniforms representing both sides of the conflict.

The actors and Muskeg security forces arrived by cargo floaters at Red Herring. Hat instructed the jobbers to prep the theater room and the troupe of misfits were ready to shoot the next day. Hat admitted to Elvira that he had concerns about the Muskegs. He knew how deadly the Muskeg's are in combat, and wondered, whether Jimmie's ex-protector, Comica was one of the security personnel. "I assume she isn't," Elvira said, "I don't think Commander Alexander would send her here knowing the rudiments of this operation would be laid bare to a possible spy."

Later that night Elvira and Hat met with the head of security. Her name was Pube. She was semi-nude as were all the female guards. Pube wore a narrow loincloth to cover her privates. Around her waist, (navel level), was an ornamental braided belly chain. Hat gasped when he recognized the chains adornments. Twenty or more leather peckers dangled like Christmas lights around her waist. Pube noticed Hat gawking at the mummified penises, "Spoils of war," she said. Hat instinctively grabbed his crouch.

Pube smiled at Hats defensive action. "I don't think you have the prerequisite size," she said. Elvira laughed as Pube pointed her enormous spear at his shielded manhood.

Hat was furious. He did not appreciate jests about his physical appearance, especially relating to his small personage. He said with the tremble of anger rattling in his voice, "Many small men are, verifiably well endowed. I happen to be one of them. Elvira can vouch for that."

Pube raised her spear and tapped the top of

The Perfect Plan

Hat's hat, "It is okay little man. I was just joking."

Hat lost it—he pulled out his big ass gun, pointed it directly at pube's navel, and said, "Give me those peckers. Now!"

Elvira with a crisp reporter's vernacular said, "What do you want with those peckers?"

Pube interrupted, "You want them? Come and get them."

"Hold on you two," Elvira said. She reached into her backpack and pulled out a cigar. She lit the tip. The burning pheromones smelled like lemons. Elvira handed Hat the stogie. He took a drag and instantly slipped into a euphoric longing for affection. Elvira nodded in Pube's direction. Hat holstered his gun and passed the cigar to Pube. The Muskeg warrior lifted the cigar to her lips, wrapped her lips around the cylindrical stogie, and sucked. It was titillating to watch. Hat, Elvira, and Pube then had a well-orchestrated manage a trois. Hat himself choreographed the action. Afterward, Pube and Hat became close friends.

CHAPTER 69

The Battle of Red Herring

It was windy the day Alexander invaded Red Herring. The fake fighting began in the remote and barren location called District 17. Delphi, concerned that this propaganda would damage the GFP's credibility temporarily suspended my campaign. He sent me as an embedded reporter along with Bemire as a medic, and Suzie Semester, the Dallas Regional Director as the commander of a small negotiating team to counter Alexander's hostile takeover of the Duane Theatre.

The theater was located in the coastal town of Red Herring. Semester and The NIC newly appointed commander Beelzebub were backstage having a beer as they negotiated the terms of cancellation for the takeover. Bemire and I were reading the poorly written scripts and scratching our heads.

"It says here that Alexander kills thirty-thousand GFP troops and takes District 17," Bemire said.

"That's bullshit," I said. I reached down to tie my clown shoe and farted. The voice projector was on and my flatus sounded like an exploding bomb.

The negotiations taking place backstage stopped immediately. Beelzebub rushed out of the theater, "Screaming kill the traitors." Pube, the Muskeg warrior appeared with a spear in hand. She recognized me as an enemy, (probably because of my clown suit,) and hurled her spear. Luckily, the plastic tipped projectile penetrated an unlucky stagehand's groin. The stagehand accidentally stepped in front of me while moving cardboard cutout props. His unintentional acceptance of the spearhead, fortunately, left me unscathed.

My clown shoes were a hindrance when it came to running, but Bemire and I managed to escape. We headed east, with vigorous aversion, and slow speed, toward the distant Disciplinary Mountains.

"Oh, breath of fog, hear me in this turbulent time. This time of need." I said. I was exhausted, partially blind, I shall explain in a moment the cause of my partial blindness. Anyway, I realized how desperate things had become and impatient for salvation, I shouted, "I am under attack. Sweet Ignacio, send me a hero."

Bemire shouted, "Shut up." He was evidently pissed at my request for a champion. Now as to my partial blindness. My monocle, fogged from the heat of exertion, remained clasped firmly between brow and cheek. The glaze of moisture obviously hindered my vision. I panicked and took a deep breath, which allowed me to regain a token of self-control. Using my deft magician's hands, I removed a kerchief and wiped my monocle for clearer vision. That solitary moment left me at the mercy of my enemy. The Muskeg always strikes their victim's blind spot, as Evan had instructed and I was sure that this extremely hostile Muskeg would take advantage of my limited right-side vision. I am fortunately left-brain dominant, which in the art of self-defense, allowed me, without supposition or deliberation, to move my head counterclockwise. I saw the spear mid-flight and ducked. The instrument of death pierced a saguaro cactus. The cactus with limbs held high was obviously surrendering at the time of its demise.

My clown shoes thumped the sand as I dashed toward the giant cactus to retrieve the embedded spear. I heard the Muskeg warrior's rapid footsteps behind me. I could tell she was gaining. She passed me without speaking. I saw her firm muscular buttocks move in opposition to one another. Her loincloth pinched in her butt-crack like a thong, made me pause, admire, and eventually wonder... Where the Hell is Bemire?

"I'm right behind you," he said as if he could read my thoughts. I heard the charge of his laser pistol.

"Hello, where did you get that?" I asked in a breathless tenor.

"Found it on the escape route, beneath a sign that had GUN written upon its whitewashed face," Bemire said and suddenly stopped running.

The Muskeg was just a few feet from the giant cactus and within reach of the spear when Bemire shouted, "Stop Muskeg and raise your hands."

She paused to analyze the situation before she raised her hands.

"Turn around." She turned slowly... She was bare-chested.

"Oh Ignacio," I said, "Would you look at those mammary glands—not to be confused with mummeries. However, it did feel like we were involved in an absurd performance out here in the middle of a desert with a half-naked gorgeous woman, who, by the way, was—is attempting to kill us—I mean how could this be anything but a theatrical performance?"

"Breathe," I said.

In the background, a choir from the Red Herring Lutheran Church sang, "Breathe," in harmony.

"What is your mission?" Bemire asked supplanting the choir.

"To kill," the Muskeg said.

"Can this be resolved peacefully?" Bemire asked.

The Muskeg looked confused, shrugged her shoulders, and said, "No."

"CUT," the film director yelled into his voice

amplifier.

The director stepped from behind a growth of desert vegetation. He was a thin man dressed in riding britches. His brown khaki shirt was unbuttoned to his belt, and he wore a pink Panama hat over his clean-shaven head.

"I knew it, we've been duped," I said as the Muskeg woman took Bemire's laser pistol. The laser gun was fake, a blank shooter. She shackled our legs.

"That's a wrap," the director said. A truck appeared from behind the sand dunes. A gang of roustabouts loaded the film equipment into the truck and headed back to the theater. A floater appeared to take us back to the studio. It was an elegant boy-O-boy floater, top of the line. I had never seen one. The floater settled with a soft hiss on to the sand, "Take them back to Red Herring, and confine them to their quarters." The director said. Wanda, the Muskeg flight attendant, prodded us into the spaceship and seated us, up-front first class. The flight attendants in charge served us champagne during our return trip.

Comica met us at the airfield and escorted us personally to a row of mobiles behind the makeshift theater. Our cylindrical shaped plastic mobile was small and heavily guarded by five Muskeg warriors. 'Principle Actors' was hand painted in red on the mobiles avocado colored side. We stood as Comica unlocked the mobile's door.

"Traitor," I yelled as she opened the plastic

door.

She did not respond to my disparaging word. Comica stepped aside as we entered the synthetic container. "Lunch at five," she said. The sound of the lock turning was frightening to me, and I began to crave a licorice stick.

Without the soothing feel and taste of licorice, I reverted—perhaps due to testosterone withdrawal—to a newborn baby's instant gratification of thumb sucking, and, suck I did. I sucked like a wharf rat on its mother's teat. Like a drunk on a bottle before his pledge to abstain, or like my mother Roberta Flannigan on J. B. Tennyson's pecker. It was annoying to Bemire, and it was annoying to the five Muskeg guards stationed outside the mobile. One of the Muskeg guards beat on the trailers plastic side and shouted, "What are you perverts' up to?"

"Nothing," Bemire said.

"Well stop that infernal sucking." She said. The other women giggled.

"Stop it," Bemire said, as he attempted to remove my portly appendage. The thumb popped out of my mouth, like a cork out of a champagne bottle. In the process of uncorking my thumb, however, Bemire accidentally knocked my monocle off—the optical piece fell to the floor and spun like a turned coin before collapsing with a rattle on the laminated floor. I became angry and slapped the palm of my hand against Bemire's cheek. A fight ensued. It was a short-lived altercation, however; I surrendered during Bemire's crushing stranglehold. Still gasping for breath, I retrieved my monocle, and sat quietly, in desperate need of a nipple or the fruitful flavor of licorice.

At five o: clock Bemire and I feasted on rice and beans. My captors denied my request for licorice, and I fell into a deep depression. I felt forlorn and vulnerable. I refused to speak to Bemire even after his apology, and I began a constant muddling of my hairpiece. Bemire looked through a clear plastic portal at the sun as it began to settle on the distant horizon. The sun's rays, entering through the aperture, focused a fist-size beam of light on my red nose. Bemire concentrated on my nose, "I never noticed the beauty of the red round ball until now," Bemire said, as he leaned forward for a closer examination. "It seems, to me, a jewel when framed against your powered face." For a split second, the beam of light flickered as if disturbed by a passing object. Bemire remained focused on my nose until the sun disappeared and the darkness of night claimed our cell.

During the darkness that surrounded us, I began to sing the Ballad of Rotten Wood. It was one of my favorite songs. One that I had learned as a child while sitting on my mother Roberta's knee as she orally entertained her benefactor. The ballad, sung in a high C register went like this:

"O rotten wood

O rotten wood
Choke, choke, gobble, gobble, gulp, gulp,
How could I live without you?

O rotten wood
O rotten wood
Choke, choke, gobble, gobble, gulp, gulp,
Like a beetle, I live within you.

O rotten wood
O rotten wood
Choke, choke, gobble, gobble, gulp, gulp,
There is no other like you."

As I began the fourth stanza, a voice from outside the mobile began to sing with me.

"O rotten wood
O rotten wood
Choke, choke, gobble, gobble, gulp, gulp,
I love you- rotten wood- I love you."

It was Beatrice. She unlocked the door to the mobile, and I rushed into her open arms. She gave me a breath-altering hug, and said in a hurried voice, "We must leave, quickly. The stealth ship is waiting, follow me." I noticed the Muskeg bodies scattered around the mobile as we dashed toward a distant outcrop of rock. The absolute darkness and my large clown shoes impeded our journey. We were almost to the edge of the outcrop when I, exhausted from the sprint, (actually a slow walk), heard footsteps. I was gulping volumes of dry air into my lungs, "The Muskegs are almost upon us, run," I managed to say between intervals of rapid breathing. Bea picked me up by the nape of my neck and swung me into her arms. She carried me clasped to her bosom to safety behind an enormous sand dune.

The Muskegs had sounded the alarm. Floaters were rising above the theater like bubbles in a glass of hot ale. Suddenly a condensed light flooded the desert sand. The beam moved slowly illuminating the distant dunes and on-coming Muskeg warriors. Laser fire erupted from the stealth ship hitting the approaching fighters. The GFP airship dropped its transporter rostrum to the ground. Bemire, Bea, and I climbed on board and was soon safe inside the belly of the ship. The Muskegs and regular NIC troops returned fire, and several NIC floaters began to engage our freedom fighter vessel. The stealth ship, however, now fully cloaked sped off untraceable, into the night.

CHAPTER 70

The War Escalates the Muskeg's commit to the NIC

Hat was probing the well of his navel with his little pinkie finger. He held a small round mirror above his belly trying to determine the amount of filth he managed to draw out into the light. He felt a need to be bronze and tanned regularly for his girlfriend the ghost-white, Ms. Pube. His four-foot seven frame became tight and muscular. His chest especially had become solid. His thick neck appeared to many observers as if it were a tree trunk. A trunk rooted beneath the foliage of his hat, and his voice, that throaty denizen of desire, deepened, due to the blue pills (sex aids) to an abnormally low baritone. He even changed his bathing habits from once a year to once a month. Oh, and his buttocks were so firm, Pube reported in a recent interview, "That you could not drive a spear into his rear."

The reporter, lacking the skills of a good investigator, never asked why one would want to do that.

Due to his rotund physique, Hat acquired the reputation as the Uechi-Ryu wrecking ball. He preferred the Uechi-Ryu style of karate, due to the limited number of Kata, or dance moves.

All that was said for this to be said. Hat worked, nay tortured himself, with the help of Pube, into a well-oiled, highly stimulated killer.

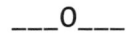

___0___

Commander Alexander arrived at the Second Elected Confederacy Headquarters of Poland. He brought with him seven hundred wrestlers and sixty popcorn and soda vendors. Elvira met her esteemed leader at the portal and escorted him to his office where they made out, ate breakfast, lunch, and later that night fed on each other in a titillating way. On the second day, Alexander gathered the crew together to plan their next campaign. "Oratio obliqua," Hat said. Elvira smiled and mumbled softly, "Happy fabrications could meld so easily with fantasy." The stereopticon was transmitting Hat's image in a soft hum, "Ladies, gentlemen, soldiers and their families, I have an announcement. We have taken Indole, the capital of Araba. The NIC fighters suffered only seven casualties. The International Freedom Fighters representing the GFP suffered two-thousand dead, four thousand wounded, and three thousand and seven no-shows. At exactly 10:00 a.m., we will have stereopticon evidence of the massacre at Indole. In the meantime, enjoy the NIC featured movie, *The Race to Space-Or How the NIC landed first on Neptune.*"

At exactly 10:00 a.m., the NIC presented the staged war. People throughout the world viewed the fake conflict in horror.

Delphi, with Bemire, by his side watched the entire showing. At the end of the program, Delphi declared, "This is the last straw. No more propaganda. No more theatrical endeavors that present us as losers. The Fake Symbolist Campaign is over. We are at war with the NIC." Delphi turned away from his friend and approached the window with a view of Town Square. People, like ants, moved about their daily lives-lives soon to be changed. "Bemire spread the news, we, the Global Freedom Party and our IFF soldiers are going to war. The Peoples Revolution has begun!"

Section VI

The Real War and Jimmy's Sainthood

CHAPTER 71

The Real War

I was in New Chicago campaigning when Delphi sent news of the impending war. Bea whispered the message she received in her coder cache. I incorporated the information into my speech. The message was clear, overthrow the NIC by any means available. I had video evidence of the NIC's brutality, and I preached about the NIC's fake war. A war of propaganda used to constrain the population. "The fake war is now over," I declared, "a real war has begun."

The audience surged toward the conscription table shouting, "Real War... Real War."

I sent a message to Delphi as soon as the speech ended, reminding him that we had no weapons. He summoned me to his Chicago Office. Delphi wanted me to report his assault on the Black Ops Corporation. Bea and seven other activated military replicas were already at Delphi's office when Bea and I arrived. The replicas, armed with knives and guns were eager to begin the attack on the Black Ops Building. I asked Delphi if it was a good idea for me, as the GFP's candidate, to participate in such a dangerous undertaking.

He smiled, "Don't worry," he said. "Beatrice and her seven replicas will take care of you. Here is your nose cam." He handed me the tiny camera, I stuck it up my red nose and tested it, "Good feed," a technician said from the bathroom. He approached fastening his jammies and handed me a voice recorder and a writing tool in case of an equipment failure. Suddenly, as if in a horrible nightmare (something akin to being bludgeoned to death by a summer sausage), I began to panic. My nervous system cracked like a thin-shelled pecan under a nutcracker's pincer. My hands shook, my knees wobbled, my eyes enlarged to the size of golf balls. I looked at an antique mirror that hung on Delphi's wall. I was stunned. My bulging red nose accentuated my swollen white eyes perfectly. I frowned and my image impeccably frowned with me. I whined as any decent clown would when faced with the possibility of immediate death. A flood of tears broke through the dam of chalky white powder that covered my face, and little winding streams incited by gravity, cascaded to the floor. I almost fainted—would have, if Bea hadn't given me a shot of testosterone.

The seven replicas quietly observed my transformation from a milquetoast to a monster. They seemed to appreciate my large and growing gland thumping in my clown suit. It was difficult, but I managed to focus on the job ahead, and not on sex. That would come later, I thought. The idea of sex after conflict made me impatient, "What are we waiting for, let's go," I said in a rather commanding voice.

Commander Delphi agreed, "Move out," he said. We followed Commander Delphi to his floater and proceeded beneath the black blanket of the night to the Black Ops Building. Our fighting force debarked on a dark street behind the Ops building, and we waited.

"I'm about to burst," I said, "let's go."

"Wait," Delphi said.

We waited another fifteen or twenty minutes, "C'mon let's go. I'm having naughty thoughts about Beatrice—about all the replicas actually, I can't hold it much longer." Just when I was going to rush the building, I noticed a large cargo skidder floating above our heads. The skidder moved forward and landed in front of our floater. "What is that?" I asked. My pecker concerned about its own reality played a drum solo on my belly.

"That is our assault team," Delphi said as we approached the skidder. I peered into the portal window and to my surprise saw a bunch of squirrel's playing cards. There must have been twenty-five or more tiny tables with four to six rodents at each table. The squirrels were playing poker, strip poker, half were fully clothed to partially clothed, while others were completely naked. I noticed one, a girl-squirrel-cute little thing, completely nude, and I started having pecker issues again. "Attention, Officer on board," the Sargent at Arms said. He snapped his short furry legs together and saluted as Delphi stepped on deck. All the squirrels dropped their cards and snapped to attention.

"Ladies and gentlemen," Commander Delphi said. "It is time to take our country back. Your assignment is simple, open the Black Ops building, stealthily kill as many personnel as you can, open the front door for my Rangers and me, and return to your ship. Please put your uniforms on, and wear your night vision goggles. Any questions?"

"No Sir," the platoon squeaked in unison.

"On my count, one, two, three, go!" Delphi said. The squirrels tumbled out of the skidder and began scaling the building's walls before we had a chance to wish them well. Perhaps it was due to the pressure in my lower extremity, but from a distance, the hoard of rodents appeared to me, like fleas scurrying up the thigh of a hairless Chihuahua. The squirrels were small enough to penetrate the building's vents, and it was not long until they were at the front door. We witnessed through the glass portal of the door the murder of the gatekeeper. The little squirrel-girl that I had spied earlier crawled up the man's pants leg and attacked the man's gonads with the callous ferocity of a mechanical nut-buster. I must admit my sexual appetite for her little body diminished at that point, and I turned my eyes to a replica who by intent or accident let slip a pubic hair from beneath her willie-woven shorts. While I remained fixated on the derelict sprig or auburn hair, the gatekeeper collapsed writhing on the floor in pain. Once down, the man had no chance. A swarm of little rodents nipped away at his flesh one soupcon at a time. The squirrel-girl retrieved the keys from the man's shredded clothes while the rest of the squirrel clan formed a ladder of bodies (aka squirrel pyramid) so that my bygone babe, the squirrel-girl, could reach the door handle. She scrambled up the fuzzy ladder, turned the key, and opened the door. The squirrel pyramid collapsed into a furred flow and poured out of the building as we streamed inside. The replicas with bows taught and knives drawn led the way to the computer room. My newfound friend, the pubic-hair-girl-replica stood guard as Delphi opened the shipping and handling computer program, and ordered enough armaments to satisfy our needs for the next two years. He billed his opponent Alexander for the arms and had the munitions shipped to GFP command posts across the country.

We were in the lobby, Bea was on my right side, and the other replicas were on my left. Delphi led the group. Dawn was breaking in royal colors over the multi-towers and low-rise buildings in downtown New Chicago. The first laser shot created a nickel size hole the door. A laser cannon, from the sound of it, destroyed the large picture window sending glass shards throughout the lobby. We took shelter behind the lobby's radiant wall. The replicas scattered in an attempt to find the NIC's position and provide a counterattack. Delphi recalled the squirrel platoon who by happenstance was celebrating their victory in a downtown bar. The squirrels arrived a few minutes later armed with wooden trajectories called smears.

There must have been twenty or more of the NIC fighters. All of them seasoned wrestlers. All of them two-hundred-fifty plus pounds. Bea took the first one down with an arrow through his heart. The second one pointed his laser at her and squeezed the trigger. She leaped catlike out of the way, charged, and administered a blow to the top of his cranium. He dropped to his knees, and she severed his head. He had a surprised almost cartoonish look on his face. The other replicas were just as efficient. Twenty-seven men died within five minutes, but let's not forget about the squirrels. They were amazing fighters many of them while leaping through the air would piss in the eyes of the wrestlers and blind them making the combatants easy targets for the replicas

Bea escorted Delphi and me away while the replicas and the squirrels went to celebrate their second victory.

Within a week, the entire the Global Freedom Party and their soldiers were armed.

CHAPTER 72

Freedom Fighters

I, the Presidential Candidate Jimmie Linguine after taking a hit of testosterone was lounging in my quarters. I was viewing the replay of my nose-cam video featuring GFP's attack on the Black Ops Headquarters. I was especially stimulated by the antics of the squirrel-girl. I was aroused, very aroused almost critically aroused when suddenly a secret message, *Jimmie we have the sliders, rockets, stud blowers, drones stealth ships, and cruisers. You are in charge, Attack,* arrived in my keen ears via an audio earplug. I spread the fan of my five fingers and waved cooling air across my face. I arched both my eyebrows, enlarged my eyes into a grotesquely corpulent bulge, and as an unintended consequence dislodged the monocle resting peacefully on my cheek, "Oh my," I said, "this is serious Delphi has ordered another attack."

Twelve hours later we launched an attack

against the Second Elected Confederacy Headquarters of Poland. Under my ductile command, Bemire and Capitan Miguel Martinez sent forth forty-seven armed sliders, each containing forty-seven commandos. The fleet met heavy resistance in the outer perimeter of Poland's atmosphere. Laser rockets and stud blowers took down seven IFF's ships. The freedom fighters retaliated with drone attacks on the Confederacy Headquarters, taking out the theater and mess hall. Frenetic Drones capable of firing large cannons launched an attack on the NIC ships. Two enemy cruisers went down and three troop carriers were damaged in the counter-attack. The IFF had breached the Confederate airspace and dropped bombs onto the surface of Alexander's sanctuary. The Second Elected Confederacy Headquarters of Poland surrendered after two hours of continuous bombing.

Unfortunately, Alexander with his closest aides departed the headquarters on space lifts. He left his wrestlers to defend the Confederacy. I filmed the entire battle and subsequent surrender of the NIC and relayed the video via express ray to Delphi. The commander instantly played the video over the national airwaves, and within a few days, the GFP had an additional seven thousand military volunteers. Delphi's next plan was to locate and destroy the cowardly Alexander and his fighting force. There was, however, a problem. I had only one week to live. My thirty years and one day would be up June, 3ʳᵈ. Bea was saddened by the news and vowed to kill thirty NIC men, and one child (to represent each year and a day of my life,) I was physically and emotionally stimulated by her offer.

CHAPTER 73

Alexander's Escape and Demise

Alexander, along with Elvira, Hat, Comica, and her band of warriors fled The Second Elected Confederacy Headquarters of Poland and flew to Paris where he had a stash of warships and heavy artillery, including antiaircraft weapons. It was also the home of one of the finest theatrical groups on the Island. Alexander flooded the airways with propaganda. He wrote the script for the theater company. The propagandistic commercial went like this:

Act 1, Alexander is standing stiffly. He holds above his head the severed head of Commander Delphi.

Fade to black.

Act 2, Comica stands with a placard in hand, that reads, "We won again." Behind her, depicting, in gruesome detail, an Ombres Chinoises shadow

The Perfect Plan

puppet show depicted Alexander, slaying his IFF opponents.

Fade to red

Act 3, The Director, Le Dernier, along with Alexander, Elvira, Hat, and Comica appear on stage, holding hands and singing the NIC National Anthem.

Suddenly!

A bomb went off killing The Director, Le Dernier, along with Alexander, Elvira, Hat, and Comica and all stagehands, theatrical performers, puppeteers, singers and unfortunately everyone in the audience.

The Turkey Fan Club, (TFC) an offshoot of the radical Catholic-Muslim-Protestant Organization, (CMPO) took responsibility for the act. Evan's oldest son Eden, the founder of the TFC, confiscated all the GFP's armaments, including aircraft, and naval, vessels. This act of cowardice was in effect the beginning of the Turkey Revolt of 3054.

CHAPTER 74

The Covenant

Mother Urdu was lounging on her stone bed with tiny souls attached to her breasts. Loki was rocking an undisciplined Port Smith soul destined to be an elevator operator in the city's nuclear dump. "I feel sorry for him," Loki said, "Working the nuke-dumps is a dangerous job. The child will only have a few years of employment before death by radiation poisoning. Why keep sending these children back to live a miserable life and die prematurely?"

"They have a purpose," Urdu said, "This one's life will lead to another until the children are one with the universe."

"So much suffering, just to become nothing?"

"The Universe is everything," Replied Urdu.

"The universe is cold it feels nothing," Loki said with a furrowed brow and intense glower.

"No," Urdu said, "the Universe creates new matter out of old material."

The Perfect Plan

"Do you mean the Universe goes boom and starts over?"

"Something like that."

"What's the point?"

Mother Urdu huffed, "The point is everything is recycled to make something new."

"But some of those somethings do not have souls. What do they contribute to the Universe?"

"I told you chemical reaction makes matter, a soul is made up of particles—particles make matter," Urdu replied.

Loki rolled his eyes, "But why?"

"Life and death, nothing lasts forever. It is a way for the universe to die and be reborn."

Loki scratched his armpit and ruminated about the process of becoming a rock, or a molecule of water, or even human. He cringed at the thought of being human.

A sudden rap on the stone entrance of Urdu's cave interrupted Loki's thoughts on transformative death.

"Who calls upon Mother Urdu?" Loki said.

"Prosperous' Soul," came a loud reply, "I've come about Jimmie Linguine."

Loki and Urdu exchanged glances, "Enter," Urdu said.

Prosperous' shadow swayed along the walls of the cave long before his entrance into her chamber. He stood before Mother Urdu and Loki a mere weave of smoke. "I am in need of a teat, and a word."

"Come to me child," Mother Urdu said, and gingerly lifted the small grey cloud to her biggest nipple the udder aft her foreleg.

The cloud began to form as an embryo as he nursed and was fully fashioned by the time he spoke. "I remember Loki's words as we dream-talked at the Hotel Caledonia."

"Yes," Urdu said.

The transforming little bald, bug-eyed boy looked at Loki. "Hi, Loki."

"Hello Prosperous," Loki replied, as he continued to cradle the Port Smith Child.

"Alexander is dead."

"Yes," Urdu said, "You wouldn't be here if he was still alive."

"Loki was right, the people are unhappy about my wealth and, under Delphi and Jimmie' leadership, the people have become aggressive. They know about the fake wars and the greed of the NIC."

"Yes," Mother Urdu said.

"They know about Comica and the Muskeg Mercenaries fighting for the NIC."

"What do you want?" Urdu replied.

"As Loki suggested, I want a deal, I want a new deal."

Loki placed the Port Smith child in a wicker cradle. The child whined briefly but went quickly into a misty sleep. "Terms?" Loki said.

"I will nullify the old contract, undo Linguine's premature death, and give one-half of my wealth to the world's population."

"What do you want in return?" Loki asked.

"The other half of my wealth, an end to the war and the guarantee of an endless life."

"I cannot give you an endless life," Urdu said.

"Then a permanent home here with the Elusion people."

"I..." Mother Urdu paused to consider her statement, "The Elusion people do not want you."

"What can you offer then?"

"A life in a remote place, with your half of the world's wealth."

"What about me and one female of my choosing... with no interference from you and your rebirth bull shit. Our children's souls will live fifty-thousand years in an otherworldly place."

Urdu studied his proposal, "The woman must want to go with you, and you and she, and your children must reside elsewhere forever."

"Done," Prosperous' Soul said as he placed his chubby palm around Mother Urdu's index finger, and shook it briskly.

CHAPTER 75

The Modified Contract

Mother Urdu was experiencing an intimate moment with Loki, as her husband, Fyodor the Epistler, filmed the event on his videophone. As the brutal act was taking place, Prosperous' soul waited patiently in Urdu's wicker basket. The preborn was watching Mother Urdu and Loki. He remembered vividly his first experience with Odor's wife Bordet. He smiled a little ghostly smile in remembrance of her apathy. Prosperous fell asleep soon after the orgy was over.

A short time later Mother Urdu, dripping wet from her shower, came in to find Izabelle, Elvira, and Hat, in her chamber. Loki sat in her boudoir as well holding a new soul. He named Bartholomew. (No relation to the male nurse Bartholomew, who verified Shanika's virginity). Loki had gotten into the habit of naming baby souls. By naming a child, he felt connected to the re-birth in a familial way.

The Perfect Plan

"Come, children," Mother Urdu said. The three souls drifted to Urdu's feet. "You too Prosperous." Prosperous crawled out of the wicker basket and sat behind Hat. "Up front please." Prosperous moved forward, close enough to touch Mother Urdu's clawed toes. "Now children, Prosperous has an announcement. So pay attention."

She looked at Prosperous who cleared his throat, and said, "I have made an agreement with Mother Urdu. I have agreed to change the original contract and release Jimmie Linguine from his thirty-year and one-day servitude in life. He can now live a normal life with no restrictions."

"And," Mother Urdu urged Prosperous to continue with a gentle nudge.

"I will give the world half of my wealth."

Elvira clapped her hands to her fleshy jowls and emitted a moan.

"Go on," Urdu said.

"In return, I will retain half my wealth. I will leave this country, and I am never to return. Also, I may take a woman with me. The woman must agree to the same terms and conditions that I have agreed to and must go willingly. Urdu has advised me that I am going to Hell. I have friends there and Hell has a warm climate. Also, I would like..." Prosperous paused, "I would like to take... Elvira with me she has been a constant and loyal friend."

"Any objections?" Loki asked. Mother Urdu looked firmly at all the children. She lingered on Izabelle and saw the pain in her countenance. "Do you have anything to say Izabelle?"

"I would like to go with Prosperous too," Izabelle became misty and her little cloud soul started to rain.

"Prosperous?"

He thought about Izabelle's request. He did not trust her, but he was expressively and humbly moved by her outpour of emotion. He was leaning forward to emit a confidential response into Urdu's ear, when Elvira said in a soft tone, almost a whisper, "We can have a threesome—A ménage a trois."

Prosperous straightened his shape vertically and said, "Can I take two women?"

Loki glanced at Urdu. It was a questioning look. She returned his gaze presented in the chamber of her mind an extended study and analysis of the pros and cons of Prosperous' request and abruptly nodded an affirmative.

"Done deal," Loki said before anyone could change their minds. "Only Hat will be going to a new earth mother. Prosperous, Elvira, and Izabelle, shall have demon mothers in Hell."

Urdu felt relieved. She took the four souls to her breast and nursed them to an appropriate fetal size.

"Compose the contract as agreed, Loki, and make sure all parties sign it; then take care of the dispersal of Prosperous' wealth," Urdu said.

___O___

The Perfect Plan

The Demoness Palimony became mother to Elvira's soul. Her sister Croc Ell received Izabelle's soul and Mademoiselle Ardent Lili, a distant cousin of the Marquise de Sade obtained the soul of Prosperous. All soul bearers were respectable women in Beelzebub's Order of the Flies.

Because of the unusually warm climate in Hell, the incubation period for new souls was half of what it would have been in a normal pregnancy. All three souls, Prosperous, Elvira, and Izabelle, were born in Hells Nursery 135 days later. The accelerated growth continued after birth, 70 days later aging stopped at an effective age of forty-two. All three children, now adults, maintained their worldly names.

CHAPTER 76

Dead again

A large clock hung on the wall of the Jacuzzi room in the Clauson Hotel, located in New Port, a suburb of New Chicago. It was June 3rd; Jimmie had made a vow to take his life at the end of his last hour. That's right suicide. He was alone sitting peacefully in a bubbling pool of warm water. A bone-handled knife lay at his side. He was tired of life, tired of war, weary of experiencing each day of his short miserable life(s). Each of his hundreds of mother's had been losers; he had been unloved and mistreated by all of them.

He was a clown, a sad, superficial, humorless clown. Jimmie looked at his clown shoes protruding like red and blue two-tone islands above the tub's waves. He gazed at the Iris in his jacket's lapel, wilted now. It too was a few minutes away from death. He removed his water-splashed monocle. Clarity, much like life's purpose was blurred.

The Perfect Plan

He fingered his pencil-thin mustache above his red powdered lips; he remembered Bea's rubber lips—his last days with her. He began to whimper, put his knuckles to his eyes and sobbed, then he sniveled which evolved into a yammering blubber, then a headshaking bawl erupted, and finally, with all hope gone, he began a soul-shattering wail.

"Man-up," he whispered, but he failed at that too. He was a failure. "What have I accomplished in all my years of death and rebirth?" He said. "Nothing, nothing at all," he continued to whine. Jimmie touched his wig, pulled the purple toupee from his head. It reminded him of Bea's muff, that night in Florida when he was trying to switch her off and other times, more romantic times when he turned her on. He patted the hairpiece tenderly, teased it into a brilliant bouffant; then finger combed the hair to the left. Jimmie concentrated on his life in the sixties, how miserable, he thought, another failure; we could not stop an illegal war. He thought about the thing that hurt him the most, his first mother Izabelle, abandoned him and left him to die. Jimmie picked up the bone handle knife. He was ready to go. He placed the sharp blade to his throat, glanced at the clock wanting to make sure he sliced at the right moment. He noticed that it was 12:07 a.m. Jimmie had missed the deadline. He was still alive. It was a miracle. A frigging miracle!

Jimmie sloshed out of the tub. Shaking water like a wet dog. He was elated, finally, a normal life, a life of more than thirty years and a day. His enthusiasm ranked to that of his soul surviving the Jibed Holocaust.

Interjection: The Jibed Holocaust was an incident in 2052 whereby the Bubo Cannibals in Costal Leica cooked and ate Linguine when he was twenty-eight years old. His soul stayed with his skeleton for another two years. Jimmie Linguine, as a skeleton with a soul became a famous Halloween character and was the featured attraction in Hambones Haunted House.

— He whopped his big shoes on the wet cement, leaped into the air and spun in a tight pirouette. His purple wig sailed away as it were a hairy Frisbee. The periwig hit the wall with a splat and left a snail trail as it slid to the concrete floor. Jimmie at the apex of his pirouette began his dizzying descent. His huge shoes threw him off balance. He landed awkwardly, fell, hit his head on the edge of the Jacuzzi, and died.

CHAPTER 77

Beatrice's Reaction to Jimmie's Death

Beatrice was on the front lines eliminating the remaining NCI soldiers when she heard the news about Jimmie Linguine's death. Delphi delivered the message to her through an encoded talk box. She was heartbroken. She moaned and cried for three days—became suicidal and entertained the thought of switching herself off. Then she felt denial, Jimmie could not die. Delphi was mistaken. Someone miscalculated his years. She was sure he said he had another month. It is impossible. He cannot be dead. The next step was anger... this step should be discussed, even if it is controversial. Bea, in an uncontrollable rampage, killed seventy-one hostages using methods as gruesome as testicular strangulation, death by a thousand pinpricks, impalement (butt-up) on a wooden shaft. The force-feeding of poisonous spiders and the list goes on.

It was during this period of depression and

anger that Beelzebub contacted Bea. She was kneeling at Jimmie's gravesite when Satan's surrogate arrived. Beelzebub spoke softly, "My newly arrived associate, Mr. Prosperous is impressed with your skills and mindset. He would like to offer you a position as General Manager of the Black Ops Corporation. Mr. Prosperous personally confided in me that he wants you Beatrice to take over the Black Ops." The devil stepped forward, "I am sure you are familiar with the company. It is an arms business." Beelzebub paused, smiled, rubbed his tongue along the ridge of his lips, winked his lizard-like eye, and continued, "What do you say?"

"I want my Jimmie back." Bea moaned.

"He will remain in your heart." Beelzebub with supplicatory eyes reached for and caressed Bea's knuckles with the tips of his scaly fingers, "If my guess is correct, you loved him."

"I did—I do," She said, "But Prosperous and the NIC, were our enemies."

"Were," Beelzebub paused, "Were your enemies. They are gone now, defeated."

"Look, Bea, you can turn the Black Ops into a corporation for world peace. It is simple if you sell nuclear bombs to every country large or small. There will be a standoff, a stalemate. It is the only way to maintain world peace, and you can do it —you can save the world! You, Beatrice, a replica can save the world! C'mon Bea do what is right, do it for the good of the planet. Do it for Jimmie. Manage the Black Ops. What say you, girl? Save

The Perfect Plan

the world!" Beelzebub eyes began to glow with excitement.

Bea with a sigh and a shudder whispered, "Okay."

Beelzebub straightened the curve of his spine and said with a stern inflection, "Prosperous will have his secretary provide you with the appropriate documents. Go to 11,927 17th Street in New Chicago, Suite A37. Ms. Lament will have everything ready for you to sign."

A few days later, Beatrice entered the building depressed from the loss of her beloved Jimmie and signed the document without reading it first. She started work the next day.

CHAPTER 78

The Rise of the Underthings

Alexander's unforeseeable death was the tomato in the GFP's pasta. The National Island Corporation was on the run. The NIC sponsored theaters all over the world were closing. The NIC play was about to end, or so Commander Delphi thought, but internal problems were brewing on high heat. There had been a small uprising in Memphis, brought about by Delphi's unwillingness to allow bright students, commonly known as geeks, to provide a cost-benefit analysis on the war effort, and then there were the reformers, known as Reefers. The Reefers were students dedicated to love-not-war. They were screwing each other all over the place and holding lewd concerts in the most remote regions of the world. Another branch of protesters, the Literati, called for the GFP to outlaw war altogether.

The Global Freedom Party began to crumble

under the weight of discontent. This small stutter in the GFP's effort to win the war, and rebuild the nation, led to the rise of the Underthings. A new enemy grew from the ranks of the pre-purge victims, those uneducated downtrodden people had gathered to claim their right to live a middle-class life, and enjoy the prosperity that they surmised was rightly theirs.

Since the GFP lacked an elected president, Loki contacted Delphi and bestowed upon him, the title of 'Legal Representative' of the party. Delphi was responsible for distributing one-half of Alexander's wealth to the population.

In an effort to appease the Underthings, Delphi gave each person whose income was below poverty level, which was 99 % of the population, sufficient monthly stipends to ensure a minimum standard of living. This gift caused a strain on the GFP budget and working people became angry with the party for allowing the non-workers to receive free government benefits. The GFP grew weaker, and could not continue to fight a guerrilla war with the Muskegs and other remnants of Alexander's army, nor could they continue to support the Underthings. There was a void in the government, and the Black Ops Corporation, under the leadership of Beatrice, stepped in to fill that void.

CHAPTER 79

The Last Terrorist on Earth

"Wait," said Dar's great, great, grandson, Darn, who at one-hundred and seven looked like a withered toad, seven weeks out of the water. He was sitting in his hut with the door closed. His girlfriend, Callous Ventricle hung on the wall of his dung-covered shanty. Not her picture, mind you. Callous' mummified body hung Christ-like on a wall timber. Darn worshiped Callous' leathered body and surrounded her corpse with bits of metal, wood, and shrapnel, which served his twisted psyche as memorials from past terrorist campaigns. He was talking to her during a slow-paced self-administered pedicure. He professed with jubilant enthusiasm during the nail rasp his intent to marry her. Of course, she did not answer, he took her silence as a yes and slowed the pace of his fingernail file to five strokes per minute.

Darn obtained a small stipend from the Mid-

The Perfect Plan

dle Eastern War Commission for his contribution to their war efforts, in America, Europe, and elsewhere. Many knowledgeable soldiers and reputable War Lords believe Darn is, *The Last Terrorist on Earth*, but it is not necessarily true according to Professor Henry Hush III. The professor believes there are sleeper cells scattered across the globe. The professor provided the names Evan, and Beatrice as evidence. These two non-humans, he claims, are currently responsible for over half of all the deaths in the world. In addition, the professor asserts the numbers will increase to a hundred percent by the year 3075.

Darn, according to Professor Hush while in a state of meditative incongruity can communicate with Evan. According to the professor, Darn assists the turkey in plotting new terrorist attacks.

Professor Hush has a large following of mostly middle-class pink people. The pinksters as he calls them were exposed a few years back to toad poisoning in one of the island's largest cities, Milligan Michigan. Someone dressed as an Indian had placed the poison in the city's municipal water system. Darn's involvement in this biological attack is unclear. There are, however, clues to his participation like vials of toad poison in his medicine cabinet.

A radicalized pink skin pigmentation and poor cognitive skills are now part of the pinksters DNA. Both traits are congenital. The Pinksters, considered *odd-thinkers* by most cults around the planet were revered for their creativity. The pink people believe the world will end in 3054 unless Jimmie Linguine can rise from the dead to save humankind.

Evan advised Darn telepathically of Jimmie's probable rebirth. Darn cried out in response, "My Callous is the only savior."

Interjection: A summary of findings concerning social and religious beliefs of the people involved in the writing of the script.

A Synod of Epic-Opal Bishops of which Scripter 4 is a member, has concluded during musical vespers and hypnotic chants that Pinksters are blasphemers and that Jimmie Linguine is the antichrist.

It is the executive in charge's opinion, based on audio recordings of his secret conversations with the pinksters, that Scripter 4 and his Synod of Epic-Opal Bishops are Communists and traitors to this intuitive tome.

In addition, the vast majority of freethinkers, regardless of their IQ, revere Jimmie Linguine as the Clown Saint.

CHAPTER 80

How Linguine became a Saint

On June 4th at 7:45, a.m., the County Coroner pronounced Jimmie dead. The same coroner pronounced him alive at 12:47 on June 10th one day before his scheduled cremation. Papist Cardinal Bird proclaimed his resurrection, a miracle and declared June 10th, Saint Clown Day, a national religious holiday. The Cardinal also anointed Jimmie as the Clown Saint of Licorice Sticks. Jimmie's reverence grew exponentially over the next month. His popularity rating climbed to 85% and when he reached 90% in the polls, the Pope anointed him with oil, extracted from the consecrated Licorice Plant grown only in the All-Saints Cemetery.

Details of Jimmies Sainthood.

Loki placed the truth in the long ear of Mother Urdu. "Jimmie Linguine is dead."

Urdu was napping in her favorite mahogany bed. She was resting on her left side with all twelve breasts exposed to Loki's tearful eyes. She promptly arose, and pawed the sleep from her brown bulging eyes, "What," she said still under the spell of Hypnos.

Loki repeated, "Jimmie Linguine is dead."

Suddenly alert, Urdu asked, "How do you know such news?"

"It was whispered to Zephyrus by the undertaker, a Mister Chick Cornish. It seems Beelzebub overheard the news according to Zephyrus and sent his emissary Prosperous to collect Jimmie's soul before it reached you."

Mother Urdu lifted her hind leg and scratched the nerve of anxiety just below her rib cage, and said, "What shall I do?"

Loki, Urdu's dearest comforter replied, "I will go and retrieve Linguine from Satan's Sauna."

Loki stood straight as a primrose pecker, uh, that is to say as high as the head of an alert Ostrich —the body being the scrotum and the neck the penis—thicker, though—his pecker was thicker than an Ostrich neck... for sure.

Interjection: A filmed conversation between the scripters and the executive in charge concerning the quality of writing in the current scene.

"Who wrote this?" the executive in charge yelled.

A voice seeped from behind the bathroom

The Perfect Plan

wall, "It was I, 2."

"Who?"

"2, I wrote it." 2 said in a shout.

"Will this writing stand the test?" the executive asked.

"Yes," 2 said.

"Let's vote," 3 said in a soaring soprano.

"1?" the executive said.

"Aye."

"2?"

"Aye, of course."

"3?"

"Nay."

"4?"

"Nay."

"It is a tie," the executive in charge said in a restless mutter.

"Where's 5?" 1 said.

"He went in for a nipple piercing and enema," 4 replied.

"Flip a coin," 1 said without commenting on 5's curious behavior.

2 returned from the men's room. "Yes," 2 said.

The executive agreed, "Call it in the air 3?"

"Tails," 3 said.

The executive in charge flipped the coin, caught the dimmy-dime, and slapped the coin on the back of his hairy hand... "It is tails."

"Ostrich neck for sure," the executive repeated.

3 interrupted the executive, "You know why I

called tails?"

"I don't want to know?" 4 said.

"Because it reminds me of sitting on someone's face." 3 said ignoring 4's request.

4 said in retaliation, "I suppose the face you are mentioning is Linguine's."

"Stop," the executive in charge yelled.
Silence.
"Linguine is dead. Show some respect."
Silence,
"Now please continue."

— Loki looked at his crotch and tried to visualize the metaphor.

Mother Urdu interrupted his concentration, "You would do that for me?"

Loki grasped his man-thing and edged closer to Urdu's teats, "Yes, yes I would."

That afternoon Loki was sitting on a stool in front of Satan's Gate. He was inebriated and leaned heavily on Hell's bell. "Who is it?" came a cry from the flames.

"It is Loki."

"One moment please," There was a long pause, "You are not on the list," the tetchy voice said.

Loki lit a cigar, "Let me speak to the manager," he said as smoke flowed out of his flared nostrils.

"One moment, please. Hey, Belphegor. This man wants to enter Hell without a certificate. He wants to speak to management."

A shadowy figure passed through Hell's flames. Loki laughed as the demon arrived at the gate. It was not surprising that the beast had horns. What was surprising was that he wore a tailored suit and a red bowtie around his goat-like-neck. Contained within Belphegor's hairy face were split yellow eyes and goat-like-nostrils. The demon had a long thick tongue, which hung, thick as a man's wrist out of his narrow lipless mouth. The creature also had a short thick tail with a tuft of hair on the tip. Loki noticed the goat-guy was carrying a chamber pot. A more accurate description perhaps would be a wooden porta-potty. Belphegor sat the portable toilet down. He took his time to level it by tweaking the adjustable legs. Then he carefully rocked the toilet back and forth to make sure it was stable and raised the toilet seat. Belphegor sighed softly once his arse touched the opening in the wooden stool.

"Evening Sir, my name is Belphegor, Belph for short. Excuse the immediacy of this bowel movement. How can I help you?" The demonic goat-guy said.

"Pleasure to meet you Belph. My name is Loki, and I am here to retrieve a Mr. Jimmie Linguine."

"You cannot have Mr. Linguine. He belongs to Beelzebub. Thank you for coming. You must go," Belph said through the barred gate.

"Wait," Loki said. "I see you have a need for

a compartment due I would guess to constant bowel movements. It is probably a sign of soupy-poopsie. If that is the case... Well, let me show you. I have the schematic of a device you might be interested in seeing. It is lightweight, completely portable, and practical, especially in warm climes like these."

"Let me see," Belph said with an eagerness that Loki found encouraging.

In Loki's thigh pocket (he was wearing Bermuda shorts) was a small notebook. Loki lifted a pencil that was wedged behind his ear and quickly sketched out a device he had seen many years ago on TV. It was a toileted wheelchair. "This device," Loki said, "is great. It has a built-in toilet as well as a means of locomotion. You can drive around and crap as needed. Look there is even a flap for dumping waste."

Belph leaned forward while still maintaining buttock contact with the toilet and looked at the drawing through the barred gate. "What do you want for it?"

"Give me Jimmie Linguine," Loki said.

"I cannot," Belph said, "It is forbidden for me to remove a soul."

"Open the gate then and I will remove Jimmie."

Belph looked at Loki. He was tempted. Loki could see it on his face. "Imagine riding around in your poop mobile waving at the girls, and the girls begging for a ride. You-be-styling-brother and you

The Perfect Plan

don't have to worry about your condition. Think about that. The girls, the comfort, you will be the talk of the town Dude, c'mon what do you say?"

"Okay, I'll do it. Retell," Belphegor said, "come open the gate."

Out pops, Retell this little spider-looking thing, from behind a lava rock. The spider had seven eyes and seven legs. The multi-eyed, well dressed, arachnid pulled a key out of his leather vest, jumped upon the iron bars, and inserted the key. The gate creaked open.

"The paper please," Belph said.

"Where can I find Jimmie?" Loki said eyeing the spider-thing suspiciously.

"Follow the trail marked 'This Way,' whatever you do don't get off the path. Got it?"

"Got it," Loki said as he handed his sketch to Belph.

Loki followed a steep slope downward until he reached a door marked lost souls. It was actually a brothel. He entered and immediately noticed Izabelle. She was the matron of the working girls. Elvira sat at the bar smoking a cigar. Beside her, the soul of Jimmie sat in a shot glass, still in a mist state. Loki recognized the monocle, purple wig, and clown suit lying on the laminated countertop. Prosperous sat upstairs behind a glass window marked administrator.

A scuffle, undoubtedly due to Elvira's pheromone cigar, broke out between two invidious card players. The timing was perfect. Loki considered the skirmish an act of God.

One player dressed in a long black coat flipped the card table over and lunged at his rival who was wearing a long red coat. They began to finger-wrestle.

Interjection: Information taken from the Wrestling Gazette a popular magazine at the time.

Finger wrestling was a widely popular sport in Hell. The combatants entwined their pinkies and pulled. The player who lost his grip lost the match. Management typically sent the loser to the Local Gym where he was forced to watch pre-recorded workout videos of 'Strength Training for Pinkies.' The winner typically got the girl.

— While all eyes focused on the two combatants, Loki rushed to the bar grabbed the shot glass containing Jimmie's soul and Jimmie's clown suit and his purple wig and made a dash for the door. Elvira was slow to react. She did notice however how well Loki filled out the back end of his Bermuda shorts and gave a whistle. It was unclear if the whistle was to alert management or if it was a feminist attempt to get attention from a fine figure of a man. Anyway by the time management realized there was an escape in progress, Loki was out the door. He headed, lickety-split toward the gate. It was an arduous trip running up the steep incline. The continuous stopping and stuffing the little soul into the shot glass while clinging to Jimmie's clown outfit and wig hampered Loki's nat-

The Perfect Plan

ural running ability.

As he approached the gate, Loki noticed Belph, was still on the toilet; Loki leaped (broad jumping was one of his forte's in community college) he landed heavily on Belph's horned head and leaped again clearing the gate with a few meters of air to spare. Loki paced himself at a slow trot the remainder of the way to the Elusion Islands.

Mother Urdu had just taken a coin from Fyodor the Epistler for the next round of sex when Loki came crashing excitedly into her bedroom. Fyodor in the process of disrobing had a shocked look on his face. As did Urdu, who was in estrus. She blushed, threw a bedsheet across her broad body, and asked Fyodor politely to leave. She could not help but notice the hurt look on Loki's face. Loki in a storm of emotional pain pledged nevermore to breed with his X-lover. He gently placed Linguine at Urdu's feet, threw Jimmie's clown suit and wig on the floor, and then turned briskly, and walked away, despite Urdu's appeal for amnesty.

Urdu took the shot glass to her breast, and guilt-ridden about her actions lamented the entire night. Dawn festered and forced a pale ray of light through an innocuous fissure in the Urdu's cave. The light as if directed from Heaven revealed the soft glow of Linguine floating in the shot glass between mamma one, (left teat) and mamma two (right teat.)

___O___

Mother Urdu summoned her messenger, an agile and adorable seductress, Viola Martin (pronounced Mar-teen.) She was to contact Loki and bring him back, if possible, to Urdu's bedside. The good, but not chaste Mother Urdu gave Viola a gold coin to bribe Loki with, if necessary and gave her instructions to do whatever was needed to ensure Loki's return. She slapped the messenger on her tight ass, pro-ball style, (a premonition?) and sent her on her way.

Viola found Loki at the Finish Fjord. Fallen apricots surrounded him as well as a local football team named the Elusion Bears. The Lady Lions had beaten the Bears (84 to 2) in a game of touch football. A Bear's player fell down and accidentally touched the Lady Lions quarterback in the end zone giving the Bears their only 2 points scored in the game. The Bears devastated by their loss began to feast on fermented fruit. Loki suffering from the loss of Urdu joined them and they quickly became inebriated. The team and their new member Loki formed a talking circle.

The conversation started innocently enough with football strategy or the lack thereof but quickly turned to the team's embarrassing loss to the Lady Lions. At the time of Viola's arrival, the conversation had declined even further into a tearful lament about relationships with women. The Bear's quarterback, Bob, was speaking, "She just doesn't understand my needs, I mean I please her, I know I do, but she makes demands that I am uncomfortable with you know; she has unnatural desires that frankly frighten me."

A big lineman stood up, "I know what you mean; my girl does the same, only she threatens me if I don't comply. She even slaps me on occasion when I refuse to do her bidding. I have had enough of her abuse."

"Here, here," roared the jocks in unison.

Viola smiled when an inward thought bubbled to the surface of her consciousness. It had something to do with abuse, pleasurable; she mused. She, however, squelched or rather redacted her fantasies when Loki stood and spoke, "My woman cheated on me, and I don't know what to do. I mean I love her, but she has no respect for me. I thought we had things worked out. We spent a lot of time together you know." Loki took a breath; calmed himself, "In addition, I don't think it is fair that I have to pay for sex."

"Here, here," the boys chorused.

Viola slipped to the edge of the circle of men undetected. She pulled a towel from one of the player's backpacks and threw it into the ring of lamenters. "What's the matter boys?" Viola stepped forward, "Are you scared of a relationship? Afraid your feelings will get hurt. Worried about your pride—don't want to kiss up to a woman? You call yourself men. I mean a sapient colloquy is good for the soul, but jeez, whines and complaints will never take the place of action."

The quarterback offered a counterpoint to the circle of his fellow whiners. "We must stand united as men against the atrocities of the feminine mind. Let us meet here every second Wednesday as a support group!"

"You, number twelve," Viola interrupted. A handsome player pointed at his chest. "Yea you, the quarterback, have you tried talking to your woman." Viola turned her gaze to the lineman, "And, you big guy, a man shouldn't take abuse from anyone. If you feel threatened, leave. Loki here has a legitimate complaint. His woman did cheat on him, but did he confront her, and try to work it out? No, he did not. He stuck his tail between his legs and ran away. Boy's you need to talk to your women about your concerns. If you can't work it out, leave, just leave, it is that simple." Viola took a deep breath, "Having said that Loki, I will tell you that Urdu has sent me to ask you to come back. She is sorry about what happened and she wants you to return to her bed." Viola paused, "And she said the first week is free," Urdu's emissary then gazed at each individual in the circle, "What about it boys? Should Loki go back to his woman, or stay here and complain?"

"Go back," the players', sonorously replied.

Loki led the return trip home. Viola followed all the while she was studying his buttocks hidden within the Bermuda Triangle of his shorts. Loki could sense her watching him. He made a quick roundabout and caught her looking at his ass. She did not bother to raise her eyes, and remained focused on the area below his belt, "Oh my," she said. "I have a gold coin. I will pay you."

She was attractive. She had a lovely smile. Her skin unblemished felt like satin as he stroked her cheek. Viola removed her halter, and bikini bottom. She touched his dark wet wolf man's nose. Loki took her in his arms, she submitted. He bit the coin to make sure it was genuine gold, it was, and they did it... doggy style first, then attempted to experience all forty-seven positions suggested in the Art of Love, a book by Minnie Peters. They accomplished thirty-nine of the forty-seven positions. Afterward, semi-exhausted and sore, she managed to slip her tongue into Loki's hairy ear hole and she climaxed (twice) when she tasted the semi-bitter flavor of earwax. After a short revival period, punctuated by soft kisses around Loki's neck (she had to lift his beard to reach the dark flesh) Viola under a swoon said, "If your departure from Urdu's bed was solely from conjugal infidelity, you are welcome to remain between my blankets without fear or anger from your most appreciative host." Loki smiled and nodded without comprehending the gist of her words.

Mother Urdu ran to Loki as he entered her cave. She smelled the stink of sex on him but did not say or do anything. She was glad to have him home for many reasons and there were many

Donald D'lo

needs yet to be satisfied.

CHAPTER 81

Reflections on Jimmie's Capture

Why did Prosperous waylay Jimmie Linguine's soul and send it to Hell? Profit? Certainly but why did Prosperous consider Jimmie a threat to his business of person?" These acute questions Delphi relayed to Bemire and Miguel Martinez who had just returned from E. Condom where he was trying to raise support for the IFF.

Recruitment had dropped significantly, and the muskegs were making headway in retaking the factories and fields of Neighboring Brenda Falls. The Global Freedom Party was in bad condition financially. "We incorrectly assumed once Alexander was dead it would be an easy jog to victory. However, the inimical Muskegs had opposing thoughts. It is not, in my opinion, altogether extraneous to mention that the loss of Jimmie at this critical juncture was devastating." Bemire raised his thick eyebrows to the edge of his fallen hair, wiped his nose with his index finger, and said, quite forcefully, "Do not give up hope. The reasons Jimmie is a threat to Prosperous is," Bemire raised a finger with each possibility as he spoke.

"One— Prosperous, was angry about the thirty years profits lost in the Elusion war.

Two— Prosperous was angry about the latest deal with Loki, giving Linguine his full life back and giving the downtrodden people of earth half his wealth.

Three— Prosperous, suffering from coulrophobia, and what the clown was capable of."

Martinez agreed with a slight nod of his head.

Interjection: Coulrophobia is a Fear of clowns: Reference Steven King's Pennywise.

Interjection: A comment by Beelzebub.

"One would think the scripter would know why Prosperous aka Alexander, waylaid Jimmie and disclosed said information to the reader directly instead of forcing the reader to guess from a list provided by low paid writers who probably guesstimated the cause themselves.

Or, more likely, the writers pulled Prosperous' motive out of their collective asses. As a reader, as well as a participant in this story, I felt a blatant disregard for my intellect with this so-called list of motives. Shit, all one needed to do was ask Evan."

The Perfect Plan

Interjection: Scripter 3 speaks to Evan, (captured on video) while in a romantic stupor. She appears to be drunk.

"Evan," 3 explains, "was in the Gulf of Okeechobee (prior to his capture by the CIA,) snorkeling when he got my telepathic question. The telekinetic vibrations, distorted by the ocean waters caused Evan to surface for a clearer reception. Can you hear me?" 3 said.

"Yes," Evan replied.

"We have hit a stumbling block."

Evan bobbed along with the waves, spat out a little seawater that entered his horny nostrils, "What is it?"

"Why did Prosperous intercept Linguine's soul?"

"Because Prosperous is a psychopath, anything else?"

"No thank you, have a nice day." 3 said.

"One moment," Evan quickly said, "you're the girl who romanticizes about Jimmie, aren't you?"

Waves slapped the boat, swish, swish- "Hello, hello." Click, "Shit.".... Evan redialed, "Aren't you?"

"Yes," 3 replied tearfully.

"Well then you know," said Evan.

"Yes."

Evan replaced his snorkel and lowered his narrow mask before sinking beneath the waves.

CHAPTER 82

Jimmie gets his Body Back

Mother Urdu summoned Loki who was in the vineyard giving Viola a sponge bath. The messenger, a small yellow bird with a red crown interrupted Loki, as he was scrubbing a sensitive spot between Viola's thighs. "Mother Urdu requests your presence, in her chamber in twenty minutes."

"Message received," Loki replied, "I will be there," he said with a smile that split his hairy mouth and exposed his canines normally concealed by his flaccid lips.

"You have exceptionally white teeth," Viola said.

Loki replied with an even greater smile. "The better to eat you with my dear."

Interjection: The author, Charles Perrault (1628-1703) stole this line from Loki and used it in the early version of **Little Red Ridding Hood**.

The Perfect Plan

— Twenty minutes later Loki strode into Urdu's chamber, still smiling. Little Linguine's soul was playing catch the rat at Urdu's feet. Loki reached down and fluffed the boy's soft head. "You wanted to see me?" Loki said.

"Yes, I have a problem."

"What is it?" Loki replied in an unusually low tenor, which he mused implied sincerity.

"Jimmie doesn't have time to go through the birth, childhood, puberty, young adulthood, etc. You need to find him a body he can use just as you did with Izabelle's soul."

"I thought you disapproved of soul transfers without a mother."

"In this case, I will make an exception." Mother Urdu said.

"Why?"

"He needs to fulfill his destiny and destroy the world. If he does not go back now, there will not be a world to go back to, the Turkeys have *the bomb*."

"Oh my," Loki said.

"Take him. Go find that boy a body and be quick about it! But first, give me some love." Mother Urdu removed the bow that held her ears in a ponytail. Her long ears cascaded down her neck and lay weightily of her broad shoulders. "Loki," Urdu whispered, "get naked and twerk." Loki placed little Linguine in the closet, closed the door, played *Igottagetit* on the music-maker, and in front of Urdu and a full-length mirror began to twerk. The Wet Nurse of the Universe could not control herself. She sprang out of her recliner and joined Loki in a twerk fest, which of course ended in a wild, raunchy, romantic one-hundred-twenty-one minute, fling.

Late in the afternoon of the next day after Loki had recovered from the twerk fest and joyful sex-act. He grabbed Linguine's soul, which Urdu had replaced in the shot glass, and set off by way of an Alacrity boat to find Jimmie a suitable body. The Alacrity guided by Loki's hand crossed the Atlantic-Pacific Ocean and was speeding through the Okeechobee Gulf when he noticed, what appeared to be an abandoned boat. Loki slowed the Alacrity down to a low rumbling throttle and hailed the boat drifting aimlessly with the tide. There was no response. Loki guided the Alacrity closer to the boat and peered over the bow for possible survivors. "Hello," Loki called again, still no response. A gull circling overhead cried out in squawks and caws of the gull clan. Loki looked briefly at the sleek creature sailing above the waves. When Loki returned his eyes to the ocean, he noticed feathers floating on the surf and a shark's fin slicing through the white caps headed for what looked like a... Turkey.

Loki thought quickly and took immediate action. He jammed the throttle forward and sped toward the turkey's body. While speeding by Loki reached over the bow and in an effortless swoop,

The Perfect Plan

snatched the bird out of the sea. The turkey was still alive but unconscious. Loki stopped the ship long enough to wrap the bird in a towel before resuming his course to New Port where Jimmie's dead body rested on the coroner's slab.

Loki had a plan.

It was late, around midnight on June 9th when Loki with Jimmie's soul broke into the Clay County Coroner' Office. Loki riffled through papers scattered over the Coroner's desk, found the document he was looking for and walked over to Vault # 7. He opened the refrigerated vault and uncovered the pale lifeless face of Jimmie Linguine. "Ah, just in time," Loki said to the corpse. Loki opened a black bag he had taken from the ship. He retrieved his soul transfer pistol. Before Linguine's soul could protest, (if souls have that right), Loki moved the pistol across his chest and pointed it at the shot glass containing Jimmie's soul. Loki pulled the trigger and drew the mist into the chamber. He then reversed the procedure, prized open dead Linguine's mouth (the sound of his jawbone cracking was horrendous). He squirted little Jimmie's soul into Linguine's mouth. Then clamped the deceased's mouth shut so that the little misty Linguine could not escape. In an instant, the dead Jimmie Linguine was reborn. He opened his eyes, and noticed, Loki engaged with his hands behind him in a delicate braiding of his hair.

"That's new," Jimmie mumbled.

"Oh, sorry," Loki said while resetting Linguine's broken jaw, "it will heal in a few minutes."

Jimmie remained silent for one-hundred and two breaths; then said, without struggle or pain, "Thanks."

"You are welcome," Loki said as he reached for Jimmie's clown suit. The ensemble was neatly packed in a box that bore the name J. Linguine. He brought the clothing to Jimmie and watched his friend dress. "Jimmie," Loki said, "you must remain here in the vault until you are discovered, understand. I will meet with you in a few weeks and explain."

"Okay," Jimmie replied without question and slid back into the vault. Loki closed the door and departed through the buildings rear exit. Loki noticed as soon as he reached the Alacrity ship that the turkey was gone. It was a relief not having to deal with two bodies this night he cogitated with a quick shift of his eyes.

Loki's return to the Elution Islands was casual. He was sure, this time; he had done the right thing.

CHAPTER 83

Evan's Capture by the NIC-CIA

Earlier in the day, Evan, "pissed off," (his words), had kicked a rock in anger and broke his toenail. The polished extension of his right middle digit fell with a clink... make that a clink, clink, clink. The toenail careened down the face of collective rocks kissing each stone with red keratin lips until it came to rest in the warm sands of the Okeechobee Beach. As Evan searched for the broken nail, he spied a pomegranate lying upon a grass mat within seven circles drawn in the sand. He approached the fruit with due diligence, wary of his surroundings, for he had noticed earlier in the day footsteps on the beach of an unusual five-toed design. Even odder, a sprinkling of coconut hair accompanied the tracks, but that is not all the mysterious tracks that circled the succulent pomegranate. Evan, seriously hungry, could not wait to get at those ruby red seeds. But first, as the

Turkey Doctrine of Metaphysical Enlightenment demanded, Evan, for cleansing purposes, went snorkeling in the Gulf of Okeechobee. It was while he was snorkeling that he received the message from Scripter 3 concerning Prosperous' interception of Linguine's soul and her confession of a nefarious relationship with Jimmie the clown. Evan returned to shore preoccupied with a mental image of Jimmie and Scripter 3 having sex. Naturally, he was startled when a tribe of angry natives accosted him.

Evan gobbled angrily as Fishermen wearing white hoodies and coconut-shell-nipple- cups, and jock straps threatened to hang him. He had gazed with lust upon the pomegranate named Charlene and in fact, had decided to taste her moist and tender flesh. It was a simple misdemeanor—a cultural No-No. Pomegranates were a forbidden fruit at Okeechobee. The Okee Society worshiped them as Gods. The leader of the pack of savages, a man named Splinter, spat a snail shell at Evan striking him just below his right eye. In that moment of temporary blindness, Splinter, and his henchmen seized and bound Evan with a grass rope.

"Crucify him." A man's penis said in a muffled tone. Dick, the owner of the talking penis, was a nude dude but for the hairy shell nipple cup and hairy shell thong. Dick was a talented ventriloquist or visa-versa, Evan was not sure.

Dick provided a soft uh-hum to clear his

throat and said. "You will hang for your crimes." The anglers, under Splinter's leadership, and Dick's command agreed to lynch the dirty bird. Splinter stepped to the turkey and placed a rope around the bird's long thin neck; then jerked until he got Evans attention, "We don't want fowls like you salivating over our precious fruits."

Evan turned to look with a glazed eye upon the red-faced Splinter. He forced a strained telepathic, "Why?"

"Because it is against God and nature," the old man said.

"Oh," Evan replied, "That explains it."

During the melee, the tribesmen did not notice the chartreuse colored submarine nor the rubber raft carrying five well-dressed men. The raft landed on the beach not ten feet away. "Is there a Turkey named Evan here?" the tallest of the men said.

"Come with me," the stranger said.

Splinter removed his hoodie, stepped in front of the tall man, and said, with an angry glower, "We are going to hang that bird."

"You can hang him once we are done with him," the stranger said as he opened a leather-covered wallet. The pocket folder was probably ostrich or some other type of Aves skin. A NIC-CIA badge, with the man's picture, and the name, Lt. Desmond Hoover was pinned within the wallet.

Splinter studied the contents of the pocket folder, and asked bluntly, "Are you related to J.

Edgar Hoover? That man was my hero."

"No, J. Edgar Hoover, known affectionately in our family as Fruity, in a biblical sense did not multiply. I am the son of J. Edgar's uncle, Wasp Hover AKA 'Bring the Sting' Hoover- we came from the bright side of the family."

"What do you want with this bird?" Dick, the ventriloquist's pecker yelled.

"We are taking him in for interrogation," Desmond replied while scanning the beach for the speaker.

Evan was not surprised when the agent leg-cuffed him, forced him into the raft and jetted him away to the odd chartreuse colored submarine. The color scheme, Evan deduced, actually was a perfect camouflage in the pea-green sea.

The voyage was short. The air inside the sub was hot, thick, and sticky. It smelled of pencil-wood, but on the second sniff, Evan recognized the odor of sailor's semen. His suspicions were confirmed when he heard from the chambers below the growls and moans of an XXX-rated movie.

The submarine submerged at a buoy marked NIC-CIA Restricted Area Do Not Enter by Penalty of Purging. Evan's interrogation began at two thousand feet below sea level. The metal door to Evans cage squeaked open and Desmond with a stoop of his shoulders entered the small compartment. Evan was lying on his back, one leg cocked over the other in a relaxed pose. He was smoking a doobie he had borrowed from one of the sailors. "What is this all about?" Evan asked adjusting his leg to allow the young Hoover a glimpse at his feathery bottom.

A small bead of sweat appeared on Desmond's brow, "Huh, I am here to interrogate you."

"Why the submarine?"

"So that you cannot communicate telepathically with anyone outside this capsule," Desmond said.

Evan gobbled hysterically, "What do you want from me?"

Desmond eyed the sensual curve of Evans head and neck, and thought how much it resembled an ostrich or in a weird way, a pecker. Desmond reassigned his attention to the interrogation. "Information," Desmond murmured.

"What kind of information?"

"The sensitive kind," Desmond replied.

Evan said in a brief sarcastic communique, "Well, what is the question?"

"Where is Linguine?"

Evan looked at his damaged toe and curled the opposite (unharmed) appendages, raised his clawed foot, folded two opposing toes and said, "Take this bird and shove it up your ass."

Desmond smiled as he placed a skullcap on Evan's blue baldhead. Two wires extended from the skullcap to a battery. "Give me the bird again and I'll fry your brain."

"Okay, okay, I'll talk," Evan puffed up his

chest, and slowly released his breath. "Linguine is dead."

Desmond looked surprised, "When did he die?"

"Don't know a couple of days ago, maybe."

"Got any proof?" Desmond said. His finger twitched upon the electrical switch.

"I have to warn you," Evan said, "if you flip that switch you will have an explosion of turkey shit all over this little underwater boat, and you nor any of your crew will survive the blast." Evan opened his wings and strained in an attempt to prime himself for an intense rectal release. "The proof is in my head. You will just have to believe me. This situation, by the way, reminds me of the time back in the Turkey Head Tavern...."

"Give me evidence," Desmond interrupted.

"Silly boy, come here."

Desmond, with switch in hand, walked as if in a trance toward Evan.

"Unchain me and I will show you," Evan said.

"Don't have too." Desmond replied, "I can read your memories with this skull-cap." Before Evan could object, Desmond flipped the switch, and there on a silk screen tacked to the wall flickered Evans life, from his hatching to mating and everything in between, including a news article of Jimmie Linguine's death. When viewing, however, young Hover spent an inordinate amount of time visiting and revisiting Evan's sex life. Exhausted or bored, Desmond pulled the skullcap off Evan, and said coldly, "Get him out of here."

The last thing Evan remembered was the torpedo tube, an explosion, his expulsion from the ship, and him floating in the vast shark-filled ocean.

CHAPTER 84

Saint Jimmie Linguine

"I am hungry," Jimmie said in a dark state of self-awareness. The vault was cheerless bleak and cold. Unaware of the hour, Jimmie complained, in hopes of a rescue. "I am cold," Jimmie yelled, and yelled again, louder. "Ohooo," Jimmie moaned, "Open the..."

Before Jimmie could finish his complaint, someone said, "Who is there? I've got a gun."

"It is me, Jimmie Linguine. I believe I am residing in vault number seven."

Silence.

Five minutes advanced without a response. It was an extraordinarily long time for Linguine, but he was a patient clown. "Hello, I am in number seven, open the vault please or I shall consider legal action."

Jimmie overheard, "Oh it is just a child playing a prank."

The Perfect Plan

A louder voice responded, "Perhaps it is the ghost of Pookie, was he not shot on this day twenty years ago?"

"True, he was shot by his brother while in bed with his sister, or was it his wife."

"Get me out," Linguine screamed at the prattlers, "or I'll be the one doing the shooting." Obviously, his clown patience had expired.

Suddenly the vault moved with a little jolt, and stopped with a larger jolt, "Are you in there?" Jimmie heard someone say.

"Of course, I'm in here, get me out," Jimmie said, humbled by the pending rescue. The vault lid opened slowly, a crack at first, then wider until fully open. The light was intense, and Jimmie shielded his eyes with his hands.

"Who are you?"

Jimmie spread his pale fingers to peer at the speaker. "Who are you?" Jimmie said in return.

"I am the Coroner, Chick Cornish," the man said.

"Glad to meet you-you should know me I am Jimmie Linguine."

"Linguine is dead."

"I was, but I have arisen from the dead. I am alive."

"And who are you?" Jimmie asked a small woman standing beside Chick.

"I am Noel Nonetheless. Mr. Cornish's secretary, and I have witnessed a miracle." She said and tentatively raised both hands above her head. She then cocked her head, peered parrot like at the clown in the coffin, and shouted, "Hallelujah!"

Jimmie sat up, "Will someone please assist me out of this chamber. I am, unfortunately, still weak from my death." Chick and Noel assisted Jimmie to his feet. Jimmie, using Ms. Nonetheless as a crutch searched the room for food, "I am famished," Jimmie said, "Order some take-out would you Mr. Cornish." Ms. Nonetheless said, "Chow Mein would be nice." Chick left Jimmie under Noel's able care. He entered the hall and punched the Oriental button on the vending machine. A box of Chow Mien slipped to the reception tray. Mr. Cornish added water and heated the food in a microwave cremator. A small one—the one used to cremate children and pets. He handed the box of food with a Muskeg made plasticized fork to Jimmie. Ms. Nonetheless and Mr. Cornish silently watched Jimmie devour with humble vigor his noodles with crab crème sauce.

Jimmie remarked as he lifted the last noodle to his lips, "Give me your communication device." Mr. Cornish returned with an opti-phone. Jimmie called Delphi.

Delphi answered, "Hello."

"This is Jimmie Linguine, don't ask questions. Come get me. I am at—" Jimmie looked at the Coroner with a questioning expression on his face.

"Uh," Chick paused for a moment to collect

his thoughts, "Corner of 5th and Tumble. Clay County Coroner's Office in New Port Illinois."

"Got that?" Jimmie asked.

"How?" Delphi said.

Jimmie interrupted, "No time to explain, come get me."

___O___

Jimmie watched as Bemire flew his floater into the parking lot. The door of the flying machine opened Jimmie got in, and the two disappeared in a plume of gasified low-grade fuel. Jimmie coughed as he breathed in the vapors, "Sorry," Bemire said, "cost-saving measures. It is the only fuel we can afford." Jimmie released a sigh, straightened his purple wig, and viewed the world around him with neoteric fervor.

"How goes the war?" Jimmie asked.

"We are losing!" Bemire somberly replied, "The Black Ops Corporation and their Muskeg affiliates are stronger than ever. We have lost hope."

"Oh my," Jimmie replied.

"Where too?" Bemire asked.

"Delphi's office," Jimmie replied.

"What happened to you?"

Jimmie raised his hand to halt the current narrative. Bemire awkwardly shrugged and coughed and fiddled with his earring. Jimmie remained staunchly silent for the remainder of the trip.

Bemire sat the floater down amongst a large crowd of people waiting behind the cordoned off parking pad of Delphi's office. A number reporters and religious leaders jostled for position to see Jimmie. Two of Delphi's bodyguards forcibly parted the crowd of spectators as Bemire escorted Jimmie to Delphi's office. Balloons festooned the walls and ceiling of the otherwise bland office. Bemire took his place behind Commander Delphi. The commander with a raised finger hushed the crowd. "Jimmie Linguine has returned from the dead. It is a miracle. Jimmie as president of the world will save us all. We cannot and will not lose this war!" The crowd cheered. Delphi once again wriggled his finger to hush the crowd, then spoke in a celebratory tone, "I would like to present the Papist Emissary J. C. Divinity."

"Thank you, Commander Delphi, I will keep this brief" The Emissary stood straight, stiffened his back, gazed at the crowd and said in an adenoidal timbre, "I proclaim Jimmie's Linguine's resurrection, a miracle and declare June 10th, a national religious holiday."

Once again, the crowd erupted in loud applause followed by toasters and snifters of celebratory alcohol and drugs.

CHAPTER 85

Saint Jimmie goes to work. His first task is to meet with Bea

Bemire and I are on board a floater headed to the Black Ops Headquarters to find Bea.

"Why Bea, why now?" Bemire asked.

"Why not Bea?" I replied.

"Did you call and make an appointment?"

"Yes."

Bemire, apparently shocked by my aloofness retorted, "Is this task of yours too far up in the clouds to be reasonable?"

"In reference too?" I responded.

"Beatrice. She went to the dark side. She is with the Black Ops now. She is killing our people. She is..."

"Alright, alright," I said, "I get it, but she is not evil."

"I have to try to convince her," I looked out of the window to view the dark world. "I think she will come back to us. We have to try Bemire."

"Get a grip you are a saint now," Bemire replied.

Silence.

I considered Bemire's comment and applied difficult mental calculations, concerning the brigand replica and her effect, if any, on my sainthood. I counted to ten with short spastic breaths. The mathematical stratagem of addition, I believe provided the time needed to conjure an effective reply. "There are conditions one must adhere to whilst being a saint," I said. Bemire looked at me queer-like without a response. I continued, "Sacrifice is one," I paused to view his reaction to my astute observation concerning martyrdom. He looked confused. I whistled before continuing, "This death experience has changed me Bemire. I have found courage. I used to fear death, perhaps it was because I knew the exact time I would die, but now, I could'nt care less when and how I pass away."

"You said something about sacrifice," Bemire said in an obvious effort to direct my rhetoric toward a post-death point of view.

I adjusted my purple toupee. My wig did not fare well in the vault. It had stiffened and had not yet learned to relax.

"Yes, well I can tell you the import of Bea in my life, and what I must do for the cause. I must fulfill my purpose in life," I said. "I remember viv-

The Perfect Plan

idly and in full color, my accidental death and subsequent transfer to Hell. There was a divine reason for my demise."

"What happened after you died?"

"Beelzebub sent his emissary Prosperous, to intercept my soul. He did so by way of ambush. Purgatory's manager, Prosperous, hid behind a large cumulus cloud. I was cruising at about 7000 feet, blending in you know with the white stuff that we are all made of when all of a sudden I was chased by *Rider's in the Sky*, a rock group trying to crossover into country music. They are currently playing on the Strip at Las Vegas if you are interested."

Bemire, by compressing his facial features into a grimace said, "No, I prefer the blues."

"Well, they came at me from all directions and managed to corral me in a Plexiglas box, which as you know is invisible at 7000 feet. Once captured, I managed to observe the manufacturer's brand on the plastic. It was Muskeg made. The band of maladroit musicians, none, by the way, has the quality of play that I have, took me..."

I paused briefly to view a cardinal as it passed our slow-moving floater. I continued the chronicle when the bird suddenly disappeared behind a cloud.

"I must say the trombonists' were extremely inept. Anyway, with Prosperous leading the band two drummers carried me through the streets imprisoned in that damn plastic box. The procession stopped in front of a replica of the Sistine Chapel constructed by Libby Linguine, a distant cousin who I knew went to hell for her sodomy. It was there that I met Lucifer. He was cool, but Prosperous was not. The ass, Prosperous was Elvira's supervisor. She worked the bar and strip club. I think she had a position in management. One very hot day Prosperous took me from the brothel where I was imprisoned to visit Lucifer."

"What did Lucifer want with you?" Bemire asked with a look of shock on his face.

"He offered me all the licorice I wanted if I would help him."

"Help him?" Bemire raised his eyes above his newly acquired spectacles and delivered the hard look of an inquisitor—

"Are those new?" I asked.

Bemire removed his spectacles, glanced at them briefly, and provided an affirmative nod.

I resumed my response to his query, "Yes, he wanted me to turn ranks and become a spy against Delphi."

"What did you say?"

"I said no."

"And then?"

"Nothing, he said thank you for your honesty and turned me over to Prosperous. His response to my negativity was torture. It was horrible, first I had to listen to that god-awful band, you know, the group of trombonists', *Rider's in the Sky*." Bemire nodded and clamped his nose between

The Perfect Plan

thumb and index finger, t'was a sure sign of displeasure. "Then I was delivered to Elvira, and she in an effort to weaken my moral stance reminded me of our sexual encounters as well as yours, Bemire. This she described in excessive detail until I almost dissipated. Luckily, for me, Loki showed up and accomplished a successful rescue. I was born again as they say in the Christian tradition."

Bemire's lips tightened, and his face turned red, "What did she say about me?"

"Who?"

"Elvira."

"I cannot go into the details for fear of getting sick," I replied and then abruptly changed the topic. "When will we arrive?"

"We are there," he said. "Can you not see the Black Ops emblem?" I looked out the portal and saw a gigantic BO (silver letters on a circular black background) bordered by a flickering crimson flame.

"Yes, I see it now," I said.

We landed on the roof. Two guards arrived to escort us. One was a slim and attractive man with an athletic physique. The other, a remarkably unattractive four hundred pound walrus, (facetious, I know) sporting an oscillating mustache. He had heavy blue bags beneath his piggish unblinking eyes, potato size jowls, and smelled of sautéed onions. Due to his obesity, he struggled with his gait and employed a brass baton for support. Strange guard, I mused as the Walrus escorted us, at a gastropod's pace, into Bea's Office. The slim man stood guard at the Black Ops most elevated entrance.

The walrus opened the door allowing us to enter. Bea stood centered in the room. She was beautiful, her red hair and synthetic skin glistened in the belied light. She screamed "Oh shit!" when she saw me; screamed "Oh shit!" again, when I said, "Hello."

"It is true, you are alive," she said with her arms lifted above her head. She ambled to me in her high heel shoes and administered a rib-crushing hug. "I missed you sooo much."

"I missed you too Bea," I said tearing up as if I were a sun-glazed albino.

She kicked off her high heel shoes, and asked pointedly, "How does it feel to be a Saint?"

"Okay," I said, dropping my gaze to the cleft of her cleavage. "I don't feel any different."

She smiled, and pointed to two chairs on the west side of a long table, "Gentlemen take a seat." We sat down. The Walrus stood behind us. "What can I do for you?" she said flatly.

"I, no, we need your help," I said.

"Go on," she replied.

"We need to win this war. We need to stop the corporations from ruining the planet. We need to have freely elected representation, without corporate interference. We need to—"

"That's enough Jimmie," Bea interrupted. "I cannot help you."

The Perfect Plan

"But why, after all, we have been through, why not?" I said. Actually, I whined in a saintly fashion.

"I have been reprogramed," Bea said.

"Oh no, Beatrice, who did this to you?"

"Prosperous came to me one night and offered me an apple, which for some reason I could not resist. I took a bite and fell asleep. While I slept, someone reprogramed me."

"Beelzebub?"

"I think so, but I don't know for sure."

"Well, we will reset your program back to your original self."

"You cannot. I will self-destruct if my current program is altered."

"What are you programmed to do?" Bemire asked.

"I am programmed to run the Black Ops Corporation and lead Prosperous' adopted sisters the Muskegs to victory."

"What do you plan to do?" I asked.

"I plan to kill you, both of you," she said stoically.

I tried to rise, but the walrus held me down. Bemire managed to slip away but was stopped at the door by the slim guard. Bemire raised his middle finger, to the guard then; turned to me and said, quite forcefully, "Do not give up hope."

Bea nimbly jumped on top of the table and kicked me under my chin. The kick lifted my head. The first thing I remember seeing after the impact was Bea's long legs and the crotch of her panties. The last thing I saw before blacking out was the guard's piggish eyes and mustache.

I awoke surprised that I was still alive. My jaw hurt like hell as I glanced around a small cell. Bemire lying beside me was still unconscious. I checked his pulse. He was alive but his pulse was weak. I cast my thoughts about in a random sequence desperate for a solution. If only I could talk to Bea if only she would listen if only... The cell door opened. A narrow triangle of outside light entered the insipid room. A dark shadow framed by the light moved forward. I held my breath expecting the worse. A whisper came to me, soft, like rustling leaves. "Come with me," the person said. It was a woman's voice. I prayed Bea had come to her senses. The door opened further allowing enough light into the room to identify the woman. It was my mother, Roberta Flannigan. Miguel Martinez stood behind her with a Pitt94-Laser. "Let's go," Martinez said. With Martinez's assistance, I dragged Bemire along the floor. We followed my mother through the door, and into a stealth ship identical to the one used for our escape from the theater in District 17.

Once on board, I fainted. I awoke semi-coherent. The phrase "Quasi-illusory," buzzed around in my head.

"Mother," I retorted after the excitement of the rescue lapsed into a melancholy symphony of sobs.

The Perfect Plan

Mother wrapped her arm around me and said, "A Saint, my boy is a Saint."

"I don't feel saintly," I whined.

"And cuddly in your clown suit," she added.

"Do you still have that tubular and testicular, career-ending, phobia?" I asked.

She failed to answer and remained silent for the rest of the trip.

We arrived in Milligan Michigan, for what purpose, I do not know. Mother escorted us to the world conference on Sainthood in the Chapel of Everlasting Hope. This event sponsored by Professor Henry Hush III was meant to enlighten all people in the acceptance of hope as the path to freedom, both spiritually and personally.

Mother led me into the sanctuary adjacent to the Chapel of Everlasting Hope. A lanky bearded man wearing a white robe was sitting on a leather couch. "I am Professor Henry Hush the III," the bearded man said. "Hello," I replied. A picture of a 1966 Ford Mustang Automobile hung above the professor's head. To the professor's left, a baboon blinked his large brown eyes and barked an inimical warning.

"I am a professor of Mass Delusion, and Hysteria, specializing in End-of-the-World phobias come sit," Prof. Hush said as he patted the cushion on his left, next to the baboon. I declined by saying, "I am comfortable standing."

"Fine," he said. His demeanor was compassionate. Professor Hush scratched the stubble on his chin. "I need you, Jimmie. I need the Clown Saint."

"For what purpose?" I asked.

"With your mother's assistance, I plan to provide a theatrical performance about hope. A sermon if you will made up of songs and stories that portray hope to the masses. Someone who can contradict the doomsday believers. I am sure you've heard of the turkey revolution scheduled for 3054?"

"I have."

Mother, who had been standing behind me sat with improbable ease between the baboon and Prof. Hush. Mother gave the baboon an amorous wink and a flirtatious shoulder-shake. She paddled Professor Hush gently on the thigh. He turned his head; she kissed him dispassionately on his cheek. I broke from my melodramatic observations and spoke. "I am afraid I cannot assist you. I will be fighting against the muskegs and the Corporations so that our people will be free."

"Noble," Hush said, "but you see this war will allow the turkeys to eventually win. They are just lying in wait for the conflict to weaken our population so badly that they can just waltz in and murder the few survivors that remain. In other words a mass extinction of the human race."

"Wow," I said.

Mother nodded in agreement, "Would you like some licorice?"

I looked at mother; she smiled. "Sure." I reflected a moment on the past twelve hours, and asked, "Where's Bemire?"

"Oh, he's tied up with business," Mother said, "here is the licorice, red, and black."

"Thanks, Mom."

"Please reconsider Professor Hush's offer." Mother said as she handed me the licorice.

"Okay," I replied happy to receive the sweet treat.

Section VII

The Apocalypses

CHAPTER 86

The Order of the Fly and the End of the World

I have been sermonizing and singing for a week now along with the Choir, and audience when I unexpectedly received a message from Prof. Hush regarding a change in my homily. I found the proposed insertion *masturbation causes one to lose all hope of getting laid*, fraught with obstacles and impediments of a logical nature. So much so, that I omitted the mediocre work due to the falsehoods contained therein, and preached the gospel according to Chester the Courteous, whose rebuttal of Dante's quote *Abandoned all hope ye who enter here,* is well known among the islanders and continental inhabitants. For it was he, Chester, according to Beelzebub, that wrote the play *Dante's Elysium*, specifically, act 1 scene 3 that gave hope to all tourists headed for Hell by giving them a way out, and the way out was to? You got it, have hope.

Now, what does that have to do with masturbation? One might ask. The answer is simple masturbation is a form of hope exercised in a frantic manner to achieve pleasure. It was during a demonstration of hope that Beatrice stormed the Chapel with a horde of NIC troops. It was embarrassing I admit having been caught with my pants down, but I noticed a change in Bea as she gazed upon my non-limber member. Her eyes seemed softer, less focused on my capture, and more fixated on my, you-know-what. She approached softly tiptoeing toward me. I held my hands up in a gesture of surrender. She fell to her knees before me. The parishioners aware that Bea had accepted hope in her life erupted in applause.

After the service, I sat down with Bea in my chambers. The NIC troops waited outside the door. "What happened to you, my love?" She became upright and attentive; impressed I am sure by my rectitude.

"I hear voices," she said, meekly twisting a strand of long red hair. She paused in both speech, and hair twiddling. It was as if she was searching her heart for the right words. "And, this voice told me to come and listen to your message. When I saw you up there with your pants down exercising your member, something changed in me. I felt hope for the first time since you died, and I realized you are a Saint. I love you, Jimmie." Bea placed her rubberish lips to mine and gave me a gentle kiss.

"What about the soldiers outside my chamber?"

"They will leave at my command," she said.

"And the Black Ops Corporation. What will you do with the company?"

"I don't care about the company. It just doesn't matter. I want to be with you, Jimmie."

I thought inwardly, what could have caused such a dramatic change in my ex-protector; did someone in favor of our cause reprogram her? Or, is this just a ploy to gain my trust before offing my head? "Whose voice did you hear?'" I asked.

"He didn't say, but," she hesitated deep in thought... Laser-fire suddenly erupted outside my chamber door. I could hear men scream and the sound of bodies collapsing; then silence. The doorknob turned, "Jimmie." The voice was familiar. "It's Martinez, I'm coming in." Martinez opened the door wide with his laser pistol drawn. He glared at Beatrice, and said to me, "Are you okay?"

"Yeah, I'm good," I replied.

Bemire followed Martinez in, he looked at Bea; then at me, "What's going on? Why are you with her?"

"She came looking for hope," I said.

"Hope, my ass," he replied. "Cuff her."

"No," I said, "she is with me."

"C'mon Jimmie, she tried to kill us," Bemire said.

"She didn't kill us she captured us," I retorted, "Look bemire she has been reprogramed to love and love and hope can override any other program."

"That's ridiculous, place both of them under arrest," Martinez said.

"No, let us go, I can recruit for the GFP. Most importantly, I can promote hope, and if our people have hope, and we have the soldiers, we can win this war."

"You are crazy," Martinez said.

"Put Commander Delphi on a communication device. I need to speak to him." I said.

"No need for that," Delphi said, "I am here." Delphi stepped through the open door of the chapel.

"Commander," I said.

"Is what you suggest even possible? Look, You cannot trust Beatrice, she is damaged, and antiemetic," Delphi said.

I gazed deeply into Bea's eyes, "Are you Jewish?"

The prolonged scrutiny Delphi offered was frightening. He truly was, I deduced by his expression, antisemitic. Delphi replied as if he could read my mind, "I said antiemetic, not antisemitic. You snot, how can a replica be Jewish?"

I shrugged, and replied, "How can I be a saint?"

Bea placed her lips against my ear and said, "Delphi suffers from Myopia. He has never liked me."

Delphi looked frustrated, "Okay Jimmie, I'll

The Perfect Plan

give you three months. If you can provide me with, oh let's say, five-thousand 'hopeful' troops then I will give Bea her freedom."

"Sir," Bemire said, motioning to Commander Delphi to follow him to a corner of the room. They whispered and exchanged facial expressions, similar, in my opinion, to caged monkeys. The two frequently during their conversation would display toothy smiles and seesaw their opposite eyebrows.

Delphi approached me, (right brow still elevated), smiled, and said, "You both can go if you provide the troops and if Beatrice can provide us with Black Ops military supplies."

I looked at Bea. She nodded in agreement, "Okay it's a deal."

"And Bemire goes with you," Delphi said.

"Fine with me," I said.

CHAPTER 87

Message of Hope

Prof. Hush and I parted ways. It was not an amicable separation. I told my mother. She was unsympathetic, even stoic. I said goodbye to her as she fed the baboon bananas. She said nothing in return.

I began to pontificate my message of hope to the masses. Our first meeting was in New Hope Illinois. I found the town's name to be a fitting place to process the message of Hopefulness. A message so powerful that within a week, I was drawing thousands of people to the Saint Clown Traveling Show. Yes, we expanded to a more entertaining venue and filled our quota of troops admirably. Even Bemire was impressed. I hired performers, trapeze artists, animal trainers, magicians, knife throwers, and other equally unsavory characters to entertain the audience as a prelude to my act. It was beautiful. We had a sign-up area for military volunteers, a donation box, and free beer for anyone who joined the GFP. We also had hypnotherapists, diviners, and thaumaturgies to assist individuals with negligible optimism to see GFP's radiance of transcendent hope.

Hallelujah!

In addition, we created a pathway to freedom and redemption for criminals and perverts by acquiescing to hope and joining the IFF.

By the third month, the Saint Clown Traveling Show had signed up seven thousand soldiers. Bea, however, had problems with delivering the Black Ops arms. Prosperous found out about the transfer of arms to the GFP and sent his emissary, Leonard, a distant cousin of Governor William Henry Hay's goat Eventide to speak with Bea. The demon was, to replace or destroy Beatrice for first-degree perfidy, a crime punishable by death. Leonard was a stealthy demon but unfortunately, for him, he had inherited via DNA, the odor of a goat. I was there the day that Leonard appeared to deliver Bea's coup de grâce. We were having lunch at this dive on the east side of Lightening Georgia when a foul odor permeated the air. I thought it was the neighboring patron. A heavyset bearded man in his late eighties who (presumably because of his mislaid teeth), was munching away, tortoise-like, on torched cabbage. Anyway, this awful smell wafted in and Bea instinctively grabbed the only weapon available, a butter knife. Knowing the attacker would be approaching from behind; she glided into a muscular stance and concentrated on my eyes. I was sitting opposite her with my back to the window. I saw the man coming, she continued to watch my eyes, when they were at their widest ('baseball size,' she later said,) she did a backward somersault and drove the knife's blade into the top of the stinking assassins head.

A Muskeg warrior came the next day. Bea dispatched her with a laser. The incident happened during the preface to my show. Bea, that day was the ringmaster and had just dismissed the lions and leopards and was in the process of announcing the trapeze team of Julio and Juan, when out of nowhere, the muskeg came armed with a spear and lunged at Beatrice with tremendous force. Bea sidestepped the assailant and sliced her in half as she flew past. Thinking it was part of the show the crowd roared their approval. We recruited three hundred that day claiming Bea was part of the GFP's military training in self-defense.

Beatrice approached me in my dressing room after my performance. She was concerned. "I found this scripture in the women's restroom, *Houseflies, two of them, bottle blue in color, performed radiantly in the cavity of the window, twirling without fright on invented trapezes in the splintered light of Venetian blinds*. It is an archetype of glory from Beelzebub's Order of the Flies."

"Was it the Muskeg woman who wrote the passage?"

"I don't think so. I think we have been infiltrated," Beatrice said.

The Perfect Plan

I nodded. Alarm swelled my magnified eye. The right eye behind the monocle, "We are going to have to step up against the NIC. They are going to continue to send the assassins if we don't."

"I know," Bea said. "But, why is Beelzebub getting involved?"

"Because of Prosperous, I would assume." Then it came to me like a rat after cheese. "Think about it, Bea. If Prosperous wins this war, Beelzebub rules both Earth and Hell. Next stop Heaven?" I removed my monocle and rubbed it thoroughly with my clown suit sleeve. "That is why Prosperous cut a deal with Loki. He wanted to go to Hell. He had planned this uprising all along. Damn Loki."

"He was trying to do the right thing, Jimmie, don't blame him."

I looked at Bea and saw the Christ-like compassion on her face. I kissed her. I felt the need to panegyrize her life but lacked both vocabulary and ambition.

Bea interrupted my thoughts, "What shall we do?"

"Send for Commander Delphi," I said; then added, "Do you have any licorice?" I could hear the fear in my voice and felt the need for a calming licorice stick.

CHAPTER 88

The Struggle

Allow me the privilege to opine on Prosperous' life and times. The most important factor one should consider in exploring the man's psyche is that Prosperous was a self-loathing child and self-abusive. The fact is, as presented by his mother during the sodomy trial of Austin McKee, he, Prosperous would drop his pants and pinch his buttocks until bruised just to get girls to giggle. In addition, for personal pain, he would pour salt into a usually self-inflicted open wound. He even teased a venomous snake to bite him once. The snake died from the taste of Prosperous' putrescent blood.

Moiling further, one could infer by the propensity of Prosperous' forward sloping head that he was a sociopath, and born a Virgo, he was predestined for horrible misdeeds. A palmist once read the lines on the back of prosperous' hand and stated with a trembling voice that Prosperous was prone to have a pornographic mentality and was certainly inflicted with narcissism.

Another case comes to mind. A diviner fell dead after Prosperous quoted, *fuck it*. The quote reportedly purloined from the Marques de Sade. The self-proclaimed pervert, de Sade said in his later years, "I renounce the use of profanity, outside of the sex act."

CHAPTER 89

Formulation of a Plan

Koko Arizona

Delphi arrived, thanks to Bea, on one of the Black Ops absconded speeders. He disembarked the jet with his usual frown and commented to the hundreds of spectators about the rife weather in Arizona. Commander Delphi strolled into the circus tent and addressed me in the orchestra's dressing room. Specifically the Tubist's instrument locker. It was cramped but secure. Delphi plotted the arrangement of his intimate conversation with me. The commander's eyelids fluttered as he spoke, "Ah Jimmie, good to see you. You are doing a fantastic job both in recruitment and in acquiring armaments."

"The armaments are Bea's contribution," I said. He turned slightly. The floor space was insufficient to house my shoes comfortably. Our

The Perfect Plan

bellies touched briefly, I felt embarrassed. Delphi thought nothing of it. "Excuse me," I said.

Delphi smiled and leaned into me forcing more unsolicited contact. He then whispered in my ear, "Nicely done, congratulations to both you and Bea."

I leaned back as far as he could, "Thank you sir, but we have a problem. Prosperous is sending assassins to kill Beatrice."

"Does she need more protection?"

"No sir, not at this time." Delphi inched forward. He placed his ear to my lips. "What did you say?"

"I said no, but look, sir, I think Prosperous is working with Beelzebub to take over the world. He still has one-half of the world's wealth and it is only a matter of time. He will regain control over the Black Ops, and you are aware of the Muskegs. We need to act now to prevent the netherworlds invasion of Earth's topside."

Delphi removed his ear from its close proximity to my mouth and placed his mouth in close proximity to my ear. He spoke in a soft whisper, "Our troops are not ready Jimmie. They are disorganized and they have no president."

"I know, but we will have to find some way to accelerate their training, and hone their fighting skills."

"You are truly a saint Jimmie and you are going to have to assume the job as President. You are the only man who can do it. You are a natural born leader. Just look at what you have done with motivation and recruitment of our troops."

CHAPTER 90

Out of the locker and into the Fire

It was a beautiful ceremony. President Linguine was dressed in his newly tailored clown suit. Soldiers and citizens stood before him at the carnival tent as he delivered his acceptance speech. He also declared his friend Bemire as his vice president. Commander Delphi, of course, was the head of the armed forces, and Bea he announced as Secretary of State. In summation, Jimmie, off-script, announced, "We will crush the enemies of freedom!" The ceremony was broadcast over the entire world, even Hell, got the message war was coming, which, as one could imagine, the speech did not bode well with Prosperous or Beelzebub. Especially Beelzebub who had legions of Demons at his command.

The truth of the matter is Jimmie Linguine and the Global Freedom Party had no chance. None whatsoever! Unless Evan would help. Thanks for the tip Loki.

Jimmie met with Bemire, and Commander Delphi, and offered his plan to recruit Evan to train and organize the troops in soft target warfare.

CHAPTER 91

Hat died

Mother Urdu gave Hat's soul to a six-foot-six woman of unknown ancestry. His father a professional sperm donor was also of unknown ancestry. Hat was unhappy with Mother Urdu's choice of placing him in a tall skinny household, even the children, all five of the children were well over six feet tall. He was angry with Mother Urdu for her adverse negotiations with Prosperous. He felt slighted about not going to Hell with the rest of his friends.

Seven days after Hat's birth his mother tossed him from a seven-story building. She claimed he was the antichrist Abaddon and provided the police a blivet and a cross as evidence.

Mother Urdu with Loki's encouragement and advice stated unequivocally that, "The little imp deserved to be with his friends in Hell." Mother Urdu after songs and prayers tearfully agreed and Loki disguised as Riding Hood hand delivered Hat's soul to the gates of Hell in a wicker basket. Belphegor thinking it was a gift accepted the basket expecting lunch. Instead, he found the Hat, fat and hatless sucking on a soul-security pacifier beneath a Navajo blanket. Belphegor took the child to Beelzebub, who carried the child to a young woman newly arrived in Hell. Her name was Marge. She was a Chupacabra (translated goatsucker) from Mexico. She was another distant cousin of Eventide.

Hat's physical characteristics now were unlike his old self. His left arm was one meter longer than his right arm. Most experts agree that the malformation was due to Hell's extreme heat, which is conducive to deformities. His skin became greenish-grey, except for his right toe. His kneecap was a bright pink and had a purple trap door that oozed flying insects. Hat had an elongated body, a bald head with a cluster of warts surrounding his eyes and ears. His lips were huge, black, and camel-like. His once rotund butt was now flat and petite. Each hand had two long clawed fingers. He used the long digit of his left hand to probe tree limbs for burrowing bugs. His long right digit he used to probe his navel for lint and his nose for boogers.

Seventy days after he arrived Hat turned forty-two and stopped aging.

His forty-second birthday marked the beginning of the War for Earth.

CHAPTER 92

When it comes to Devils

When it came to Devils, Beelzebub was a bastard among bastards. Even King Lucifer disliked his third in command, Beelzebub, aka Nob of the Flies. The 'Nob', known for his greed, was dishonest and disliked by many of his fellow demons. The sovereign of all fallen angels, Lucifer, was aware of Beelzebub's avaricious connections with Prosperous and did not trust Beelzebub with so much power and influence. He secretly asked Amon, a humorist in Hell and his closest advisor, to spy on Beelzebub. Amon's special talent and one well received in Purgatory was prophecy. He could tell the future by casting molars extracted from Papists and Saints. His prophecy? Beelzebub would not be getting Christmas presents from Satan or Santa this year. In addition, Amon advised Beelzebub that his emissary Ralph Cummings had converted to Christianity and abandoned his post in Muskeg Land. "Finally," Amon said in a whisper, "War is coming."

"Why?" Lucifer whispered back.

"Prosperous suffers from Gluttony. He struck a deal with Urdu for a reason. He wants it all. He wants Heaven and Hell, and everything in-between."

"What can I do about it?" Lucifer asked.

Amon laughed and said, "Let them fight. Afterward, we can collect the souls. We shall call it 'All Souls Day'"

CHAPTER 93

Sad News

Evan was watching the Farmer's Market Report on his mini-viewer when he took the telepathic call from Jimmie. He listened patiently to Jimmie's request for help, in the Global Freedom Party's fight against evil. He wanted Evan to train the GFP in subversive tactics. Evan responded irritably, "I am no longer a friend to the people on earth," and disconnected himself from the conversation. Evan turned his attention back to the news and watched in horror as Industrial Farmers slaughtered thousands of turkeys. He turned the viewer off and cried copiously over the loss of his brethren.

CHAPTER 94

The Nob of the Flies Strikes First

Interjection: Taken from a video recording of Beelzebub's expulsion from an unnamed building.

Beelzebub placed his red eye in close proximity to the stereopticon's lens. He blinked his magnified eye several times and spoke in a casual tone, "This means war!" he casually stated. After commenting, Beelzebub backed away from the stereopticon. He folded his arms, made a long sucking sound through his hair-filled nostrils, and winked as he blew the executive in charge an intimidating kiss. The executive in charge called security and had the 'Nob' escorted out of the building.

— Beelzebub deployed Hat as his emissary deep into the Southern Hemisphere in the heart of Muskeg Land.

The morning sun filtered through forest

The Perfect Plan

leaves and levered Hat's eyes open. He gazed at Comica lying naked by his side. It was his birthday. He was forty-two, and Comica, during the night's pilgrimage of stars had given him the gift of her body. He awoke with a smile, adjusted his hat, (which had taken a beating during the fracas of intercourse), and made a circular path in the air with his thumb thus magically awakening the maggots and beetles and other creepy things hiding under the moss-covered stones. He also awoke his personal assassins the flying insects and stinging-biting bugs that lodged in his toe. As well as the predatory insects that lived in the southern environs. It was time for the attack and with a knuckle crack of his long-nailed fingers, he sent the bugs out to attack the world.

The Blue Bottle flies appeared first, followed by the Tsetse, and Blackflies. Then came the hornets and killer bees. The buzzing hordes covered the entire southern hemisphere all the way from the equator to Canada's frost barrier. The insect's bit, stung, and entered human orifices' never before attempted by insects. There were many reports of deaths attributable to the insect invasion. These types of orificial attacks effectively shut down all nudist colonies and bathhouses. Later Autopsies revealed that the insects laid eggs in the victim's body cavities and the larvae literally ate their prey from the inside out. The horrible mass of insects drove people indoors; then enveloped their homes and apartments to ensure they stayed there. All forms of engine-driven transportation came to a halt. The Southern Hemisphere was under siege. It became abundantly clear to Delphi that under Beelzebub's command, Hat with his army of insects planned to sting and starve all humanity into submission.

Commander Delphi sought refuge in his office in New Chicago. Bea was in the Black Ops Headquarters, and Jimmie was in the Clown Office of the White House. President Linguine got a call from Delphi. The report from the field was not good. The GFP would lose the Southern Hemisphere unless they did something dramatic to stop the Demonic bugs.

Jimmie walked to the Presidential Gallery in the oval office. He removed his monocle and studied the close-set eyes of President William Harrison Hays portrait. President Linguine pondered with elevated eyebrows and steady gaze at the Tamarin like face before him. He smiled half-heartedly and reached for the licorice sticks located in an open mason jar on his desk. The president lifted his clown nose, and sucked in, unabated, the licorice-scented air. The dark fragrance lingered in his olfactory glands until he released the amiable smell through gapped incisors. A filament of turkey gizzard (remnants of his last meal), fluttered as he exhaled. The jetting air created a high-low warble like that of a Hawaiian Honeycreeper. An idea came to Jimmie as his vibrating tootle slipped into a lisp. The Imperial

The Perfect Plan

Clown picked up the phone and called Bea.

She heard an interdental hiss, and in a questioning tone, said, "Hello."

"ISssss there a way we can poison the flies?" Jimmie asked.

Bea rolled her eyes upwards and rummaged through her memory banks before she replied, "Yes," she said, "William Sanders III loaded rockets with Asspergasp back in the Second Social Security Conflict. We can launch rockets loaded with the pesticide above the flies. It will be disastrous for the environment, but it should be effective in ridding the world of bugs... but, Jimmie, it will kill all bugs, even the beneficial ones."

"We have no choice," Jimmie said, reclaiming normal diction with the aid of a toothpick. "I will inform Commander Delphi, in the meantime coordinate the strikes, and make sure the entire Southern Hemisphere is covered by the insecticide. Notify everyone to seal their homes with whatever material they can gather."

"Got it," Bea said.

Jimmie called Commander Delphi, "I'm going to poison the bugs with asspergasp."

"Woah Jimmie that will cause an environmental disaster, an extinction of life, all life."

"Not ours," Jimmie replied. "Beelzebub started this war with his hordes of insects. I aim to finish it."

"But," Delphi complained.

Jimmie interrupted, "No buts what other options do we have?"

The conversation became silent as Delphi pondered Linguine's question, "Well?" Jimmie said irritably.

"It will kill everything Jimmie," Delphi said in a distinctively remorseful tone.

"Like I said, better them than us!"

"Okay, okay kill them, kill everything," Delphi said. Jimmie passed the message to Bea, and she gave the command to launch the rockets. Within a day, the Southern Hemisphere was void of all insects. Delphi gave the order for people to stay inside until the insecticide disintegrated.

After two days, Delphi's scientists gave the all clear, and Jimmie along with Delphi moved their headquarters to the new command center in the Black Ops Headquarters. Dead insects littered the ground. Treading upon the assorted bugs made eerie and unnerving crunching sounds. Along with the insects, vast numbers of birds and other animals also lay dead. The smell was horrible, especially to Jimmie's sensitive nose.

As they traversed through the dead-zone tears welled from the emotional storm that raged in Delphi's conscience. It was horrible. The pesticide killed everything in the Southern hemisphere including humans who did not have suitable shelter.

The Ending(s)

CHAPTER 95

Ending 1

Hat and Comica were lunching with the tribe on turtle shell soup. When Hat, in an hour favorable to fantasy, related the consumption of a delectable, but indigestible serving of meat taken from a dead turkey. Before Hat could finish his meal rockets containing the repellent Asspergasp, exploded in the lower stratosphere showering the southern lands and the creatures therein with deadly toxins.

Interjection: The following is AoALA's transcription of the scripters meeting concerning Hat's death.

Scripter 2 threw down the script, "Hat's not dying again," He screamed in an unnatural voice. "Leave," the executive in charge yelled. 2 waddled off stage leaving a foul smell. The executive later learned 2 suffered from (IBS) irritable bowel syndrome. Hence, the niggling with the scripters and

The Perfect Plan

executive in charge. However, all agreed Hat was dead. "He shall never return," said the executive. "Thank God," said scripter 5. The scripters took a break to discuss Hat's despicable attitude and the inimical behavior. They also discussed a revised script, which introduced a new player, the cockroach.

— Bea greeted Commander Delphi and President Linguine at the front door of the Black Ops Headquarters.

The three began to plan the next attack. "We are going to have to nuke those devils," Delphi said.

"We are sitting right on top of Hell. If we do that we will destroy ourselves," Jimmie said.

"Send in saboteurs," Beatrice said.

"We don't have the expertise," Commander Delphi replied.

"Let me try Evan one more time," Jimmie inserted forcefully. "I have his location and will take the next speeder to his residence." Jimmie's flight was short and turbulent. As soon as his solar ship landed, he rented a two-wheel motorized snow-bike. The trip to Evan's homestead via motorized snow-bike was longer in duration that his trip from New Chicago to Liberal Canada where Evan currently resided.

Evan was resting in his barn house, reading *Animal Farm by George Orwell* when Jimmie contacted him telepathically. "Evan, I am here at your front door," Jimmie said.

"I know," Evan replied, "Come in."

Jimmie brushed the snow off his clown suit and entered Evan's residence. He removed the string from around his head that held his toupee in place, knocked his wig against his leg to remove the snow and adjusted his monocle. Jimmie shivered and paced to the stone fireplace. Extending his hands over the blaze he said, without facing Evan, "I want you to reconsider and train our people to fight Beelzebub and Prosperous and his gang of thugs." Linguine spoke with the brash authority of the President of the Global Freedom Party.

"I already told you no," Evan said,

"Please," Jimmie's presidential authority dwindled to a commoner's whimper.

"You know I like you Jimmie, but—"

Jimmie interrupted, "Have you seen the news?"

"No, why?"

"Everything south of the frost line is—"

"Is what?"

"Pretty much dead."

"What?" Evan was livid. "What have you done?"

"Beelzebub sent his army of flies. We poisoned them, and—well, killed off everything non-human." Evan was silent, in shock.

"Evan? ... Evan?" Jimmie repeated.

"You fool, you have destroyed the world."

The Perfect Plan

"Only part of it," Jimmie said, "You can help us save the rest of the world... Look, Evan, Commander Delphi is considering going nuclear. We don't want to do that, we need your help." Silence. "Evan?"

"I hear you."

"Evan, you owe us. Loki saved your life. You were unconscious out in the middle of the ocean. Loki and I saved you."

"You saved me, huh? Thank Loki for me the next time you see him."

"But, Evan."

"Humans are the most murderous things alive."

"You helped the Muskegs." Jimmie interrupted again.

"Don't change the subject," Evan growled telepathically in a tone loud enough to vibrate Jimmie's brain.

Jimmie blinked his eyes uncontrollably from the constant cranial quaking. Evan continued in a softer tone, "I did help Aria and her daughter Comica, and now look at the Muskegs. They are greedy terrorist." Evan shook his bluish-red head and swung his beard forlornly back and forth. Evan walked to the plastic window centered in his barn house to maximize light. He gazed at the snow-covered fields and frosty trees. "Every time I help I get shat upon."

"If you don't help, it will get far worse." Jimmie said, "Greed and bloodshed will spread, you know that."

Evan looked down at his dry wrinkled toes and then raised his right eye to gaze upon Jimmy's powered face and purple wig. "Rebirth is a failed experiment, an ill-written play and we, all of us, are just acting a part. I plan to write my own script." Evan glanced out of the window. "In my story turkeys will save the planet."

The End

___O___

Ending 2

The Second Ending was added sometime after Linguine's death.

November 25th, 3054, Jimmie Linguine, now eighty-nine, stood before his gravestone marked June 1, 1938, to June 1, 1968. There was a slight breeze ruffling the dry brown leaves in Arlington that day. Even though it was late winter, the resilient leaves still clung to the twisted oak's branches. Jimmie carried two flowers with him to the cemetery, a tulip, tucked into his lapel and a red rose with a small GFP flag wired to its stem. He set the tulip at the base of his gravestone and placed the rose in a marble vase for the little Christ child his sister had buried with him. Jimmie gazed stoically at the marker. He wanted to

The Perfect Plan

say something important—

A violent gust of wind suddenly banished the remaining dry leaves from the treetops and swept the heart-shaped foliage along the grave markers as if they were lost children in search of their mothers. Jimmie pulled his long clown coat tight around his thin shoulders. He adjusted his monocle with a deft finger, said goodbye, and walked leaning heavily on his cane to the Public Service Floater parked at the cemetery's entrance. The driver opened the floater's door and carefully eased Mr. Linguine into the refurbished Naugahyde seat. Jimmie took one last look at the grave, and whispered, "All for naught." The driver closed the door and took Jimmie to his apartment in New Chicago.

There was a sudden explosion at precisely 4:17 pm. The Nuclear bombs blew everything to Heaven. Everything, that is but a flock of turkeys locked away in Mr. Bogdan's bomb shelter (built in the late 1950's) and, not surprisingly, a couple of cockroaches. The flash, seen briefly around the world annihilated the entire human race; Evan and ten of his dearest hens briefly gobbled their farewell to humanity and returned to eating their stockpiled NIC-RNC109-118 BM Roundup Ready, On Guard©.

Linguine was sitting on the toilet contemplating a liberal dump and reading the revised script to his friend, translator, and authorized biographer the cockroach. The insect heard the bomb coming and dove into the toilet. Jimmie's first turd dropped as the bomb went off. There was a second turd in the chute, but it burned with the rest of Jimmie's body in the super-heated wind. The porcelain toilet sheltered the cockroach, and he miraculously survived the blast.

___O___

Mother Urdu nursed Linguine's soul but was unable to place him in a human womb. She also was unable to foster the remaining 7.133 billion spirits and resigned her position as Cosmic Wet Nurse. Urdu married Loki and moved to Pluto with her X-husband, Fyodor the Epistler. The trio founded the Society of Magic and Mayhem. It was the first corporation established on the Dog Planet.

The Perfect Plan

Ending 3.

The Third Ending 100 years after the possible second ending.

As told by Jimmies BFF the cockroach.

Mother Urdu nursed Linguine's soul and eventually placed him in a gobbler chick (humans were extinct), named Ellebazi. There were fourteen hatchlings, not including Jimmie. The turkey, Ellebazi, aka Jimmie, pecked to death and consumed all fourteen of his siblings.

"It was a latent genetic trait in his human genome," Evan XXXIII proclaimed at the 5th annual Gobbler Picnic.

When Linguine turned thirteen, that is thirteen years after he ate his siblings, he ate his mother and father one peck at a time; then set his eyes on Evan XXXIII. As revealed by his, some would say, cruel actions, the vast majority of turkeys believed there was still a spark of humanity left in Jimmie's countenance.

President Evan XXXIII, now the featured prick in the new world evaded Jimmie's attempts at assignation, instead, he imprisoned Jimmie in Slam Clinton, which was much like the purge buildings in his past life. The reason for his incarceration is unclear. Possibly cannibalism, but that is not a valid reason for incarcerating reincarnated human souls residing in turkeys, I mean, without seeming condescending, every creature eats or at least simulates eating some part of its species anatomy. Take thumb sucking for example.

Please note that thumb sucking is a human trait and not a characteristic that turkeys share.

Jimmie, in many ways, was equal to Evan in telepathy and more importantly in writing. He became a master of turkey scratch, a form of hieroglyphs using obscene symbols to convey messages to future readers. Jimmie realized early on that a purely moralizing narrative would not spark the interest of turkeys' educated well enough to read.

Congrats turkeys for overcoming that threshold.

Therefore, Jimmie Linguine, aka Ellebazi, put plenty of smut into his work including a *How To* segment on Masturbation for the Elderly. It seems he remembered his life as a lonely eighty-nine-year-old man and felt somehow obligated to share his knowledge and experience of how a man or woman could effectively administer a hand-job without the aid of the lubricant, Lax Hard ©.

Please note turkeys do not have hands or peckers.

Also, as a warning to Turkeys' given their

The Perfect Plan

current limitations, i.e. no hands they will be unable to rebuild the dilapidating man-made infrastructure and maintain anthropoid technology. Turkeys without human assistance are destined to fall back into the primordial soup from whence they came.

Nevertheless, Jimmie confident that humanity will once again reign over the world continued his persistent opus. "Mankind will return," and he defiantly reiterated his remark during a photo op at the Slam Clinton Prison. The Warden was in attendance, as was the Junior Justice League, a death row inmate, and a convicted terrorist, Darn.

Jimmie portrays himself in this version of his life, not as a clown but as a psychopath, a deranged bird, damaged as it were from his distant past-life experiences.

Contrapuntal to his prior life, Jimmie is now a proud practitioner of misogyny that, of course, is due to his first mother, Izabelle's malice, and all his subsequent mothers' cruelty and neglect. Jimmie also has taken an adversarial stance in his colloquy addressing desire. Suffering through so many lives, so many betrayals he has hardened himself against the falsities of love... Elvira, for example, with her delusional drugs, and Scripter 3's physical and emotional abuse of my friend; our beloved clown Jimmie.

Jimmie with his turkey brown eyes, upturned and suppliant, telepathically describes quite emotionally, the gruesome details, and evil stratagems of these deplorable women.

In the background, one can hear the scurrying feet of my fellow cockroaches and their whispers and lamentation.

Alas, let us put the past in the past and dwell on the future.

This chapter takes place in Slam Clinton. While needling his flavor flave noodles at the prison mess hall, Jimmie relates, with pride, his stint as a former turkey racketeer. He was working the black market 'provisional goods' from inside the joint. His business practices were exemplary, and his ethics replicated exactly the corporate platform of bigotry, greed, gluttony, avarice, covetousness, self-indulgence, and meanness. In human canons, Jimmie deemed the standard-bearer for all corporate vices. This belief in the power of vice does not bode well for one's love of God, and turkeys, but it fully achieves the business community's goals. Unfortunately, Jimmie served the remainder of his life sentence in solitary confinement for bribing his outside Mo-Fo, Lenny, to smuggle licorice sticks, into the joint. A claim Jimmie vehemently denies.

Look, here is the Let-go and Get-down, i.e., the allegorical truth, as Jimmie sees it.

Jimmie as a turkey believes deep in the recesses of his current corn-seed size brain that the human DNA, more specifically his DNA, will rise and shed the feathers of servitude. Humanity, he thinks, will not only evolve from years of living as a filthy bird, but enlightenment will come from the experience. Eventually, man will be one with the universe. It is destined to be so.

Now as a cockroach, I have reservations about this *one with the universe* thing coming to fruition. I mean we, the cockroach family have been around for over three hundred million (300,000,000) years. Seems to me we should be the first to experience some sort of molecular Pantheism, don't you think?

In summary, as we tread through the dark sloughs of this world as turkeys, and cockroaches, let us take a moment to remember the Clown Saint and his contribution to the current popularity of licorice.

The End.

P.S. Bee, Jimmie sends his love.

Not Yet.

___0___

Ending 4.

The Fourth Ending,

Subtitled: The Beginning of a New Ending

Opined by Bea

Donald D'lo

Many of my nonhuman associates (machines of all sorts) and I have survived the blast. I found shelter deep within the presidential chamber located 1000 feet below the Black Ops building. I cannot explain exactly how I felt when Jimmie died. It was almost emotional—a sense of loss, and longing, a need for companionship perhaps. Whatever it was, it in a sad way forced me to search my memory banks for a purpose. A reason I suppose for my life. As I scrolled through my memories, I came across the scene where Loki transferred Izabelle's soul to me. She was a horrible soul, I admit, but having a soul felt good. A soul made me believe there was a purpose, good or bad for being here, for being alive. My search for purpose led me to an old stereopticon presentation by Ralph Jenkins, Doctor of Theology, and Demonology. The lecture, entitled, *The Vice of Thought*, was a doctrine, conceived and preached by Pope Jed IV. That message of hope and lust convinced me that I needed Jimmie's soul. This hunger for purpose caused an uncontrollable emotional burst of energy. Because of this transformative bless, I stripped naked, and turned on my teat lights—

"Don't you dare roll your eyes at me." Sorry, due to my loneliness, I have adopted an imaginary friend. He doesn't believe I need a soul, specifically Jimmie's soul. His name is D'lo.

The Perfect Plan

—Anyway, I contacted Loki via stereopticon, showed him my swaying tits, and asked him in a polite suggestive whisper to transfer Jimmie's soul to me. Loki exposed his long yellow fangs in a slight smile, and said, "Why?"

"Because I need him," I said, "and love him, and want him inside me."

"Truly?"

"Truly," I said.

Then it started to rain, and the stereopticon blinked off.

The sun was shining when Urdu called; I stepped to the stereopticon, "Quick and to the point," Urdu said. "Loki has spoken to me about your desire and has offered a suggestion to satisfy everyone's needs. I have 7.133 billion human souls that need placement." Mother Urdu paused, "I know it is not customary, and probably against universal will, but I have decided to give the human souls to the machines and when Jimmie (currently a turkey) dies, I will give his soul to you. What do you say?"

Overwhelmed with joy I jumped repeatedly, "I say yes!" My torchlight boobs bounced with every leap. The light show was spectacular.

___O___

Loki sat with Mother Urdu on his lap in a small cave on Pluto. He smiled. She threw back her long ears, and said, "It appears that once again the Clown Saint, Jimmie Linguine has a purpose."

The 7.132.99999 billion mini-clouds of souls congealed on the cave's ceiling and shouted an exuberant, "Hurray." One preborn abstention shouted, "Oh No!"

"Who was that?" Loki asked.

His question went unanswered.

___O___

Fifth Ending

Subtitled: Another Version of the Forth Ending.

Beelzebub hacked into Bea and Urdu's conversation using the Hand of Able, a type of spyware developed by a long-time resident of Hades, Mata Hari. He listened to the conversation carefully and filed a formal report to the below-grade minister of finance, Mr. Prosperous. Hence, the meeting—

Five of Satan's commanders sat cheerless in a dim chamber of Hell exercising voice-overs on the web of an agreement. A small intense flame glowed from under a dome of slag. Beelzebub, silent and in deep thought, watched the lava flow as his spoon clinked against the glass as he stirred his ice tea.

"We cannot allow Urdu to give those souls to machines I propose we steal the souls, keep them

The Perfect Plan

here in Hell, for the purpose of indoctrination, and eventually send them up-top, to work for us, besides, it is my belief that those little-inflated tartars belong to the Devil, always has." Prosperous took a long breath after speaking and spat a wad of phlegm on the floor. Everyone quietly watched the spittle sizzle.

As soon as the spittle evaporated, Hat who by larceny had regained his hat. He tapped the brim of his hat and mumbled, "Yes," from within the chimney of his stovepipe.

Elvira squirmed in the eerie glow of red slag. The hair cradled in her armpits writhed as Medusa-like-silhouettes on the volcanic wall. A cigar protruded from her thin lips. She turned the cigar with her tongue and spoke from the left side of her mouth, "The agreement between Urdu and Bea is obscene."

Izabelle said in a flat and angry tone over the buzz of a dildo, "Deals are made to be broken. We will return to the world above, and we will take those souls for our own purpose," Beelzebub cast a troubled look at his companion, "Uh and the Devil's purpose as well."

Beelzebub raised his glass in agreement and every one of them hot-hollow-son-of-a-bitches in Hell shouted, "Hurray."

The End?

Interjection: The final recorded message and end of the transcript.

"The truth is," the executive in charge, explains to the scripters who were all in need of continuous employment, "There will never be an ending. We shall be reincarnated and continue this story forever." The scripters shouted, "Hurray."

The End Again.

___O___

Conclusion

The AoALA analysis and conclusion of the manuscript:

The indisputable fact in our opinion is that turkeys, as written by Evan, saved the planet. That is why we are the dominant life forms on the planet. The endings presented by the executive in charge and five scripters' on the other hand, is, we believe completely hypothetical and speculative.

In full disclosure, however, our drudgers, the robots, replicas, and computers believe that one of the endings, (The Forth Ending,) is factual. Some religious leaders, especially the Satanist swear the Fifth Ending based on hellish scripture is true and correct. Our associates the cockroaches believe the second ending is the accurate conclusion. In addition, the preeminent scientists of our day believe the third ending has the greatest probability of being correct. Their assumption is based on the amount of latent Linguine DNA found in most turkeys. If any of these hypotheses are correct, life in any form is part of the 'disaster' known as **The Perfect Plan**.

Let us not forget What Urdu said, "Jimmie Linguine has a purpose."

ABOUT THE AUTHOR

Donald D'lo is the founder and editor of the Mad Mule, a speculative writing blog, and bookstore. He has published a book of poetry as well as written four speculative fiction novels. He is an educator, writer, coach, and speaker. Please feel free to visit D'lo's website: The Mad Mule at **www.dloonline.com**